WARHAMMER
40,000

KASRKIN
EDOARDO ALBERT

BLACK LIBRARY

A BLACK LIBRARY PUBLICATION

First published in 2022.
This edition published in Great Britain in 2023 by
Black Library, Games Workshop Ltd., Willow Road,
Nottingham, NG7 2WS, UK.

Represented by: Games Workshop Limited – Irish branch,
Unit 3, Lower Liffey Street, Dublin 1,
D01 K199, Ireland.

10 9 8 7 6 5 4 3 2 1

Produced by Games Workshop in Nottingham.
Cover illustration by Marc Lee.

A CIP record for this book is available from the British Library.

ISBN 13: 978-1-80407-302-5

See Black Library on the internet at

blacklibrary.com

Find out more about Games Workshop
and the worlds of Warhammer at

games-workshop.com

Printed and bound in the UK.

For Justin Hill, who made this possible.

For more than a hundred centuries the Emperor has sat immobile on the Golden Throne of Earth. He is the Master of Mankind. By the might of His inexhaustible armies a million worlds stand against the dark.

Yet, He is a rotting carcass, the Carrion Lord of the Imperium held in life by marvels from the Dark Age of Technology and the thousand souls sacrificed each day so that His may continue to burn.

To be a man in such times is to be one amongst untold billions. It is to live in the cruellest and most bloody regime imaginable. It is to suffer an eternity of carnage and slaughter. It is to have cries of anguish and sorrow drowned by the thirsting laughter of dark gods.

This is a dark and terrible era where you will find little comfort or hope. Forget the power of technology and science. Forget the promise of progress and advancement. Forget any notion of common humanity or compassion.

There is no peace amongst the stars, for in the grim darkness of the far future,
there is only war.

PART I

BIG YELLOW

 CHAPTER 1

'Looks big.'

'Bigger than you think.'

'Suppose it's hot too?'

'Hot enough to fry a grox steak on the cowling of a Leman Russ.'

'So why not send a squadron of them in then?'

'Heard they tried – didn't get more than a mile before they started sinking.' Sergeant Shaan Malick adjusted his helmet. He wasn't wearing it; he was sitting on it. Beside him, Trooper Torgut Gunsur stared out from the relative cool of the precious shade under the stubby wings of the Valkyrie, his eyes squinting against the glare.

'It's all yellow.'

Sergeant Malick laughed. 'It's the Great Sand Sea. There's a clue in the name.'

Trooper Gunsur unclipped his rebreather and spat, the phlegm arcing out from the precious shade and landing on the sand. It sizzled.

Malick shook his head. 'Keep your spit – you're going to need it.'

'I don't start no mission without spitting on the ground I'll be treading.'

Malick looked at Gunsur. 'Why?'

"Cause it ain't Cadia, and I spit on ground I fight on that ain't home.'

Malick looked away, staring out into the heat haze but not seeing it.

Trooper Gunsur glanced at his sergeant. 'Not so stupid, is it?'

But Sergeant Malick did not look back at him. His fingers strayed to the little plasteel vial hanging from a chain around his neck. The plasteel had been finger-burnished bright by the Cadian rubbing it between thumb and forefinger. The two men were sitting in the jet-blown bowl of sand beneath the wing of a Valkyrie, one of three that had brought the squad of Kasrkin here.

Malick pointed out in front of them. 'It's not all yellow. Some of it is brown and I reckon it goes white in the distance.'

'You mean, where the heat haze hides the horizon?'

Sergeant Malick laughed, then coughed. 'Throne. Wish I hadn't done that. Even the air is hot.'

'Everything's hot on this damned planet.'

Malick turned and stared at Gunsur. 'You saying you don't want to be here, trooper? That's treason.'

Gunsur shook his head, suddenly unsure. 'You playing me, Sergeant Malick?'

Before Malick could answer, another voice spoke.

'Yes, are you playing him, Sergeant Malick?'

The two Cadians scrambled to their feet, the sand beneath their boots crunching.

Sergeant Malick looked at the man standing in front of them.

He was wearing fatigues that gave no indication of rank. He was even barefoot. But everything else about him suggested 'officer'. Malick decided to play it safe.

'Yes, I was playing him. Sir.'

The man nodded. 'Good. I rather hoped you were. It would mean that you might have the wit to lead this team.'

Malick blinked. 'Sir?'

'Assemble the rest of the squad.'

Malick stared at the man. 'Who are you? Sir.'

'Bharath Obeysekera.' The man regarded Malick through sun-slit eyes. 'Captain Bharath Obeysekera. For your sins, you have been given into my command. Now call the troopers.'

'Yes, sir.' With a definite order to carry out, Malick made the aquila and spun off to see it done. 'Fall in!' he roared, in his best sergeant's voice, the sound of it filling the dead, empty desert air.

It was a voice that had Captain Obeysekera putting his hand on Sergeant Malick's shoulder and saying so that only he could hear: 'Use the squad vox-channel. This will be a mission of silence. Best you start getting used to being quiet, Sergeant Malick.'

'Yes…' Malick cut off the second half of his barked reply. 'Sir,' he finished.

'Good man,' said Obeysekera. 'Assemble the squad in the shade – we will all have had enough sun soon. Colonel Aruna will address you first, then I will fill in the details.'

Captain Obeysekera turned away, his bare feet quiet on the sand, and slipped away into the deeper, darker shadows of the interior of the Valkyrie.

Sergeant Malick picked up his helmet and keyed the squad vox-channel, sending alerts to the other seven troopers in the unit. He saw on the auspex integrated into his helmet that they had all acknowledged. Tracer runes showed them all moving to the location he had marked on the auspex, the outlying troops converging from the sentry positions Malick had ordered them to after the Valkyries had landed.

Gunsur leaned over towards Malick. 'The only time I ever saw a captain dressed like that, he'd been stripped and had his ribs opened out by those Gallows Cluster traitors. You sure he is a real captain?'

'Didn't you see?'

'See what?'

'When he went back inside. He's proper 'kin, all right – he's got the eagle on his neck. Besides, I reckon I've heard of him.'

'Yeah? Where?'

'The Sando retreat. He sent his 'kin squad to hold up the 'nids while he marshalled the civvies onto exfiltration vehicles.'

Gunsur looked at his sergeant. 'Yeah? So?'

'None of them got out, but *he* did.'

Gunsur nodded. 'One of those officers.'

Malick shook his head. 'Don't know. But I'm keeping this beauty to hand.' The sergeant picked up the hellgun that was leaning against the ticking plasteel of the Valkyrie. He ran his hand over the use-polished stock of the hellgun, its paluwood the colour of aged honey. 'This beauty will put a hotshot through the eye of any xenos at a mile.'

Gunsur gestured towards the desert. 'You reckon we'll meet any bluies out there, sarge? Don't look like the sort of place they'd be interested in.'

'They're xenos scum,' said Malick. 'Who knows what they're interested in. Besides, from what I hear, there's plenty on this planet to draw the attention of the bluies.'

'Yeah, sand,' said Gunsur. 'Lots and lots of sand.'

Malick cuffed Gunsur on the shoulder. 'There's stuff under the sand's worth more'n most subsectors. That's probably why we're here on…' The sergeant paused and gestured out from the shadow under the wing to the vast dry world that surrounded them.

'It is called Dasht i-Kevar.'

Sergeant Malick and Trooper Gunsur turned around to see Captain Obeysekera, now dressed in the grey and tan of the Kasrkin, standing at the top of the rear ramp of the Valkyrie holding, of all things, his dress cap in one hand.

'Colonel Aruna will brief you on your deployment here and the strategic objective. I will cover the tactical situation.' Captain Obeysekera pointed over to the next Valkyrie, standing stark and outlined in the sun. 'You don't want to keep the colonel waiting, do you?'

'No, sir,' said Malick. The sergeant glanced at the auspex; the other squad members were drawing in towards the mark.

The three men stepped out of the shade under the Valkyrie's wing. The sun hit them with the weight of lead, pressing down upon their heads.

Captain Obeysekera put his dress cap on his head. 'Only time this has been any use.' He looked at Malick and Gunsur. 'Here, helmets are barely better than bare heads – you want a cap and scarf.'

Malick shook his head. He pointed at various gouges and scratches on his helmet. 'I wouldn't be here without this. Besides, we might need the rebreather.'

'We might need lots of things, but none of them will matter if we can't get to where we need to go.' Obeysekera looked at Malick. 'You're from Kasr Vasan. Hear it had the best logistics on Cadia. You're used to having the right weapon on hand when you need it. I grew up in Kasr Gesh. We were lucky if we had a power pack to go in our lasrifles, let alone a spare. On this mission, we will be on our own. We carry in everything we need, and when we run out we make do with what we've got left over, and when we run out of that we'll use our hands. I expect every man to be able to adapt. If you can't, I'll get someone who can. Understand?'

Malick stared back at the officer. Obeysekera regarded him mildly but steadily.

'I have never failed on a mission.'

'Which is why I asked for you, sergeant. Your record suggests a soldier who is willing to use his brain and think. Is that true?'

Malick paused, staring at Captain Obeysekera, and then, slowly, he began to smile.

'Yes, sir, it is true.' He pointed at Gunsur. 'Not so sure about Gunsur, though.'

'That's all right, sergeant. We can't have troopers thinking, can we?'

Obeysekera set off over the hot sand, his feet, now booted, sinking small pits into the ground as he went, with Malick and Gunsur following, heading towards the command Valkyrie. Reaching the bowl of sand blown out by the Valkyrie's turbofans when it landed, they crested the rim and started down towards the machine squatting in the middle of the wide crater. The sand slid away under their boots, slipping like liquid so that they all but skied down the inside of the bowl. Fifty yards away, the command Valkyrie stood, its lower half hidden by the sand bowl. Other men were centring in on the Valkyrie, some from the third craft that made the other base of the landing triangle, the rest from the perimeter positions that Malick had assigned to them.

The Valkyries themselves were not sitting silently on the sand. Their turbofans rotated gently, pushing air through the vents to placate machine-spirits grinding sand between their plasteel teeth. The pilots sat ready in the cockpits, eyes hidden behind black goggles, while the heavy bolters mounted on the Valkyries continued to track over the landscape, empty though it was. But the heat haze, rising all around them, reduced visibility: anything over half a mile away dissolved into rising columns of heated air, twisting slowly under the sun.

It was a strangely flat landscape, unrelieved by shade, even though the sand rose in static waves to their east as it stretched into the Great Sand Sea. To the west, the land was rock and salt-flat, studded with shallow outcrops and basalt columns.

'There're no shadows,' said Malick. He pointed down at his feet. 'Where has it gone?'

Obeysekera laughed, the harsh sound cut short by the dry heat. He pointed straight overhead. 'Up there.'

Malick squinted up, cricking his neck back and back, the flare guards in his goggles activating. Above him, the sun that squatted over Dasht i-Kevar rode, a white eye sitting on top of the sky arch.

Malick looked back to Captain Obeysekera. 'I don't understand.'

The captain grimaced. 'Don't worry, it won't last.' Obeysekera looked up into the sky too, his eyes becoming slits as he did so. 'Thankfully.' He glanced back to Malick. 'With no shadows it's impossible to judge distance. Speaking of distance, let's not keep the colonel waiting.'

The Kasrkin sergeant saw the sweat pricking through Obeysekera's skin, only for it to evaporate as it appeared.

'This is hotter than Prosan,' he said.

Captain Obeysekera looked back at the sergeant. 'It's about the same in terms of climate. But there are other things…' His voice trailed away as his eyes, squinting against the overwhelming light, took in the Great Sand Sea. 'Let us hope we do not meet them.'

As they neared the command Valkyrie, Malick saw the rest of the squad assembling in the shade under the wings: some squatting, others sitting on their helmets, hands resting upon their treasured weapons, the hotshot lasguns they nicknamed 'hellguns'. The last of the perimeter troopers were walking in, hellguns cradled on forearms. Malick glanced at his auspex: they were all here.

Just as he was about to look away from the display, he saw movement traces and, glancing up, he saw a man in a high-ranking officer's uniform emerge from the Valkyrie.

Aruna. The colonel's reputation had spread sector-wide. He had led the defence of Krack des Chavel against an insurrection of Chaos cultists, woken to frenzy by the great purple bruise that split the night sky. He had planned and led the assault on the ork warband led by Grashbash the Grabbler that had laid waste to three systems. And the word among the Guard was that Colonel Aruna was the brains behind the unusually subtle attempts to retake the Imperial worlds in the subsector that had succumbed to the blandishments, diplomatic and militant, of the T'au Empire.

In Malick's previous experience, whenever the Guard had retaken Imperial worlds that had been lost to the enemy, be that Chaos or xenos, it had been necessary to repopulate the planet after the victory. Aruna had managed to retain a viable population on two of the planets he had wrested back from the t'au.

Colonel Aruna came down the ramp and stood on the sand among the squad of Kasrkin. The 'kin regarded the colonel with battle-hardened eyes, then, slowly, one by one, stood and saluted him. The troops, looking upon the colonel, measuring him, saw him as one of their own: a soldier who had stood in the midst of battle without flinching, a man who had faced death on as many occasions as they had and not let fear prevent him from doing his duty to the Emperor.

As the Kasrkin acknowledged the colonel as their equal, the

colonel returned the salute. Seeing Captain Obeysekera, he nodded to him then turned to the waiting, silent 'kin.

'We have lost a general. You are going to find him and bring him back.'

The Kasrkin greeted the news in silence, but it was a silence that held a wealth of unanswered questions relating to the conduct of the mission and the chance of carrying it out successfully.

'General Mato Itoyesa, commanding officer eastern sector, was returning to headquarters when his Valkyrie was attacked by t'au Barracudas. Attempting to evade the xenos, the general's pilot flew into a sandstorm.'

Colonel Aruna paused as he said that, looking around the watching Kasrkin. They said nothing but Malick saw, from the tightening of muscles, that they all knew what such an action meant: arriving on Dasht i-Kevar, it was drummed into every combatant, be they ordinary soldier, Kasrkin or Imperial Navy, never to deliberately enter one of the planet's sandstorms. Such was the violence of the storms that an unprotected soldier would be flayed in a few minutes. Aircraft such as Valkyries had their engines clogged, their machine-spirits choking on vast quantities of sand, while even the normally indomitable Leman Russ would grind to a stop as the corrosive grains insinuated themselves into gears and bearings.

'Transmissions indicated that the general's aircraft managed to land successfully, but we have only very approximate indications of its location. No further transmissions have been received, despite our efforts to raise General Itoyesa. As the commanding officer of the eastern sector, I do not have to tell you how important it is that the general does not fall into xenos hands.' The colonel paused and looked around the watching, silent Kasrkin. 'It is your job to ensure that he does not. Questions?'

Malick looked at the surrounding troops. There were many
questions that could be asked, but they were 'kin: they did the
jobs no one else could do. He expected no reply.

But a voice spoke.

'That is what I don't understand. Why did the general's pilot
fly into the sandstorm? It was strictly against the orders of the
lord militant.'

The questioner stepped forward out of the deep shadows of
the loading bay and into the softer shade under the Valkyrie's
wings. He was a young man, with all the leanness of youth, but
his leanness was sheathed, despite the heat, in the long drapes
of the coat of a commissar of the Officio Prefectus.

Colonel Aruna turned towards the young man and shook his
head. 'It is a question we shall put to the pilot should he be
recovered in a state to answer. I am sure your father will be as
keen to learn the answer as you are.'

'I am sure he will. Lord Militant Roshant is… concerned that
one of his key generals has disappeared.'

'As are we all, Commissar Roshant,' said Colonel Aruna.

At the name, all the men listening stiffened slightly. Commissar Roshant gave no obvious indication that he was aware
of their regard, but Malick saw the halo of self-regard that clung
about one of the appointed of the Imperial elite, as invisible
and as impenetrable as a refractor field. The Kasrkin sergeant
squinted. There was a subtle phase effect around Commissar
Roshant that suggested he might actually be employing a
refractor field.

'That is also why my father, the lord militant, has ordered me
to accompany your men on their mission.' The young commissar
paused slightly as he said this. The Kasrkin, no strangers to the
ways of Imperial commissars, knew well that he had paused so
that he might assess their reaction to this news. What physical

reaction they gave was minimal: some tightening of the eyes, quick glances, nothing more.

For his part, Malick looked to Captain Obeysekera, seeking to judge if he had had any warning that the lord militant's son would be accompanying them on their mission. But at the news, the captain's expression remained as blank as the desert on the day after a storm, when the windblown sand had scoured all tracks from its face.

Commissar Roshant, evidently satisfied with what he saw in the faces of the watching Kasrkin, turned back to Colonel Aruna.

'Should we find the general alive, it will be imperative to assess immediately whether he has been compromised. Should we find the general dead, the same question will arise. And should we fail to find the general, the question will become even more urgent. My father has given me the task of answering these questions.'

Colonel Aruna nodded. 'Very well, commissar. But, unless you have received new orders from the lord militant, operational command of this mission remains with Captain Obeysekera.' Colonel Aruna paused, making sure that all the men present were listening and would be able to hear the answer.

'Yes, that is correct.' The words sounded forced, as if Commissar Roshant said them against his will. Malick, face impassive, smiled inwardly at imagining the son pleading to his father for command of the mission and that permission being denied.

Colonel Aruna nodded. 'Thank you, commissar. So that there might be no misunderstanding, you will be attached to the mission as its commissar, with responsibility for the political and religious welfare of the men, but answerable to the mission commander, Captain Obeysekera. Is that clear?'

Commissar Roshant stared at Colonel Aruna, then glanced at Captain Obeysekera. 'Yes, it is clear,' he said through narrowed lips.

'Very well,' said Colonel Aruna. 'I am glad we have cleared that up before the mission begins.' The colonel began to turn away, but before he could do so, Roshant spoke again.

'While it is true that Captain Obeysekera has operational command of the mission, it is also true that Lord Militant Roshant has asked me to write a full report on this operation. I will of course note any instances where Captain Obeysekera fails to adhere to my advice – the advice of a commissar of the God-Emperor's Imperium.' Roshant looked from Aruna to Obeysekera. 'Is that clear, too?'

The colonel looked at the commissar. 'Perfectly clear.'

Roshant turned to Obeysekera. 'Captain?'

Sergeant Malick saw the danger light in the captain's eyes, a glint even in the deep shadow under the Valkyrie's wing.

'I understand, Commissar Roshant,' said Captain Obeysekera. His eyes broadened and he smiled. 'For my part, I am grateful that you will be writing a full report of the mission as that will save me the labour of filing my own account.' Obeysekera turned to the colonel. 'Now that is settled, shall I start the mission briefing, sir?'

'Yes, please do so.'

Captain Obeysekera paused and looked at each of the watching soldiers. His glance caught on something on Gunsur's uniform.

'Take off your campaign medals and kasr tags. That you fought in the Haetes Second Star campaign or which kasr you hail from is of no interest to me. For what it's worth, you are now part of First Squad, One Hundred and Fifty-Fifth. But I don't really care about that either.' Obeysekera looked round the waiting soldiers. 'All that matters is the mission.'

He waited.

Slowly, first in ones or twos, then followed by the rest, the Kasrkin removed their campaign medals, stowing them in pockets, and tucked their kasr tags away out of sight.

When they were all simply Kasrkin with no other identifying marks, Obeysekera nodded.

'Thank you. Uwais. Ha. Prater. Ensor. Chame. Quert. Lerin.'

Malick glanced at Lerin as her name was spoken. He had heard of her reputation with heavy weapons.

'Gunsur. Malick.'

As the captain called out each name, Malick realised that Obeysekera already knew who each soldier in the squad was.

'Sir,' he said.

Obeysekera paused, drawing the listening troopers in closer. 'This mission will test even the very best. For we will not only be facing the enemy, we will be fighting a planet.' Obeysekera gestured outwards, his arm taking in all the unseen expanses of Dasht i-Kevar. 'This world kills. All of it is deadly, but we will be going into the most dangerous area of Dasht i-Kevar, the Sand Sea. It kills with heat and exhaustion, it kills by blinding and wearing down, it kills the stupid with ease and the clever with indifference. Our survival on this mission, and its successful accomplishment, will rely upon exact attention to detail and an ability to maintain concentration under the most difficult conditions that you have ever known.'

Captain Obeysekera stepped forward. He looked at his squad, the Kasrkin gathered around him in the shade below the wing of the Valkyrie, and he smiled.

'I've got something to show you,' he said.

 CHAPTER 2

Captain Obeysekera lined his men up along the rim of the Valkyrie's blast crater. The sun of Dasht i-Kevar had slipped from the zenith, and with the return of shadows the world had depth again. He peered into the east, shading his eyes with his hand, then turning his head to listen.

Yes, there. The distant, cyclic thrum of turbofans.

Obeysekera glanced along the line of soldiers. They were 'kin: they had picked up the sound. Those wearing their helmets would have received warning from the in-built auspexes, tracking the inbound traces. They stood with their weapons lightly held but ready: hellguns, the hotshot lasrifles that were the standard-issue weapons for the Cadian elite. Obeysekera had seen a hellgun take the head off an ork at two miles. As the noise of the turbofans grew, the hellguns were slowly raised, without command from either him or Sergeant Malick, until only a minimal movement would have them ready for use.

Obeysekera glanced towards the commissar. Roshant was looking from side to side, then to the approaching noise. Under the sun's weight, sweat was pricking through his skin, but the aridity of the air dried the liquid as soon as it appeared, leaving only salt streaks on the skin.

Feeling the gaze, Roshant looked at Obeysekera.

'What are we waiting for?' he asked.

Obeysekera could see the flush in the man's face as his animal spirits pushed blood to the skin in an attempt to cool it. But the air was hotter than blood: there was no cooling there.

'You will see soon, commissar,' said Obeysekera.

He squinted east. The sand was boiling, rising in abrupt gusts from the desert. Running before the sand, coming directly towards them low over the ground, were the splayed M's of three approaching Valkyries. They were shapes familiar to all the men watching. But hanging beneath the mid-point of each ship was another, smaller outline.

Obeysekera glanced again along the line and saw, from the grins spreading across a few faces, that some of the men recognised what they saw.

The Sky Talons approached, their outlines emphasised by the clouds of windblown sand rising behind them. The note of the turbofans changed as they began to slow, the pitch rising from the regular low thrum of level flight to the headache-inducing scream of landing. Only, the Valkyries did not land. Reducing their speed, they crawled closer, the sand billowing up further from the downdraught of the turbofans. Then the clamps beneath the three aircraft released, and the vehicles they were carrying fell the final few yards onto the soft sand.

Their loads delivered, the Valkyries reared away, up into the sky towards the sun, like horses freed from their riders. The sand-churn chased up after them before falling back.

Captain Obeysekera felt the colonel's regard and looked over to him. Aruna raised an eyebrow.

'Not my idea,' said Obeysekera, spreading his hands in innocence. 'They must be in a hurry to go elsewhere.'

'Indeed,' said Colonel Aruna, looking up into the sky. The three Valkyries had dwindled to dots.

Sergeant Malick pointed at the vehicles the Valkyries had left behind. 'Those our rides, captain?'

'Yes, sergeant. They are indeed our rides.'

Sergeant Malick grinned. 'Three Tauros Venators.'

Obeysekera pointed at the leftmost vehicle. 'Twin-linked multi-laser. That will be my command vehicle, call sign *Holy Fire*.' He pointed at the right-hand vehicle. 'Twin-linked lascannon. Call sign *Divine Light*. That one is yours, sergeant. Both modified to take driver and navigator as well as gunner.' Then he indicated the central vehicle. 'Modified as a troop carrier – driver, navigator and up to eight men in the back. Call sign *Saint Conrad*.'

The sergeant's smile broadened. 'Always wanted to try out one of these ever since I saw the One Hundred and Eighty-First Elysians use them on Patanal. Never seen anything Imperial move so fast on land.'

'They're light, fast and quiet,' said Obeysekera. 'Exactly what we need. Have three men bring them over. We'll need to load them up.'

'Gunsur, Ensor, Prater, bring them over...' Malick paused.

'One by each Valkyrie, sergeant,' said Obeysekera.

'You heard the captain.' The sergeant grinned at the three men. 'Don't ever say I give you all the worst jobs.'

Gunsur, Ensor and Prater, smiling at the jealous calls of their overlooked comrades, made their way over the sand towards the three Venators, while Malick, at a gesture from Obeysekera, set the rest of the squad to unloading the supplies from the Valkyries.

While the troops shifted the crates of powercells, supplies and, heaviest of all, barrels of water, Obeysekera moved so that he could get a better view of the Tauros Venators.

Gunsur, Ensor and Prater each climbed into their seats, strapped the webbing around their torsos and, with swift prayers to each vehicle's machine-spirit, engaged the galvanic motors. Obeysekera nodded as instead of the usual promethium-laced roar that accompanied the start of most Imperial vehicles, the Venators hummed, sounding more like the idle buzz of a chainsword than a herd of stampeding grox. With their six large wheels ploughing shallow grooves through the sand, the three Venators approached, each peeling off towards its own supply ship, where the troopers began loading the supplies, strapping water drums into the racks welded onto the sides of the Venators and stowing the powercells in the armoured ammunition boxes lining the interior of the vehicles.

'There's no roof,' said Roshant.

Obeysekera looked round. He had been so absorbed with overseeing the loading of the vehicles, running his hand over the rough plasteel to get a sense of their machine-spirits, that he had not heard the approach of the commissar. He chided himself for that. It did not do to allow his senses to become so focused that he could not notice someone coming closer.

'No, there isn't,' agreed Obeysekera.

The commissar was sweating, even though he was standing in the shade of the Valkyrie. The dust-dry air of Dasht i-Kevar sucked the sweat from his skin as soon as it formed.

Roshant took off his commissar's cap. 'Out there, we'll need all the shade we can get.'

'Agreed,' said Obeysekera. He pointed towards Malick, who was stringing tan-coloured netting over the driver's and navigator's compartment of the Venator. 'Which is why we have that. It will provide shade and allow air circulation.'

Roshant sniffed. 'Not sure if I want air this hot circulating anywhere near me.'

'Better it moves than it doesn't,' said Obeysekera, 'even if it feels like being in an oven.'

Roshant pointed at the water drums. 'They're on the outside. If they get holed by the enemy, then...'

'Then we die of thirst,' finished Obeysekera. He pointed at Roshant's water flask. 'You've got that – we're all carrying personal rations. But there is no room to carry water drums inside the vehicles. At least water makes effective armour. So we'll survive the ambush.'

'To die three days later.'

Obeysekera shook his head. 'Not three days. Not here. Personal flasks will be good for about a day. After that, without water, we won't last another day.'

Roshant nodded. He reached to his hip and, taking the flask from his belt, raised it to his lips and drank. 'I find that talk of death by dehydration makes me thirsty.'

'You might think about leaving behind the coat and cap, then.'

Roshant stared at Obeysekera. 'If the commissar cannot command his body against the conditions, how can he expect the men to command themselves in the face of the enemy?'

Obeysekera shook his head. 'From my experience, 'kin respect officers on the basis of what they do, not what they wear.'

'I am a commissar. I do not ask for their respect – I demand their duty.'

'Very well.' Obeysekera pointed at Roshant's flask. 'Better drink up before we set off. Water will be rationed when we begin.'

'Oh, I will, I will.' Roshant took another long draught then headed towards one of the barrels, to refill his flask.

'There's water in the Valkyrie,' said Obeysekera.

Roshant sniffed, continued to the water barrel and reached for the tap. But before he could turn it, Malick knocked the commissar's hand away.

Roshant drew back. His other hand went to his bolt pistol, drawing it from his shoulder holster and pointing it at Sergeant Malick.

'Striking an officer, let alone a commissar, is a capital offence,' Roshant said. 'Tell me why I should not execute the sentence at once.'

'Because Sergeant Malick was following my orders,' said Obeysekera, stepping forward and putting himself between the commissar and the Kasrkin soldier. 'He has strict instructions that no one may draw water from these barrels without explicit assent from me.' Obeysekera reached out a hand and rested it on one of the barrels. 'On Dasht i-Kevar, and even more in the Great Sand Sea, water is life.'

Commissar Roshant notched the barrel of the bolt pistol back, so that it pointed slightly above Obeysekera's eyes. Then, his finger tightened on the trigger.

The bolt-shell sizzled past Obeysekera's head, close enough for the captain to feel his hair, which he had allowed to grow longer than the usual Cadian crew cut, crisping.

Sergeant Malick's hellgun appeared, levelled and ready, pointing steadily at the centre of the commissar's chest.

'Try that again...' the sergeant began, but Obeysekera held his hand up.

'No need for that, sergeant.' He gently put his hand on the barrel of Malick's hellgun and pushed it down. 'I am sure the commissar has an explanation.'

Commissar Roshant smiled. 'My father, the lord militant, received this oath when I swore myself to the Emperor's service – that I would never draw weapon without discharging it. So by discharging it, I was fulfilling my oath to the Emperor – as must all who serve Him.' The commissar twirled the bolt pistol, allowing Captain Obeysekera to see the carved ivory of the grip, before replacing the weapon in its holster.

Obeysekera paused, then asked, 'Amphant ivory?'

Roshant nodded. 'Yes.'

'Impressive.'

'Indeed.'

The commissar looked towards the Venator. 'Inform me when the vehicles are loaded. I will make a final report before we depart.' With that, Roshant turned and made his way back into the relative cool inside the Valkyrie.

When he was out of earshot, Sergeant Malick turned to Obeysekera.

'Amphant ivory? Really?'

Obeysekera nodded. 'I think it was. It had the patina I've read about – a sheen of gold.'

Malick blew air through his teeth. 'This is a first, going on mission with a weapon that's worth more than we are.'

Obeysekera grimaced. 'In the Guard, that is scarcely unusual.'

Malick grunted. 'Point. But you could buy ten years of luxury on Venera with it.'

Captain Obeysekera turned to his sergeant. 'Better not tell the men, then.'

'I won't have to if he keeps waving it around like that.'

Obeysekera looked at Malick. 'I want the commissar alive when we return, understood?'

Malick nodded. 'Of course. But you know how it is in battle – things go missing.'

'Malick...'

The sergeant grinned. 'Just joking, sir.'

'Besides, you're wrong about the bolt pistol being the only valuable thing around here. Dasht i-Kevar is the most valuable world in the system by far.'

Malick waved his hand, the gesture taking in the wide expanse of nothing beyond them. 'This exceptional piece of the Emperor's estate? I heard there's something precious under the sand, but I'll be damned if I can see it.'

Captain Obeysekera nodded. 'It's true. They get aqua vitae from here.'

'Life water? Is that what it sounds like it is?'

'Yes. The most effective rejuve treatment in the sector. A bottle of the stuff costs more than a Custodian's armour. All rejuve and none of the unpleasant side effects most of the other treatments have.'

Malick gestured again. 'But where's the water? Where's the life?'

Obeysekera shrugged. 'I don't know. No one knows, save the desert tribes who trade it – or who used to trade it, before the bluies turned up.' He grinned grimly at his sergeant. 'That's why we're here on this planet – to ensure that our generals and planetary governors stay thirty-four when they're really two hundred and forty.' The captain laughed but there was little humour in the sound. 'We die so they can remain beautiful.'

Sergeant Malick stared at his captain. 'Throne. Is that it? Is that why we're going into the fire?'

Hearing the sergeant's tone, Obeysekera looked up and out of his introspection.

'No, that's not why *we're* doing it, sergeant. We're doing it because we're Guard and we do what we're ordered to do, even if it's stupid and pointless, which most of the time it is. We're doing it because we're Kasrkin and we do the jobs no one else can do.' The captain's face suddenly broke into a smile and he pointed at the Venator. 'And we're doing it because we're going to get the chance to gun these flat out with no one around to tell us to back off. You ready for that?'

Malick's smile matched that of Obeysekera. 'Oh, I'm ready, sir.'

 # CHAPTER 3

The Tauros Venator *Holy Fire* drove up the slope, its six fat tyres sending rivers of sand tumbling back behind it. But the tyres dug deep into the shifting surface, finding purchase, and the machine surged forwards. The other two Venators, *Divine Light* and *Saint Conrad*, flanked it as they followed it up the dune, cutting channels through the sand, following the contours of the desert like boats over an ocean of water.

Captain Obeysekera sat in the navigator's seat of *Holy Fire*, map spread on his knees, chrono in one hand, stylus in the other, tracing their track upon the thick paper. As they neared the crest of the dune, Obeysekera looked up, checking again the dials on the minimal panel before him: speed, distance and compass bearing. Beside him, he could hear Trooper Gunsur crooning to the machine-spirit of the Venator, urging it on and encouraging it as its wheels, suddenly encountering slicker sand, began to spin.

'Come on, you can do it, come on, yes, yes, come on.'

The tyres bit, finding traction, and the Venator pushed upwards, its front nearly forty degrees above its rear.

'Yes!' Gunsur slapped the steering wheel. 'Come on.'.

'Trooper.' Obeysekera, still following their course and speed without allowing his concentration to lapse, tapped the driver on his arm. 'Halt just after the crest. I want to take a look.'

'Sir.' Gunsur tapped the steering wheel again. 'She'll get us there, you'll see she will.'

Obeysekera looked ahead. The final slope of the vast sand wave rose above them, its flank growing steeper as it reached the crest. He was thankful for the galvanic motors that powered the vehicle. Even with the machine-spirit straining to drive the Tauros up the slope, the Venator was quiet. If he had been leading a trio of Sentinels – the machines that the lord militant's headquarters had suggested for the mission – the howling of the machine-spirits and the grinding of their gears and engines would have alerted any enemy within ten miles of their approach. Dasht i-Kevar was a quiet world and the Great Sand Sea was quieter: only war brought noise and movement, sound and fury to its surface.

Obeysekera glanced at the other two Venators that formed his squad. They were fifty yards distant on each flank. On the left, in *Divine Light*, Trooper Chame was cycling the twin-linked las-cannon through targeting options, the head cloth that Obeysekera had demonstrated to his men wrapped loosely over her face and blowing behind her in the wind of the Venator's passing. In the stripped-out driver's seat, Obeysekera saw Sergeant Malick with Trooper Prater beside him in the navigator's position.

On the right, Trooper Ha was driving the Venator carrier, *Saint Conrad*, with Lerin the navigator and Roshant squeezed into a third seat behind them and the rest of the squad in the back. Obeysekera reminded himself to move Roshant when they stopped. The commissar had barely hidden his displeasure at being assigned that post. Obeysekera suspected that the discomfort of the seat was a lesser factor than the perceived slight of not accompanying the commanding officer. So long as it did not compromise the mission, it would be better to keep Roshant happy.

Obeysekera heard the pitch of the galvanic motors increase and he looked ahead: the slope was rising to the final crest.

'Take us over, then stop,' Obeysekera said to Gunsur.

'Sir.'

Another advantage of the Venator, Obeysekera thought, was that the machine was quiet enough for the driver to hear his instructions without having to speak on the vox-circuit.

The nose of the Venator tipped up and sand splashed over it, spraying across Obeysekera's face. The cloth he had wrapped around his nose and mouth stopped him spitting sand – the particles were so fine they could work their way into a rebreather – but he had to wipe his goggles clear and shake off the residue from his map. As he did so, the world tilted forward, suddenly, precipitously, and the galvanic motors whined to their highest pitch as the rear wheels, free of the sand drag, spun without hindrance. The Venator balanced for an instant on the crest of the wave and then, as Trooper Gunsur throttled back, it began to settle, its weight digging it into the dune. The wheels, front and back, made contact as the Venator sank lower, and its balance – knife-edge before – broadened.

Obeysekera let out the breath he had not realised he had been holding. He looked over to Gunsur.

'Good driving, trooper.'

Gunsur nodded. By the sweat pricking through his skin, Obeysekera knew that the trooper had not been sure of holding the Venator on the crest. Now it was up to him to use the position as quickly as possible: the skyline was not a good place to linger.

Obeysekera stood up, grabbing the roll bar to steady himself. 'Watch out, sir. I could have taken your head off.'

Obeysekera looked behind him to see Trooper Quert peering at him from over the barrels of the twin-linked multi-laser. She was tracking off south and Obeysekera realised that if Quert had swept them central while he was standing up, he would have been crushed against the roll bar.

The captain raised his hand. 'Point taken. I will make sure to warn you in future if I am going to stand up.' Obeysekera turned back and, raising his hand to shield his eyes from the sun, he peered into the west.

From the top of the two hundred-yard-high sand dune, Obeysekera saw the crests of other dunes winding across the erg, running roughly north to south, some cresting to a height matching the dune he was balanced upon, others lower but broader. It was still early in the morning and the distance had the clarity of the night. He stared at the horizon, searching for some sign of what he was looking for.

There. Rising above the erg in a series of smooth humps, like some monster rising from the depths of the Great Sand Sea: the Tabaste. Even at this distance – some fifty miles – Obeysekera could see why it was also called the Old Mountain: time had smoothed and worn it, leaving the rose-and-orange nubs of the vast volcanoes that had once risen above the sands of Dasht i-Kevar.

The Tabaste was the location of the last signal from General Itoyesa's Valkyrie.

It was as well they had crested the rise early to look for the Tabaste; by mid-morning at the latest, the heat haze, rising in shimmering, dancing columns from the desert, reduced visibility to little more than a mile – and that was without the sandstorms.

Obeysekera tried to take a reading on the Tabaste so that he could plot the bearing on his map, but even here, just a handful of miles into the Great Sand Sea, the auspex was becoming unreliable. Obeysekera tapped it, and the readings finally settled. But he knew it would not be much longer before it became completely unusable. There was some anomaly within the Great Sand Sea that affected instruments, causing the machine-spirits to falter and the readings to vary wildly or fail utterly. Only basic magnetic compasses and vox continued to work with any degree of reliability, but even they could not be trusted entirely.

Hence the maps that Obeysekera carried and his careful logging of distance, time, speed and direction. They were the only sure way of getting back.

Even as Obeysekera took and checked his bearings, the two flanking Venators reached the crest of the dune and settled there, sinking into the ridge, the three vehicles fifty yards apart.

Obeysekera sat down and traced further lines on his map. Beside him, Trooper Gunsur was silent; Obeysekera subconsciously noted the quiet ratcheting sounds as Trooper Quert rotated the twin-linked multi-laser, scanning over the erg ahead.

'I never knew there could be so many yellows.'

The words were quiet. If Obeysekera had not just finished the final plot he might not have heard them, but, map work done, he was looking up when Gunsur spoke. Obeysekera glanced at his driver. Gunsur was staring ahead, looking out over the still waves of the Sand Sea, and his eyes were full of the colours of the desert. The netting, stretched over their heads, stippled the shade on Gunsur, but the open windscreen allowed the slight early morning wind to play over their faces, still cool enough to bring some relief from the heat. Later in the day, the wind would rise, like bellows stoking a furnace, and its touch would only heighten the discomfort of the afternoon.

Obeysekera looked back out over the erg and he saw what Gunsur saw.

'You are right. I did not know there could be so many yellows, either.'

Gunsur jerked and looked to the captain. 'I didn't mean to speak aloud, sir.'

'Don't worry.' Obeysekera grinned, although only his eyes showed above his face cloth. 'I am glad to have had it pointed out to me.'

The captain looked back, at the steep slip face descending before them and the rising and falling waves of sand stretching into the distance with the smoothed-out mounds of the Tabaste on the horizon.

'You know, sometimes, I think that if only there weren't so many things trying to kill us all the time, the galaxy could be a beautiful place.' Obeysekera grinned again, but it was bleaker this time, as his eyes squinted into the distance. 'But it seems like we were made only for war.' He nodded towards the Sand Sea. 'So it's good to see somewhere that war has left no marks upon, eh, Gunsur?'

The trooper nodded. 'Yes, sir.' He hesitated, then continued. 'You know, sir, I've seen some sights in my time – the Kefahuchi Reach, the sun rising over the Caducades, the Twelve Sisters – but this is as pretty as any of them.' He fell silent for a moment as he stared out at the desert and all its myriad shades of yellow below the vivid blue arch of the sky, then lowered his gaze. 'You're right, sir. It's good to see somewhere peaceful. But now we're here, I s'pose it won't stay peaceful for long.' Gunsur looked back to Obeysekera. 'Shall I start her up, sir?'

Obeysekera was about to give his permission, when he stopped. He glanced along the ridgetop, at the other two Venators poised there, on a solid but shifting wave, remote from the sound or sight of war.

It was quiet here. Peaceful.

The realisation came upon him as he looked at the Sand Sea.

It was pure, unmarked. If any had perished near them, enemy or Guard, the desert had covered all trace.

In the silence, the only sound the ticking of the plasteel expanding under the sun's lash, Obeysekera heard the echo of a galaxy at peace. Cadia, lost and broken. Cadia had been the eternal fortress against Chaos, its people the warriors who kept the rest of the Imperium safe through the sacrifice of their lives. He had known nothing but war; his world had known nothing but war until it died. But sitting there in silence, atop the still wave in the Sand Sea, Obeysekera heard a still, small voice, as quiet as his blood, whisper peace.

'Wait here.' Obeysekera held his hand up to Gunsur, unstrapped the webbing, then swung his legs out of the Venator and stepped down onto the sand. The dune, softer than sea mud, swallowed his feet up to the ankles.

Inside him, a voice – the voice of discipline and duty and the veteran Guardsmen who had trained him – was muttering madness. But another voice, quieter but more compelling, told him to walk.

Obeysekera walked. Pulling his boots out of the sand, he waded along the ridgetop. As he did so, the sand, pulled and pushed by his passing, started to shift, sliding in small and then greater sheets down the slip face of the dune.

And the sand began to sing.

At first it was gentle, a sound akin to the wind blowing through the paluwood groves of Cadia. Then it grew and deepened, taking on the register of the Caducades Sea breaking upon the hundred-mile-long shingle breakwater that protected the Manhof Reach from the sea's full fury.

Had protected, Obeysekera corrected himself.

But the sound continued, deepening, broadening, assuming overtones that hearkened to the mournful music of the tsiranope, the ancient pipes of Kasr Gesh, his home.

The desert was singing.

Obeysekera looked up as he walked along the ridge. He had not realised it – and would have taken the other direction if he had – but he was heading towards the Venator that was carrying Commissar Roshant. For a moment, Obeysekera thought of turning round and returning to his vehicle. But he wanted to hear more.

Wading along the ridgetop, the desert singing its bass threnody for the galaxy, Obeysekera walked in wonder.

As he approached the waiting Venator, he realised that part of the reason he had kept going was that he wanted to know if they heard the song too. Perhaps he was going mad. But the gestures from Ha and Lerin, and Ensor and Uwais in the back of the Venator, pointing to their ears, told that they too were hearing what Obeysekera was hearing. Some of the faces were looking alarmed, but Obeysekera raised his hands, palms downward, to let them know all was well. With the song resounding in his lungs and in his blood, he was loath to break its music by speaking through the squad vox-channel.

'What in the Emperor's name is that cursed moaning sound?'

The voice, all too clear, cut into his ear from the micro-bead in his shoulder pauldron. Obeysekera had a link to the squad vox-channel in his helmet and another embedded into his carapace armour should he have to remove the former.

Obeysekera held up his hand, but Commissar Roshant got out of the Venator and started struggling towards him along the ridgetop. Instead of accepting that each step would see his boot sink into the sand and adopting a wading motion, Roshant was trying to kick a channel through the sand and sinking deeper with each step. Obeysekera waved at Roshant, trying to get him to stop, but the commissar had his head down as he ploughed forwards. He was setting off larger and larger slides of sand down the slip face of the dune. Obeysekera looked beyond Roshant. The sand was slumping towards him, at least two yards of the ridge collapsing towards the desert floor.

It would be like being caught in an avalanche.

A voice, tiny, treacherous, whispered, 'Let him.' But Obeysekera pushed forward, trying to run through the sand, and the desert moaned its song as he went, the sound rising to a rumble that sank down into the deep on the far side of the dune. As he rushed onwards, Obeysekera called into his vox-bead, 'Stay still, you idiot, stay still.'

But Roshant was talking to himself over the vox-channel, not hearing Obeysekera's order. Some small corner of the captain's mind, a corner that never could be anything other than an officer of the God-Emperor's Imperial Guard, noted that he would have to cite the commissar for failure to follow correct vox-protocol. The rest of Obeysekera's mind, and his body, was occupied with getting to Roshant before the collapsing ridge caught up with him.

The song of the sand grew louder, deeper. As Obeysekera pushed himself forwards, he realised that it had taken on a new tone, a sub-bass note that he felt in his bones as much as he heard. It was the sound of the heart of a world breaking, and he had heard it before.

It was all that he could do to stop the memory overwhelming him, as it had done through so many long night watches, when sleep would only come again if he drank himself into unconsciousness. But now the sound came in the waking hours, under the brightest light, beneath the beat of the sun, and it was rising from the sand: the song of the desert.

Roshant had never heard that sound. But nevertheless he paused, looking around him, suddenly aware that something was happening.

Obeysekera called to him, by voice and vox. 'Get back from the edge.'

Roshant, hearing him at last, looked towards Obeysekera, now only a few yards away, and then, realisation dawning, back the way he had come just as the collapsing sand reached him.

The commissar threw out a despairing hand as the world fell away beneath him, sucking him down. Obeysekera reached and grabbed the out-thrust arm, fingers locking around Roshant's wrist. Digging his feet into the ridge, he started to pull the commissar back from the brink.

And then the sand collapsed beneath Obeysekera.

The two men fell, tumbling downwards, the sand falling with them, over them.

Some reflex kept Obeysekera from releasing the one solid grip he had, the hold on Roshant's wrist, as he fell, although the arm twisted and turned and pulled as Roshant slipped and slid down the face, Obeysekera falling after him.

The sand fell with them, over them, under them.

The world went yellow.

Sand in his face, his ears, his eyes, his mouth. His nose.

Obeysekera, feeling the sand blocking his airways, tried to hold his breath while with his free hand he reached for the rebreather mask. He continued to tumble down the slope, the world turning over, the sand in his eyes and ears, all the while keeping hold of Roshant with one hand while the other pushed the rebreather over his mouth and nose.

The fall was slowing.

They had stopped rolling. Now they were just sliding. But the face of the sand dune was sliding with them, as if they were riding one of the waves of the Caducades as it broke on the shore, the surf washing over them.

The sand, heavy, crushing, immobilising, covered Obeysekera, layering over his legs, his chest, his face, his arm.

The world went yellow once more, then dark.

He could not move. He was fixed in place, as if rockcrete had been poured over him rather than sand. The only movement he could make was to squeeze the wrist he still held, but there was no response from Roshant.

The rebreather hissed. Its vents were being clogged with sand. Soon, there would be no air.

Obeysekera, with the air he had in his lungs and his body, with the last of the air of the rebreather before it failed, pushed with every muscle, straining upwards; up against the weight of the sand, up towards the light, towards the air. He pushed with all the strength he had, pushing against death.

Nothing moved.

Nothing moved at all.

He was going to die.

A memory of training in the Rossvar Mountains: the old instructor telling his raw Whiteshields that, if caught in an avalanche, they had five minutes before they suffocated, drowning in their own dead air. The old man had smiled. 'Don't worry,' he had said, 'it's a quiet death.'

Obeysekera did not want to die. Not now. Not here.

But even as fear threatened to unman him, he heard again the song of the sand. Now, with the sand surrounding him, he felt its call in every bone and fibre of his being, so that it seemed that he too was joining in the music of the desert.

Where before fear had surged up hot through his gut, now a great peace flowed through him. He could still feel Roshant's wrist in his hand and he squeezed it, trying to pass on fellowship and communion to another dying man. Although he disliked the commissar, all Roshant's privileges had served only to bring him to the same hole in the sand where he would die alongside the low-born son of a kasr. War, at the front line, was nothing if not egalitarian.

As he squeezed Roshant's wrist, Obeysekera felt a movement, a straining. The commissar was still alive too. It would not be for much longer, though. Obeysekera could feel his mind beginning to fog, as if he were on the point of sleep.

The song of the sand grew louder, more encompassing. Now he could feel the air in his lungs and the air cavities in his face resonating with the low, thrumming sound that enveloped him.

This was the long sleep, the one from which there was no waking.

Random memories played out in Obeysekera's mind: his mother, holding him by the hand as his father marched off to join the 27th accompanied by the regiment's drums and tsiranopes; the message of his father's death, flashing upon the screen; the Caducades Sea, calm after a storm; the sun, huge and livid, setting over the parched plains of Prosan; the face of the first dead man he had seen, mouth still wide with the shock of his dying; the face of the first man he had killed, eyes widening in the realisation that his dark gods had betrayed him; a smile, glimpsed through lho-smoke. A ragtag collection of impressions from a life unnoticed.

A grab, something pulling his arm.

Obeysekera, mind dim and confused, could not understand it. There was something pulling at him. The sound of the sand was growing louder around him, more open, more expansive.

Light.

Yellow, filtered ochre, but light.

Even as his mind fogged over, some deeper level of thought tightened Obeysekera's grip on the commissar's wrist.

Sand, running off his face in rivers, blurred shapes behind, digging, scrabbling, pulling.

'Get the rebreather off.'

Fingers fumbling at his mask, digging into the sand that still cradled his head, pulling the mask off.

Air.

Hot. Gritty. Sandy.

Life.

Obeysekera's chest heaved as, like a baby new born, he breathed in life.

'Pull him out.'

His vision was still blurred with tears and sand, but Obeysekera could see the shapes of the men clustered around him, scraping and pulling with their bare hands like human moles. One face resolved into that of Gunsur. Obeysekera grabbed the trooper with his freed hand.

'Under me. Roshant.'

Gunsur nodded. 'Dig,' he yelled to the others.

'I've got him,' said Obeysekera, his mind coming back to him. 'Follow my arm down.'

Scrabbling and shoving, flinging sand up and away, the men dug in down the length of Obeysekera's body, following the track of his arm until he felt their hands close about the wrist that he had never let go.

'Got him,' Gunsur said to Obeysekera. 'You can let go now.'

Obeysekera released his hold. His body free of the sand, he began to slide down the slope, and for a moment the memory of the first panicked fall came back to him. But the slide stopped and, lying spent and exhausted on his back, he looked up from the trough of the sand wave and saw the sky as blue as he had ever seen it, untouched by cloud or smoke.

He turned his head, just a little, and saw the men gathered

around the pit they were digging, and the figure emerging from it, like a sculpture appearing as the sculptor pared away the rock. Obeysekera tried to call up, to ask if the commissar lived, but his voice had dried away to a husk under the sand and only a whisper breathed from his lips.

Then he saw Sergeant Malick turning to him, his face breaking into a smile, and the thumbs-up gesture he sent down to him.

The commissar was alive.

As Obeysekera drifted on the edge of consciousness beneath an endless sky, it occurred to him that he had never before seen Guardsmen so pleased to see that their commissar was still alive. The sand shifted beneath him, then settled into silence. The music was over. Now the only sound was the coughing of the commissar and the few words of his men, faced with a recovering political officer and not sure what to do or say next.

Captain Bharath Obeysekera of the God-Emperor's Imperial Guard forced himself to sit up. He was in command. He had better do some commanding.

He tried to stand up. It did not work. Instead he sat, coughing, the phlegm gritty with sand. His mouth and throat were rough with it, his ears half-blocked.

He tried to stand again, and this time staggered to his feet. The sand felt firm beneath him. He looked up. The slip face of the dune rose a hundred feet and more above him, but here, in the wave's trough, the sand was hard-packed. If only the troughs turned in the direction they were going, the way would become so much easier.

As he stood, still swaying, the men started bringing Commissar Roshant down the short distance to the bottom of the slope, half carrying him and half sliding him, with shears of sand following. But their initial fall had dislodged the greater part of loose sand on the slip face; what slipped and slid now posed no danger.

Trooper Gunsur was beside Roshant, Sergeant Malick had hold

of him on the other side, and the rest of the troops who had
come down to dig them out – Obeysekera noted with approval
that Ha, Lerin and Prater had remained with the Venators – slid
and waded down the slope beside them.

As they came closer, Obeysekera saw that the commissar had
turned yellow. His immaculate greatcoat – how he had kept it
so clean in the desert was a mystery to Obeysekera – was now
streaked and stained, with trails of sand leaking like yellow oil
from every crease and crevice. His cap was gone, still buried
under the sand. His hands, clutching convulsively on the men
helping him down the slope, were as yellow as a wedge of pico-
giallo cheese, apart from a band around his right wrist where
Obeysekera had been holding him. And his face was the colour
of curdled starch-milk, streaked with the trails of tears and spit
and phlegm from eyes and mouth and nose.

The men slid Roshant down to the base of the slope, where
he sat, not moving. Obeysekera went over to the commissar.

In the yellow that was his face, Roshant's eyes were islands of
white and blue, but the whites were traced with red. The commissar was staring into a distance only he could see. Squatting
down on the sand in front of Roshant, Obeysekera put himself
into the commissar's line of sight, but still the far focus of his
eyes did not change.

'Commissar. Commissar Roshant.'

There was no flicker of acknowledgement on Roshant's face.

Obeysekera reached out and grasped Roshant's wrist, the wrist
he had held when they were buried. At his touch, the commissar
started.

'No, no, no.'

He started to pull away, but Obeysekera tightened his grip
and pulled Roshant back towards him so that their faces were
almost touching.

'You're out,' he said. 'You're out.'

Slowly, Roshant's gaze returned from the far distance where it had been lost and focused on the man right in front of him.

The commissar nodded. 'Yes. Out.' The words were thick, barely audible.

'Permission to spit,' said Obeysekera.

Roshant turned his head, hawked and spat a yellow glob of mucus into the sand. Then, putting his free hand on Obeysekera's shoulder, he levered himself back onto his feet.

Obeysekera stood up in front of the commissar and stared into his face. 'Commissar Roshant?'

The sand crust on Roshant's face began to crack. Little trails of yellow particles streamed down from his forehead, down his cheeks, his chin.

'I thought I was going to die.'

Obeysekera put his hands on Roshant's shoulders. 'So did I.'

For a moment, the commissar allowed the hands to remain there, then he struck one aside and turned away. Pointing at Gunsur, he said, 'Get me some water.' Roshant coughed, a long, body-shaking fit.

Trooper Gunsur's eyes tracked to Captain Obeysekera, who gave a fractional nod.

'Sir,' said Gunsur and, getting to his feet, he started on the long climb back up the dune. But Obeysekera stopped him.

'No need, trooper. I'm going to call the Venators down to us.' Keying open the squad vox-channel, Obeysekera ordered the Kasrkin who had remained with the three Venators to drive them down the slope. He looked up as the whine of the galvanic motors starting up came faintly down from above, then signalled to his men.

'Pull back from the slope in case they set off another fall.'

At his words, Roshant all but ran away from the slip face. The rest of the squad followed: Obeysekera's expression told them to guard their own expressions, facial and verbal.

Obeysekera stepped back himself, then stopped to watch as the Venators descended the face of the dune, slip-driving down like the great predatory seals that had surfed the waves of the Caducades Sea, launching themselves off the crests to snatch low-flying seabirds from the air. He wanted to hear if their movement triggered the song of the sand, but all he heard was the whine of the galvanic motors and the wave crush of sand turning under tyres.

Part of Obeysekera had thought that the strange music had been produced purely by the movement of sand on sand, but if that was the case then why weren't the Venators producing the same noise? There must be another factor.

The Venators reached the trough and came to a stop, still maintaining the regulation distance between the vehicles.

Obeysekera nodded. This squad was good. Turning to Gunsur, he motioned the trooper to get some water and take it to the commissar while he called Prater and Lerin, the navigators of *Divine Light* and *Saint Conrad*, over to *Holy Fire* so that they could check their reckonings against each other's map plots.

Torgut Gunsur looked after the receding back of Captain Obeysekera. The captain's reputation suggested he was a competent officer, but Gunsur was a trooper in the 'kin, not a servitor water-carrier. He shook his head, only slightly, but enough for Malick to spot the movement.

'Get moving,' Malick said. 'Captain's told you what to do.'

'All right, all right.' Gunsur trudged over to the Venators, filled a water flask from one of the barrels, his throat pricking with thirst as he did so, and turned to look for the commissar. Hopefully, Roshant would not use all the water and he could drink what was left over: it was a couple of hours yet before the next water break.

Roshant was still walking away from the Venators. Gunsur shook his head again and started after the commissar. The water sloshed in the flask, the sound reminding him of the waves of the Caducades Sea washing against the outer ramparts of Kasr Osmun. The memory clutched at his throat with all the intensity of unexpected remembrance for that which was lost, all but stopping Gunsur in his tracks. He clutched his head, trying to force the memory from his mind. Kasr Osmun was gone, along with all the people who had tried to defend it at the end. What was left was the long revenge. Gunsur squinted ahead. The commissar had finally stopped and was standing with his back turned to him and the rest of the men.

Coming closer, Gunsur realised that the commissar's body was shaking.

The man was crying.

Gunsur stopped himself. He did not know what to do. Roshant was a commissar and not just a commissar but the lord militant's son to boot. He wanted to back away, but then he looked down at the bottle he was carrying. The captain had ordered him to take water to the commissar.

He could just hand over the bottle and get away.

Gunsur coughed.

Roshant gave no sign that he had heard. His head was bent, his hair still covered in sand, and his shoulders were heaving with silent sobs.

Gunsur tapped the commissar on the shoulder.

Roshant started.

'Commissar, I have the water for you.'

Roshant turned around. His face was smeared with tear tracks. He wiped a hand across, but it served only to spread the mess further.

Gunsur held out the water bottle but Roshant did not seem to see it. He looked at the trooper, his eyes red.

'Your water, sir.'

Roshant took the water bottle, but the action was automatic, like a servitor carrying out a task it had been programmed for.

Gunsur made to turn away.

'By my stupidity, I endangered the mission.'

Gunsur stopped. 'Most everyone's done that some time or other, sir.'

Roshant looked at him. 'Have they?'

'There was one time when I had the map turned up the wrong way and took my squad the opposite direction we were supposed to go. I got lucky that time – we ran into the heretics that were trying to outflank us.'

Roshant nodded. 'Thank you.' He looked beyond Gunsur to the men clustered around the Venators. 'And them? Will they think the same way? I am the lord militant's son.'

'What happens on a mission stays on a mission, sir. That's the 'kin way. You're one of us, now.'

Roshant stared at Gunsur, his eyes growing wider as he looked. 'One of you…'

Gunsur nodded. 'Yes, one of us.' He pointed at the bottle. 'If there's any water left over when you've finished, I could do with a drink.'

Roshant nodded. 'Yes.' He held the bottle up to his mouth and drank, then poured a little onto a cloth and wiped the sand from his eyes. 'Have the rest.'

'You sure, sir?'

'Yes, quite sure.'

Gunsur, bottle in hand, headed back to where Sergeant Malick was standing in the shade of one of the Venators. Once there, he handed the sergeant the bottle – Gunsur had left a finger of water in the bottom – and, turning to Malick, said, 'You'll never guess what the commissar was doing when I took him this water...'

As Gunsur told the story, Sergeant Malick turned to watch the commissar walking back towards them.

'What do you think of that then, sergeant?' asked Gunsur.

'If you hear or see anything else about our commissar, you come tell me, Gunsur, you understand?' Malick turned towards his corporal. 'You tell me and no one else, got it?'

'Sure, sergeant, I understand. But what's the problem?'

'Some things are better kept quiet, Torgut. If you don't keep them that way, I will cut out your tongue.' Malick smiled. 'Understand?'

Gunsur nodded. 'Give me the rest of the water, then – I keep quiet better when my throat isn't dry.'

Gunsur tipped the bottle and sucked the last few drops from it but, as he did so, he sneaked a look at Malick. The sergeant was staring after the commissar with all the eager intensity of a sniper lining up a kill.

CHAPTER 4

They had beat along, over crests and down troughs, crossing the waves of the Sand Sea, for the whole of the parched day with no further incident, stopping twice to move men between the Venators – Obeysekera found that rotating the crew of each vehicle served to keep the troopers sharp.

The only man that Obeysekera had not rotated during the course of the day was Commissar Roshant. He had kept him by his side, teaching the commissar how to navigate across the markless expanse of the Great Sand Sea. Roshant had taken on the task of keeping and plotting the map with wordless gratitude. For his part, Obeysekera was glad to have the chance to swap the navigator's seat for the driver's cockpit; it was like riding shotgun in a ground-hugging Valkyrie but without enemy shooting at you. As he, and the flanking Venators, whooped their way up and down the ridges, Obeysekera felt the shock of being buried alive gradually recede into the distance. As the day's end drew near, even Roshant had recovered enough to offer a quiet oath the next time the Venator breasted a crest and drove down the slip face, outrunning the sand-slide.

With the sun lowering towards the horizon, Obeysekera took a hand from the driving wheel and held it out at arm's length, fingers together and horizontal.

'What are you doing?' asked Roshant. He was holding the map tight on his lap, but glanced over to Obeysekera as he spoke.

'There's some anomaly under the Great Sand Sea that plays havoc with machine-spirits – even the chronometers start acting up. No idea what. Nothing shows up from orbit, so they reckon it must be underground.' The Venator hit a glancing blow on a sand bar and slewed sideways, forcing Obeysekera to put both hands back on the wheel to correct. Back on track, he held his hand up again. 'A palm's breadth between sun and horizon gives us about forty-five minutes until sunset.'

'Days are shorter here than Terran normal,' said Commissar Roshant. 'About twenty hours.'

'We need to stop soon and camp. I don't want us driving after dark – we'd lose our position on the map.'

'What's wrong with using the auspex?'

'Same as the chronometers. Something throws them off. One of the reasons that our aircraft are forbidden entry to the airspace above the Great Sand Sea – come in here, and they're lost.'

'You said that's one of the reasons. What are the others?'

'There's one,' said Obeysekera, pointing south. 'Sandstorm. They rise most days, by the evening at least. We've been fortunate not to encounter one sooner.'

The sandstorm was looming over the whole southern quarter, a wall of yellow gloom flecked with flashes.

'Sand-lightning,' said Obeysekera. 'We're going to have to find somewhere soon.'

'I heard that the sandstorms can flay a man's skin off.'

'So have I, but I haven't seen it happen. Probably just soldiers' stories, but on the other hand we don't want to find out that they're true.' Obeysekera keyed the squad vox-channel so that he could speak to *Divine Light* and *Saint Conrad*. 'We'll camp for the night in the lee of the next dune. That should provide protection against the storm.'

'If this is protection, I wouldn't want to be out in the storm.'

Sergeant Malick could only hear the words because Prater was yelling them into his ear as they lay under the Venator. They were using the Tauros as their shield against the storm, with Quert, the gunner, squeezed in beside them.

Malick turned his head so that he could shout into Prater's ear.

'You've got your skin – or most of it – so stop frekking complaining.'

'Not complaining, just saying.'

'Say nothing, that way I won't have to listen to you.'

'How long do you reckon we'll be stuck under here?' asked Prater. 'I've heard these storms can go on for days.'

'You're well named, ain't you.'

'What? I don't understand what you mean, sarge,' said Prater.

'Oh, shut up,' said Malick, turning away and pushing himself further into the lee of the Venator's rear tyres. Even with them hiding under the Tauros, the wind was still sending blasts of abrading sand through.

Prater turned towards Quert. 'Don't know what's up with the sergeant,' he said. 'Anyway, what do you reckon on Roshant? Noble, hothead or commissar?'

'Oh, shut up, Prater,' said Quert.

'Come on,' said Prater. 'We're stuck here until the storm is over. Roshant – noble, hothead or commissar? I'm taking bets on which comes out top.'

While taking no part in the conversation, Malick shifted so that he could hear it better over the gravel hiss of the wind and the rumble of sand-lightning.

'Money? Right,' said Quert. 'In that case, I'll bet on noble, though he wants to be a commissar.'

'Noble. You sure?'

'Sure,' said Quert. 'He made me brush the sand out of his coat. Creep. If he wasn't a commissar, I'd have taken that greatcoat and shoved it down his throat.'

'Best not do that to the lord militant's son,' said Prater.

'Yeah, that was what I thought,' said Quert. 'I'm smart like that.'

'You reckon he's a coward?'

The two troopers rolled over so that they could see Sergeant Malick.

'Didn't know you were listening, sergeant,' said Prater.

'Why do you think the commissar is a coward?' asked Malick.

Prater peered at Malick, trying to make out the sergeant's expression in the gloom under the Venator. 'I'm not going to get into trouble about this, am I?'

'No.' Malick leaned forward and grabbed Prater's arm. 'But first make sure your vox is off. You too, Quert.'

While the troopers checked, Malick looked out from under the Venator into the storm. Only the sand and wind were moving, their skirling skeins lit into tableaux by the strobe of the sand-lightning.

'He's a bully,' said Prater. 'Sure, commissars are all bullies – they wouldn't be commissars if they weren't – but sure as my hellgun is my best friend, he's a bully to cover his fear. You've seen it too, Quert?'

'Maybe,' said Quert. 'Maybe.'

'You've taken the bets,' said Malick. 'What are the men saying?'

Prater spat out some of the sand that had blown into his

mouth when he answered. 'I'm going to stop taking bets – no odds. Everyone's betting "noble".'

'Right,' said Malick. 'This needs to be kept quiet. You see anything, you come to me, right? It won't do us no good if the word gets out that the lord militant's commissar son is a coward. You see him cracking, come to me. I'll cover for him.'

'What about the captain?' asked Prater. 'You going to tell him?'

'He's got enough on,' said Malick. 'This is sergeant stuff. I'll deal with it.'

But as he answered, Malick realised that Prater was not paying attention to him. He was staring down at the sand beneath his face as if it were alive.

'I'm talking to you, Prater. You only listen when you're talking. Don't make me repeat myself.'

Prater turned his head to look at Malick. 'The desert is moving.'

Under *Holy Fire*, Roshant turned to Obeysekera, his face a ghastly series of strobe flashes as sand-lightning detonated overhead.

'The sand is moving,' he said.

Next to the commissar, Gunsur nodded. 'It is, sir.'

Obeysekera had already felt it himself: the sand beneath him, heaving upwards, as if the desert had turned to sea and a wave was rising. As the sand rose, he thought he was going to be crushed up against the underside of the Venator, but then Obeysekera realised that the Venator was rising too, pushed up by whatever upheaval was raising the sand.

'Throne!' Commissar Roshant grabbed at Obeysekera. 'What is it?'

Obeysekera shook his head. He did not know. Turning to look outwards, he saw the desert floor, strobe-lit by lightning, rising in fits and starts, and the Venator next to his vehicle moving up and down like a boat bobbing in harbour.

It was truly as if the Great Sand Sea had become water: the only mercy was that they were not sinking.

'Stay still,' Obeysekera said into his vox-bead, transmitting over the squad channel. 'Any observations, report to me.'

The acknowledgements flicked over his display. All readings for the men were level: despite the sandstorm and the ground moving, they were remaining calm and watchful, as their training had taught them. Only the commissar's readings were spiking, his heartbeat raised and his breathing shallow.

'What is going on?' The commissar grabbed Obeysekera and pointed at the hard-packed sand around them, rising and falling with a steady rhythm, as if the desert were breathing. 'Why is it doing that?'

'I don't know.' Obeysekera removed Roshant's hand. 'It does not seem to be dangerous. We'll ride it out.'

But the commissar was pointing past Obeysekera, his eyes widening. Twisting round, Obeysekera saw the desert rising to form a ridge.

'What is that?'

Something was moving under the sand. Obeysekera stared. Moving, or growing.

'It's big,' said Gunsur.

The ridge grew higher, cutting off their view of the next Venator. 'Really big.'

Obeysekera realised that it was moving like a wave, the sand swelling and falling in its wake. He could hear it. He realised that the sound he had previously ascribed to the storm was the sound of billions of grains rising into the ridge.

The sound rose in intensity, notes playing off each other, making a new music in the silent desert. It was the song of a million saws, the thrumming of the greenhoppers of Cadia, the buzz of the treeborers of Catachan. But there was another note to the sound: a rhythmic pulsing, almost a drumming, as if the sands of the desert were booming. Lying flat on the ground beneath the Venator, Obeysekera could see the rhythm playing out in the vibration of the sand beneath his face; it jumped at the beat, like grit upon a drum skin.

'And what is that?'

Roshant was pointing out from under the Venator.

Obeysekera squirmed over towards him. He realised as he went that he had heard the commissar's words relatively easily. The sandstorm was dying away. Reaching Roshant, Obeysekera looked out and saw the storm vortex disappearing away from them, and the sand it had raised, suddenly left without motive power, falling in dark clouds back to the ground.

'There.'

The ground was slowly settling, the sand subsiding into a trough between their vehicle and the next. The wave was sinking back into the desert floor.

But the sand still drummed.

Obeysekera looked in the direction that Roshant was pointing and saw.

At first, he was not sure what he saw. Shapes, dark shapes rising and falling over the sand, working towards the watching soldiers as they tracked the path of the ridge. Obeysekera slowly realised that the motion of the shapes matched the rhythm that was pulsing through the sand.

They were drumming upon the desert.

Not just drumming: drilling. Those closest were pushing great long spikes into the sand, boring them in along the path of the wave, while the ones further away were beating upon the ground.

'What are they doing?' asked Roshant.

'They're trailing the wave.' Obeysekera pointed beyond the

figures – they were close enough now for him to see they were human, dressed in billowing robes that flared out in the last wind of the passing storm – to the shapes following on behind. 'Mukaali.'

'Mukaali?' Roshant looked at Obeysekera. 'Xenos?'

'Non-sentient.' Obeysekera pointed again. 'That's not a neck, it's a rider.'

'What's riding them, then?'

'I think that we are about to meet the Kamshet.' Obeysekera keyed the squad vox-channel. 'The men approaching are non-hostiles, repeat, non-hostiles. Stand ready but do not train weapons.'

Roshant looked to Obeysekera. 'Are you sure they're not hostile? My data-slate briefing said their combat status was uncertain.'

'Kamshet means "Wanderers". From everything I have learned about them, they just want to be left alone.'

Roshant snorted. 'Those who do not fight for the Emperor aid those who oppose Him by their inaction. There are no neutrals.'

Obeysekera watched the Kamshet approaching, both those drumming the sand and the ones following, riding the mukaali. 'Maybe.'

'I shall speak to them. I shall call them to the service of the God-Emperor.' Roshant looked at Obeysekera and his eyes were wide and white. 'It's the duty of a commissar. It's what my father would expect me to do.'

Even as he finished speaking, Roshant began to crawl out from under the Venator. Obeysekera grabbed his ankle and pulled him back.

'What are you doing? Why are you stopping me? What do you want to hide from me?'

Obeysekera could feel the young man trembling in his grasp. Crawling out from under the Venator was, he suspected, one of the braver things the young man had ever done and, having gathered his courage to do the deed, he had been stopped from going through with it.

'There is nothing to hide,' said Obeysekera. 'But unless you speak Kamshet, it might be difficult to call the Wanderers to the service of the God-Emperor. Very few among them speak Gothic in any of its dialects.'

'And you do speak Kamshet?' Roshant stared at Obeysekera. 'What, you mean you really do?'

'A little. Hypnocaches for basic grammar and vocabulary. Enough to communicate with them, I hope. Enough to ask if they know of any Valkyries that have landed nearby.' Obeysekera let go of Roshant's wrist. 'Which is why I will go out to speak to them. Gunsur, stay here with the commissar.'

The captain began to crawl out from under the Venator. As he did so, he spoke into his vox-bead on the squad vox-circuit.

'Malick, have the men and vehicles ready. We might need to fight, or retreat. Make sure we're ready to do both.'

The acknowledgement came through as Obeysekera emerged into the aftermath of the storm.

It was different, Obeysekera noted, from a snowstorm. Sand had piled up in the lee of the Venator rather in front of it, settling in the area of calm behind the vehicle. The Venator itself had been scoured, its camouflage paint largely sandblasted away. Pulling himself upright, Obeysekera brushed his fingers against the plasteel: it felt scrubbed. From its texture he now took as true the reports he had read of the sandstorms of Dasht i-Kevar stripping skin and flesh to the bone. He would not wish to have seen his men if they had been caught out in the open during the storm.

Obeysekera looked towards the approaching Kamshet. He was standing, empty-handed to show peaceful intent, in full view.

But the Kamshet, both those drumming and piercing the sand and the ones following, riding the mukaali, gave no sign of seeing him but continued on their course, following the ridge in the sand.

Obeysekera checked his auspex then shook his head. It was reading approaching numbers flickering between one and one hundred thousand. By eye, he counted twenty men on foot, beating and stabbing the sand, their own movements tracking the rhythm they drove into the ground. Following in a rough group behind were around thirty mukaali, each with a rider sitting high upon its shoulders while the animal itself plodded stolidly on over the sand, head thrust forward and swinging side to side.

Looking round, Obeysekera surveyed the other Venators. The troopers had not needed Malick's orders; some were shovelling clear the sand while others checked the vehicles' weapons. Obeysekera saw Uwais heading towards *Holy Fire*. Good. With only Gunsur, it needed a couple more hands to dig the vehicle clear and man the multi-laser. Clearly Malick trusted the commissar to do such menial work as little as he did.

Turning back to the approaching Kamshet, Obeysekera decided to wait and watch.

The men on foot – they were now within a hundred yards – were wearing yellow robes, yellow and ochre and brown, as if mimicking the myriad shades of the desert itself. Their heads and faces were covered with only their eyes showing. The drummers struck with paddles that slapped upon the sand, making a booming sound and sending vibrations up and into Obeysekera's feet. The piercers, who were generally a little in front of the drummers, each carried spears that were some four yards long and these they raised up before driving down into the sand at an angle of about thirty degrees from the vertical. The sand was still moving at their feet and Obeysekera saw that they were following the thinning ridge, thrusting their long spears along its path as they went.

The Kamshet who followed, riding upon their mukaali, wore robes of white and blue, and were being followed by a string of riderless mukaali, presumably the mounts of the men on foot.

The men at the front were within twenty yards of him now. By their course, they would pass between his Venator and the Venator of Sergeant Malick, leaving them exposed to flanking fire. As Obeysekera had ordered, the weapons were not tracking the Kamshet, but they stood ready, with Quert manning the weapon on her Venator and Malick himself taking control of the multi-laser. Obeysekera noted the third Venator – Prater was in charge of it – shift quietly so that it could bring its own weapon to bear without catching Malick's vehicle in crossfire.

But still the Kamshet advanced, beating and piercing the sand, apparently oblivious to the men silently watching them, hellguns cradled and ready. Obeysekera noted that the mounted Kamshet had closed the gap between them and the men on foot. Now they were closer, he could see that the riders were armed, but so far as he could see their weapons were swords, spears and autoguns, not a powered weapon in sight. They carried their swords and autoguns across their laps, while the spears and bows were laid along the long necks of the mukaali, strapped to the animals with ropes.

He also saw, as the riders approached, that while some had their faces covered in the manner of the men on foot, others did not, but went barefaced, and these were all women. Old or young, the women had painted skin, a colour that Obeysekera did not expect to see on any human.

'Blueies.'

The call came through the vox, signalled from Trooper Ensor.

Through the channel Obeysekera could hear the sound of weapons being powered up as the Kasrkin targeted what looked like approaching xenos.

'Hold,' Obeysekera whispered urgently into the vox-circuit. 'Hold.' He saw the Kamshet riders pause as the xenos signal was relayed among the Kasrkin and their hellguns were moved to readiness while the multi-lasers tracked closer to the advancing nomads. But still, with all this ranged firepower pointing at them, the Kamshet dancers came on, stepping and whirling and jumping, beating and stabbing the sand.

Obeysekera held up his hand, giving the visual signal to hold fire. The foremost among the Kamshet were close enough now for him to see their eyes. He had seen eyes like that before, in troopers battle-struck, in troopers whose fingers had had to be prised from lasrifles drained of power, in troopers sitting without moving in the aftermath of battle. The Kamshet were in a trance. They gave no sign of seeing him because they did not see him, nor the other waiting Kasrkin. They were caught in the action of a ritual that Obeysekera did not understand but which was clearly connected to the moving sand ridge they were following.

But while the eyes of the dancers were glazed in trance, those of the Kamshet riding the mukaali were looking upon him with wary interest. Obeysekera signalled for his troopers to stand aside as the dancers passed between the vehicles of the squad, their bare feet crunching the sand.

With the dancers past, Obeysekera stepped forward into the path of the advancing mukaali and raised his hand.

'In the name of the God-Emperor, I greet you.'

The mukaali continued plodding on, their heads swinging from side to side and only the flaring of their nostrils indicating that they sensed the man standing in their path. But Obeysekera was not looking at the desert animals but rather at the people riding them. The Kamshet sat astride the shoulders of the mukaali, their legs gripping the base of the beasts' long necks. Mukaali were tall animals and the men riding them sat higher than head height, swaying to left and right as the animals took their ungainly, outward-rolling steps. But the riders did not slow, nor acknowledge Obeysekera's greeting; they kept on going, as if they intended to ride right past him.

Bharath Obeysekera was a captain in the Astra Militarum, an officer of the Cadian Kasrkin. He was not used to being ignored.

He stepped forward, putting himself right in the path of the first of the mukaali, and planted himself there, bedding his boots down into the sand. The animal was five yards away from him, plodding closer, head swinging left to right, its small eyes, set back on its head, swivelling towards him on each sweep.

Obeysekera looked up, past the low-swinging head, to the Kamshet sitting astride the beast. He was cloaked in white and blue, his robes spotless and his headscarf, which left only his eyes exposed, the brilliant blue of the cloudless skies of Dasht i-Kevar. The Kamshet looked straight at Obeysekera, his eyes dark, and the captain began to speak, trying to greet him in his own language.

'Azul. Nekk d Bharath Obeysekera. Tzemreḍ ad iyi-d-teseeddiḍ Aɣella.'

The words sounded harsh on his tongue, but there was a timbre to them that seemed to fit the desert that had bred them.

But the Kamshet, rather than acknowledging Obeysekera's request to speak with the chieftain of the tribe, simply looked away from the captain, as if he were of no more moment than a zephyr on the sand and, pulling on the reins, directed the mukaali to Obeysekera's left. Animal and rider walked past Obeysekera, the captain staring up at the Kamshet while the rider looked straight ahead and the mukaali plodded onwards.

They came close enough for Obeysekera to have reached out and touched the mukaali's tough, leathery hide; they were certainly close enough for him to smell the animal – the odour intensified each time it swung its head in his direction, so he knew that the smell came from its breath. It was the smell of decay, of plants rotting wetly under a hot sun. It was the smell of a Kasrkin mess hall with thirty wet and weary men and women drying off while the cooks heated fried slab; the food was as much an endurance test for recruits as the training.

Obeysekera snapped back from the memory fugue to see that the rider and mukaali had passed him. He looked round and saw the animal's rump waggling as it followed the dancers, the man swaying on top.

Turning back to face the oncoming Kamshet, Obeysekera saw three riders approaching abreast. He moved in front of them, called out the greeting he had learned from some hastily absorbed hypnocaches.

'Azul. Nekk d Bharath Obeysekera. Tzemreḍ ad iyi-d-teseeddiḍ Aɣella.'

He held up his hand, showing its conspicuous emptiness.

The three riders kept on coming, neither changing course nor slowing down.

'Do you want us to stop them, captain?'

The question, from Sergeant Malick, came in over the squad vox-channel.

'No, repeat, no. The cooperation of the Kamshet is vital. We are under strict orders not to antagonise them.'

'Understood.'

As the riders came on, their mounts looming larger and larger, part of Obeysekera wished that mission orders allowed him to use the multi-lasers targeted in on the creatures. But Colonel Aruna had emphasised the need not to rile the Kamshet. He reminded himself that mukaali would only walk over him by accident, and even short-sighted creatures could not fail to see him standing right in front of them.

And indeed they did not. The mukaali separated and walked past on either side of him, their riders continuing to ignore Obeysekera's attempts to engage them.

'This is an outrage.' The voice coming through on Obeysekera's vox-bead was that of the commissar, raised to a fresh pitch of indignation. 'These barbarians are insulting the Astra Militarum, and by insulting us they are insulting the Emperor Himself. It cannot go unpunished.'

'No!' Obeysekera hissed into his micro-bead. 'If they do not want to speak to us, I cannot make them.' The captain paused. 'But I might try something else to attract their attention.'

Obeysekera looked ahead. The next group of approaching Kamshet included three of the unveiled women flanked by men. He stared at the centre woman. She was striking in her beauty despite the blue paint in stripes on her skin, but there was a timelessness to her face that made it impossible to judge her age: she might be nineteen or ninety. Or nine hundred. On the planet that produced the highest quality aqua vitae for the sub-sector, there were rumours of people living for a thousand years or more, although how the Kamshet processed the substance into usable rejuve treatments was passed over in his briefing data-slates.

The woman herself, sitting easily upon her mount, moved with it as one born to the saddle, so that mukaali and rider seemed to be a single being. Unlike all the other Kamshet that had passed by, she looked upon Captain Obeysekera with frank interest.

'Azul!' said Obeysekera, holding up his empty hand and smiling as he moved to stand in front of the onward-plodding mukaali.

For the first time, there was a response. The woman nodded. There was no smile, but she at least was acknowledging his presence in front of her.

'Azul!' repeated Obeysekera. 'Hello,' he added in Low Gothic, in case she understood the speech of the Imperium. 'Awyet-iyi s imḍebber-nwen.'

But at his further words, her face darkened and she looked away from him. The mukaali, responding to some sign from its rider, lurched forward, its pace increasing from its customary plod to something approaching a trot.

She was sending the mukaali right at him. Obeysekera wondered what he had said to so displease her – he had simply asked to see their leader – but when she showed no sign of turning the lumbering animal aside, he had no choice but to step out of the way. The mukaali rolled past him trailing the stench of fermenting cabbage. Obeysekera looked up and saw its rider staring down at him, her face without expression. He did not know how he had offended her, but there was no doubting that he had.

It soon became all too clear that the following Kamshet had no more intention of engaging with him than those who had already passed, so rather than wait for the long procession to finish, Obeysekera made his way back to the Venators.

Commissar Roshant was waiting for him by the side of the vehicle. His outrage at the way the Kamshet had treated an officer of the God-Emperor's Astra Militarum had not in the end outweighed his wish to remain in the shade of the Venator, and there he had stayed as the sun rose, bringing fire in its train of light. Roshant held up his bolt pistol, the amphant ivory of its grip glowing despite the deep shadow in which he stood.

'You should not allow barbarians to disrespect the God-Emperor.'

Obeysekera shrugged. 'So long as I am ordered to keep the Wanderers happy, I will do so.'

'Wanderers.' Roshant sniffed. 'They will wander into slavery to the t'au.'

Obeysekera shook his head. 'From what I saw of them, I would be surprised if they became slaves to anyone.' He keyed open the squad vox-channel. 'Get ready to roll out. Follow my bearing.'

Hearing the command, Trooper Gunsur swung up into the gun placement while Uwais made his way back over the sand to *Saint Conrad*.

Obeysekera swung himself into the navigator's seat and indicated for Roshant to take the driver's seat. As Obeysekera took the maps from their sealed container, fixed in under the dashboard, he briefly thought of moving Roshant to one of the other vehicles. He shook his head as the commissar climbed in alongside him and strapped on the restraints. While it might make for a better day for him, he could not inflict the commissar on any of his men, particularly as none of them had the rank to push back against the whims of a commissar who also happened to be the lord militant's son. Obeysekera, hunched over his maps, grimaced. Just one of the many joys of command.

 CHAPTER 5

'We're in the middle of a desert and I'm cold.' Prater looked at the other troops sitting near him. 'How's that supposed to happen?'

Gunsur pointed up at the sky. 'You noticed? It's dark too.'

'Come on, it's night,' said Prater. 'It's going to be dark.'

'I like the stars here,' said Quert, leaning back and staring up. 'It's like the sky used to be.'

'That's another thing,' said Prater. 'Why don't we see it here? The Rift. Where's it gone?'

Sergeant Malick, leaning against the cooling plasteel of *Divine Light* with his eyes closed but his ears open, sat up and looked over to the three 'kin – Prater, Quert, Gunsur – sitting round their evening rations. When no one answered, he sighed and, getting up, went over to them, a shadow standing in the dark.

'Is that you, sarge?' asked Prater.

'Just as well it is, Sill, or you'd be dead.'

'Uwais, Ha and Ensor are all picket. If anything got past them, we'd all be dead.'

Malick kicked the tyre of *Divine Light*, knocking off the sand clinging to his boot. 'Throne, I'll give you that, Sill. But what I won't give you is being so stupid as not knowing why you're not seeing the Rift.'

'Frekk, sarge, I don't care why I can't see the Rift – I'd be happier if I never saw it again,' said Prater.

Quert, still staring up, her face a starlit landscape of shadow, nodded. 'I'm with Sill there, sarge. It makes me feel ill when I see it.'

Malick gathered the sand coating his tongue and spat, thick and gritty, on the ground. 'Not knowing is what gets us dead, Etene.'

Quert glanced over. 'Sure, whatever you say, sarge.'

Malick looked at her, head back, face as blank and stupid and killable as a grox. He took a step towards Quert. But Gunsur reached out and laid a hand on Malick's hip, stopping him. Malick looked down at the hand, then slowly at Gunsur. The trooper removed his hand, holding it up, fingers spread in as unthreatening a manner as he could.

'You tell us why we can't see the Rift, Shaan,' he said. 'Etene and Sill want to know – they're just too stupid to realise it.'

Malick stopped. He slowly looked at Prater and then Quert. Even Etene had realised the danger and was staring at the sergeant.

'Not knowing is what killed Cadia. Remember that.' Malick hitched his thumb into his carapace pauldron. 'Learn, live.'

Quert nodded. 'Tell us, sarge.'

Malick leaned back against *Divine Light*. Even through the backplate of his carapace armour, he could feel the heat radiating from the metal.

'First, why you're cold, Sill,' he said, looking at Prater. 'There's nothing to hold the heat in a desert. The moment the sun goes down, the temperature starts falling faster than an Earthshaker shell and 'cause you've been cooking your balls all day, it feels colder than the Emperor's tears.'

'It's right,' added Gunsur. 'Honest, the coldest I've ever been was sleeping out on Prosan when I was training there.'

'Well, there you go then. Torgut confirms it – it must be true.'

'I wasn't riding you, sarge.'

Malick stared a moment at Gunsur then turned away. 'Like I was saying, the Rift.' Malick pointed up into the star-flung sky. 'There's more than one reason why we can't see it. One, there's stuff in the way. It looks empty, don't it? But space ain't empty – there's all sorts of stuff, dust and debris drifting all through it. Could be we're the other side of some huge dust cloud.'

'Then why don't the dust cover the stars?' asked Prater.

"Cause there're stars between the dust and us. There's a grox load of stars in the galaxy – I reckon even the High Lords don't know 'em all. Throne, probably the Emperor Himself hasn't counted them.'

At those words, Gunsur glanced about, searching for listening ears. 'Careful what you say, sarge. We've got a commissar with us.'

'I saw him. He's sat in *Holy Fire* with that greatcoat wrapped round him, head back, fast asleep.'

'Yeah, well… Go on.'

'I will. So there're stars, thousands, millions of them between us and the dust cloud. But there's another reason too which you groundhogs are too ignorant to work out, so I'm going to tell you.' Malick paused. They were watching him with the interest of men about to be vouchsafed secret knowledge. He pointed up at the sky again. 'Those stars, them up there, all of them. They could have all gone out, every one, and you wouldn't know yet. You're looking up there with your jaws hanging open and you're looking into the past. The light from that star, it's hundreds, maybe thousands of years old. All that time it's been crossing space and now it gets here and, Throne, it thinks, I'm falling into Sill's eyes. No! All that journeying, all that time, and I get seen by a frekking idiot. Same with the Rift. In realspace, nothing goes faster than light, and light is slow. It's why we travel in the warp – the only way to keep the Imperium together is to go through hell, 'cause in hell there ain't no limits. Back on Cadia we got it close up, but out here the light from when the Rift cut the sky ain't arrived yet.'

'Hang on, sarge,' said Quert. 'I swear I've seen the Rift away from Cadia.'

Malick clapped his hands, slowly. 'So there is something between Etene's ears. Course you have. Any systems close to the Rift, it's going to be right there, in the sky.'

'But I reckon I saw it when we were on our way here,' said Quert. 'How's that then?'

'You weren't looking into the warp, were you?'

'You don't think I'm that stupid?'

Malick shook his head. 'I guess not even you're that stupid.'

'She's right though, sarge,' said Prater. 'I reckon I remember seeing it, before we arrived, when we dropped.'

'And that's why. When we drop out of the warp, for a moment we drag a bit of it with us, caught up in the Geller fields as they're powering down. If you look out then, like as not you'll see the Rift.'

'Yeah, I wanted to see where we were going,' said Prater. 'I'd heard about this place – the desert of life, that's what they call it.'

'Who calls it that?' asked Gunsur.

'Saw it in a briefing pack.' Prater shrugged apologetically. 'So, I read them. Gives me something to do in transit.'

Gunsur nodded. 'I've heard it called a different name.'

'Like what?'

'Some people call it the Pit.'

Malick looked with sudden interest at Gunsur. 'Where'd you hear that?'

'Don't remember, sarge. But it came back to me today, when we were driving, and now, sitting here.' Gunsur dropped his voice and glanced around. 'Maybe it's just me, losing my nerve or something.'

'Like you haven't done that already,' said Quert.

'Shut up, Etene,' said Malick. 'I want to know what Torgut means.'

Gunsur hunched his shoulders against the night cold. In the dark, under the stars, they could all feel the day's heat being sucked greedily up into the void. He looked at the troops around him, listening, their faces shadows.

'Any of you, back on Cadia, any of you see a dirtshark pit?'

'You mean one of those little hollows?' asked Prater. 'Yeah, there were some outside my kasr. Frekking nuisance – could turn your ankle if you stepped in one.'

Quert laughed. 'You're both from Kasr Osmun. Weird stuff round there.'

'Our weird stuff lived outside the kasr,' said Gunsur. 'Not like Kasr Viklas. The weird stuff there is all inside.'

Quert stared at Gunsur for a moment, then looked away. 'Doesn't matter no more,' she said.

Gunsur paused. 'Yeah. Suppose you're right.' He turned back to Prater. 'Did you ever stop and watch a dirtshark pit?'

'Stare at a hole in the ground?' Prater laughed. 'Even when I was a kid, I had better things to do.'

'Yeah, well, I did. Don't know if you noticed, but they've all got the same slope – about fifty degrees. I got curious about this – yeah, all right, I didn't have much to do – and I started watching one, just lying there next to it one summer day. Saw a glow beetle come trundling along, heading towards the lip of the pit and I wanted to see what would happen, so I let it go on. It came to the lip of the pit and went over – at its size, there's all sorts of ups and downs – but then the dust under its legs all slipped and it slid down to the bottom of the pit. I was really curious now. The glow beetle lay there a bit, flashing like they do, then it picked itself up and started trying to climb up the other side of the pit. It would climb maybe halfway up and then the side of the pit slipped and it fell down to the bottom again. It kept doing that, again and again, but I could tell it was getting tired 'cause it wasn't getting so far up the pit. Just when I was thinking of picking it up, it slipped back down to the bottom of the pit. But this time, the pit opened, and there was a mouth there, and teeth, and they grabbed hold of the glow beetle and crunched it, cracking its carapace in one go.'

Gunsur looked round his comrades, all of them from Cadia. 'Don't know if you ever tried stamping out a glow beetle when it was blundering round, bumping into things, but they're solid right through. I never split one. But this one, in the bottom of the pit, it was split apart like an egg. Buried down in the bottom of the pit was a dirtshark.'

'Still reckon it's a stupid name,' said Quert. 'What's with the shark bit?'

'If you'd seen the way it chomped the glow beetle, you'd know,' said Gunsur. 'They live at the bottom of their pits and you never see one. They're too small to bother us, other than turning an ankle or two, but they eat – ate – anything small that falls into their pits. Turns out, they dig out their pits at the exact angle so that any beetle or ant or spider that falls into it tries to climb out, but the sides of the pit slip, taking it back down to the bottom and wearing it out, until the dirtshark, in its tunnels, hears all the commotion and crawls along and' – Gunsur snapped his jaws together – 'chomps.'

'What's that got to do with us?' said Malick.

Gunsur paused, looking around furtively once again. He looked back at Malick.

'See, there's this sense I've had since we started into the Sand Sea, and I couldn't work out what it was, not until today. Then I remembered the pit, and the dirtshark waiting at the bottom, and I knew. This desert, it's the pit, sarge, and we've fallen into it, and no matter how hard we try we ain't ever going to climb back out of it – and then, when we're spent, the dirtshark will open its mouth.' Gunsur shook his head. 'Just a feeling, sarge. Stupid, probably.'

'Yeah, you're right for once,' said Prater. 'Stupid.'

'Stupid,' echoed Quert.

'Sarge?'

'Sure don't look like Cadia to me,' said Malick. 'And, yeah, it's stupid. Anyway, time to change the picket. You three can take over from Uwais, Ha and Ensor.'

'Come on, sarge,' said Prater, 'I've not finished my rations.'

'Shouldn't spend so much time talking then, should you?'

As Prater, Quert and Gunsur headed off, grumbling, to relieve Uwais, Ha and Ensor, Malick looked around at the dark desert. Even under the light of ten thousand stars it lay shrouded in darkness. Quiet. Waiting. Patient.

 CHAPTER 6

'Whooah!'

The Venator crested a ridge, its galvanic motors sending the front wheels spinning wildly as the rear four dug into the sand, and then its nose fell, down and down, like a boat riding a breaking wave, and the wheels, all digging deep into the sand, sent the vehicle powering down the slip face, outracing the sand-slides that fanned out in a spreading V behind the racing Tauros.

Trooper Ensor, driving the Venator, yelled again as the vehicle powered across the dune. The wind – hot, dry and gritty – blew through the empty windscreen of the Venator, drying sweat before it could form: the cooling airflow was worth exchanging for the protection of a windscreen. The slope of the slip face was near to forty degrees, the fall off from the ridgetop steep and the distance of the fall to the trough at least two hundred yards. Ensor, fingers light upon the wheel, gave the Venator its head as the vehicle surged down the slip face, his face split wide in a grin of delight.

'Honest, this is the most fun I've ever had in the frekking Guard, never mind the 'kin,' he said, eyes fixed ahead but words directed to his navigator, Trooper Prater, sitting beside him, trying to keep his maps in order as the wind ripped at the sheets of paper. 'Good day when I got promoted from the Hundred and Fifty-Fifth.'

'All right for you,' said Prater. 'You're not trying to hold on to the maps while plotting distance and direction.' He slammed down on an escaping sheet, grabbed it and shoved it under his leg.

'Enjoy the ride,' said Ensor. 'You're never going to have this much fun again in uniform.' He glanced down at the navigator and himself. They were both stripped down to shorts and vest because of the heat. 'Well, some of it at least.'

'Orders. I've got to track our position.'

'Why bother? The captain's got it in hand.'

'What if we get separated? I don't keep track of where we are, we get split off from the captain and then we're driving around in the middle of more nowhere than I've ever seen with even less idea where to go. I'll keep plotting.'

'You keep plotting, I'll keep driving. What you say, Chame?'

Chame's answer came over the local vox-circuit. 'I say, faster.'

'See, even the gunner says "faster", and they always want to slow down so they can get a better shot.' Ensor grinned. 'Let's go.'

The hum of the galvanic motors raised in pitch, the wheels spun faster, and the headlong charge down the slip face became breakneck.

Prater glanced over to the left, where Captain Obeysekera's Venator had the centre. That Tauros, having been first to crest the ridge, was already nearing the bottom of the trough, but it seemed to be slowing down. With Ensor running the galvanic motors at high intensity, their Venator was fast catching up.

'Better slow down,' said Prater, 'or we'll overtake the captain.'

'Come on. Down one dune, up the next, bearing two-seven-five.' The galvanic motors were humming like a hive of angry bees – and then they got angrier. 'We'll beat them up the next dune then wait for them there.'

The Venator surged forwards, trailing its V-shaped wake of falling sand, with Ensor and Chame hollering the joy of being young and alive and in command of a ton of fast, heavily armed machinery.

Prater, having given up trying to plot the course during the bumps of the helter-skelter descent, was looking ahead, down the slip face to the broad trough at the bottom. It was strange. Rather than the usual long smooth curve into the trough that he had seen before, the slip face seemed to run at the same angle all the way until it met the sudden flat of the trough.

It was very flat.

He peered more closely.

It seemed to be moving.

Flowing.

'Divine Light, Saint Conrad, *pull up, pull up.*'

The call came over the squad priority vox-channel, the channel that overrode all other communication.

'Stop! Stop!' yelled Prater, beginning to brace himself.

Ensor stamped on the brakes. The galvanic motors, humming like a turbofan one moment, went silent the next. The Venator, sliding down the slip face, brakes on full, began to skid, its nose slewing as the braked front wheels bit into the sand and the momentum of the heavier rear of the vehicle began to turn it around its inertial centre.

'Hold it, hold it.'

'I'm trying,' said Ensor, attempting to angle the Venator back into the skid before it could turn sideways on.

Prater looked left. They were running out of steering room.

Everything became clear, sharp. He saw the slip face, still running downwards at an angle of thirty-five degrees. He saw the lip, where it met the valley bottom. He saw sand slipping over the edge. And he saw the sand of the trough moving, slowly, along the bottom of the erg. Flowing.

It was a river of sand.

Ensor hauled the steering wheel left, struggling to turn the Venator into the skid, and slowly, slowly its nose came back round. But the sand was sliding away under its wheels, falling down the slip face and tumbling into the river below.

'Got it, got it.'

Ensor crooned the words, over and over again, as the Venator's brakes slowly burned off its momentum, the wheels digging deeper into the sand.

They were ten yards from the edge.

Eight yards.

Five.

Three.

Stopped.

Prater breathed out.

'Got it,' said Ensor. He slapped the steering wheel. 'You did it.'

Prater tapped the driver on his arm. 'Look,' he whispered. He pointed to the bank.

A little wave of sand slipped over, falling into the river. Then another, larger slip, and another, and another, and each slip nibbled away at the edge.

The river of sand was eroding the bank on which the Venator stood.

'Get us out of here.'

Ensor, seeing the danger, tried to start the galvanic motors. They whirred, then died away.

'Come on, come on,' he whispered as he tried again. Beside him, Prater was mumbling whatever invocations to machine-spirits he could call to mind.

The galvanic motors hummed alive, buzzing and angry, and Ensor gunned the wheels, spinning them and sending great plumes of sand arching backwards.

The Venator lurched forward with Ensor trying to turn its nose up the slip face. But even as it started to move, the vehicle tipped over onto its left. Prater, sitting on that side, looked over to see what was happening.

'The bank's gone!'

The spinning wheels had eaten away what was left of the bank and, with nothing there to support it, the Venator was beginning to topple.

Ensor reached out, killing the galvanic motors driving the left-hand set of wheels. The Venator settled further but, with the wheels not excavating the sand, the chassis sank down upon the ground and rested there.

'Get the weight on the right,' Ensor said, throttling back the right-side wheels.

Prater unfastened his harness and climbed over Ensor, while behind them Chame swung her body and the heavy bulk of the multi-laser out to the right of the vehicle.

As he scrambled over Ensor, Prater saw that Captain Obeyse-kera's Venator, tilted over at thirty degrees, was driving over the slip face towards them, with Malick's following behind. They just had to hold the Venator for a few more minutes and then the other two vehicles could haul them to safety.

The Venator lurched again, tipping further left.

'It's the frekking water tanks,' yelled Ensor. 'They're forcing us over.'

Prater nodded. The tanks, slung on the outside of the Venators, helped even out the weight, but now with the Tauros rolling over on its side, the water shifting in the barrels was rotating the vehicle around its centre of inertia.

'I'll get them.'

He started crawling back across the Venator, moving slowly and keeping as low as he could. As he went, he drew his knife from its sheath at his waist. The handle fit snugly into his hand: Prater had used it many times before. The blade itself, sharpened at the point and cutting edge, gleamed in the desert light.

The Venator rocked.

'Hold!' said Ensor.

Prater went still. Everything settled.

'Slow,' said Ensor, 'nice and slow. Chame, can you give us more balance?'

'Trying,' yelled back the gunner. 'Okay. Far out as I can go.'

'Nice and easy,' said Ensor, looking back to Prater. 'Nice and easy.'

Prater nodded, then began to inch forward, the cutting edge of his Cadian knife held out in front. He just had to reach the straps holding the water barrels in place. The blade, honed to battle sharpness, would cut through the webbing as if it were smoke.

Nearly there, nearly there.

The Venator lurched sideways, and Prater slid forwards. Ensor made a grab for his ankle but missed. Prater snatched the webbing, stopping himself falling through the vehicle and into the river of sand. The Venator lurched again, tipping over further.

It began to slide sideways.

'Get back,' yelled Ensor. 'It's going.'

But Prater shook his head. 'Got this,' he muttered, sawing through the webbing, 'got this.'

The straps parted, pinging apart under the weight of the water barrels, and the barrels themselves started to tumble off the side of the Venator, slapping onto the sand below. Prater saw the sand part around the barrels like thick soup, then swallow them down.

The weight on the left side of the Venator released, the vehicle rocked back in the other direction, back towards the bank.

'Clear,' said Ensor.

'Clear,' said Prater. He levered himself upright, sheathing his knife.

But then the bank under the vehicle collapsed.

The Venator tipped on its side. Prater, half standing, hand at the knife sheath, flailed for a hold, missed and fell. He saw the ground approaching. He twisted, trying to stop himself going in head first, and landed on his shoulder, digging it into the shifting sand.

At the impact, Prater spread himself out, making as large a surface area as possible, splaying out arms and fingers and legs, turning onto his back and making an X shape, staring up at the sky. He had not realised: it was so blue it was almost violet.

Prater lay stretched out upon the sand but he felt it shifting, flowing, beneath him, and he found himself drifting past the Venator. The removal of his weight seemed to have stabilised the vehicle: it was balancing on the edge but not tipping over any further.

'Hang on.'

Ensor was unstrapping himself from his seat, reaching for a rope.

'I'm okay,' Prater said into the vox. 'Get the Venator clear.'

'Sure?'

'Sure.'

He could feel the sand beginning to shift under him. His legs from the knees downward had disappeared beneath the surface. He tried kicking them upwards, but the sand was thick as treacle and he could barely move them. Prater began to make slow paddling motions with his hands and arms, trying to push himself back towards the bank. The slow-flowing sand was dragging him further out.

Where was it going?

He turned his head. He could hear the whine of motors and the hiss of tumbling sand. Captain Obeysekera's Venator had nearly got to them.

Prater tried to lift his head a little, to see better.

The bottom half of his body suddenly sank, rotating downwards. Although all his training told him to stay still, at the sudden drop he could not stop himself. He began kicking, searching for some purchase on the flowing sand, some floor to stand upon.

The motion made him sink further. He was down to his chest. Prater raised his arms, tried to lay them out flat upon the top of the sand, but the surface parted like molasses and his arms went down. Now, only his head and neck were above the surface.

He dropped further. He tried to speak, to call for help, but sand trickled into his mouth and he choked. Prater turned his head upwards, spat, tried to clear his mouth then turned his head to speak into the vox.

'Hel–'

But even as he opened his mouth to call, he saw the Venator tipping as more of the bank beneath it collapsed. Men were attaching cables to it, tying it off against the captain's Tauros, which was reversing, trying to haul the vehicle back.

Ensor, looking around from the driver's seat, saw Prater in the flowsand and gestured some of the men to help him.

'No!' said Prater. 'Secure the vehicle.'

'You sure?' Ensor's voice cracked through his vox.

'Sure.'

Ensor nodded and turned back to the Venator.

Prater struggled, pushing his arms back up out of the sand. It felt as if he were pushing through a membrane, but he managed to free them. He felt his head a little clearer of the sand.

He began pulling his way through the grains, sweeping his arms back over the surface in wide arcs.

The Venator jerked backwards, Ensor engaged its galvanic motors and, with all its wheels back on sand, it reversed up the slope, away from the edge.

The vehicle safe, Prater began to raise his hand.

'Some hel–'

His leg jerked downwards.

'H–'

The sand, pouring in over his face and eyes and nose and mouth, stopped the rest of the call. The last thing Prater saw before the sand closed over him was the blue sky of Dasht i-Kevar.

CHAPTER 7

'Flowsand.'

Captain Obeysekera sat among his remaining men, the Venators parked up along the slip face. He pointed down towards the valley bottom.

'I'd heard tales but I thought they were exaggerated, stories spun to excuse a failed mission or to entertain bored troopers. We're 'kin, we've all done the training on Prosan, we know what to do in quicksand.'

Obeysekera looked around the men, sitting on the sand in the lee of the Venators, the shade providing some relief from the unrelenting sun.

'I was wrong and Prater died because of my mistake.' Obeysekera paused. 'We learn from this.' He looked towards Ensor, who was sitting, his face downcast. 'No more racing down dunes. From a distance, it's impossible to tell what's flowsand and what isn't.'

Ensor nodded, saying nothing. He did not look up at the

captain. In his hands, he held his knife. The gentle rasp told that he was honing its edge, honing and honing it again.

'For now, we go on.'

At that, Ensor looked up. 'We're 'kin. We don't leave our dead behind.'

Obeysekera pointed at the flowsand. 'If we could retrieve him, we would.'

Ensor stropped his knife back and forth, back and forth on the grox-leather strop. 'We're 'kin,' he repeated. 'We don't leave our dead behind.'

'I know. If there was any way of finding Prater, we would do it.'

Ensor jumped to his feet, knife in hand, and advanced on Obeysekera.

'We're frekking 'kin,' Ensor said. He grabbed Obeysekera and pushed him back, up against the side of the Venator. 'We don't never leave our dead behind.'

The commissar, seeing a trooper lay hands on his commanding officer, drew his bolt pistol, his face pale and determined, but Obeysekera gestured him to stand down.

Ensor put the point of his warknife up against Obeysekera's throat. 'You come in here like you're the Emperor's gift and you don't even know about that... that *stuff*, and now you tell me we're going to leave Prater behind. We're 'kin,' he repeated. 'We don't leave our dead behind.'

Obeysekera looked into the eyes in front of him. Ensor's face was pressed up almost against his own. He could smell the rank breath of days' travel through the desert without water to clean teeth.

'We did on Cadia,' Obeysekera said softly.

'What? What did you say?'

'We left our dead on Cadia. We never went back for them.'

'That was Cadia – it's where they should rest.'

Obeysekera raised his hand and pushed the warknife aside. 'Cadia's gone.'

Ensor shook his head. 'No. No, Cadia stands.'

'Cadia stands where Cadians do their duty to the Emperor. If you would honour Prater, give him some of our home to remain with him. I will.'

Ensor stared at Obeysekera. His hand went to the vial around his neck. There was a similar vial hanging from the captain's neck and indeed those of all the Kasrkin – only the commissar did not wear one.

'This?'

'Yes. We will give Prater some of the soil of our lost home, that he might find his way back there when the stars fall and the worlds are made new. You are right, Ensor. We are Kasrkin. We leave no man behind.'

The trooper stood back, nodded, let his hand fall. 'Yes, sir,' he said.

'Good,' said Obeysekera. He stepped forward, put his hand on Ensor's shoulder and spoke into the trooper's ear. 'Pull a trick like that again and I will execute you on the spot. Do you understand, trooper?'

Ensor nodded. 'Yes, sir.'

'Very well.'

'I checked on him, sir. He was all right. He signalled for me to get the Venator free or I wouldn't have left him in there. It couldn't have been more than a minute, sir, but when I looked again he was gone.'

'The responsibility is mine, Ensor. I should have had a man getting him out while the rest of us secured the vehicle. Come. Let us bid him farewell.'

Obeysekera tapped Ensor on the cheek then stepped past the trooper. As he went, the captain lifted the vial up over his neck and carefully twisted off the cap. The men around him stood and did the same, pinching a few grains from within their vials. With the men following, Obeysekera walked over to the edge of the flowsand.

'Spread out,' he said. 'We don't want the bank collapsing.'

The Kasrkin spaced themselves out along the edge, each with the hand containing the pinch of Cadian dust held over the flowsand. Roshant stood to silent attention behind them, commissarial cap on his head.

'May the dust of Cadia carry you home, Sill Prater.'

As he spoke, Obeysekera let the grains of lost Cadia fall from his fingers. One by one, the other Kasrkin did the same, the dust of their home merging with the sand of Dasht i-Kevar.

'Until the stars fall and Cadia is made new.' Obeysekera passed the prayer down the line of Kasrkin.

'Until the stars fall and Cadia is made new.'

'Until the stars fall and Cadia is made new.'

For a moment the Kasrkin stood silent with heads bent, then, one by one, they turned and walked back to the commissar, who was waiting by the Venators. Ensor was last to return. Chame and Lerin made room for him between them. Ensor sat down, using his helmet as a stool.

Obeysekera pointed along the slip face.

'We will have to follow the line of this erg until we can find somewhere to cross the flowsand.'

'That's taking us off our bearing, sir,' said Malick.

'I know. But we have no choice.' Obeysekera looked around the men. 'With the loss of the water barrels and being forced off course, we will have to reduce the water ration.'

'How many days' supply have we got left, sir?' asked Gunsur.

'Malick?'

'On minimum rations, a week.'

'That will be enough. If we haven't found the general by then, he'll already be dead. Any questions?'

'Why follow on along the slip face this way, sir? We don't know where we can cross the flowsand and this way we're heading in the direction it's going. If you're trying to cross a river, it's better to go upstream,' said Uwais.

'True, but we have no idea if this flowsand behaves like water. Do tributaries feed into it, like streams into a river? Or is it the result of sand flowing down from the slip faces all along its length? Or something else entirely? If we head this way we are at least going at a vector towards our destination – the other direction, we would be heading away.'

Sergeant Malick stood up, the sun almost directly over him so that he cast barely any shadow, and pointed slightly off the line of the slip face. 'That's nearly the direction the painted people went.'

'The Kamshet?'

'Yes, sir.'

'We'll only meet them again if they turn off their bearing. Malick, check the auspex, see if there's any chance of getting an exact bearing so that we can mark this waypoint. The rest of you, back to your vehicles. Ensor, you'll have Chame navigating.' Obeysekera looked over to where Roshant was standing, a little apart from the rest of the squad. 'Commissar, if you would accompany me.'

'Yes, captain.' Roshant saluted smartly and headed to their vehicle, leaving Obeysekera looking quizzically after him.

'The auspex is still all over the place, sir.'

Obeysekera nodded. 'Thank you, Malick. Worth checking but good to know. It will be paper and stylus for us there and back, I suspect.'

'Never thought I'd actually get to use all that trig they taught us on Prosan, sir.'

'Can't say I did either, but I'm glad you followed your lessons, Malick.'

'Barely bothered with it at the time. It's only when I was back on Cadia when… when it happened that it came in handy. Everything was down then. Used some old maps and a stylus to get my men to the landing fields. Remembered just about enough to do it. Once I was off, I took a refresher course. I wanted to be prepared, in case I ever needed it again.'

Obeysekera nodded. 'Sometimes, the old skills prove the most useful.' He looked along the three Venators. 'Looks like we're ready to go.'

'Hopefully find somewhere to cross the flowsand soon, sir.'

'Hopefully,' said Obeysekera.

Gunsur, driving *Divine Light*, glanced over at Malick in the navigator's seat. The sand thrown up by *Holy Fire* in front hung as a thin suspension in the hot air, griming his face and hands as he drove.

'When we were under the truck during the sandstorm, I thought the commissar was going to break.'

Malick looked up from his map, glanced at Gunsur, then went back to tracking their route on the map.

'Go on,' he said. 'But make sure your vox is off.'

'It is. I saw him. He'd turned away from the captain but I could see him. He was sweating and shaking, mouthing stuff I couldn't hear 'cause of the storm but looked like prayers. Then, when he wanted to go out and speak to the Kamshet and the captain pulled him back… The expression on his face – like when someone walks out from cover 'cause he can't take being under bombardment no more.'

Malick nodded. 'What I thought.' He glanced back at Gunsur. 'Remember, say nothing to anybody. I will deal with this.'

Gunsur pressed his finger to his lips. 'Silent as the Raven.'

Malick shook his head, surreptitiously making the sign against the Eye. 'Don't speak his name – you never know if he might answer.'

Four hours later, they still had not found an end to the flowsand. The slip face had slowly diminished into a gentle slope, however, making it easier to drive the Venators over the angle, and Obeysekera had called a stop to see if the end of the steep slip face had deprived the flowsand of its sources.

Standing beside it, with Malick and Roshant on either side, Obeysekera stared out over the treacherous surface.

'Can you tell if it is still moving?' he said, squinting in the fierce light. In the valley bottom, in the mid-afternoon, the air was hotter than the interior of a locked-down Leman Russ after three days fighting – and Obeysekera had seen what the tank crews looked like when they emerged from their vehicles after that. But while the air temperature was hotter than a fighting Leman Russ, it did not have the stifling mixture of carbon dioxide, fear sweat, cabbage and spilt promethium that characterised a tank. The air on Dasht i-Kevar had the cleanliness of fire.

'Don't matter if it's moving so long as it's still flowsand,' said Malick. He looked around. 'Where's a frekking stone when you want one?'

'You can throw this.' Roshant handed Sergeant Malick an amulet.

The sergeant looked up at the commissar. 'It's an amulet of Saint Xaver – you want to throw this in?'

'Either the saint will show us our way is clear or he will enter this cursed river of sand and by his presence there bless it.'

Sergeant Malick shrugged. 'It's your call, sir.' He turned the amulet in his fingers. 'Looks valuable – got the feel of proper aurum.'

'It was a gift from my father. I don't think there's much doubt it's real aurum. Any aurum smith who tried to cheat my father wouldn't live long enough to claim it was a mistake.'

'Here goes then.' Sergeant Malick balanced the amulet on his curved index finger, then flicked it with his thumb. The amulet spun up into the air, the aurum catching and splitting the light as it turned, before reaching the top of its arc and curving downwards.

The amulet landed on the sand, gold on yellow, and lay, looking innocently up at the bright sky.

'That's holding,' said Roshant.

'Not quite the weight of a fully laden Venator,' said Obeysekera drily.

'I am aware of that, captain. It's why I gave Sergeant Malick the amulet – it's heavier than it looks.'

'It was, sir,' confirmed Malick. 'Surprisingly heavy.'

'We could try something heavier,' said Roshant, 'but I don't suppose we have anything we don't need.'

Obeysekera looked at Roshant. 'You don't need a blessed amulet of Saint Xaver that your father gave you?'

'I don't need my father to give me anything.'

'It's moving.' Malick pointed. 'It's definitely shifted along, maybe two fingers. That's flowsand, sure enough.'

Obeysekera nodded. 'We'll have to go on then.'

'You don't think that maybe Uwais was right?' asked Roshant. 'We should head back and try to cross further upstream?'

'It can't be like water. There's no sand rain to replenish the springs. There's no evaporation.'

'Sandstorms.'

Obeysekera looked at Malick. 'What was that?'

'Sandstorms, sir. You said they happen almost every day here. Maybe it's the storms that shift the sand, piling it up into dunes and then the sand slips down into the valleys and makes flowsand.'

'Could be. But then, it would have to be almost frictionless, every grain worn smooth. It would take millions of years to do that.'

Roshant bent down and picked up a handful of sand. It ran through his fingers, even though he was holding them tightly together.

'Like water, you say?'

Obeysekera looked around at the dunes that marched alongside them like the curves of a wind snake. He remembered the time-worn humps of the Tabaste Mountains at the heart of the Great Sand Sea: their destination.

'Millions and millions and millions of years.' He bent down and dug his fingers into the sand. It spread, like water, and he picked up a handful, holding it up in front of his eyes. The sand ran off his palm, trickling down in little rivulets to the ground.

'Slow water.' Obeysekera nodded. 'Then, if it is…' He turned back to look at the flowsand. 'I'm afraid you have lost your amulet, commissar.'

Roshant nodded. 'I expected to, captain.'

'Let's push on. All rivers end.' Obeysekera started back towards the Venators, pretending not to hear when Malick muttered, 'Yeah, when they get to the sea.'

 CHAPTER 8

As Roshant drove, Obeysekera marked the obstacle on the map. Even the best Imperial map showed the Great Sand Sea as largely empty and featureless, with only the Tabaste Mountains as a recognisable landmark. Certainly, there was no flowsand shown on the map. Even if they did not find General Itoyesa, having the flowsand channels marked would prove a valuable piece of geographical intelligence. If it should prove possible to cross the Great Sand Sea, the chance of a flanking attack on the t'au would be opened up. Obeysekera, maps strapped to a tray across his lap, charted their course and bearing, checking and recheck- ing as they went, reading off distance, speed and time against the compass reading – a simple magnetic compass was about the only instrument whose machine-spirit could cope with the anomaly in the Sand Sea. After a few rejected attempts at con- versation, Roshant was keeping his peace, driving the Venator with increasing skill, while the other two vehicles followed in line behind. They had the best of it in front: clear air and clean sand. The Venators in their wake had to drive through the clouds of sand thrown up by the wheels of the lead vehicle, with the last having to endure the dust of both the Venators in front.

Ensor was driving the rearguard. So far as Obeysekera was concerned, Ensor would be in the last vehicle all the way to the Tabaste. While he had let the man's conduct pass, some consequences would remind Ensor to control himself better in future.

'Do you think he might be right?'

Obeysekera looked up from his map. Roshant was talking to him through their personal channel. With them sitting right next to each other he could hardly claim that the signal was weak.

'Who?'

'Uwais. About turning back and finding a way across upstream.'

'It's sand. There shouldn't be any stream.'

Roshant snorted with laughter. 'There are many things in the galaxy that should not be, but are. Against that list, sand that flows like water seems a minor anomaly.'

'It's not like water. That's what bothers me. If it was like water, it would be following a gradient. But it isn't.'

'It's not flowing uphill, though?'

'No, not that I have seen. It seems to be keeping to the flat.'

Roshant shook his head. 'I don't see the problem, then. If you spill water on a completely flat surface it will still flow. That's what the sand is doing here. Under the surface sand, the bedrock is level.'

'But if it was simply windblown sand flowing over flat ground it should spread out along every available channel, like water filling a lake. It shouldn't flow.'

Roshant shrugged. 'It's sand. Who cares what it does?'

Obeysekera looked up from his maps, covered with contours and flows, to the ridges and troughs of the Great Sand Sea that surrounded them.

'I do,' he said.

Roshant laughed again. 'You should have become a scholar, then.'

Obeysekera shook his head. 'Not much call for scholars on Cadia. Still, at least the 'kin train us to think. I am and remain grateful for that. But I think I would have enjoyed a more scholarly life – shut away in scriptoria, poring over old tomes, searching for knowledge.'

'Knowledge is dangerous,' said Roshant, 'even in the right minds.'

'That is the opinion of the Commissariat. But if we had had knowledge of what Abaddon planned, would we not have planned our defence differently?'

'To contemplate the plans of the Archenemy is to stare into the abyss. And when you look into the abyss…'

'…the abyss looks into you. Yes, I know the proverb. As with all such sayings, it defines truth, but limits it, too.'

'Captain Obeysekera, what do you mean by that?'

Obeysekera glanced over at the commissar. He had been thinking aloud. It was a habit that he must remember to curb. 'Do you agree that the God-Emperor is beyond our understanding? That He transcends all the categories of thought that we normally employ.'

'Of course. The God-Emperor is beyond mere words.'

'Then the same is true of His Imperial Truth. Of course, we try to capture it in phrases, we attempt to pin it down on the pages of sacred codexes, but the truth we are trying to express is so much more than anything we can encapsulate in any formal system of language. There, do you understand what I meant now? It is perfectly orthodox.'

Commissar Roshant glanced away briefly from his driving and looked at Obeysekera. The captain, seeing his face, was struck again by how young the commissar was. How callow.

'It might *be* orthodox, but it does not *sound* orthodox.' Roshant looked back to the way ahead, directing the Venator along the gentle slope beside the flowsand. 'Not all the members of the Ecclesiarchy are as well versed in the finer points of Imperial theology as you are, captain. It would be wise not to tax their learning too deeply.' The young commissar grinned. 'My father always said that, for sport, nothing beat pricking the pride of a precentor. Great fervour, little learning.' Roshant raised his hand and brushed away the sand from his goggles. 'But pricked pride provokes revenge. Should the Ecclesiarchy range against you, even the Commissariat would have difficulty coming to your aid.'

'I have no intention of provoking the custodians of the Imperial creed,' said Obeysekera. 'For my part, I am simply trying to understand it better, and by doing so know more fully the grace of the God-Emperor. Speaking of that, I presume they went into some detail about the Imperial creed at the schola?'

'We delve deeper into Imperial theology in our training than in the seminaries of the Ecclesiarchy, for we have to distinguish between heretical and orthodox expressions of the Imperial creed, whereas preachers merely have to preach.'

'Then tell me, what do you think of the Stinian School? According to Saint Stinus, the Emperor wills none of the evil in the galaxy but permits it as a shadow that serves to highlight His glory.'

The commissar glanced at Captain Obeysekera. 'Our commandant delivered ten lectures to us on the theology of Saint Stinus, each of them not less than three hours long, and by the end I was little wiser than I was at the beginning. But when I had to pass the final examination I studied the saint's theology and came to a similar conclusion, except I would say that according to Saint Stinus the Emperor permits evil that we be purged in the fire of war and suffering, to better become instruments of His will.'

'That's an interesting reading of his *Ecclesiarchy Dogmatics* – volume twenty-three?'

'Most of the argument was contained in volume twenty-eight but there was an important prolegomena in volume twenty-three.'

'I will look it up. But would you agree that both are permitted orthodox readings of Saint Stinus?'

'They were declared so at the thirty-eighth Ecumenical Synod.'

'Then we might say that what we endure, while not willed by the Emperor, nevertheless serves His purpose either directly, by manifesting more clearly His glory, or indirectly, by honing us, His servants, into better servants of His will.'

'That is what I concluded from my reading of Saint Stinus.'

'Then I think we can face what awaits with equanimity, whatever it entails.' Obeysekera grinned. 'Although of course, if the School of Saint Cauvin is true, then the Emperor has looked upon us and by His inscrutable will decreed that only a vanishingly small number among us shall be justified, with the rest destined for perdition. The doctrine has the advantage of removing us from vain striving, for only the Emperor knows whom He wishes to justify, but only when our duty ends in death shall we know if He has deemed it acceptable to His glory and accepted it as the necessary sacrifice to His will.'

'The Officio Prefectus, while maintaining official neutrality with respect to the orthodox schools of the Imperial creed, in practice prefers the doctrine of Cauvin over those of Saint Stinus, or the doctrine of Saint Quino or Saint Gustine.'

Obeysekera laughed. 'Of course. Cauvinism fits the Officio Prefectus like a power pack fits a lasgun. From what I have heard, the Inquisition leans towards the School of Saint Quino while the Astra Militarum naturally professes the doctrines of the School of Saint Gustine.'

'What about the Adeptus Astartes?'

'I have never been able to establish that. I suspect that most of them regard the disputes between the schools as the pettifogging nit-picks of Ecclesiarchy scholars, disputations that would be more quickly and cleanly resolved with a bolter and chain-sword, and who are we to say that that is not the case, since the disputes have endured without resolution for ten thousand years. But, for myself, I think the lack of resolution reflects what I said earlier, the inherent impossibility of framing the Impe-rial Truth in language. Language, by definition, excludes as it defines and the Imperial Truth is greater than the words with which we seek to describe it.'

'Suffer not the witch, the mutant and the alien to live. That's clear enough.'

'Perfect for soldiers – clear, concise orders. But insufficient for scholars and theologians, hence the thirty-eight volumes of Saint Stinus' *Ecclesiarchy Dogmatics*.' Obeysekera paused to shake the sand from his face cloth.

'Saint Stinus never finished the *Dogmatics*, did he?' Roshant put in.

'No. There should be forty volumes, but while writing the thirty-eighth during his retreat on the convent world Erem-ita, Saint Stinus was forced to emerge from his cell to lead the defence of Eremita against the Great Devourer. By his example and leadership, Saint Stinus repelled the Devourer from Eremita but at the cost of his own life, leaving the *Dogmatics* unfinished and, I suspect, generations of schola students giving thanks to the Emperor for His mercy – the last five volumes do get *very* dense.'

'I gave up around volume twenty-five,' said Commissar Roshant. 'Don't mention that to anyone.'

'Don't worry, you did better than most – few get through the first ten.'

'Anything on the auspex?'

'No, still the same readings. Take the speed down. I need to pay attention to plotting our course.'

Roshant nodded and they drove on in silence, the sand hissing under the wheels of the Venator and the wind of Dasht i-Kevar hot in their faces.

'*Captain.*' The squad vox-channel squeaked into tinny life.

'Malick?'

'*Captain, I'm picking up something ahead on my auspex.*'

'Ghost readings?'

'*They've stayed steady for a few minutes. Multiple contacts, stable, with fast-moving overheads – looks like aircraft strafing ground targets.*'

'I'll take a look.'

Obeysekera switched his display to the auspex, the ghost-green screen coming up in front of his eyes.

'I see it.'

'*Range about three miles.*'

'No Imperial signature on any of the readings,' noted Obeysekera.

'*Signals keep fading in and out,*' said Malick.

'More switching in and out.'

'*Think I have something in sight.*' The vox-signal flashed Trooper Uwais' sigil.

'What do you see?' asked Obeysekera.

'*Vapour trails. Two, maybe three craft.*'

'Identity?'

'*At this range, uncertain. Not Imperial. Wrong movement pattern. Very smooth. Could be t'au.*'

'You can tell they're t'au aircraft from the way they move?' asked Roshant. 'How?'

'Later, commissar,' snapped Obeysekera. 'Halt. We don't want them observing us.'

As the Venator came to a stop, its tyres settling into the sand, Obeysekera stood up on his seat, retrieved his magnoculars from his belt and trained them ahead.

He could see, over the rising and falling ridges of sand, the traces of what Uwais had reported: vapour trails. In the arid air of Dasht i-Kevar there was precious little vapour to create such trails: that they existed, however briefly, told the speed of the aircraft making them. Through the magnoculars he sought to find one of the darting craft.

There.

'Got it.' The voice was Gunsur's. 'T'au Remoras, sir. Three of them.'

The drone, smaller than a standard Barracuda but no less lethal for that, was riding the rolling level of the heat thermals, jinking through the columns of air like one of the migratory v-tails of Cadia, birds that spent their whole lives, once hatched, on the wing. Following the darting silver through the magno-culars, Obeysekera felt a nudge of appreciation: the Remora was a thing of beauty, form and function aligned in combat harmony. It was hard not to compare it to the bombast and thunder of a Thunderbolt, an aircraft that flew more by blasting gravity into submission than by any suggestion that the air was its rightful element.

It was as well, Obeysekera pondered as he put the ideas away in the secret corner for forbidden notions, that the Commissariat could not actually read thoughts: he wondered how many would be condemned from their own minds if the Officio Prefectus should ever be able to do that.

The darting patterns the Remoras were running and the weapons' flares told that the drones were strafing targets on the ground.

'Any contact on the Remoras' target?' Obeysekera posed the

question over the squad vox-channel. As he did so, he noted the flicker of surprise in the glance that Roshant shot towards him. According to Commissariat doctrine, an officer told his troops what to do: he did not ask them questions.

Obeysekera reminded himself to speak to Roshant about the differences between the Kasrkin and ordinary Cadian troops.

'*Auspex showing something.*' The vox-display showed the report was coming from Chame in the rearmost Venator. '*Multiple soft ground contacts and... and something else.*'

'*I see it,*' broke in Malick. '*Never seen anything like it.*'

'Range?'

'*Soft signal. Maybe two miles. Bearing three-four-eight.*'

'Got it.' Obeysekera stared at the auspex. Even with the strange readings that plagued the machine-spirit in the Great Sand Sea, this was unusual.

As he was looking at the auspex, trying to work out what he was seeing, Obeysekera saw the secure vox-signal flare. He keyed on the bead.

'Yes?'

'Roshant here.'

Obeysekera looked round at the commissar, sitting next to him in the Venator. But Roshant was staring straight ahead.

'Yes?'

Obeysekera saw the commissar's lips begin to move and then, lagging a moment to allow for encryption, the words reached him through his micro-bead.

'The mission calls for the strictest secrecy. I strongly recommend avoiding contact with the enemy.'

Obeysekera veiled his grin. Maybe the commissar was not quite so callow after all. He looked back to the auspex, bending closer to the screen to veil the conversation.

'Is this an official Commissariat recommendation, commissar?'

'No, captain. A suggestion, but one given in light of our orders.'

'Noted. But if the blueies have sent aircraft into the Great Sand Sea, then the most likely reason is that they know one of our Valkyries came down here and are looking for it.'

'You think they are searching for the general?'

'Not necessarily. They would be interested in retrieving a Valkyrie whatever it contained. But to venture so far as to send aircraft in here suggests that, at the least, they know there is something or someone of high value in the Valkyrie and they are willing to lose some aircraft in order to retrieve it.' Obeysekera tapped the auspex. 'There's a sandstorm rising. If they don't clear the area soon, they won't be able to.'

'My recommendation stands,' said Roshant. 'Avoid contact with the xenos.'

'They stand in our way. We sit here and wait for them to go, in which case the sandstorm will probably reach us before we can get any further, or we push on, risk the blueies spotting us, but also establish what they are attacking.' Obeysekera sat back. 'Our tactical doctrine states, when objectives clash, advance. We will advance.' Obeysekera touched his finger to the maps and bent over them. 'Thank you for raising this privately, commissar.'

'I can see that among the Kasrkin it is not unknown for soldiers to question the orders of their officers, but I have been commissioned into the Officio Prefectus – I am not comfortable with that.'

'Not question, rather clarify. But I know it can seem like insubordination. I will explain the reason why later.'

'I would appreciate that, captain.'

'Remind me.' Obeysekera switched to the squad vox-channel. 'We will advance at half-speed. Keep watch, visual and auspex. I want to know what the blueies are attacking, preferably without them seeing us.'

Roshant started up the galvanic engine, the other two Vena-tors whining into life as the machine-spirits responded to their drivers' whispered prayers, and the vehicles moved forward, their tyres hissing over the thin sand.

'Trooper Lerin.' Obeysekera addressed the Kasrkin manning the twin-linked multi-laser on the back of his Venator.

'Yes, captain?'

'You have the clearest field of vision. Tell me at once when you see the blueies. I will be watching on the auspex.'

'Anything else, too?'

'Yes, of course.'

'Will do.'

The Venator was moving slowly enough for Obeysekera to hear the machine creak of the heavy weapon set into the vehicle behind him as it swept back and forth, the pintle grinding the sand that had seeped through the collar into the mechanism.

'Lerin, dismantle the pintle when we camp – sand is getting into the mechanism.'

'Yes, sir.'

'And tell the troops in the other vehicles to do the same.'

'Yes, sir.' The second assent snapped through the vox.

Obeysekera grinned. 'Misery is endured more easily when it is shared out,' he said over the private circuit.

'That's what they teach us in the Officio Prefectus,' said Com-missar Roshant. 'In my experience, I have found it to be the most accurate precept that we were taught.'

# CHAPTER 9

'Sergeant, *Holy Fire* has slowed down,' said Gunsur. 'I reckon something's wrong.'

Before Malick could reply, the order came over the squad vox-channel. *'Reduce speed to five miles per hour.'*

Malick, driving the Venator, snorted. 'What's wrong with you, Torgut? Never known you so jumpy.'

Gunsur shook his head. 'I don't know, sarge.' He looked up from the maps clamped onto the tray and stared ahead. The lead Venator, having slowed down, was throwing up less wake and the cloud of thin sand that they had been driving through began to thin. 'Least I can see better now.'

Malick nodded. The lead Venator was some fifty yards ahead but even with that gap, and the reduced speed, they were still driving through clouds of dust. He flicked his finger across his goggles to remove the sand stick – he had learned that the lighter the contact, the less sand remained stuck on his goggles, glued there by the oils from his skin – and refolded his head cloth so a new section guarded his mouth and nose. The rebreather did keep the sand out, but by the end of a day's driving its filters were so clogged with dust as to be almost impossible to clean out. Whereas the face cloth could just be moved to a clean section. It was a practice that he and the rest of the squad had adopted from Captain Obeysekera.

'Sarge, I've got something on the auspex,' said Gunsur, his voice suddenly urgent.

'Call it through.'

'I-I don't know what it is,' said Gunsur.

'Call it through. Now.'

'Yes, sarge.' Gunsur paused, opening the channel to his commanding officer. 'Captain, I've got something new on the auspex.'

The command came back from *Holy Fire* to stop.

Malick brought the Venator to a halt, maintaining the fifty-yard separation between the vehicles that was part of their operating codex while travelling through hostile terrain. Looking into his mirror, he saw that Ensor was bringing *Saint Conrad* to a stop as well.

'*Malick, come with me,*' came the summons from Captain Obeysekera.

Gunsur looked at the sergeant and shrugged. Malick unstrapped himself from his seat and, unracking his hellgun, made his way across the sand to Obeysekera, waiting by the lead Venator. The sand crunched under his boots. Out from the shade provided by the Venator, Malick felt the weight of the sun upon his head and shoulders as a physical force. But he had soldiered on planets with gravity fields significantly higher than Terra normal: he carried on, scanning his surroundings as he went with the practised skill of a Kasrkin.

They were still driving along the broad valley made by the flowsand, the valley slopes rising gently on either side. Ahead, ridgetops of dunes running at a closing angle to the flowsand valley restricted their view. Squinting ahead, Malick saw the flashes of light fracturing upon the planed edges of banking aircraft: the Remoras.

Obeysekera was waiting for him beside the Venator. The commissar was still sitting in the driver's seat and, at the rear of the vehicle, Lerin was tracking the multi-laser across an arc of one hundred and twenty degrees, ready to engage any approaching targets.

'Got your magnoculars?' Obeysekera asked as Malick reached him.

The sergeant held them up.

'Good. Yours are better than mine. Come with me, we're going to see what's got the blueies so excited.' With that, Obeysekera began climbing up the side of the valley, boots sending Vs of sand sliding down the slip face, and Malick followed, taking a course up the slope ten yards right of the captain.

Nearing the top of the ridge, Obeysekera crouched down and began to crawl upwards, seeking to keep his profile low, and Malick did the same. The sand was hot between his fingers. It slipped over them like cinders, as if he were crawling through the wreckage of a battle not long over.

The sergeant felt the sand beneath his left boot give way and he began to slide. He spear-thrust his fingers into the sand, arresting the motion, kicked the other boot into the dune and then started up again. He could feel the sand grains here were smaller and finer than lower down, slipping more easily as he went over them.

Malick glanced left, past Obeysekera, and saw the view beginning to open out as they ascended. Now he could begin to see the crests of the dunes, running east to west, stretching away into the crystal distance. Before the heat haze of the afternoon, the air on Dasht i-Kevar was the clearest he had ever seen, let alone breathed; even when it burned from its heat, it was a clean burn, very far from the acrid, burning air of Imperial forge worlds.

And through that crystal air, Malick saw something that should not have been there.

'Sir, stop. Look left.'

At Malick's words, Obeysekera dropped flat upon the sand and turned his head.

'What in the Throne's name is that?'

Rising above the crest of the dunes, maybe half a mile away, was a tree. But a tree that in scale and appearance was like nothing Malick had ever seen before. A central trunk rose into the air then split into myriad tubes that rose further and then arched back downwards, like jets of water from a fountain. Flitting through and between the tubes, Malick saw glints of light and, raising his magnoculars to his eyes, confirmed that they were the t'au Remoras, drones. Trying to hold one in the magnoculars' field – the Remora seemed to shift and slide in his vision – he saw burst cannons pulsing as they released a sudden hail of plasma bolts. Then the Remora slipped out of his view.

Malick scanned, searching for what the Remora was firing at, and saw flashes of white, and wings.

'Sir, so far as I can see, the Remoras are shooting at birds.'

'That's what I thought.'

'How come we didn't see the tree before?' asked Malick.

'I don't think it was there before,' said Obeysekera. 'It's big enough to have shown up on orbital auspex sweeps, let alone the ones we did before setting out. It's still growing. I think it has just come up today. By the Throne, what is it? Malick, quarter the sky, see if you can locate the drones' mother ship – there should be a t'au Tiger Shark somewhere in the vicinity – and call in the

Venators, see if they're picking up anything on their auspexes. I'm going to go a little higher and try to get a better view.'

'*Holy Fire, Divine Light, Saint Conrad,* auspex scan, sixty degrees around reading three hundred and thirty degrees, distance five hundred yards.'

Malick noted the responses while scanning the sky, looking for the Tiger Shark. The Remoras were short-range drones, yet it was still possible that their mother ship was over the horizon. But even if it was within visual range, Malick knew from painful experience how difficult it was to spot t'au aircraft, visually or on the auspex. In contrast to the plasteel bulk and turbofan scream of Imperial planes, t'au aircraft were quiet and they shifted under the eye, squirming out of view like trying to hold a squito in focus to swat it.

Malick continued to quarter the sky, scanning through blocks of blue, searching for the telltale glint of refracted light. But even as he did so, his gaze was drawn back, again and again, to the tall tree-like structure rising from the desert and the white-winged birds that flew among its branches.

'*Faint target, bearing three-four-three, distance three miles.*'

The voice was Gunsur's.

Malick raised his magnoculars and, setting them to a wide field, trained them at the bearing Gunsur had called.

There. It shimmered in his sight, like looking at something through heat haze, but the Tiger Shark was high enough above the desert for the rising thermals not to affect his view of it. The broad, bat-winged craft was flying in a figure-of-eight pattern, looping back on itself while keeping its drones, and the tree structure, in view. But even as he watched, Malick saw the Tiger Shark withdrawing, pulling away from him. He checked behind, looking to see why the Tiger Shark was drawing back, and saw the southern horizon dark and billowing, with lightning chequering the clouds.

'Sir, sandstorm approaching from the south.'

Malick saw Obeysekera look back in his direction.

'How far?'

Malick checked his auspex. 'Two miles. Distance closing quickly.'

'Time before it hits?'

'Auspex playing up, sir. Maybe thirty minutes. Could be less. The t'au Tiger Shark is holding station.'

'It is? Check.'

Malick went back onto his magnoculars, calibrated them for distance and found the Tiger Shark in its field.

'Still three miles, sir. Definitely holding station.'

'Right. We'll make use of that.' Obeysekera signed for Malick to follow. 'We're going to see what that tree thing is and why the blueies are attacking it.'

Obeysekera led the way, scrambling up to the top of the sand crest with Malick following. The slip face gave way beneath his hands and feet, the sand groaning as it slid down the slope, but he ignored the singing in his haste to get to the top. He looked back south. The storm was coming up fast, the clouds seared from within by sand-lightning, its advance heralded by the almost continuous rumble of thunder. There was not much time.

He scrambled higher, digging his way up the slope, magnoculars banging on his chest from their strap. He needed to get high enough to see what the Remoras were attacking; if this ridge was not high enough to give him a field of view, there would not be time to find another.

Fit as he was, Obeysekera felt the air rasping through his mouth, hot and gritty, and his heart pushing against his chest as it worked to pump blood through his body. Climbing sand was hard.

Reaching the lip of the slip face, Obeysekera pulled himself

over the edge and lay prone on the crest of the dune, pulling the magnoculars to his eyes as he did so. Beside him, he
heard Malick pull himself up too and the whirr of the sergeant's
magnoculars searching for focus. His own magnoculars blurred,
then cleared, finding the depth of field. Obeysekera heard the
gasp that issued from his lips, but in the wonder at what he
was seeing, he barely noticed it.

Through his magnoculars he could see the broad, flat plain
beyond the last sand ridge. A part of his mind, the analytic,
tactical part, stowed away the fact that it looked like there was
a salt flat in the Great Sand Sea, an anomaly of the shifting
winds. But the greater part of his mind was staring at what was
upon the salt flat.

Cutting through about a hundred yards of the flat was the
furrow that he had marked earlier. But at its end, rising from
the ground, was the trunk of the strange tree. It rose up like a
fountain, reaching to three hundred feet in height before splitting into hundreds of fronds, or tubes, that arched out from
the trunk. Through the branches – they were not branches, but
he could think of no other term for them – Obeysekera could
see white-winged creatures, birds presumably, flying. With the
boughs so thick, he could not make out what sort of birds they
were, although they were evidently large, but he did see that
they would settle next to the buds that were sprouting on the
branches. He could not see what they were doing.

But the tree was not the only thing upon the flat.

Closest to him were the mukaali of the Kamshet, herded
together, their front legs hobbled, but pushing against their
herders in their frantic attempts to escape the Remoras, buzzing
low over them. The Kamshet herders were trying to stop the bull
mukaali bursting from the herd, wielding whips and pricking
scourges into the sensitive snouts of the beasts, stopping them

and sending them blundering backwards into their fellows. One or two mukaali fell and, thrashing upon the floor, brought others down too, only for a Remora passing above them to cut a burning trail through their midst. The smell of charred flesh reached Obeysekera, telling the tale of winds rising.

Clustered in under the tree were the rest of the Kamshet, their robes startlingly blue and yellow against the white of the flat. Through his magnoculars, Obeysekera saw that many of them were holding vessels, while others were carrying ritual knives, elaborately carved. Then Obeysekera saw a white flash in the corner of his view and turned his magnoculars to see...

He saw wings, great white metal wings, unfurl from behind one of the Kamshet and then the man, carrying one of the ritual knives, leapt upwards, carried by a launch blast from a jump pack. His wings beat, catching the leap and bearing him up into the shadow of the great tree.

They were not birds flying among the branches of the tree, but men.

As he watched, Obeysekera saw one of the winged men fly down from the heights, carrying a bud in his hands, and on landing pour its contents into one of the vessels that another Kamshet was carrying.

The water of life.

The elixir that made a desert planet a vital Imperial asset in this subsector.

The Kamshet traded it, but nobody had ever discovered where they found it. Now, he knew. And if the t'au got back to their base, they would know too. It was imperative that he find some way to destroy the Tiger Shark, the mother ship that had launched these drones.

The only way he could do that would be by baiting it closer.

Over the vox, Obeysekera heard soft curses from Malick,

indicating that he was seeing the same sight. But as they watched the Kamshet reaping their strange harvest, a Remora flashed above the giant fronds of the tree, its burst cannon pulsing, and a small explosion showed that it had scored a hit. In a bloody ruin of flesh and metal, the winged man crashed onto the flat salt pan.

But as he was about to turn away, Obeysekera saw new movement. As one of the fronds of the tree touched the ground, the salt flat beneath began to seethe, rippling, boiling. The Kamshet tapping the frond leaped away, running through the breaking ground. Obeysekera knew that he must get back to his men, but he could not pull himself away – not until he had seen what was breaking through from below.

The desert was coming to life.

In response to the liquid leaking from the great tree, stalks were pushing up from the ground, rising as quickly as a man waking, weaving up towards the sun. The stalks were springing leaves, flowers were unfurling as he watched, and in among the new growth there was movement – darting, shimmering movement. Insect-like creatures were hatching from the ground and taking wing, flitting to the newly opened blooms, creating a hum of fresh life that reached Obeysekera even through the whine of the Remoras and the harrumphing of the mukaali. But, as his magnoculars zoomed in closer, Obeysekera realised that not all those flowers were benign: some were mouths that gaped and closed upon each curious, visiting insect.

'Throne!'

Malick's exclamation broke the spell that had held Obeysekera frozen. The time for watching was over.

'Let's go. Time to reel in some fish.'

While the Kasrkin were far less prone to Commissariat-induced freezing, he had nevertheless moved Roshant to *Saint Conrad* at the back of the column. The commissar had started to object, but Obeysekera had pointed out that it would give him the chance to observe the rest of the team, and he had accepted the suggestion with a reasonable amount of grace.

They were driving ahead of the storm. Already Obeysekera could feel its outliers, skirls of wind, lashing at his face and stirring up sudden plumes of sand from the crest lines of the dunes. He checked the auspex, cursed its machine-spirit for freezing again, and leaned out of the Venator to look behind. The skyline had disappeared into lightning-pierced darkness. It would not be long before it was upon them.

'Faster,' he said. In response, Malick drove the Venator forwards, its wheels throwing up sprays of sand as he urged it on.

Obeysekera looked ahead. The tree rose above the dune crests, its highest branches reaching at least five hundred feet into the sky before they arched downwards. With the dune crests still blocking his view of the base of the tree, he could not see what was happening to the life breaking upwards from the salt flats. But he could see, with the naked eye now, the glint and flash of the t'au Remoras, moving like fish through an undersea forest, their burst cannons pulsing. As he watched, he saw the fire-trail of missiles launching – each Remora normally carried two – the weapons arching between the fronds of the giant tree and striking its thick trunk. But the explosions made barely a mark upon the dense surface, the blasts seemingly dissipated by the matting that covered the trunk, a natural form of slat armour.

The valley that Malick was leading the Venators through was broadening out, the ridge at the end of it dropping lower as they approached the salt flat and the tree. Obeysekera, scanning for enemy, saw on their left a long disturbance running parallel with them and towards the structure, as if a point plough had been dragged through the sand.

'Gunners, independent fire. Track the Remoras and destroy them.' Obeysekera gave the order through the squad vox-channel and saw the acknowledgements flash up on his display. He pulled his hellgun from its rack and cycled a charge. 'Drivers, *Divine Light* break right after the ridge, *Saint Conrad* break left. *Holy Fire* straight on. Troopers, deploy missile launchers. Load with flak missiles. We must take out the Remoras and lure the Tiger Shark into range.' Obeysekera shot a look behind him again. 'We have thirty minutes max before the storm hits. Make them count.'

'Straight on?' asked Malick.

'Straight on,' said Obeysekera.

Sergeant Malick grinned, and Obeysekera saw the fierce delight lighting up his face.

He felt the grin spreading across his own face too: battle joy. The time when everything becomes clear. It was a feeling that united the 'kin, the unspoken source of their union and their fierce, unflinching memory of their lost home.

Obeysekera turned to face the front, hellgun in his hands. The galvanic motors powering the Venator hummed higher as Malick kicked the vehicle up to top speed. Sand flew up behind the tyres as they climbed the final slope and broke the ridge.

Before them: the salt flat, the tree spouting life upon the desert, the panicking mukaali and the rushing Kamshet, and the darting Remoras carving paths of fire.

Malick gunned the Venator, sending it surging down the slope onto the flat. Above his head, Obeysekera heard the heat rasp of the multi-laser, its twin beams stabbing at the nearest Remora. Lerin had engaged the enemy without further instruction.

Obeysekera saw the Kamshet, startled, looking towards them. A quick glance left and right told him that the other Venators were breaking off across the salt flat in the directions he had ordered, each vehicle's weapons triangulating on the lead Remora. The Remoras responded, dropping their attack on the tree and the Kamshet and turning towards the Kasrkin, jinking to and fro through the criss-cross of laser shots, shimmering in and out of view like half-remembered dreams as the burst cannons cycled. Plasma pulses liquefied the salt a few yards to their left. Through the vox-channel, one of the gunners was screaming obscenities.

'Silence!' yelled Obeysekera, cutting off the cries. 'Malick, get in closer, in under the tree.'

Ahead, the mukaali were breaking across their path, harrumphing, bellowing, a frightened, confused mass of flesh, the Kamshet vainly trying to stem the stampede. The Remora was turning, rotating on its axis, lining itself up for a second pass. Lerin was desperately trying to bring the multi-laser round on target, but the pintle, its mount fouled with sand, was grinding to a halt.

Obeysekera looked ahead again. A herd of stampeding mukaali could knock the Venator over.

'Go round them.'

Malick pulled the Venator left, gunning the galvanic motors. On the hard surface of the salt flats there was no desert-induced pause as the tyres spun sand; the vehicle responded immediately, careening over the surface at an angle to the onrushing stampede that would give them enough leeway to round the leading mukaali.

'Throne, Throne, Throne!' Obeysekera could hear Lerin swearing as she tried to haul the multi-laser round. It was not coming through on the vox-channel, he was hearing the woman's shouts as she ground the weapon around on its sand-fouled pintle.

A burst of plasma cut across their way, forcing Malick to jerk the Venator right, towards the mukaali.

'Where the frekk are the others?' Malick yelled.

Obeysekera unstrapped his belt and leaned out of the Venator, lifting his hellgun into firing position while he held on with one hand. 'Keep moving,' he yelled.

The Remora was jinking back and forth, avoiding the crossfire of the other two Venators, while tracking them across the salt flat.

A predator is never so vulnerable as when it's lining up a kill.

Never taking his eyes from the Remora, Obeysekera saw the fire flash of a flak missile launching from *Divine Light*. At the same moment, he fired his hellgun, deliberately lacing the air to the right of the Remora with bursts of hotshots.

In response, the machine intelligence of the Remora jinked the aircraft in the opposite direction – right into the path of the flak missile.

The starboard engine of the Remora disintegrated, shards of its casing flying in chaotic streams outwards. The aircraft wobbled, the whine of the other engine rising in pitch as its machine intelligence tried to compensate for the sudden imbalance in thrust, but the wobble became an uncontrollable oscillation, each correction sending the Remora further out of control and shedding pieces of the aircraft.

'Watch out.' Obeysekera pointed up at the Remora.

'I see it,' said Malick, turning the Venator to avoid its course. But as he did so, the Remora lost all control, spinning wildly and crashing among the herd of mukaali. The animals, already panicking, responded to the smell and sight of their broken herd mates by breaking their final restraints. Hobbles snapped, chains broke, and the herd came stampeding towards the Venator.

'Lerin, clear a path through the mukaali,' Obeysekera ordered. But from behind he heard the grinding of the cannon's pintle.

'It's jammed fast, sir.'

'Malick?'

'Yes.' Sergeant Malick spun the Venator around, its tyres carving tracks through the salt crust, bringing the jammed multi-laser to bear on the approaching stampede.

'Fire at will,' said Obeysekera.

+Stop!+

The voice was no voice, but a command in his head, and in Sergeant Malick's and in Lerin's, too. It was a command that translated into Obeysekera's muscles and nerves without any impulse from him. Sergeant Malick, similarly commanded, stopped and the Venator, its impulse removed, slid to a halt. Although he could not see her, Obeysekera was sure that Lerin was standing frozen behind the multi-laser, finger poised over the trigger but unable to pull it.

The stampeding mukaali were coming closer, their stench riding before them, heads swinging in pendulum panic, bodies like wrinkled dozers rolling over the flat towards the Kasrkin, small eyes white in fear. Staring at them, unable to move, a stray part of Obeysekera's mind reflected that of all the potential deaths he had contemplated, being crushed by stampeding mukaali had never figured as a possibility. He could hear subdued, strained breathing, his own and Sergeant Malick's, as they both fought against whatever or whoever was controlling their bodies, each with as little success as the other.

Obeysekera stared at approaching, undignified death. The philosophical corner of his mind, the reserved voice that had allowed him to accept the horrors of his life, counselled him that death was almost always undignified, calling up images of the battlefield slain he had seen, exposed and stripped of pretension or humanity. Death took the soul and left only the flesh.

But to die under the fear-filled feet of a herd of panicking pack animals...

Obeysekera would have shut his eyes, but he could no more control his eyelids than any other part of his body. He could still listen, though. Through the vox, he heard *Divine Light* and *Saint Conrad* calling in to him, asking if he needed assistance. But he could tell from the distance of the air snaps that accompanied their weapons fire that they were both too far away to come to their aid in time.

The mukaali were mad with fear. The crashed Remora was still spitting ordnance, a broken burst cannon firing at random like a Cadian scorpine still pumping poison into its killer, even after it itself had been killed, and the plasma pulses were cutting through the herd, amputating limbs and sending animals crashing into the flat.

Obeysekera tried to close his eyes again.

He still could not move them.

He stared death in its bestial, onrushing face.

And then, death changed his face.

Before him, with her arms spread wide, was the woman he had seen, unveiled, among the Kamshet. She stood before the Venator and her eyes were cerulean blue and her mouth was madder red and her teeth were white. She stood before the Venator and spoke, uttering sounds of command, and the mukaali parted, moving to either side of her, streaming past the Venator on left and right, harrumphing and rolling and bumping into each other, but none of the beasts touched the vehicle.

The invisible locks upon Obeysekera's body were released. He glanced at Malick, saw that he was free too, then back to the woman standing in front of them.

And she spoke in Obeysekera's mind.

+I am not your enemy.+

'Sir, she's in my sights.' The message over the vehicle's vox-channel told him that Lerin had got the multi-laser working.

Obeysekera stared into the woman's eyes.

'No.' He could hear himself speaking as if through treacle: he was talking through all the years of training as a Cadian and a Kasrkin; he was saying 'no' to all the preachers he had heard denouncing the witch and the psyker; he was looking into a face that all his teachers had told him to blow apart in a stream of multi-laser fire, and he said, 'No.'

The woman's lips twitched in a smile and then she turned and stood with her arms upstretched, and the air around her spread fingers shimmered, as with the haze of the desert heat.

Obeysekera could feel Sergeant Malick looking at him. He ignored the gaze. Standing up on his seat, he stuck his head through the Venator's roll cage and scanned for the two remaining Remoras.

The las-fire from *Divine Light* and *Saint Conrad* pinpointed them for him: the Remoras were twisting through the trailing fronds of the great tree, using it as cover from the 'kin while lining up plasma pulses from their burst cannons. Only the zigzag driving of Ensor and Roshant in the Venators had kept them from harm, but as he watched he saw a burst strike near the front wheel of Roshant's vehicle, boiling the tyre away from the rim and leaving the Venator pushing the plasteel tyre rims through the salt crust, forcing it to turn in a circle.

The Remora banked round, skipping between trailing shoots.

+Rise.+

Obeysekera heard the word in his mind, the command, and he looked to the Kamshet woman of the cerulean eyes, and her arms were raised in summons.

From the flat surrounding the tree, boiling up through the breaking ground, came a cloud of creatures – insects, or their evolutionary analogue on Dasht i-Kevar, Obeysekera thought – chirring, whirring, clicking and rising in a cloud of wings and chitin up through the tendrils of the tree that had summoned them from their centuries-long hibernation. And like smoke they rose in wavering columns up into the sky, weaving in and out of the branches of the tree, forming living nets that looped around the two Remoras, drawing in tighter and tighter as the machine intelligences within them sought to find routes out from the flying mass.

From his vantage point far below, Obeysekera heard the Remoras' engine notes change, choke, cough as a thousand, ten thousand chitinous bodies hurled themselves at the aircraft, clogging intakes, smearing optics, and choking the intricately engineered engines. The aircraft were dragged from the sky, struggling with mechanical intensity against the weight of the columns of life that pulled them down, but they struggled in vain.

The Remoras broke upon the salt flat, their nano-crystalline alloy skins shearing apart on impact, their mechanical guts leaking fluids of yellow and black upon the thirsty salt. They lay there, small columns of smoke rising from them, all but buried in furious clouds of tiny chattering, chittering creatures.

The Kamshet woman with the cerulean eyes spread her arms wide. The cloud of insects rose from the stricken t'au aircraft.

'Throne!' said Malick. 'Glad she's on our side, be gladder when she's gone.'

The woman raised her hands, palms up, and the insects began to disperse, buzzing upwards in and among the fronds of the giant tree, settling upon the flowers that were breaking open over its limbs, flowers of yellow and red and blue and every shade in between.

'Roshant, can you get your vehicle over here?' Obeysekera asked over the squad vox-channel.

'*Slowly.*'

'Do so. *Saint Conrad*, rendezvous on me.'

As the two vehicles made their way over the flat to him, Obeysekera began to climb down from the Venator.

'Sir,' said Malick over their personal link. 'Shouldn't we wait for the others?'

Obeysekera, poised half in and half out of the Venator, looked back to his sergeant. 'A commissar is not going to be the best man to deal with her.'

Malick nodded. 'We'll keep you covered, sir.'

Obeysekera grimaced. 'For what it's worth... I'd say take over the mission if I don't come back but, frankly, if I don't come back then I don't expect the mission will continue much longer.'

Malick pointed south. 'You'd best be quick. The storm's coming up fast.'

'Keep scanning for the Tiger Shark. It's lost its babies – it's going to come nosing closer to see what happened to them. Make sure we have all available flak missiles primed. Fire on your command if I am otherwise occupied.'

'Sir.'

Obeysekera climbed down from the Venator. His boot crunched on the ground. He looked down. The salt glittered beneath him, crystals of white diamond. Obeysekera reached back for his hell-gun, his fingertips grasping its worn-smooth stock.

He stopped. He released it and, empty-handed, turned and walked towards the woman with cerulean eyes.

The desert, normally so silent, was filled with sound and scent: the distant bellowing of mukaali, slowly being settled by the blue-robed Kamshet running beside them, loping over the salt flat; the deep, bone-settling buzz of the insect life – although now he was closer he could see that it was by no means all insectoid – that was still swarming from the ground; the scent of flowers, thick and heavy, overlaying the petrichor of the newly anointed desert.

And the steady stream of winged Kamshet flying up to harvest aqua vitae from the tree, each holding an intricately carved knife, alighting upon a bough next to one of the sprouting buds, slicing the bud from the tree and then flying down with it in their hands, knife held between their teeth.

As he approached the woman, Obeysekera saw some of the Kamshet gathering around her, blue-robed warriors, their faces veiled but their status clear from the weapons they carried: a mixed bunch, bone recurved bows and flange spears alongside stubbers, autoguns, lasrifles and more exotic weaponry that appeared to have originated from the aeldari. But Obeysekera paid the assembling entourage no mind; they would kill him or not at the command of the woman with cerulean eyes.

She was the only one that counted.

The blue-robed warriors parted as he approached, opening the way towards the woman. But although Obeysekera kept his gaze fixed upon the woman who waited on him, he was conscious of the hisses and imprecations from the surrounding warriors: the young bloods, fingering blades and making gestures either obscene or threatening while the older warriors stood silent and waiting, their stillness more menacing than the threats of the younger men.

As Obeysekera made his way through the cordon, he spoke into his vox-bead on the channel to Malick.

'Keep the commissar with you. Do not, repeat not, allow him to follow me.'

'*Understood.*'

Obeysekera emerged from the cordon of warriors and stood in the bubble of space surrounding the woman. She stood with the tree rising above her, shaded from the fierce sun of Dasht i-Kevar by its spreading branches. But even in the deep shade cast by the tree, she appeared brighter than her surroundings,

standing out from them as a statue of an Imperial saint stands
proud from the wall in which it is carved in the cathedrals of
the Ecclesiarchy. Although around her feet life still squirmed
out of the ground in a tidal rush of birth, the woman seemed
more alive than even the creatures buzzing and crawling and
rattling up from their long sleep.

For a moment, seeing the way creatures he would have
dismissed as bugs on Cadia seethed around her feet, Obeysekera
wondered if the woman was a servant of the Plague God. The
servants of Chaos could sometimes take on fair forms to hide
their inner foulness. But none of his briefings had suggested
the Kamshet were tainted. Nor did he sense anything wrong
about her.

She was alive. Simply, wholly alive.

Obeysekera approached the woman with cerulean eyes and,
stopping in front of her, paused momentarily. He made the
sign of the aquila and then, seeing no reaction, he bowed. She
laughed. It was the sound of silver.

Obeysekera straightened up and looked into her eyes.

They were blue. All blue, save for a pinprick of black at their
centre. They were the blue of the sky above the sand on Dasht
i-Kevar, the blue of the Caducades Sea beneath a clear sky, the
blue of Alnitak, burning in the deep.

+A storm is coming.+

Obeysekera heard the words, but he did not know if they were
spoken directly into his mind or came to him by normal speech.

The woman smiled, her red lips parting. 'Both,' she said,
answering his unspoken question.

She turned and looked back, through the tangle of swoop-
ing branches that formed the great tree rising from the desert.

'It is here,' she said.

Obeysekera's vox buzzed. *'Captain, we have an auspex reading.'*

Obeysekera looked at the woman. She was staring intently through the tangle into the distance.

'It's the Tiger Shark,' he said. 'Fire when locked.'

'Can't… can't get a fix.' Malick's words were distorted in his earbud. 'Auspex fading in and out.'

'Launch on visual – guide the missiles to target.'

'It's turning back, sir.'

'Pulling back?'

'Unclear. Might have picked up the auspex lock.'

'We have to bring it back in closer.' Obeysekera paused. 'Fire one flak missile on a two-second fuse, make sure it misses.'

'No chance of it hitting without a target lock and no visual.'

'I want the t'au to see it explode so they think they've sprung the trap.'

The woman turned back to Obeysekera. 'For a trap, you need bait.'

'My men and I are the bait.'

'Poor bait for such a prize. I have something more to its taste.' The woman of blue turned and gestured. From among the warriors, one stepped forward carrying something. Obeysekera stared at it. It was fire-scorched, and held gingerly at an unfamiliar angle, but then it rotated in his mind and he saw it for what it was. He stared at the woman and his hands clenched into fists.

'That's an Imperial distress locator.'

The woman shook her head. 'It is not from the vehicle you are seeking.'

Obeysekera stared at the woman. 'You know where he is? You have him?'

'We know where he is, but we do not have him. This came from one of your aircraft that crashed when first you came to our world, but it will serve.' The woman pointed at the distress locator. 'If you would bring your enemy closer, let them hear its call.' She looked past Obeysekera. 'The storm is close.'

Obeyesekera nodded. He took the distress locator and laid it on the salt flat, inspecting the device. Although it was fire-scorched it seemed undamaged. Breathing an invocation to its machine-spirit, Obeyesekera keyed in the activation code.

The distress locator lay inert and unresponsive on the ground. He stared down at it. He looked up at the woman.

'Try again.'

Obeyesekera nodded. He muttered the prayer to the machine and entered the code once more. The distress locator lit. Lights, red and green and yellow, flashed in random order before settling into a repeating sequence: the identifying call sign that told other Imperial aircraft the identity of the Valkyrie and its position.

'Malick.'

'Sir.'

'Have *Divine Light* and *Saint Conrad* stand ready. The Tiger Shark has been baited.'

'They're ready, sir.'

'Fire everything we've got when you have a lock.'

'Yes, sir.'

Obeyesekera nodded. He looked down at the cube sitting on the desert flat, marked with the aquila. It was, in its own way, as deadly as a bolter. He remained kneeling beside it, listening in on the squad vox-channel as each Venator crew dialled through their auspex settings, trying to get locks on the shifting signal of the t'au Tiger Shark.

'Closing.'

'Signal phasing.'

'Can't get the lock.'

'Switch to delta rhythm.'

Malick's voice, cutting through the chatter. 'Divine Light, *set auspex to standard pattern*. Saint Conrad, *set to Imperial pattern. Phase shift settings.*'

In his mind, Obeysekera could see what Malick was trying to do: calling up the auspex feeds from the other two Venators to the display on *Holy Fire*, he was superimposing the two readings upon his own, hoping that the false readings caused by the t'au Tiger Shark would cancel each other out, allowing him a clear fix.

'*Nearly, nearly… Got it! Lock!*'

'*Lock.*'

'*Lock.*'

The voices of troopers Ha and Chame in the other two Venators, called lock almost simultaneously.

'*Fire.*'

The three flak missiles flared up into the sky, trails converging. Obeysekera turned to watch their flight. The fire-trails were pointing up, but not very far up, on the further side of the great tree. The Tiger Shark was coming in low. He peered through the shifting fronds of the tree, trying to trace the missiles.

A flash. It came from low down, nearly on the horizon, lighting the shadows under the tree. Before the sound of the first explosion could reach Obeysekera, there came a second and a third flash, but not at the same spot as the first.

Obeysekera hoped that meant the trailing missiles had followed the course of the Tiger Shark and struck it a second and third blow; he feared that they may have exploded on chaff, distracted by the decoy launchers on the t'au aircraft firing off streams of reflective strips and lures when it detected the missile trails.

The distinctive sound of the vector thrusters of the t'au Tiger Shark, a smooth hum comparable to the noise of a hive of Cadian flower mites converting the pollen of a hundred thousand flowers into winter comb, quickly told him that the enemy aircraft had not been seriously damaged and that it was coming closer – much closer.

'*Rearm.*'

Through the vox-channel, Obeysekera could hear his men doing that without his orders.

'Fire when armed.'

Obeysekera did not wait for Malick's response – he knew the sergeant was on it – and instead made to move out from under the cover of the tree so that he might see more clearly what was happening.

'Wait.' The voice was gentle but imperious.

Obeysekera stopped moving, his legs utterly immobile. But he could still move his upper body and he turned to look at the Kamshet woman – their queen, he presumed.

'Let me go,' he said. 'I must help.'

'Wait,' said the woman again. As she answered him, she turned to look back south.

Immobile, Obeysekera heard the fizz of ion cannons, the energy beams burning the air itself. He turned to see twin, parallel finger trails of fire moving over the salt flat, drawing lines towards *Divine Light*. The salt liquefied, bubbled, then vaporised where the ion beam struck it. It smelt like burnt plasteel.

Obeysekera saw Roshant, in the driver's seat, engaging the galvanic motors. The Venator jerked into motion. Trooper Chame, manning the lascannons, was firing bursts at the oncoming Tiger Shark, the beams hissing across each other in the air. Ha was shouting into the vox, the system automatically cutting out the higher ranges of his cursing. Standing beside the Venator, Quert stood, the flak missile launcher balanced on her shoulder, lining up the missile on the onrushing Tiger Shark.

The fire fingers reached across the flat towards them.

The Venator's machine-spirit answered Roshant's frantic prayers and it lurched forward as the fire tracks reached them, the ion beams cutting through the desert behind the vehicle, Chame still loosing off laser bursts.

Trooper Quert stood her ground, waiting for the target lock, waiting, waiting, then keyed the release. The flak missile flew, gouting fire, and Trooper Quert threw herself aside.

Too late.

The right-hand ion beam burnt through her waist as she leapt, vaporising it, leaving her two legs twitching upon the salt and, two feet away, her chest and arms and head.

Quert's life signs on Obeysekera's display flashed critical, then lined.

The flak missile that Quert had died to fire off flared above their heads, changing course, then exploded harmlessly among the chaff cloud.

'If you are going to do something, lady, now would be good,' said Obeysekera. The Tiger Shark hissed past overhead, a shadow upon the desert, its vector thrusters a whisper in comparison to the ground rattle of an Imperial Marauder, already banking so that it might come round on a fresh pass, the stabbing fingers of the Venators' multi-lasers frizzling out on the streams of countermeasures that surrounded the t'au aircraft.

'Not me.' The woman with cerulean eyes raised her hand and pointed. 'See.'

The invisible shackles holding his body immobile fell away. Obeysekera turned, with the same sense of looming presence that accompanied his turning in dreams – but in his dreams he always woke before he saw that which was behind him. This time he did not wake.

The storm.

Dark. Vast, reaching up to overwhelm the arch of the sky, broad as the expanse of all that he could see. Reaching.

Reaching out towards the banking Tiger Shark.

Dark, dancing columns of twisting sand laced with sand-lightning were advancing in front of the storm bank. Sand tornadoes spun forwards like the battle tops he had played with as a child, rebounding off each other, lightning striking across them as they fought too.

Obeysekera saw the Tiger Shark, its velocity too great to turn away before it was caught up in the maelstrom, pull its nose back and back: the pilot was trying to climb up and out of the storm. A silver-and-grey fish against the black, the Tiger Shark rose, climbing all but vertically now, its pilot twisting it back and forth as black columns danced towards it and lightning bolts set jittering patterns of light playing over its skin.

Obeysekera had never seen an aircraft flown so well. Over the vox, he heard the men, whispering its downfall as they watched with as much awe as he: the storm appeared a thing alive, hunting, and the Tiger Shark a bird, fleet and flying.

The dark closed upon the silver.

Obeysekera breathed out. He had not realised that he had been holding his breath.

The Tiger Shark burst out from the black, vector thrusters shredding the black columns of sand, sheets of electric charge crawling all over its silver skin, and put its nose down, diving towards the ground, enlisting the gravity of Dasht i-Kevar to escape from the storm.

'It's getting away,' said Obeysekera and he felt a strange thrill of joy at the words.

Then the desert shivered, as an animal waking from sleep – shivered and shook. Under the salt flat, through the Sand Sea, the desert moved.

The Tiger Shark powered downwards in a shallow dive, vector thrusters pushing it away from the dark of the storm. As it neared the desert floor and the pilot pulled back its nose to bring it to the level, the desert rose up to meet it. First little geysers of sand, spitting upwards. Then explosions, gouts of sand and salt, blowing up in front and underneath the Tiger Shark, the grains sucked into the intakes of the aircraft's thrusters. Obeysekera heard the engine note change, shifting from a deep hum to a screaming, shredding whine. Smoke plumed from the starboard engines. Fire flicked from the port engine array. The Tiger Shark started to judder, shaking as it flew, the pilot fighting to keep the aircraft under control as it began to yaw, its nose pulling from one side to the other, bleeding speed.

And the storm pulled it back into the dark.

The great body of the storm surged forward, jumping almost as if it were alive, enveloping the lithe silver fish into its lightning-jagged darkness. This time, the Tiger Shark did not re-emerge.

Obeysekera listened for the sound of the crash, but he heard nothing: only the crack and rumble of the sand-lightning and the hiss of the windblown sand. It was as if the Tiger Shark had never been. He stared up at the rolling dark, then started and spoke into his vox.

'Get under the Venators.'

The storm was all but upon them.

He felt a touch, light as light, upon his arm, and Obeysekera turned round.

'There is no need,' she said. 'The storm will come no further.'

He stared at the woman. 'You can do this?'

'Not I.' She turned away and started walking towards where her people waited for her.

'Wait.'

She stopped.

Obeysekera ran after her. She did not turn around. He saw the warriors watching him, death in their eyes, but none approached.

'Great lady.'

At the honorific, the woman turned back to Obeysekera and

inclined her head slightly, assenting to the title the captain had given her.

'Will you aid me, great lady? I would do your people no harm.'

The woman raised her hand and pointed past Obeysekera. 'I hear truth in your words. But will you answer for these others? Your Imperium has no love for people such as mine. Will you answer for them that I might know my trust shall not be repaid in betrayal?'

Obeysekera felt his skin prickle, the hairs of a far distant ancestral past standing up at the purport of the promise that would carry over into an equally distant future. He was being asked to pledge his honour, and for him that was being asked to pledge his very being.

'I…' He hesitated.

The woman waited. And as she waited, Obeysekera realised that the sounds and movements of the outside world had stilled and stopped. He glanced around, not turning his head but only his eyes, and he saw the world waiting.

'Great lady,' he began again, 'gracious queen, you ask much.'

'No less than I ask the rest of my children.'

'I am not one of your sons, great lady.'

'But you are, dear one, you are.'

Captain Obeysekera stared at the woman of blue. 'How may this be? I was born far from here, I have come but recently to your world, it is not possible…' His words trailed away. 'I answer for them, great lady. On pain of my soul.'

The woman in blue smiled. 'You may call me by name – Mother.'

Obeysekera shook his head. 'I may not do that, great lady. My mother's name is Sashma and I honour her memory.'

'All mothers are blessed in dutiful sons. What would you ask of me?'

'I ask your aid against the enemy that seeks to take this world.'

The woman spread her arms wide, taking in the world. 'From whom would these enemies take this world?'

'From you, great lady.'

But she shook her head. 'You are mistaken, dear son. This world is not mine, although my sons people it, and harvest its living water. The living water that is valuable to your people, and to the blueskins that seek it too.'

'We are your people. The blueskins are xenos, aliens.' A memory, unbidden, flashed through Obeysekera's mind, of the way the Tiger Shark pilot had fought to save his plane, with all the skill and courage of any human pilot. 'As aliens, they must be either subjugated or destroyed.'

The woman looked at him, not answering. Obeysekera had to turn his gaze away. Never had he seen such deep sadness.

'I am old, Captain Obeysekera. In all my years I have known peace only here, in the desert, among the Kamshet.'

Obeysekera glanced towards the nomad warriors. Even fixed outside this bubble of time in which he spoke to the Mother of the Kamshet, they looked fierce and warlike.

At his glance, the woman laughed, a sound of silver.

'It is true – my sons do not present a peaceful front. But they fight only when necessary. Many would trade with the Kamshet for the water of life, that which you call the aqua vitae, and not all of them are men of honour.'

'There are many rejuve treatments, but none so effective, and with as few side effects, as aqua vitae – the trade from this planet, I hear, reaches as far as Holy Terra itself.'

'And none know the wells from which the Kamshet draw the water of life – none save you, Captain Obeysekera, and your men.'

'If you fear that this will mean people will try to harvest aqua vitae directly, you have nothing to fear. When I saw you and your people before, I thought that you were herding some monster. Now I understand that you were following, maybe guiding, the root to the surface.'

'Dasht i-Kevar was once a world of streams and lakes, a gentle world of water. The water remains, buried deep beneath the sand for generations beyond number, and there it has become purer, refined by the heats of this world and filtered through its sand. The life of the world sleeps, dormant, beneath the sand, waiting only for the water of life to spring up and live. The creatures you see about you will live their lives in the space of a few hours, and leave their young to sleep a thousand years beneath the sand until next the water of life shall vivify them. The tree itself shall wither, its branches fall and its trunk shrivel before the next day dawns, leaving but a mound upon the desert floor that the wind will cover in a few days. It is no easy matter to hear and guide one of the deep tendrils of the world tree when it quests towards the light. Your Imperium has neither the patience nor the humility to learn this skill.'

'I fear you speak the truth, great lady. But we will protect you against the t'au.'

'They have sought to deal with us. From that which I have seen, they seem no more rapacious than the traders who come to deal with us already?'

'The traders are at least human, great lady.'

'In form, yes. At heart, many are no longer so.'

Obeysekera nodded. 'It is the privilege and burden of men, great lady. We come into this world as human beings but may leave it as angels or as beasts.'

'How will you leave it, Captain Obeysekera?'

He looked into her eyes, their blue as bright as the lost seas of Cadia.

'Gladly.'

He had not known he would answer so. She nodded, and Obeysekera saw again the deep, deep sadness behind the blue.

'You asked for my aid. I will give it.'

Obeysekera bowed. 'Thank you, great lady.' He looked up and saw the smile that lifted her lips. 'You smile?'

'Such courtesy is rare from a soldier of your Imperium.'

'Then I apologise for their lack of manners.'

The woman smiled again. 'Before I spoke with you, I had determined to have you and all your men slain.' She looked at him. 'I see you smile, now, Captain Obeysekera.'

'I would have expected that, great lady. You have no reason to trust us and more to fear. But we would not have died without killing many of your sons.'

'They will die for me if I command.'

Obeysekera nodded. 'As would mine for me.'

She nodded gravely. 'I see that they would.'

Obeysekera stopped, thought. 'But I would rather that they live.'

'What would you ask, faithful son?'

Obeysekera paused. 'We are searching for one of our own. Do you know where we may find him?'

'The aircraft?'

'You are right, great lady. We seek the man who was travelling aboard the Valkyrie. Do you have him? Or know where we may find him?'

'My sons watched as far as they were able where he went.'

'The Tabaste?'

'Yes.'

'Then that is where we must go.'

The woman shook her head. 'The great mountain is forbidden.'

'Nevertheless, it is where I must go. For what reason is the mountain forbidden?'

The woman looked at Obeysekera. 'It is tabu.'

'We are not of your people. Does the tabu apply to us?'

The woman stopped. Her gaze moved within, the blue of her eyes clouding as she thought on the matter.

'Very well. You may travel to the great mountain.'

Obeysekera bowed. 'I thank you, great lady.'

'But beware. Do not go under the mountain. Those who do, do not return.'

'My orders do not include cave exploration. The only reason I would enter any caves would be to seek the man I have been tasked with finding.'

'I say again – remain in light. The dark beneath the mountain is the haunt of strange and terrible creatures.'

'What is the nature of these creatures?'

'They are not creatures of the desert. Flee them.'

Obeysekera looked at the woman. If she was frightened of whatever lived in the caves beneath the Tabaste Mountains then he would certainly avoid them.

'I will, great lady.' He bowed. 'Thank you.'

'Is there anything else you would ask of me?'

Obeysekera looked into her face again. 'There is one further favour I would ask of you, great lady.'

'Ask it.'

'We have been unable to find anywhere to cross the flowsand. Would your people show us a place where we might safely do so?'

'The desert is difficult to cross for those who do not know its ways. I will send one of my sons with you, to guide you to the mountain.' The woman looked deeply at Obeysekera. The captain realised that she was taller than he.

Captain Obeysekera bowed once more, the full formal bow of an officer of the Astra Militarum of Cadia. 'I thank you, great lady, with all my heart.'

The woman with the cerulean eyes smiled. 'I, too, thank you, Captain Obeysekera.'

Obeysekera looked at her in surprise. 'What have I done for you to thank me?'

'You have shown me that at least one of the servants of the Imperium is worthy of being spared – and where there is one, there will be others.'

Obeysekera nodded – there was not much more he could say to that – then he saluted, turned smartly in his best parade-ground manner and started marching back over the salt flat to where Sergeant Malick was waiting for him in the Venator with Lerin still manning the multi-lasers, their barrels turned towards him in cover.

Over the vox, Obeysekera heard Sergeant Malick say, *'One of them is following you, sir.'*

'That's all right. I've got us a guide. Call *Divine Light* and *Saint Conrad* in.'

As Malick ordered the other two Venators to close with his vehicle, Obeysekera turned around.

The woman, the great lady of the Kamshet, had disappeared among her people, who clustered close around her. The first of the mukaali, having been calmed and restrained, were returning, led or ridden by Kamshet herders, and the animals were being loaded with the casks into which the Kamshet had decanted the aqua vitae collected from the great tree. Obeysekera looked up at the tree itself. Already, its long trailing branches were going limp and starting to wither; that it should have decayed to a great mound of manure by the next day no longer seemed unlikely to him. The creatures that had swarmed up from the ground when the tree burst from the flat, insect and arachnoid and others for which no classification existed, had already almost all dispersed, their explosive life cycles all but at an end with only the search for somewhere to lay eggs still to complete.

CHAPTER 11

Obeysekera looked at the Kamshet walking over the flat towards them. Like the other men of the tribe, he was dressed in robes of white with a blue headscarf that covered all his face save his eyes. He walked easily across the salt, his gait as smooth as that of the mukaali was rolling: the sort of walk that could cover thirty miles a day and start off fresh the next morning. The Kamshet was carrying an autogun. So far as Obeysekera could see, the man carried no other weaponry although he was sure the Kamshet had one or more knives under his robe.

He walked up to where Obeysekera was standing, stopped, and waited, saying nothing.

For his part, Obeysekera held silence too. The Mother of the Kamshet had given the warrior to him as guide: the man would do as he had been bidden. Nevertheless, faced with the Kamshet's silent, blank regard, Obeysekera felt his lips begin to twitch.

He was saved from saying the first words by the arrival of the other two Venators. *Saint Conrad* arrived smoothly, Trooper

Ensor bringing it to a halt beside Obeysekera's command Venator with barely a whisper from the galvanic engines. But *Divine Light* crunched up alongside the other two vehicles, its shredded front tyre carving a squealing track through the crust of the salt flat.

Hardly had the vehicle come to a halt than Commissar Roshant swung out of the driving seat and came striding over towards Captain Obeysekera.

'A word, captain,' he said, as he approached Obeysekera, gesturing the captain away from the three Venators.

There was little time, but over the years Obeysekera had learned that it was usually quicker to follow the more urgent requests of Imperial commissars. He followed Roshant, walking twenty or thirty yards away from the Venators. While the troopers remained with the vehicles, Obeysekera noted that the Kamshet warrior followed, remaining ten yards back but following nonetheless.

'What did you want, commissar?' asked Obeysekera, turning to face Roshant.

The young commissar looked at Obeysekera, his face incredulous. 'You have to ask, captain?'

'I have to ask because it is not apparent to me that I have done anything wrong – and from your appearance and tone it appears that you consider that I have.'

Roshant shook his head. 'I can't believe it. I saw you, Captain Obeysekera, you, a hero of the Imperium, openly consorting with a witch.' Roshant ran his fingers over his face. 'You, Captain Obeysekera, talking with a witch. I wouldn't have believed it if I had not seen it myself.' He looked at Obeysekera, his eyes wide like a disillusioned child. 'What do you have to say, captain?'

Obeysekera stared at the young commissar. One of his hands, the one that was rubbing unconsciously up and down the side of his leg, was trembling. His face was flushing. But Roshant's other hand was resting upon the amphant stock of his bolt pistol. It was still holstered, but Obeysekera noted that Roshant had unfastened the safety flap that held the gun in place: commissars were trained to draw and shoot in a single smooth movement.

'I assume you read your briefing slates, commissar?'

Roshant blinked. 'What do you mean?'

'It is a simple question, commissar. If you are unclear, then I will remind you. The Imperium is perfectly aware of the powers of the lady of the Kamshet. Appendix Three-C contains the Inquisitorial seal, granted a century ago, allowing her continued presence here under the auspices of the Holy Ordos.'

Roshant shook his head. 'I-I did not see that.'

'Then I suggest in future you read all your briefing documents before embarking upon a mission.'

Roshant opened his mouth, closed it, then nodded. 'Very well.'

He turned and stalked away. Obeysekera watched him go, slowly allowing the tension in his body to drain away. There was no appendix Three-C.

Obeysekera turned to the Kamshet warrior. 'We must go to the mountain,' he said.

The Kamshet inclined his head. 'It is forbidden, but Mother has given me leave to take you there.'

'Can you find a place for us to cross the flowsand?'

'Yes.'

'Far?'

'No.'

'One day?'

The Kamshet warrior pointed to the mukaali. 'On those, a day.' He pointed to the Venators. 'In those, three hours.'

'We can get there and cross before nightfall?'

The warrior glanced to the sky, looking for the sun's position along its great arc.

'Yes.'

Obeysekera activated the squad vox-channel. 'We're moving out. Get *Divine Light* repaired and ready. Gunsur and Lerin, retrieve Quert. We will bury her where we camp.'

The Kamshet held up his hand. 'You have water?'

'Water?'

'Water.'

'Yes.'

'Give me water.'

'What for?'

The Kamshet warrior pointed to the mouth hidden beneath his headscarf. 'For the tongue. It is dry.'

'Malick, pour a water measure,' Obeysekera said over the vox-channel.

'The men have had their rations.'

'It's for our guide.' Obeysekera turned back to the Kamshet warrior. 'What is your name?'

'Amazigh.'

'Amazigh, go to Sergeant Malick. He will give you what water we can spare.'

Amazigh inclined his head, hand on heart, then turned and made his way towards the lead Venator, where Sergeant Malick was pouring out a small measure of water.

Obeysekera walked over to Roshant. 'Your vehicle's tyre has been replaced. Are you fit to continue?'

Roshant nodded. 'I am ready.' He stepped back in some disgust as the last of the insect bloom from the eruption of the tree swarmed up out of the ground and seethed into the sky. 'I have heard of people dreaming of making the desert bloom,' he said, 'but I suspect that this was not what they had in mind.'

At the joke, Captain Obeysekera threw back his head and laughed, a clear laugh and pure, the sound of clean joy.

Commissar Roshant grimaced. 'I don't think it was that funny, and I made the joke.'

But Obeysekera clapped Roshant on the shoulder. 'It was. Come, let us go, commissar. We have a few hours until sunset and the Kamshet, Amazigh, promises to guide us to a place where we can cross the flowsand. The mission can continue – and we have done enough already to earn ourselves promotions.'

'You have recorded this position?' asked Roshant. 'So that we can find it again?'

'Of course,' said Obeysekera. But as they walked back to the Venator, he glanced behind. As the lady had said, the fronds of the great tree were already shrivelling under the weight of the heavy sun, while the trunk showed signs of beginning to decay. By the morrow, there would not be much left: in a week's time, Obeysekera suspected there would be no trace of the eruption of the great tree and the efflorescence of life that it had produced. Remembering how the Kamshet had guided the runner from which the tree had sprung, it was likely that the next time the desert produced a tree of life, it would grow in a completely different part of the Great Sand Sea, one that only the Kamshet knew. If an Imperial observation station was set up at this location, Obeysekera thought they could wait a thousand years and never see what they had come to observe. The extraordinarily rapid life cycle he had witnessed among the creatures hatching at the tree's eruption suggested animals adapted to spending hundreds, if not thousands, of years lying dormant beneath the surface of the Great Sand Sea, waiting for their time to come. Even more reason to believe that returning to this same spot would not yield a harvest of aqua vitae.

As they reached the Venator, Obeysekera wondered if he would put that in his report.

'I will drive, sergeant, with the Kamshet, Amazigh, as my

guide. Make sure that the navigators in *Divine Light* and *Saint Conrad* keep a proper record of our route – I will not be able to as I am driving.'

Sergeant Malick nodded and slid from the driver's seat and out onto the flat. 'Should be easy going so long as we keep to this flat, sir,' he said.

'Take the commissar with you on *Divine Light*.' Obeysekera switched to the private channel. 'See that the commissar is kept as far away from the Kamshet as possible.'

Sergeant Malick nodded again: he was no stranger to orders directed towards ensuring the smoother running of the squad through the careful regulation of the contact between highly trained and sometimes volatile killers. 'I'll do that, sir.' He paused. 'We have put Quert's body into *Saint Conrad*.'

Obeysekera nodded, his previous light mood flattened out by the reminder of the squad's loss.

'Emperor willing, we shall find a suitable place to bury her.'

'If we don't?' Malick squinted up at the sun. 'It's hot. She won't keep long.'

'Then we'll cover her with sand and mark the grave as best we can. Let's move out, sergeant.'

Malick saluted. 'Sir.'

Obeysekera looked up to Lerin manning the twin-linked multi-lasers mounted on *Holy Fire*. 'Have you cleared and cleaned the pintle, Lerin?'

'Cleared, sir,' said Lerin. 'No time to strip it down and clean it now. I will do that when we camp.'

'Make sure you do, Lerin.' Obeysekera pointed to the navigator's seat. 'That's where you sit,' he said to Amazigh. For the first time, he saw a ripple of concern pass through the Kamshet's desert-clear eyes.

'Is it not possible for me to sit atop the machine?' he asked.

'No, it is not possible,' said Obeysekera. 'One skid or drop and you'd be sailing off the top and like as not cracking your skull on the one rock in this whole desert.'

Amazigh stared at him. 'There is more than one rock in the desert,' he said.

'Even more reason for you to be strapped to the seat,' said Obeysekera. 'Come on, jump in. It's a Venator. It won't bite.'

'Ven… itor?'

'Ven-A-tor,' said Obeysekera. He tapped the navigator's seat. 'You're here. I am there' – he pointed to the driver's seat – 'next to you. That way, you can tell me where to go.'

'And you will be close to kill me if I should lead you false,' said Amazigh.

'Exactly,' said Obeysekera. He grinned, showing his teeth. 'So do what you said – find me a way to cross the flowsand and you will live to see the stars in the sky tonight. Fail, and you will be meat in the morning.'

'Mother gave me to you – I will not fail,' said Amazigh.

'I'm sure you won't. Now get in, we're wasting time.'

While the Kamshet warrior climbed gingerly into the Venator and strapped himself into the navigator's seat, Obeysekera took a final look at the great tree and the Kamshet harvesters. Already, half the tribe had saddled up their mukaali and were moving out, great panniers of aqua vitae strapped across their beasts' shoulders and haunches. The rest were loading up. Obeysekera searched for some sign of the Mother of the Kamshet, but from this distance he could not make her out, although a cluster of blue-robed warriors suggested her presence in the centre of the tribe.

Obeysekera went round to the other side of the Venator and climbed into the driver's seat, strapping himself in.

'Ready?' he asked Amazigh.

The Kamshet nodded. Although, in profile, Obeysekera could not even see Amazigh's eyes, it was a nervous movement. Obeysekera started the galvanic motors. The Kamshet grasped the edges of his seat, knuckles whitening.

'Which way?' asked Obeysekera.

Amazigh raised his hand to point straight ahead.

Before he could renew his grasp, Obeysekera gunned the Venator, its instant acceleration over the hard crust of the salt flat pushing them both back against their seats. The Kamshet warrior cried out in alarm. Obeysekera accelerated faster, taking the Venator round the decaying remains of the tree.

With Amazigh breathing fast and loud next to him, Obeysekera sped the Venator past the remaining Kamshet. As he went, the warriors parted and he saw the Mother, her face uncovered, turn to look at him. He raised his hand in salute and then they were past, on over the salt flat, into the great desert.

CHAPTER 12

Commissar Roshant, driving *Divine Light*, was staring ahead, eyes fixed on the horizon, his foot pressed down hard.

'What are they doing?' He gestured ahead to *Holy Fire*, its wheels skimming over the desert, sending up showers of sand in its wake. 'Do they think this is some sort of race?'

Sergeant Malick, strapped into the navigator's seat beside the commissar, laughed. 'If it is, we'll win it with you driving, commissar.'

Roshant glanced over at the sergeant. 'You think so?'

'You're one of the best drivers I've ever seen,' said Malick. He checked his display. All his external vox-channels were switched off. No one else could hear what he was saying.

The commissar nodded, smiling.

As he did, he looked like the boy he might once have been: eager, enthusiastic, petulant when crossed but desperate for praise. Malick layered on some more.

'Good to have you with us, sir.'

'But I've hardly said anything to the men,' said Roshant. 'No speeches, just a few words when we've stopped.'

'Just like all the best commissars – they act, they don't speak. It's your presence that helps keep us going.'

'You think so? Captain Obeysekera's not said anything like this to me.'

'He wouldn't, would he.'

'No? No, of course he wouldn't.'

Malick pointed ahead. 'Maybe watch where we're going.'

Roshant jerked the wheel of the Venator, just missing a stone outcrop, but driving into the skid following while barely losing any of the vehicle's velocity before bringing it back on track.

'Nice driving,' said Malick.

'Thank you,' said Roshant.

'You know, it's a shame that you won't get the credit due to you for this mission.'

Roshant looked over at the sergeant. 'What do you mean?'

'No offence, sir. But, lord militant's son, fresh from the schola of the Officio Prefectus... No one's going to believe how big a part you played in everything. It will all be ascribed to nepotism.'

Roshant stared ahead. He said nothing. Malick saw his knuckles whiten on the steering wheel.

'Mind if you check your vox is off, sir?'

Roshant looked at Malick. 'Why?'

'Something important – better kept between us for the moment.'

'It's off.'

Malick checked his display – as sergeant, he could see the vox and life signs of the members of the squad. 'Your father is the lord militant – he has enemies?'

'Of course. Officers he has looked over, or demoted, let alone the enemies we all fight.'

'You know how many commissars fail to return from their first battle postings?'

Roshant nodded. 'Yes.' Malick saw him swallow. 'It's called fragging. They mentioned it in the schola. Discipline is the answer, they said.'

'It's battle,' said Malick. 'Stray rounds can strike anyone. One hotshot las-round looks pretty much like another, whoever fired the gun.'

'A heroic death in service of the Emperor.'

'A death, nevertheless. Now, like you say, your father has enemies. Wouldn't be too hard for someone with money and influence to buy the service of a poor trooper, even a 'kin.'

'Are you saying that one of your men has been paid to assassinate me, sergeant?'

'Where'd you get that idea, sir? No, I'm not saying that. They're all good men, I'd swear for each and every one of them. I've served with them for years.'

'But not Captain Obeysekera?'

'I am sure he is beyond doubt.'

'But you have only recently met him?'

'At the start of this mission.'

'He was Colonel Aruna's choice.'

'Colonel Aruna is a rising star – on the grapevine I hear many people expect a great future for him.'

In his peripheral vision, Malick saw Roshant glance over towards him. The sergeant kept looking ahead.

'You have fought many battles, sergeant?'

'Too many, sir.'

'You have much experience.'

'I've seen many men die, sir, if you call that experience.'

'Perhaps you could help me.'

Malick turned to look at Roshant. 'You are a commissar, sir. It would be my duty to help you.'

Roshant nodded. 'Then maybe you could keep an eye open for me, your ears too – tell me if anything is afoot. There are enemies everywhere.'

'I will, sir, I will.'

'I will see that you are rewarded, sergeant.'

'I'm sure you will, sir.'

Roshant glanced at the sergeant. Malick stared ahead, his eyes set upon the Venator in front.

'Good.'

'I'll watch your back, sir. No one gets near you. Like I said, in battle one las-round looks pretty much like any other.'

'Do your duty, sergeant.'

Malick turned to the commissar and smiled. 'Oh, I will, sir. I will.'

CHAPTER 13

Amazigh, whooping with excitement, yelled, 'Faster, faster!'

Obeysekera shook his head. 'I liked you better when you were scared,' he said, the wind of their driving whipping his words away from his mouth. The Kamshet wasn't listening in any case. Despite Obeysekera's remonstrations he had unstrapped himself and was now standing on his seat with his head and shoulders through the roll bar, laughing and singing to himself in between asking Obeysekera to speed up. If he should roll the Venator, Obeysekera knew, the roll bar would cut the Kamshet in half. But he could not complain about their progress. After a nervous first half hour, Amazigh had settled into travelling through the desert at the speed of a Venator rather than the slow-motion roll of a mukaali. As he had promised, he had shown them to a place to cross the flowsand before nightfall, a ford where the flowsand formed a thin skin over hard bedrock, and the Venators had driven across, spraying sand up on either side of their tyres.

The far bank had been rock and stone, and they had made good progress until nightfall, when they had camped. The morning had seen Amazigh installing himself in the navigator's seat before the rest of the men were even ready, and the day had seen the Kamshet urging them on to ever greater speed, a speed that had been made possible by the hard rock surface over which he took them. Obeysekera had worried that jagged rocks might shred a tyre, but he soon realised that the exposed surface had been smoothed to round undulations by the sand blast of millennia of storms. The only problem was that the undulations transmitted up through the tyres into the Venators, shaking the occupants as if they were being put through a blender. But while Obeysekera felt as if his teeth might rattle loose, the Kamshet, standing now, just shouted louder and urged them faster.

'How… far… now?' Obeysekera asked, his teeth banging together as he tried to talk.

'Not far,' said Amazigh, turning to look down at the captain. Although he had kept his scarf on throughout their evening meal, simply raising it a little to carry food to his lips, his eyes told the tale of his joy to Obeysekera. The Kamshet was having the time of his life.

'Can you… slow down… a little… captain?'

Obeysekera tried to see on his display who was talking to him but it was shaking so much he could not make out which ident rune had lit up.

'Who… is… that?'

'Ch-Chame… sir.'

The gunner on Roshant's Venator.

'I think… I'm going… to be sick… sir.'

'Me… too,' said Obeysekera. He yelled up at Amazigh. 'I am going… to slow… down.'

'There!' said the Kamshet, pointing ahead. 'There it is. Tabaste. The mountain.'

Obeysekera braked, slowly bringing the Venator to a stop, with the other two vehicles ranged behind him. Over the vox-channel he heard the murmur of the men's complaints and relief, but he struggled to stand – his legs felt like they'd been turned to hypogel – and stuck his head up through the roll bar to look where Amazigh was pointing.

With his head above the shadow netting, Obeysekera felt the full impact of the sun, now nearing its zenith, upon his head and shoulders. The sweat that the wind of their speed had evaporated immediately now lingered a moment longer until the dry and thirsty air sucked it from his skin. But he relegated those impressions to insignificance as he took stock of their surroundings.

Tabaste.

The mountain forbidden to the Kamshet. The redstone heart of the Great Sand Sea.

It rose over the sand and rock in ridges and humps that looked nothing like the jagged peaks of Cadia. Tabaste was smooth and worn, its ascending series of summits more like the boils made when the bulge mite laid its eggs under the skin than a mountain serif. To Obeysekera's eye it presented a series of overlaid mounds, climbing upwards and then rounding out at a broad and knobbly summit.

Obeysekera, and the drivers, navigators and crew of the other Venators, looked at the mountain for a while. The mountains of Cadia had always given the sense of strength and vigour, of the planet thrusting up against its own gravity. As a child, growing up in Kasr Gesh, he had looked out from the city's defences to the jagged range of the Karakora Mountains that defined the horizon. As a boy, training to be a Whiteshield, Obeysekera had camped in the Karakora. The memory of days spent in the high passes, with the wind never ceasing and the creak and break of ice falls from the higher ridges, was among the most vivid of his childhood. The Karakora had inspired awe in the young Bharath. He imagined that, if by some unimaginable chance, he should ever set foot upon Holy Terra, he would feel as he did when standing beneath the sky-churning mass of the Skyspear.

The Tabaste produced its own sense of awe, but it was very different from the feeling he had had when looking up at the Karakora as a boy. There, beneath the Skyspear, he had been overwhelmed by the majesty of the mountain, of its strength and power. He remembered old Sergeant Yannek, pointing up at the majesty of the Skyspear and saying to them all, 'You want to know what the Emperor is like? That's what He's like.'

Looking at Tabaste over the intervening desert, Obeysekera also felt a sense of awe, but where the Karakora had dwarfed him by their size, the Tabaste made him insignificant by its age.

The mountain was old. It was old beyond his comprehension, old beyond the understanding of any mortal human. Time had worn the Tabaste smooth. Millions of years of sand and wind had rubbed away every jagged edge and cleft from its surface. What was left was the testimony of time: the red-rock bone underlying this desert world. Staring at the Tabaste, Obeysekera, and all the men looking at it, felt their own insignificance: they were nothing more than dayflies, playing out lives that the mountain, lost in the dream of time, would never even notice.

Obeysekera took his magnoculars from their case and trained them on the Tabaste, setting them on a wide field of view to start with as he scanned the red rock for any signs of the general's Valkyrie.

'See anything, Malick?' Obeysekera knew his sergeant would be searching the Tabaste for the target too.

'Nothing, sir.'

'We'll move in closer. Too much to expect to see anything from this range.'

Obeysekera slid back down into the driver's seat and slid the magnoculars back into their case. He tapped Amazigh's leg. The Kamshet, still standing, pulled his gaze away from the mountain and looked down at Obeysekera.

'Get down. We're moving on.'

Amazigh sat down and began strapping himself in. Obeysekera looked askance at him.

'Why are you doing that?' he asked the Kamshet. 'You wouldn't before.'

Amazigh, still fitting buckles into clasps, glanced over at Obeysekera, his eyes blue glints above his cheche.

'It is the Tabaste.'

'I know. Why are you putting on the straps now?'

'It is the Tabaste.'

Obeysekera was about to repeat the question, then thought again, shook his head and started the galvanic motors. The Venator gently stirred itself back into machine life, humming softly. Obeysekera could tell that its machine-spirits had come to like the desert: sand and grit needed to be cleaned out of bearings at every camp, but the dry air suited the vehicle.

The Venators moved off, Obeysekera leading, the other two following at fifty-yard intervals. The Tabaste disappeared behind a ridge, only to reappear as they crossed the rocky crest and started on a long, gentle decline towards a wide, flat plain. The Tabaste rose from the centre of the plain, climbing up gently from the sand.

Obeysekera stopped the Venator. 'We have to cross *that* to get to the mountain?'

The plain upon which the Tabaste stood was table-flat, and

roughly six miles in diameter. There was no cover. Crossing it, they would be absolutely exposed.

'There is another way,' said Amazigh. 'On the other side of the mountain there is hard ground that comes closer.' The Kamshet made a circling gesture. 'But the ground is difficult. It will take two or three days to go around the... the... I do not know the word in your language. We call that the uzayar.'

Obeysekera shook his head. 'Too long. Can we cross that... you called it uzayar?'

Amazigh pointed ahead. 'There is a way,' he said. 'Mother told me the signs to look for.'

'You have not been to the Tabaste?'

Amazigh shook his head. 'The mountain is forbidden. Only Mother has walked there, and that was when the mothers of our mother's mothers were still children. But she told me the way.'

Obeysekera stared out over the plain. 'Why is the uzayar so flat? Surely the wind should leave some mark upon it?' For even as he asked the question, he could see zephyrs of wind tumbling over the plain, raising spumes of sand, but in no place did these plumes settle to make the ridges and troughs of the rest of the Sand Sea. The uzayar was flat, utterly and completely level.

The Kamshet looked at Obeysekera. 'You do not know?'

Obeysekera shook his head. 'No.'

'It is flowsand.' Amazigh pointed out over the uzayar. 'All the channels of flowing sand wind their way here.'

'All?' Obeysekera looked around. The Tabaste rose from the uzayar, but around the uzayar there was a great bowl of dunes and rock. 'Won't it...?'

'Do you ask if someday the flowsand will rise up over the mountain? I do not know, but Mother tells us that it was not always so. The flowsand channels wandered through the land, some spilling out into the plains beyond. But the desert shifted and the sand started to flow here, making the uzayar, and it is true, its level rises. When I was a boy it was not so high as it is today. But whether it will one day cover the mountain, I do not see how, for the land around the uzayar is not so high as the mountain, although it seems to me, coming back after many years not seeing the uzayar, that even the land around the uzayar has risen.' Amazigh pointed to the rock bluffs to their right. 'I do not know if rocks may grow, but these seem taller than my memory makes them, and I have heard others of my people speak the same.'

Obeysekera stared where the Kamshet pointed. 'Mountains may rise, but they don't generally do that within the memory of people.' He turned back to the Kamshet. 'According to the Imperial surveyors, this is a stable world – there is no tectonic activity on it.'

'Yet the rocks are higher now than I remember, and my memory does not fail,' said Amazigh.

'My memory fails me all the time,' said Obeysekera. 'How can you be so certain of yours?'

'Because if we do not have memory, we have nothing,' said Amazigh.

Obeysekera nodded. What the Kamshet said was true: nomadic peoples tended their memories for they were all the history they had.

'Very well. I must write it down as another of the mysteries of Dasht i-Kevar to go alongside all the others – the rising rocks surrounding the Tabaste. But nevertheless, we must still reach the mountain. Is there a way across the uzayar?'

'Yes. Mother told me where to find it. But the way is narrow and the flowsand is deep on either side of the way. You must go carefully. Come off the track and the sand will swallow you.'

'*Divine Light* and *Saint Conrad*, did you read that? There is deep flowsand on either side of the track we will follow to reach the Tabaste. Follow exactly in my tyre tracks.'

The two Venators acknowledged Obeysekera's message from their respective waiting positions. *Divine Light* was on the crest of the final ridge and its driver and navigator – Roshant and Malick – could see the flat plain of uzayar, but *Saint Conrad* was waiting on the reverse slope: Ensor and the rest could only wait to see what the rest of the squad were looking at.

'*Slow and steady,*' said Malick, '*and right in your tracks. Ensor, you follow me.*'

'*Got that,*' replied Ensor over the open squad vox-channel.

'Take us through,' said Obeysekera to Amazigh.

'Drive down to where the uzayar begins,' said the Kamshet. 'I must get out there and walk before you to make sure of the way.'

Obeysekera started the galvanic motors and eased the Venator down the incline, making sure that shifting sand did not start to slide away beneath the tyres and roll them down too fast for him to stop the vehicle.

'Stop,' said Amazigh.

They were nearly at the level of the uzayar.

The Kamshet got out of the Venator and, wrapping his cheche more tightly around his face to protect his lungs from the sand spumes blowing up from the uzayar, he made his way down the final few yards of the incline. Reaching the start of the flowsand, he turned sideways on to it and started walking along the edge of the uzayar, stopping every so often to bend down and test the sand.

Obeysekera sat, waiting and watching. He hoped that Amazigh would find the way soon: he did not relish the prospect of driving around the edge of the uzayar, for the slope down to it quickly grew steeper and rougher. But the Kamshet had not gone more than fifty yards when he stopped, tried the sand, tried it again a few paces further on, and then walked out a little way into the uzayar.

Standing there amid the flowsand, Amazigh turned and beckoned Obeysekera to him.

'You see where we have to go,' he said over the vox. 'Drivers, follow exactly in my tracks. Everyone else, stay alert. Gunners, have the weapons cycled. We will be as exposed as it is possible to be out there.'

One of Obeysekera's private vox-channels flashed and he saw that it was Roshant calling him person-to-person.

'Commissar?'

'*Shouldn't we wait for dark to cross? We won't be so obvious.*'

'The greater risk is that we drive off the path and fall into the flowsand. Besides, we do not have the time to lose.'

'*Captain…*'

'Moving out, commissar. I am driving – don't distract me.'

Obeysekera started the Venator, the hum of the galvanic motors telling of the eagerness of the machine-spirit. He carefully engaged the wheel drive and set off around the edge of the flowsand to where Amazigh was waiting.

The Kamshet waved him to a stop as he reached his position. 'The way starts here,' Amazigh said, 'and stops here,' he added, walking across to the other edge of the track. It was barely four yards wide, sufficient to take the Venator's six tyres, but there was little leeway.

'Does it stay that width all the way across?' asked Obeysekera.

'We will see,' said Amazigh. 'Follow.'

He began walking out into the uzayar, and Obeysekera drove the Venator after him.

Speed was the primary defence for the lightly armoured Venators. Now they were crossing three miles of flat and featureless plain, with no cover, with the sun still high in the sky, at walking pace. Obeysekera was not sure if he feared the arrival of the usual afternoon sandstorm, or hoped for its cover.

Like beetles crawling over a table without end, the three Venators followed behind the blue-and-white-robed Kamshet as they took the way across the uzayar to the Tabaste. After the first mile, Obeysekera found himself struggling to maintain concentration. The uzayar had no features whatsoever. It was simply flat sand, stretching in either direction, with only the Kamshet walking in front of the Venator and the Tabaste looming ahead to give any relief to the monotony.

The track that Amazigh was taking them on, a ridge of rock cutting through the flowsand, was straight, barely deviating. In fact, it was so unwavering that Obeysekera began to wonder if it really was a natural feature: it ran more like a road, or a pilgrim path nearing its final objective.

Obeysekera keyed on the squad vox-channel. 'Read it off.'

'Clear.'

'Clear.'

'Clear.'

The replies came in from every member of the squad, squinting out into the white light or poring over the auspex, apart from one.

'Commissar?'

'Captain?'

'Do you see anything?'

'No.'

'Then tell me next time I ask.'

Roshant went silent.

'Did you hear me, commissar?'

'Yes. Captain.'

'Good. Everyone keep sharp. We're completely exposed out here and there's nowhere to run to. I don't expect to see t'au aircraft this far into the sand, but keep watching the auspex.'

As Obeysekera was speaking, he was watching Amazigh walking steadily in front of him. There was something strange about it. Then Obeysekera realised what it was. Although Amazigh was walking on sand, he was leaving no tracks. The thin skin of flow-sand that lay atop the ford filled his steps as soon as he lifted his foot.

The Kamshet was barefoot. Obeysekera wondered how he could endure the heat of the sand, but he walked without flinching. Obeysekera squinted past him. Here, in the middle of the uzayar, with miles of sand reflecting the heat, the Sand Sea settled into its flat heart and simmered under the copper sun. Columns of rising air, cooked by the desert heat, rose in gyrating funnels, twisting the sand where they touched the ground. The sand there swirled, as if it were being slowly stirred, but as the columns of hot air wavered and wandered over the desert, the sand settled sullenly back into place as soon as the thermal had moved on, giving no sign of the agitation that had previously disturbed it.

The Tabaste, which had seemed clear from the far side of the uzayar, now appeared ghostly and insubstantial behind the heat haze. It shimmered and shifted, a red-orange dream that seemed to grow more distant as they crawled across the uzayar, three black beetles pinned under the sun.

Obeysekera sucked a little water from his reservoir. It was warm, a little brackish from the purifier, but it was at least wet. He felt himself sweating it out almost as he drank it, while fighting the urge to stop Amazigh and ask him how much further. If it was hard for him, how much more difficult must it be for the Kamshet, walking barefoot over sand that could cook an egg, protected from the full weight of the sun only by his robes?

But Amazigh walked on without faltering, his steps smooth

and steady, and Obeysekera blinked the sweat from his eyes, realising that he was veering off course. He brought the Venator back in line.

Just keep following the Kamshet. That was all he had to do until they got to the mountain. But it was like driving on water. There was nothing to distinguish, by sight, the solid way from the flowsand on either side. Nor was there any way of telling if the path should narrow, allowing a man to walk unhampered but precipitating one or other set of wheels into the sand.

'*Divine Light* and *Saint Conrad*. If you come off the path and start tipping into the flowsand, everyone bail out. I don't care about losing one vehicle – I do care about losing the men on it.'

The acknowledgements came back, after the slightest of baffled pauses.

'We've already lost two soldiers. If we lose any more, our operational effectiveness will drop and our chances of making it back will dramatically reduce. If we lose a Venator, we'll just have to strap the general in underneath.'

The splutters of laughter told Obeysekera that the joke had hit its mark. He keyed the vox-channel to silent and squinted at Amazigh's back as he walked carefully along in front of them. How far was it across the uzayar? From the start of the causeway it had looked like it must be two or three miles, but without any features on the plain, it was almost impossible to judge distance. It might be one mile, but it was at least unlikely to be much more than three since the horizon on Dasht i-Kevar, a planet with a circumference and gravity very similar to that of Holy Terra itself, was about three miles and he was reasonably sure that he was able to see the base of the Tabaste from the start of the causeway.

Obeysekera checked the readings on the Venator. They had come over a mile across the uzayar already. He squinted ahead through the shifting heat haze. The Tabaste did look significantly closer. It also meant that they were right out in the open, in the middle of the uzayar, as obvious as a stinkbug crawling across a data-slate.

If he were a watching enemy, this was when Obeysekera would attack.

He keyed on the channel to Chame in *Divine Light*. 'You've got a clearer view up there,' he said. 'Any sign, movement?'

'The only thing moving is us, captain,' said Chame, *'and it's so hot I'm not so sure about us.'*

'Malick, make sure you have someone on the auspex. If the blueies come in by air, we won't have much time.'

'On it, sir.'

Ahead of him, Amazigh trudged on, his footprints flowing away as soon as he made them. Obeysekera felt his vision narrowing to a tunnel. To open it out again, he looked rapidly left and right, stopping for a moment at the end of each sweep to allow his eyes to focus on the horizon.

Pulling his gaze back to the Kamshet, he felt his peripheral vision return. Everything about the conditions on Dasht i-Kevar – the heat, the monotony, the constant, nagging thirst – militated against the sort of awareness that allowed soldiers to remain alert to the stealthy approach of an enemy, so Obeysekera was relieved to have regained some of his focus. It had saved him on more than one occasion.

He squinted at the Kamshet. Amazigh had stopped moving. He was staring ahead, like a carnodon that had seen prey. Obeysekera slowly brought his Venator to a halt. The auspex told him that *Divine Light* and *Saint Conrad* had stopped too. They sat under the sun in the middle of the uzayar, its weight heavy upon them.

Obeysekera was about to stick his head out of the Venator and call to the Kamshet when Amazigh abruptly turned round and came back towards him, glancing over his shoulder as he did so.

'You have magnoculars?' Amazigh asked Obeysekera when he reached the vehicle. In answer, Obeysekera handed him the device. The Kamshet turned back to the Tabaste and, raising the magnoculars, scanned the mountain, his movement soon settling on a particular point.

'What do you see?' Obeysekera could make out nothing but the red-orange rock of the Tabaste.

'There,' said Amazigh, handing the magnoculars back to Obeysekera and pointing. 'In front of the gap that looks like your letter "Y".'

Obeysekera took the magnoculars and raised them to his eyes. The lenses whirred into focus, pulling different parts of the Tabaste into view.

Then, he saw it.

Jutting out from behind a ridge, the distinctive drooping tail fin of a Valkyrie. The rest of the aircraft was hidden behind the ridge, but there was nothing about the position of the tail fin to suggest that it was the broken remains of a crashed vehicle: the Valkyrie had put down under power and control.

But if it had not crashed, then why had it not taken off again?

Obeysekera remembered the sandstorm. The engines could have been destroyed and the Valkyrie immobilised. He scanned the immediate vicinity of the landing site, searching for any sign of the Valkyrie's crew and, in particular, General Itoyesa, but there was nothing.

'Valkyrie in view,' Obeysekera said over the squad vox-channel. 'Bearing two-eighty.'

The other two Venators were stretched out in a straight line behind his own: it was unlikely that either would have a better view than he, but at least they would know the target location.

'*I have the Valkyrie in view,*' said Malick from *Divine Light*. '*Unable to confirm identity.*'

'*I see it too,*' said Trooper Ha in *Saint Conrad*. '*Can't identify.*'

'Move on. Gunners, keep watch. We're as exposed as a White-shield helmet out here.' Obeysekera started the galvanic motors. Amazigh began walking, but he had not gone more than two or three paces when he stopped again. This time, however, he was looking out to the left, over the uzaγar, the table-flat expanse of flowsand that laked around the Tabaste. Obeysekera looked where Amazigh was staring.

The flowsand was rippling. The ripples were V-shaped, and the apex of the V was pointing straight at them.

Something was coming.

Amazigh looked back at Obeysekera. Even with his face covered, the captain could see the fear in the Kamshet's eyes.

'Awsaḍ.' Amazigh paused a moment. '*Run.*'

The Kamshet turned towards the Tabaste and began running.

Obeysekera gunned the galvanic motors and the Venator's tyres spun, then cleared the thin layer of flowsand and bit on the rock of the causeway. The vehicle surged forward.

'Gunners, target left, approaching fast.'

From behind him, Obeysekera heard the grind of the multi-laser's pintle as the bearings, still not entirely clear of sand, turned to bring it to bear. Behind him, the other Venators were doing the same.

'Fire at will.'

The first burst of las-fire seared through the air as the Venator caught up with the fleeing Kamshet. Amazigh, hearing its approach, moved out of the way, teetered on the edge of the causeway, then jumped into the Venator.

'Straight on?' asked Obeysekera as Amazigh tumbled into the vehicle.

'Straight on,' said Amazigh, righting himself.

Obeysekera mentally drew a straight line to the Tabaste and set the Venator off to follow the line. He kept his eyes fixed ahead, knowing that glancing left to see where the Awsaḍ was would only serve to drag him off line and send the Venator careering off the causeway and into the flowsand. He could hear the snap-hiss of the las-fire, and the crack of superheated sand where the multi-lasers struck into it. The sounds were coming closer, tracking in towards the lead vehicle.

Obeysekera tried to measure the distance ahead. Not far now. The Tabaste rose up from the flowsand in a series of levels, the transition flagged by the change in height and colour, the yellow of the flowsand giving way to the red rock of the mountain.

Not far now.

But the lasers were firing off at close range, the snap-hiss of the Venators' weapons joined by the individual jolts of hell-guns. With his peripheral vision, Obeysekera could see the apex of the V-shaped wake of waves in the flowsand approaching, pointing towards his Venator like an arrow. It was coming in fast – faster than anything had any right to move through sand.

Obeysekera concentrated his gaze ahead, striving to drive in as perfectly a straight line as possible over a road that had no markings.

'What is it?' he asked Amazigh.

'Pray you do not learn.' The Kamshet stuck his head through the open side of the Venator. 'Faster. Faster. We are nearly there.'

Obeysekera gunned the galvanic motors, their hum overlaying the rasp of sand as the waves arrowed closer. He risked another glance to the left. The apex was about a hundred yards away now.

The Venator lurched left, the front wheel falling off the side of the causeway, the rear starting to slew around as the motors drove the rear tyres on. Obeysekera cut the drives to the right-hand wheels and turned into the slide.

The front left tyre bit on the side of the causeway, slipped back, then the Venator's forward momentum brought it back up against the rock and this time the tyre gripped and pulled the front back up onto the way. Obeysekera flicked the right-hand drives back on, compensating with the steering while the drives kicked in, then slewed the Venator back onto the straight line, driving it on towards the Tabaste.

Not far. He could see the red rock rising up from the flowsand not more than one hundred and fifty feet ahead. He gunned the motors, putting every bit of power the Venator could generate into its tyre drives, and it surged over the hard rock of the causeway towards the mountain.

Obeysekera stopped himself looking left.

'How far?'

'Keep going.'

From behind, Obeysekera could still hear the snap-hiss of the multi-lasers.

'Are they doing any good?'

'Burning sand.'

'Cease fire. Wait for a target above sand.' Obeysekera keyed off the vox-channel. 'Will it come out from the surface?'

'When the Awsaḍ rises from the sand, it is too late.'

Obeysekera keyed the vox-channel on again. 'Max speed, feed everything to the drives.'

The three Venators, now bunched much closer together than Imperial Guard tactical doctrine allowed, surged forward over the final stretch of causeway while the V at the point of the arrow burrowed in closer. Fifty yards now. Forty. Thirty.

The ground sound changed, sand hiss giving way to rock roar, and Obeysekera knew he was out of the flowsand. He arced the

Venator left, pulling away from the flowsand but giving Lerin a clear field of fire.

He twisted back, saw that *Divine Light* had crossed clear, and spoke into the vox, 'Malick, break right, converging fire.'

The two Venators were moving so that they could focus their fire on whatever emerged from the sand, while the third vehicle crossed the last of the causeway onto the solid rock.

The flowsand waves surged the final few yards as the last Venator, galvanic motors rising to their highest pitch, drove pell-mell over the remaining causeway.

'Nearly there, nearly there.' The words were coming from Amazigh.

Obeysekera did not look round at the Kamshet. They both stared at the race reaching its climax before them.

Last few yards.

The Venator was about to cross onto the hard red rock of the Tabaste when the leading sand wave slapped into the side of the causeway, flowing over it and knocking the Venator sideways. Its front right tyre slipped off the causeway and it heeled over.

But before the wave could carry it off the causeway, the wheel caught the edge of the hard rock of the Tabaste, bit, and pulled the Venator back upright and onto the mountain.

The Venator, hard rock beneath all its wheels, surged forward as the second sand wave splashed harmlessly over the causeway behind it. Obeysekera saw Ensor, face staring ahead in the driver's seat, pushing the vehicle on up into the safety of the rock.

Behind the Venator, in the flowsand lapping up against the causeway, Obeysekera saw the waves reduced to a roiling mass and, beneath the churning sand, through the furrows that opened and closed in it, he glimpsed something moving, deep and dark and huge beyond thinking.

'Awsaḍ,' breathed Amazigh.

'Awsaḍ,' said Obeysekera.

The seething sand whirled, then began to settle and slowly sank lower.

'It's going?' asked Obeysekera.

'Yes,' said Amazigh.

'You know, I am interested in xenobiology, but on this occasion I am glad not to have been able to satisfy my curiosity.'

'The Kamshet are not curious – we follow the old ways and we survive.'

Obeysekera shook his head. 'The world is changing. I fear the old ways will have to change too if you would survive.'

Amazigh turned to the Kasrkin captain. Obeysekera could see the Kamshet's blue eyes through the gap of his cheche.

'If we survive at the expense of who we are, do we then still really live?' asked Amazigh.

Obeysekera nodded. He said nothing to that but turned towards the other two Venators and spoke into the squad vox-channel.

'Gunners, keep alert – that thing under the sand might still decide it wants to climb out and grab itself a snack. Make sure if it does that it gets a mouthful of fire. The rest of you, get ready to move out. We had a sight of a Valkyrie. We'll get as near as we can with the vehicles, then climb the rest of the way. Do a quick vehicle test, then we move out and up.'

CHAPTER 14

They had come as far as the Venators could bring them.

'Keep in visual contact with each other,' said Obeysekera. 'Squad pattern aleph. Vox silence unless you see the general, his Valkyrie and its crew, or an enemy.'

'Any enemy expected, sir?' asked Gunsur.

'According to intel, no. But I won't have to remind you that it's precisely when intel tells you there's nothing to worry about that you've got most reason to be cautious. Watch for blueies. They shouldn't be able to get here, but they know we've lost a general, and they'll be searching for him too. Just depends on whether they want him more than we do.'

'And what could we want more than another general?'

'Thank you, Ensor,' Obeysekera said over the guffaws of the rest of the Kasrkin. 'General or not, it's our job to find him and bring him back, in one piece if we can, bagging up the bits if we can't.'

'What's the use of bringing in his body?' asked Uwais. 'It'll slow us down.'

'The lord militant either wants him alive, or proof that the blueies haven't got hold of him. No coming back with a finger. We'll need enough of the general to prove that the t'au don't have him wired and singing.'

As Uwais started another question, Obeysekera held up his hand. 'We'll leave the discussions as to how much and which bits of a man constitutes him to later. Now, we move out. Uwais, on point...'

The trooper grinned, stropping his warknife against his carapace armour.

'Amazigh is lead scout. Keep sharp. Let's go.'

The troops started up the mountain, tramping up the smooth slopes, with the Kamshet, unencumbered by weapons and with only a small skin of water, going lightly ahead.

The Kamshet led them up and into the mountain. As they climbed higher, sweating out the altitude but feeling a blessed coolness about them, Obeysekera slowly realised that the mountain was not a single peak but rather a series of peaks and plateaus, rolling upwards in waves. As he followed Amazigh, Obeysekera had the recurring sense that what he was climbing reminded him of something. Then, as they cleared the next ridge, only to see another rising beyond, he realised that the Tabaste was like the layered defences of a kasr, with bastions covering bastions in a rising sequence of emplacements.

Obeysekera stopped for a moment, pulled his cheche back and let the sweat on his forehead evaporate. Up here there was a breeze, as the air, heated on the uzayar around the Tabaste, rose up the flanks of the mountain. He looked back. That way lay the flats, lying like a lake around the Tabaste. He shook his head. Without air support, this was as close to a trap as he had ever let himself enter; an enemy planting an explosive charge on the causeway would effectively maroon them.

'Bit out of breath, captain?'

Obeysekera looked round and saw Malick watching him.

'Looking at the lie of the land, sergeant.'

Malick nodded. 'One way in, one way out.'

Obeysekera looked at Malick. 'I know my job, sergeant.'

'Of course you do. I wasn't suggesting anything else.'

'Good.' Obeysekera stared at Malick a moment longer, then turned back to looking where they were going. 'Still a long climb ahead of us.'

'At least it'll get cooler as we go higher.'

Obeysekera nodded, not looking at Malick. 'From furnace to fire.'

'What was that, sir?'

Obeysekera shook his head. 'Nothing. Just a memory.'

'A good one, I hope.'

'Just a memory. Who's on point?'

Malick checked his display. 'That's Ha, sir, though I don't rightly know where the Kamshet savage is.'

'Time to swap him over. Put Uwais on point again.'

As Malick called the orders through on the vox-channel, Obeysekera looked at him, waiting on him to finish. When the sergeant looked up in confirmation, Obeysekera said, 'Why do you call him "savage"?'

'It's what he is, sir. A savage.' Sergeant Malick regarded the captain with the bland gaze of a long-service squad leader. 'It is a mild term compared to what others call him.'

'Amazigh speaks Gothic. It would be best that he not hear the names you have for him.'

'Indeed he does. I have hardly heard him quiet.'

Obeysekera nodded. The Kamshet did not cleave to the stereotype of the laconic barbarian. 'His help is useful. I would not have it ended by careless words, from you or the men.'

'It won't be, sir.' Malick pointed. 'Shall I go ahead?'

'Yes, see if there is any sign.' Obeysekera looked back down the slope. 'I will wait for the commissar.'

Malick peered back too. 'You may have to wait some time, sir.'

The commissar was labouring upwards. Even from their distance, they could see the blood suffusing his cheeks and the sweat trails on his face. Sensing their regard, Roshant looked up. Seeing his expression, Obeysekera said to Malick, 'Go on, sergeant.'

As Malick started up the slope, his boots rasping on the smooth orange-red rock, Obeysekera stepped back to wait for Roshant.

'You... don't... have... to wait... for me.' The words came gasping over the private vox-channel.

'I differ on that, commissar,' said Obeysekera. He scanned the surroundings – it was as automatic as breathing – and sat down on a rock to wait. An oath, ten seconds later, told that he had forgotten how hot rocks became under the unrelenting sun of Dasht i-Kevar, even high up on the Tabaste.

Obeysekera stood to wait for the commissar. He tried to find some shade, but there was none to be had: millions of years had worn the Tabaste to smooth folds and humps, lying exposed under the press of the sun.

Roshant eventually came toiling up the slope, panting in the heat, and Obeysekera held out a hand to help him the final few steps. The commissar looked at the hand, then batted it away. He struggled up to Obeysekera and stood, swaying and sweating, in front of him.

'How much... further?'

Obeysekera shook his head. 'As far as finding the general – or the wreck of his Valkyrie.'

Roshant nodded. 'Very... well.'

'You could wait here.'

The commissar shook his head. 'I must… go on.'

'In a minute or two. I could use a breather too.'

Roshant looked at Obeysekera. 'You could?'

The captain unclipped his water flask and unscrewed the top. 'Yes.' He drank, at length but not deeply, letting the water wash his mouth and trickle down his throat.

'In that case…' The commissar unshipped his own water bottle and drank. Obeysekera watched over the lip of his own bottle to make sure Roshant drank enough. Those inexperienced in desert conditions would sometimes deny themselves immediately needed water for fear of not having enough later, only to collapse before the later arrived. But it appeared that Roshant had no difficulty not denying himself.

'Good.' Obeysekera resealed his flask and clipped it back onto his carapace armour. 'That's better. Are you ready to go on?'

After a moment's hesitation, Roshant said, 'Of course,' and put his own bottle away. But before they could begin up the mountain, the squad vox squeaked into life.

'*I see it.*' Obeysekera recognised Uwais' voice.

'How far?'

'*Five hundred yards, elevation one hundred. Definite Valkyrie.*'

'Hold there. Malick, confirm when you reach.'

'*Will do.*'

Obeysekera looked at Roshant. 'Looks like it's not much further.'

The commissar nodded. He squared himself, unhitched the latch over his bolt pistol. 'Let's go.'

They started up the mountain.

'*Confirmed Valkyrie.*' The sigil was Malick.

'Any sign of life?'

There was a pause. '*No.*'

'Run an auspex scan.'

'*Already done it. It's all scrambled – just fuzz.*'

Obeysekera's gaze refocused, under the impulse of years of training, to his auspex, but Malick was right: here, at the centre of the Sand Sea anomaly, there was only fuzz and random signals – he could not even read squad locations clearly.

'Approach but do not enter. Remain alert for blueies.'

'*Yes, sir.*'

Obeysekera saw, over the sergeant's direct channels, that he was sending Gunsur and Chame out on flanking approaches. Then a couple of words to Uwais told that Malick and he were taking the straight path towards the downed Valkyrie. The captain looked ahead, but a ridge blocked the view.

'Ensor, Ha, hold the flanks. Take sniping positions.'

The troopers acknowledged as Obeysekera hurried up the slope, the commissar labouring behind him. Reaching the crest, Obeysekera laid himself out flat and reached for his magnoculars.

Roshant joined him as he was adjusting the focus. 'See anything?'

'No. Damaged, but not catastrophic. Could be survivors.'

'Vox?'

As Obeysekera adjusted the vox to make a clear call to the downed Valkyrie, he saw Uwais, crouched low, hellgun couched under his shoulder, moving towards the aircraft along a smoothed-out gulley in the rock. The Valkyrie itself was half-hidden by the rock outcrop where it had come to rest. Malick was taking a parallel track but was further back. As Obeysekera watched, he saw the Valkyrie move.

The door-mounted heavy bolter began to track round.

'Uwais, get down!'

But the trooper did not respond.

'Uwais, down.'

Still there was no response from the trooper. From his position, the bolter's movement was all but invisible.

Obeysekera realised, with a muttered curse, that in trying to switch frequency to the clear channel he had lost contact with the squad. He pushed it back.

'Uwais…'

The bolter coughed. Uwais fell back.

'Hit, I'm hit.'

Hellguns flared, to the left and right, as Ensor and Ha, Gunsur and Chame returned fire.

'Hold fire, hold fire!'

But Obeysekera's order was lost under the sound of Uwais. He was keening. A high-pitched, tearing noise. Obeysekera had seen this before on the battlefield. A trooper, hit, immediate shock, then pain and panic overwhelming the shock reaction. Uwais must have taken shrapnel wounds; a direct hit from the heavy bolter would not have left enough of him to be crying out.

The hellguns flared, las-shots sputtering against the Valkyrie, pitting its armour, but the bolter began to track over towards Ensor and Gunsur.

Obeysekera overrode Uwais, cutting the keening from the squad vox-channel.

'Hold fire! Hold fire!'

The hellguns went dark. But through his magnoculars, Obeysekera could see the bolter continuing to track to target.

'Get down!'

The bolter coughed, spitting out bolt-shells, and the rock split and shattered, stone shrapnel flying. Through the squad vox, Obeysekera heard the cursing of troopers peppered by stone shards, but by their oaths, Ensor and Gunsur were being protected by their armour and helmets.

'Stay down. Hold fire.'

The bolter's chatter stopped. Silence returned to the silent mountain, but threading through the quiet there came the rattle-grind of the pintle, tracking the bolter towards fresh targets, and low moaning as Uwais tried to fix a field dressing over his wound.

'Ha, go to Uwais. Stay low.'

The trooper acknowledged and started to move, keeping low, using the cover, while Obeysekera struggled to switch his vox to clear.

'Here.'

Obeysekera looked round and saw Roshant lying next to him, proffering his vox-bead. Obeysekera bent his head to it.

'Valkyrie, hold fire, repeat, hold fire. Valkyrie *Eternal Flame*, respond. Hold fire. Hold fire. We are friendlies. Hold fire. Valkyrie *Eternal Flame*, please respond.'

'It's stopped tracking,' whispered Roshant.

'I say again – Valkyrie *Eternal Flame*, hold fire, hold fire. Friendlies. Calling *Eternal Flame*, respond.'

Then, over the clear channel, faint and crackling: *'Identify.'*

Obeysekera paused. The identification codes were changed every three days. General Itoyesa had gone missing before the current set of identification codes were set. The previous set... He scrabbled through his memory.

'The Emperor is merciful...'

Thin, but clearer, *'...but His justice precedes His wrath...'*

'...and His mercy is completed in victory...'

'...*victory over death.'*

The vox went silent a moment, then crackled into life.

'You took your frekking time.' There was a pause. *'I thought you were hostile.'*

Obeysekera checked Uwais' life signs. 'The man you shot should live.'

'That's a relief... Who the Throne are yo–?'

The final part of the question dropped away. Then the general spoke again.

'As you have come so far to find me, perhaps you could ask your guide not to kill me.'

Obeysekera looked round, then spoke urgently into the vox. 'Amazigh, do not kill the general. Repeat, Amazigh, do not kill the general.'

The vox crackled. *'Master. He tried to kill you.'*

'Amazigh, thank you for protecting me, but now, as your master, I am telling you not to shoot the general.'

The vox went silent. Obeysekera stared at it, willing the Kamshet to stop. There was no time to get any of his own men into the Valkyrie.

'He lives.'

PART II

DEEP GREEN

CHAPTER 1

The Kinband moved up over the time-smoothed, red-rounded rock with the ease of meat mates. They ate together, they moved together, they thought together. They fought together. Shaper Tchek stretched his neck, feeling the vertebrae extend, and from behind the cover of the rock ridge, looked around. His eyes, the eyes of a kroot Shaper, were preternaturally sharp, able to absorb the contours of the land before him in a single look and then focus in on a single point while still retaining a general view of his surroundings.

The Kinband were spread out over the side of the mountain: there, Stalker Krasykyl, ascending that smooth face through the aid of the rock talons that he had communed from the pit apes of Canopus Minor. There, Tracker Cirict, beak down almost to the ground, tongue flicking, tasted the air and the scents it carried to senses he had honed from the warhounds of the Doge Loredano: the contract had cost Tchek the lives of three of the Kinband but the Harvest Feast it brought, when they had all shared the flesh of one of the Doge's prime warhounds, had been worth the price in blood. Tchek paused, sniffing, head turning, the movement combining the stop-motion of their avian ancestry with the canine warhound genes they had communed at the Feast.

As he turned his head, the wind hissed and feathers sighed. Tchek saw the colour flash of the pech'ra as it flared its wings. Cirict held out his arm. The bird landed, its talons fitting into the score marks that it had made through the years on Cirict's bracer. The Tracker and his pech'ra were not master and servant, nor nestlings but rather companions in the hunt, the bird providing eyes and seeing things that even the eyes of Cirict the Tracker did not see, enhanced though they were from the Feast. But the pech'ra, born of Pech itself, could see a mole rat from two miles and guide his Tracker to it. Now, it spoke to Cirict, turning its head and clacking its beak as it shared what it had seen. Cirict nodded and clicked back, preening the breast feathers of the bird then taking a stinkbug from the pouch on his belt and feeding it to the pech'ra. The bird must have payment for the knowledge it brought. Tchek, impatient for information in the past, had learned that no Tracker would speak until his pech'ra had had its reward. So Tchek waited, listening while Cirict crooned the name of his pech'ra, singing its praise in the time-honoured way of kroot Trackers.

'Far-eye, bright wing, sharp claw Flet.'

The pech'ra took the stinkbug as its due, ignoring Cirict as it ate. Although it was not something he would ever say to his Tracker, Tchek suspected that the pech'ra only had two categories of creature in its fierce little mind: those to eat and those to fear – and the latter category only comprised the spider-apes of Pech, who netted creatures flying through the jagga groves in their webs. Cirict, as a creature who provided food for the pech'ra, possibly managed to inhabit the category once held by Flet's parents, but Tchek suspected that if Cirict died the pech'ra would pluck the eyes from the Tracker's skull with no more sentiment than it ate the stinkbug he was feeding it.

Flet fed, the Tracker turned to the Shaper and spoke. The notes, to the ears of any listeners ignorant of the semantics of song, sounded like trills and runs and squeaks. To the kroot, it was more than language, but it served as language too.

'He is close. I can smell him.'

And it was true. Although Cirict had naturally consumed the greater part of the warhound's flesh and communed most deeply with the animal's spirit, all the surviving members of the Kinband had partaken too, that they might each have a small share in the gifts of the rest, and Tchek could taste something of what the Tracker sensed upon the wind.

It was the smell of man.

A rank smell, of turbid flesh and violent mind, with tangs of metal and chemical and underlying it all, the distinctive smell of tumour.

For humanity smelled like cancer.

Then Cirict whistled again, the notes trilling alarm. 'There are more. The smell is too strong for one.'

'How many?' Tchek whistled back, the harmonics telling Cirict the calmness of the questioner while also offering ritual thanks to the Huntress, Vawk, for bringing blessing before them.

'Shaper, I can taste them on the wind – there are many. Ten perhaps.'

'How far?'

The Tracker pointed. 'Beyond the next rise and the one after.'

The Shaper's crown quills rustled. The quills of the Kinband rattled in answer, subtle colours fluting through and up and down the quills, like light broken upon iridescent feathers.

'Keep Flet on the arm – I do not want the humans to suspect any living creature draws near.'

Tchek signalled and the kroot Kinband spread out, rifles ready, taking their positions. Shaper Tchek stepped aside as a rangy kroot moved up beside him, muscles cording beneath his skin. Slung upon his back was the standard kroot rifle, the wicked barb turned carefully away from its head, but in his hands he held a fighting staff, made of the light, hard, flexible wood of the jagga tree. The light glittered upon the cutting axe at its tip, and split upon the spear point at its base.

'Chaktak, stay with me.'

The Cut-skin's quills rattled in answer, splitting white light to red.

Shaper Tchek looked back. The last of the Kinband followed behind, as was his place: the Bearer, Kliptiq, carrying upon his back the pot from which the Kinband would feast following the hunt, the pot that told the tales of all their hunts, each one leaving its trace in their communal memory.

Kliptiq's rattle flashed his knowledge of the Shaper's regard. The Bearer lifted his rifle: although he carried the communal pot, he was not without a weapon, but Shaper Tchek had put before him meals of beasts of burden sufficient for him to both bear his load and not to cavil at being required to do so.

'Put it down,' said Tchek, pointing at the rifle. 'Before you shoot something you should not shoot.'

Kliptiq's quills drooped but he did as he was told: the Bearer, fed upon beasts of low intelligence, was only of use in battle to fire at something that was pointed out to him.

'Follow me,' said the Shaper. 'Do not fire at anything unless I tell you. Do you understand?'

Kliptiq's quills flared. This was something he could understand.

'To live is to hunt,' said Chaktak. 'For what does not hunt is prey. I am glad I am a Cut-skin. Not the Bearer.'

'We are all the Bearer,' said the Shaper. 'Until we have tasted all.'

'When the Chained shall be loosened,' said the Cut-skin.

'The Wind Lord return.'

'And the Free will fly to Him and leave this universe behind.'

As Shaper Tchek spoke the words, he felt his old, tearing, familiar flight yearning. Part of him wished to return to the air, but he knew well that without the right material the Feast would reduce him to the state of Cirict's pech'ra: a brain bright with fierce desire but stripped of everything else. The tremors and colour flashes upon the quill crests of the Cut-skin and the Bearer told the same for the other two kroot. The secret language of the kroot was sound and light, harmonics and spectrals, in which syntax and semantics were all but united: for the kroot, the meaning was the sound and the sound was the meaning.

The Creed spoken, Shaper Tchek whistled his instructions to the Kinband, using the ultrasonic frequencies that allowed the kroot to communicate over long distances without machines. Few other species in the galaxy could hear in that range, so the communication was doubly secure: ultrasonic and in a language indecipherable to any outsider. Not even the t'au knew the secret language of the kroot.

Tchek sent Stalker Krasykyl higher, instructing him to look for the humans from the heights. He told Tracker Cirict to continue towards where he smelled the humans, advancing with caution, with Long-sight Stryax flanking him. He would follow, with Cut-skin Chaktak flanking him and the Bearer, Kliptiq, at the rear.

It was the usual search-and-contact formation employed by the kroot; it should have enabled the Shaper to acquire the necessary intelligence about the humans before issuing instructions on whether to consume, to fight or to fly. It should have worked.

But the sun had sunk the space of only a single quill in the sky, still high and fierce, when the standard plan of approach moulted and the feathers came out.

The squad was in standard advance formation. A few words over the squad vox-channel had been enough: the 'kin knew what to do. Obeysekera had checked – visually, the auspex was still useless – that the men were in the right places and then signalled the advance. He was following, with the general and the commissar, behind a screen of the best troops in the Imperium. Chame was helping the injured Uwais, far enough behind the command group that they would not all be killed by any but the largest ordnance. Fifty yards further back, Gunsur was rearguard.

A few steps along the way back down the mountain to the waiting Venators, General Itoyesa signalled Obeysekera closer.

'Yes, general?' asked Obeysekera. They were close enough not to need the vox.

Itoyesa gestured to the screen of Kasrkin making their wide way down the Tabaste.

'Cautious.'

'Yes,' said Obeysekera. 'Having found you, general, I don't intend on losing you.'

Itoyesa shook his head. 'Too cautious. I must get back and this formation slows us down.' He pointed at Lerin, who had moved into the lee of a redstone outcrop to assess the way ahead. 'Look at her. She'll take three minutes checking everything is clear before voxing us to move up. We need to move faster.' He turned back to Obeysekera. 'Switch formation – we can march out of here.'

Obeysekera shook his head. 'Such a formation leaves too much chance of us walking into a trap.'

'A trap?' Itoyesa snorted. He swept his arm wide, taking in the whole expanse of redstone sloping down before them. 'There's nothing here. I've been stuck on this rock for three days and I haven't seen anything bigger than a sand fly. Unless you're worried about being ambushed by sand flies, we need to get moving.'

'I'm afraid I can't do that, general.'

Itoyesa snorted again. 'Do I have to remind you who is the ranking officer here, captain?'

'Do I have to tell you who is in operational command of this mission, general?'

Itoyesa stared at Obeysekera, then looked away, shaking his head. 'The men who will die because you took your time shall be on your conscience then, *Captain* Obeysekera.'

'The men who have died because of my decisions have always weighed upon my conscience, *General* Itoyesa.'

Itoyesa waved Obeysekera away. 'At least go and check on your advance line, try to speed them up.'

Obeysekera paused, looked towards Roshant, then nodded. 'Very well, general. I will see if we can move a bit more quickly. Commissar, stay with the general, please.'

Obeysekera caught the tail of Roshant's protesting expression but ignored it. He was already moving ahead, scuttling down the mountain towards the forward scouts, keeping low and breaking up movement by periods of stillness and watching. It was the standard movement pattern for traversing enemy territory.

Stopping in the partial shade of a dry gulch, Obeysekera scanned for movement, but saw nothing. His own wayfinders were still for the moment, fanned out to either side of the main party with Ensor on point. Backed into the shade, Obeysekera took a moment to appreciate the lifting of the sun's weight from his head and shoulders. The shaded stone felt cool against the back of his neck.

Obeysekera turned his head and looked down the gulley. It was in shadow, and going down it would shield them from the sight of any watchers. He took a bearing on its direction against his compass. It was only ten degrees from their direction of travel. But the wayfinders had passed it. Looking back, Obeysekera could see why. The gulley sloped upwards, dying away, and from the higher level it must appear as nothing more than a brief break in the redstone.

'Hold your positions.' Obeysekera voxed the scouts on the channel he had set apart for them, then started down the gulley. There was no point calling the scouts back if the gulley petered out within a few hundred yards.

It was blessedly cooler there. The floor of the gulley alternated between scoured-clear rock and deadfalls of accumulated stones, pebbles and larger rocks. Having scrambled past the first two deadfalls, Obeysekera stopped at the third.

The only thing he could think of that could sweep the sand and rock down the side of the Tabaste and into the gulley was rain. But he had heard no reports of rainfall within the Great Sand Sea from any of the Imperial forces on Dasht i-Kevar: so far as the soldiers of the Emperor were concerned, it never rained on the Sand Sea.

Standing in the lee of the deadfall, Obeysekera scraped away some of the sand at its base. Human skin is sensitive to tiny concentrations of dampness. Having scraped a pit into the sand, Obeysekera propped his gun against the wall of the gulley and pushed his fingers into the compact sand, feeling, feeling. If there was water there, hidden under the surface, it could be important, both for him and for future expeditions.

The sand scraped at his skin as he wormed it deeper. Was that it?

Yes. He could feel the sand change. He reached a little deeper, grasping, and pulled a handful out, raising it to his face. It was dark, darker than the other sand, and he sniffed the water on it, feeling the sublimation of the water molecules as the fierce heat pulled them out of the suddenly exposed sand.

Water. He smiled and looked up, over the deadfall, further along the gulley.

Movement.

Movement.

Tchek threw himself towards the deadfall in the gulley while pulling the long barrel of his rifle round to bear on the human. As he juddered into the ground, he loosed off rounds, the slugs splintering off the rocks around the human, the kick of the recoil nearly jerking the rifle from his hands.

'Contact, contact!' Obeysekera spun behind a rock as the rounds chipped the redstone around and in front of him, rock splinters flying into bare skin and bouncing off his carapace armour.

'Enemy, enemy!' Tchek whistled, the frequency high above the low thud of his rifle as he pushed up above his sheltering rock and loosed more rounds to keep the human down. As he lay behind the deadfall, reloading his rifle, Tchek thought again how right his old kill-broker had been. No plan ever did survive contact with the enemy. He had intended to watch the humans from a distance until he had determined which of them was his target, then plan an ambush to kill the others, consume any who had been particularly worthy foes, before returning with the human the t'au wanted. Now, he was scrunched behind a deadfall that was slightly too small to cover all of him while the human did the same to him that he was trying to do to it: keep him pinned down while the rest of its squad arrived.

Hunched in behind a deadfall that was too small to cover all of his body, Obeysekera cursed while calling his men back to flanking

positions and at the same time shooting, almost blind, over the top
of the rock to try to keep the xenos down.

'Malick, Roshant, Amazigh, get the general down to the Venators.'

As the hotshots sizzled against the rock, Tchek suddenly considered whether the human firing at him was the one he sought.
It was unlikely. He was valuable to the humans too. They would
be trying to get the general down the mountain while maintaining a screen to delay pursuit.

'Krasykyl, Cirict, wide flank down the mountain. The humans
will be trying to get their general to safety. Cirict, fly Flet.'

There would be a few more seconds before the xenos could call
further rifles in upon him – any flanking shots would find his body
behind its inadequate cover, and at these short ranges even carapace
armour would not stop the rounds.

'Gunsur, Ensor, Lerin, cover fire, I need to move.'

In response, hellgun fire came sizzling through above him, well
above, for the men were still too far back to get direct line of sight
on him, but their concentration would make the approaching xenos
stay low.

The human was calling in suppressing fire, trying to keep him
pinned down. If he was the human commander he would be
trying to roll out and get away, down the mountain, keeping a
screen to protect the general. Time to get clear.

Time to roll clear.

Shaper Tchek crouched behind the deadfall, pushing himself down, compressing the muscles in his legs, folding both
leg joints, tightening.

Captain Obeysekera crouched behind the deadfall, holding the
hellgun round the redstone and shooting off more rounds blind as
he got his balance.

Shaper Tchek released his sprung muscles, jumping into the
mouth of the defile.

Captain Obeysekera pushed off, scrambling back up the gulley.

Cut-skin Chaktak was running up. Tchek stopped him, hauling the Cut-skin back when he tried to push past him, the fight blood rising.

'Round, cut them off,' said Tchek. 'They are trying to get down the mountain. Stop them.'

Chaktak, his staff in his hands, his eyes livid with fighting blood, shivered, quills rattling. He could smell the Feast that would follow battle, taste the worlds that waited. The Hunger was upon him. It was upon them all. But Tchek was Shaper because he could still think and plan when the Hunger rose, and the Kinband would listen.

'That way.' He pointed, left, towards a downward-folding defile. 'Listen for Cirict and Krasykyl – they are moving round to cut off the humans.'

Chaktak raised his quills in answer, the light splitting upon them, and bounded off in the direction Tchek pointed, whistling his position to the rest of the Kinband.

Tchek whistled for Long-sight Stryax. 'Pick the humans off. But for your soul do not touch the general.'

The Long-sight, hidden in the rock folds, whistled his reply, and began to hunt, the Hunger building within him as it was in the others. They must feed soon or the Kinband would turn upon itself.

The Shaper turned back to the Bearer, Kliptiq, the last to answer his summons.

'You come with me,' he said.

The Bearer held up his rifle: its barrel was cut shorter than those carried by the rest of the Kinband. 'Shoot?'

'Soon,' said Tchek. 'When I say. Follow.'

The Shaper, with the Bearer following, started down after the human, moving at an angle to its descent. It would not be long before they caught up with the human rearguard. The plan was to engage it while the other Kinbandlings killed the humans escorting the general. Then they would feast, and assuage the Hunger, before bringing the general to those who wanted him.

Tchek's quills rattled. No plan survived contact with the enemy, but a good general adapted.

Obeysekera scramble-rolled down the slope, tumbling to a stop up against the redstone and pulled himself round, hell-gun pointed up the mountain, as he scanned for the xenos.

Silence.

He looked, listened, put his senses and experience into the red-rock world, while checking his auspex. It was scrambled, putting up ghost notes and noise, even his own squad flicking in and out and transposing positions. A distraction. Obeysekera keyed it off, the display disappearing from before his eyes.

Better. Eyes and ears, wit and craft against these xenos.

Kroot. The label came up from his hypnocache. T'au allies and mercenaries. Low technology in comparison to their masters. That was why the t'au had sent them in after the general. Neither the anomaly nor the desert would disable their simple weapons; they did not rely on complex equipment to track and find their quarry, only sight and sound and smell.

Obeysekera grinned, baring his teeth. It was going to be a good fight.

'Gunsur, Ensor, Lerin, hold your positions. I am pulling back past you.'

As the troopers acknowledged, Obeysekera started making his way further down the slope, working his way from one piece of cover to another.

'Report contacts.'

The xenos had disappeared. Obeysekera saw Gunsur, tucked

in behind an outcrop, peering through the sights of his hellgun as he scanned the higher ground. Looking past him, Obeysekera saw Ensor and Lerin in covering positions.

Where had the enemy gone? More to the point, why were the xenos here?

Lying on the sun-warmed rock, Obeysekera realised that he was facing a snatch team, sent by the t'au to find and capture General Itoyesa. He had sent the general on down the mountain with Malick, Roshant and Amazigh to get him to safety, thinking this was a simple enemy contact. If the kroot were after the general, they might bypass him and go after Itoyesa. Still, so long as Malick and Roshant got the general down to the Venators, the twin-linked multi-lasers and lascannons mounted on the vehicles should be enough to drive back any attack these xenos could launch with only light weaponry.

'Uwais? Location?'

The answer came back after a pause, voice strained and taut over the vox.

'Can't keep going, sir.'

'Who's with you?'

'It's Chame, sir. I can carry him.'

'No, sir. There are enemy. I-I will hold them.'

'Where are you?'

'Cave mouth, sir,' answered Chame as Uwais coughed, the liquid cough of a man whose lungs were filling with blood. 'About a hundred yards below you.'

'Malick, Roshant, where are you?'

'Fifty yards past Uwais,' Malick answered. 'Heading down.'

'Watch for ambush. I think the xenos are trying to flank us.'

'Will do. Could do with another gun, sir. There's only me and Roshant with the general.'

'Where's Amazigh?'

'No idea.'

'Throne! Continue down the mountain. Get the general to the Venators, wait for us there.'

'Yes, sir.'

Obeysekera scanned the mountainside, but there was no sign of the Kamshet. With no vox, he could not speak to him. There was nothing he could do.

'Fall back pattern beta.'

Ensor, Gunsur and Lerin acknowledged, with Lerin starting back down the mountain under the cover of Ensor and Gunsur.

'Keep contact. I will go ahead.'

Obeysekera started down the slide, moving from rock to shade, stopping at each waypoint to observe and listen. Above him, on the mountainside, he could see Gunsur, Ensor and Lerin covering each other's retreat. But there was no sign, nor sound, of the xenos.

Where were they?

Where were they?

Tchek stopped, his frame hidden by the gulley he was using to cover his descent, and listened. Behind him, Kliptiq waited, eyes vacant, the empty pot upon his back waiting to be filled.

The Shaper could hear no movements. He turned his head, smelling, but he did not have a sense as refined as Cirict the Tracker. He could smell the humans – the scent was all but overpowering – but he could not separate it out or locate its different components. It was too strong. But scents that strong meant the humans were close, even if he could not see them.

They were skilled, these humans, not like most he had encountered in the past. Those had advanced in solid lines, marching stolidly to their deaths, and retreated the same way. It was no difficult task to pick one out among such multitudes and take him for the pot. But these humans were different. They moved with the near silence of his own Kinband. After the barrage of their first contact, the humans had withdrawn as quickly and efficiently as the kroot had followed, but they had so far avoided further fighting.

Tchek risked lifting his head up out of the gulley, looking for any sign of them, but conscious that the quills that identified his rank also stood in stark, jagged, coloured contrast to the surrounding redstone, making it easy for any watching eyes to see him.

Nothing. Just the folds and rills and humps of redstone, tending downwards towards the great plain that surrounded the Tabaste. There were many places to hide, and more ways to get down the mountain than he had anticipated. It would be easy to miss their target, moving quietly down through gullies and declines, safe from all but the most direct sight.

Tchek whistle-called the Long-sight, the Stalker and the Tracker. 'Have you sight of the target?'

His whistle-call disappeared into the still air, but there was no reply. Down in the gulley, the redstone was channelling the sound along its length. For his call to reach left and right, he had to climb out into the open again.

Tchek pushed his foot talons into the rock and began to lever himself up the few feet necessary to take his head above the lip of the gulley. But as he reached its edge, he heard a sudden explosion of rifle fire and the answering sizzle-crack of the enemy's weapons. Following the sound, he looked and saw, a few hundred yards away, the rock-smoke of fierce fighting.

They had found the humans.

CHAPTER 2

'We're pinned down.'

As Sergeant Malick spoke urgently into his vox-bead, another round from a kroot rifle glanced off the redstone above his head, striking sparks and fragments that bounced off his helmet. He was crouching with his back against a boulder, with General Itoyesa beside him and Commissar Roshant on the other side of the general.

'Where are they?' said the general, pushing himself up to peer over the redstone.

A further rifle round chipped splinters from the boulder as Sergeant Malick hauled the general back down.

'Unhand me,' said General Itoyesa, striking Malick's hand away from his tunic. The general was dressed in the field uniform of a commanding officer of the Astra Militarum, with the stylings of his own Tekan Janissaries. Lighter than usual on the braid and gold epaulettes, but still gaudy in comparison to the tan and brown of Malick's uniform.

Malick held up his hand. 'Just trying to keep you alive. Sir.'

General Itoyesa smoothed the crease made by Malick's grab from his jacket. 'I have survived worse than…' – a kroot rifle round skimmed the top of the redstone, just above the general's head – '…than this, sergeant, and I fully intend to survive this too.'

'Maybe get just a little lower then, general,' said Malick, twisting round and firing off a suppressing burst from his hellgun. 'They're trying to get above us.'

'Why don't you do something, commissar?' said the general, turning to Roshant. 'Your bolt pistol is hot, but I have not seen your shells hit the enemy.'

Roshant, his face pale, gave the general a look that was part grin, part grimace. 'When my bolts hit an enemy, there is not much left of it for you to see, general.' He turned and fired off another shell in the direction of the last series of shots.

The commissar spun back under cover before a volley of kroot rifle rounds – the bullets might be little more than crude balls of metal, thought Malick, but a crude ball of metal fired sufficiently fast and at close enough range could still sear through even the best carapace armour – struck the redstone above Roshant's head.

'Captain, we are under attack,' Roshant said into his vox. 'We need assistance.'

But the anomaly that rendered auspexes unreliable in the Sand Sea was stronger here than anywhere else on the Tabaste; all they could hear in answer were squawks and stutters, words cut off and cut through.

'Captain!' Roshant repeated, nearly shouting now.

'They don't work better if you shout in them, son,' said General Itoyesa, touching Roshant's hand with his own. The commissar jerked, then nodded dumbly as another volley of kroot rifle rounds ricocheted off the top and side of the boulder.

Malick pointed to the stone shards. 'They are working round to flank us, general.'

'I know.' General Itoyesa smiled, his teeth white in his face. 'As the word "retreat" is not in the tactical vocabulary of the Guard, I suggest that we advance backwards instead.' The general pointed down the slope about fifty yards. 'See that deep shadow under the rock outcrop? I think it is a cave entrance. Get in there and we can hold it against these xenos scum.'

'We will also be trapped in there, general,' said Malick. 'If they have any grenades, we will be in trouble.'

General Itoyesa looked at Malick. 'I am not accustomed to sergeants questioning my decision, sergeant.' Then the general smiled again. 'But then again, maybe this is the Kasrkin way of which I have heard so much. If the xenos had explosives, they would have used them by now.'

Almost by way of answer, another burst of rifle fire scored the redstone, the angle indicating that the xenos were getting closer to successfully flanking their position and opening them up to attack.

'We can't stay here,' said Roshant. He held his hand to his face and it came away red. 'I've been hit.' He was staring at the blood on his fingertips with something approaching disbelief.

'A rock splinter,' said the general. 'A scratch. Your father will be proud to hear of your courage.'

Roshant looked at the general. 'He will?'

'It does depend upon someone getting back to tell him,' said General Itoyesa. 'And for that I am going to need a volunteer to make the run for the cave.'

'I-I am not scared.'

'No?' Itoyesa's voice grew suddenly soft. 'Well, I am. So let's get out of here until some help arrives.' He pointed at the cave entrance. 'One at a time. Covering fire from the other two.' He looked at Roshant. 'As you volunteered, you first, commissar.'

Roshant stared at the general, his face blank, as if he did not understand what Itoyesa was saying. Itoyesa put his hand on Roshant's shoulder and his face close to the young commissar, looking him directly in the eye.

'You are your father's son.'

'Besides, going first is safest,' said Malick. 'They won't be expecting the move.'

'Get ready,' said Itoyesa. He shifted his bolt pistol to his left hand, drew his power sword from its scabbard, the blade humming quietly as it emerged into the light, as if excited at the prospect of drinking new blood.

'Ready?' asked General Itoyesa.

Roshant took a deep breath. 'Ready,' he said.

'Sergeant?'

'Ready, sir.'

'Then let us give them a taste of hell. On my count. Four, three, two, one.'

As the count reached its end, General Itoyesa and Sergeant Malick swung round to either side of their concealing boulder and started spraying rounds, quick bursts of semi-automatic fire, targeting any obvious gaps and mounds that might conceal the enemy. At the same moment, Roshant sprang to his feet and sprinted down the redstone slope towards the dark shadow of the cavern mouth, the hiss-snap of Malick's hellgun forming a harmonic to the low cough of the general's bolt pistol, all overlaid with the noise of las-round and bolt-shell hitting and shattering the redstone.

Malick, keeping one eye on his power pack, pulled back under the cover of the redstone as General Itoyesa did the same. In answer, there came a volley of kroot rifle rounds, smacking into the rock and covering them with splinters.

Malick pointed down towards the cavern. 'He made it.'

'Try your vox again,' said General Itoyesa.

Sergeant Malick fiddled with its settings, trying to get something beyond static and jumbled words. 'Still nothing,' said Malick.

'Then I think I shall have to go next,' said General Itoyesa. He began to crouch down.

'W-wait!' Malick held his hand up. 'I've got something.'

Through his vox, faint but distinct, the captain's voice.

'...are you? Say again, where are you?'

'You hear the shooting, sir?'

'I hear it.'

'That's where we are.'

'Very well. Stay under cover. We will come to relieve you.'

Another fusillade of shots hissed past them, the bullets expending their energy on sand and redstone.

'It's pretty hot here, sir. We're going to have to move.'

'That's a no,' said Captain Obeysekera. 'Stay where you are. We will find you.'

General Itoyesa leaned over and spoke into Malick's vox-bead. 'I am a general, Captain Obeysekera. You will find I outrank you. We will retreat into a more defensible position.'

'General, I must...'

'Look for us in a cave, captain.' General Itoyesa looked back at Malick. 'Ready?'

'Yes, sir.'

'Then let's go.'

As the general started running down the slope towards the cave entrance, Sergeant Malick and Commissar Roshant began firing, hosing the immediate area down with bolt-shells and las-rounds, trying to keep the heads of the xenos down lest they lose their own.

But there were only two weapons – Itoyesa was too busy

running to fire as well – and kroot rifle fire began again from other areas than those they could see, the rounds bursting against the redstone. Glancing back, Malick saw the general running on regardless even as incoming fire curdled the rock beneath his feet. Sergeant Malick squeezed off another burst of las-rounds, in the process draining one of the power packs for his hellgun, then swung back into the blessed shadow of the rock, panting hard. From the rock's shelter, he saw General Itoyesa dive into the darkness of the cave.

Just him left, then.

But the kroot would know where he was going. Malick, with all his experience of battle, looked over the course he would have to run, judging where he was most open and therefore most vulnerable, looking for scraps of cover at those points.

The vox wheezed back on. It was Roshant; his voice was breaking up again, but enough came through for Malick to know that they were ready for him to make his move. He was about to go when he saw something. It was moving in from his left, a shape tracking through the stark shadows of the rocks.

The xenos were moving to cut him off.

Malick started up, running, hellgun held at his hip and firing in the rough direction of where he had seen the xenos, hoping to keep it pinned down. As he ran, Roshant and the general opened up with everything they had, spraying rounds above and around him. From the whistle crack of supercharged air, some of the shots were not missing him by much.

Malick kept going, boots pounding over redstone, splitting his gaze between watching his footing and watching where that xenos was coming from, sliding along one of the rock gullies that criss-crossed the slope.

Then it jumped up in front of him: taller than a man, face a hybrid of the avian and the human, crowned with a rattle of quills that were flashing through the colour spectrum and on to colours he had never even seen. It was swinging a great staff with an axe blade at one end and a spike at the other, and it ran towards him over the cracked slope, jumping each gulley with the hopping motion of a carrion bird rather than the gait of a man.

It was running at him, its face a hideous devolution of the simian, featherless like a newborn chick, and raising its weapon as it saw him, its mouth opening in a shout and challenge, while Chaktak, the Cut-skin, swerved, turning off either leg so that he might present a moving target to the humans sheltering in the cave's mouth.

Malick, running as rifle rounds chipped into the redstone at his feet, pulled round his hellgun and tried to fire on the move, squeezing the trigger, but the las-rounds pulled left, hissing into the stone behind the xenos.

Chaktak jagged left, reversing his fighting staff to reach its maximum reach, ready to step in close and swing it round in a descending figure of eight: the axe would take the human at the point on his shoulder where helmet met chestplate, the point where there was nothing to protect against weapons from the front, swinging down into where neck met shoulder. He would cut the human across the diagonal.

Running with rifle rounds chewing at his heels and the covering fire from General Itoyesa and Commissar Roshant hissing past his head, Malick saw the xenos swing its long battle axe up into the start of a killing arc. It leapt forward, bounding over the rock like a big bird as Malick pulled his hellgun round to target it.

But before he could bring his weapon to bear on the xenos he felt a blow on his shoulder, heavy as a hammer, and he fell forwards, turning as he did so, hellgun beginning to fall from suddenly nerveless fingers. He had taken a round from his own side, leaving him exposed to the axe-strike of the xenos. And as he fell, Malick looked at the xenos closing on him and all that went through his mind was the thought, *I am going to be killed by a frekking bird*, and the incongruity was worse than the death that strutted towards him.

The Cut-skin could smell the prey as well as see it; it filled his whole vision, moving with all the uncertainty of prey when it belatedly realises that though it had thought itself the master of the universe, here, in this place and this time, it was the prey. Chaktak stepped closer, his blade hungry, singing for blood in the ancient life-tongue of the kroot, remembered and sung at all their Feasts. But as Chaktak lifted his axe to bring it swinging downwards, he felt something grasp his ankle, something cold in this world of heat, and jerk him back towards the rill that he had just jumped across.

Malick, grounded, his shoulder throbbing with pain but also with unexpected life, resumed crawling for the cave entrance, trying to look backwards to see what that creature was doing while also inching towards the general and Roshant. The two men were at the entrance of the cave, urging him on while keeping up a barrage of suppressing fire to make the xenos stay low.

'Keep going.'

The vox was working now.

'Shoot the frekking fowl,' Malick said, crawling slowly, for the pain in his shoulder was stopping him using his right arm at all: his hellgun he was just dragging along beside him by its strap, the paluwood of its stock rubbing ochre up against the redstone. As he crawled, he expected a strike from the creature, but nothing came.

Where had it gone?

More bolts hissed past his head, striking redstone but not the xenos. Malick heard the captain's voice, coming through tinny and high-pitched above the roar of the bolt pistols, breaking between the static that was feeding back through the vox-channels.

'*General, commissar, can you hear me?*'

Malick could hear it from his own vox and from up ahead: he must be getting close to the cave entrance.

'*Bit busy here, captain,*' he heard the general answer.

'*Two minutes away,*' said Obeysekera.

'*Make it one,*' said General Itoyesa.

A fresh volley of kroot rifle fire spattered into the redstone around Malick and then, suddenly, there was silence from behind him. Only the flash and percussive roar of the bolt pistols firing from the cave mouth, and those too died away as Malick crawled the final yards into the cave.

'Made it,' said Malick. 'Safe.'

'Not so sure about that,' said General Itoyesa, pulling the sergeant to his feet and into the dark of the cave. He pointed deeper inside. Eyes stunned by the bright light of Dasht i-Kevar, all Malick could see at first was darkness. But then, as he acclimatised to the gloom, he began to see details: the roof and walls of the cave, smooth as glass, angling downwards. And there, at the vanishing point of the tunnel, the faintest hint of livid green light.

Chaktak, pulled like a bird on the line, tumbled into the rill, turning head over heels as he fell. But he still held his hunting staff and as the images of his fall spun past him, confused in their speed, he maintained his hold on it, ready to strike out when the falling stopped. Landing on his back, Chaktak went to spring up, but his ankle was pulled from under him and he sprawled again even as he swung out with his staff. It struck, the axe connecting with something hard.

The smell. Only now did he notice the smell.

He was being dragged along the floor of the rill like a sack, the redstone rubbing against his back. Chaktak looked down along the length of his body for what was pulling him, while he tried to find purchase on the smooth rock with his hands to grab something and stop himself.

It had its back to him. In the deep shade of the rill, it was hard to see more than a shape – that smell – but it was dragging him along as if he were a nestling. Chaktak scrabbled against the redstone, but he could not stop his progress. Where was the creature taking him?

He saw, ahead, a deeper darkness at the end of the rill, as if the channel led into a tunnel. That was where it was dragging him. Chaktak seized his hunting staff and brought the axe head down upon the shoulder of the creature.

It bounced.

The creature did not even look round. And they were nearly at the tunnel entrance. Something that Chaktak had never truly known before rose up his throat: fear, choking and enveloping as gas.

The Cut-skin realised that he was going to have to call for help. But before he could utter the whistle call of alarm that would bring the rest of the Kinband to his aid, the creature dragging him stopped. It turned towards him.

For a moment, Chaktak thought it was human. But then he saw the blood weeping through the empty space where the eyes had been, and he realised that the thing was wearing a human face as a mask – a mask that from the blood seeping down over the skin had only just been cut from its owner.

Chaktak would have called out then, called as loud as he might, not to save himself but to save the others, but he could not, for fingers that were colder than the space between the stars, wielding a knife that could slice electrons from atoms, reached round his throat and sealed his cry there, while another hand slowly held a knife up before his face.

# CHAPTER 3

Shaper Tchek crouched down beside the Long-sight, Stryax. From their position, in a large hollow under a wind-carved rock, Stryax could see the entrance to the cave and the slope down to it.

'Kill any human that tries to get to the cave,' he instructed the Long-sight, 'but do not shoot any human that comes out from the cave – one of them is the human we want.'

Stryax said nothing, but the nictitating membrane that slid across kroot eyes to protect them from wind and storm flicked back and forth in answer and his quills rattled gently in response.

Tchek had Krasykyl the Stalker covering the far side of the slope down to the cave mouth, while Cirict and Kliptiq waited further back, in the deeper shade under the rock.

The Shaper looked around. 'Where is Chaktak?' When silence greeted his question, Tchek moved beside Stryax and whistle-called for his Cut-skin, the sound high beyond the range of human hearing.

There came no answer.

Tchek called again, the string of high-frequency notes resonating from his quill crown. But still there was no reply.

The Shaper looked towards the Seeker. 'Where is he, Cirict?
Where do you smell him?'

The Seeker, the smallest and slightest of the kroot, crawled
forward to the edge of the bowl, head turning as he sought
scents on the still air.

Cirict turned to Tchek. 'His smell is… strange. It comes from
more than one direction, as if he is in many places. I will send
Flet higher, that he might see.' The Tracker turned his head up
and whistled, calling the pech'ra further towards the zenith,
and from below they saw the flash of its wings as it ascended.

As Obeysekera, Gunsur, Ensor and Lerin worked their way down
the mountain, advancing through rills and gullies, stopping
and covering while one man moved then proceeding down in
sequence, Obeysekera tried to raise Uwais and Chame on the
vox. There was no answer from either of them. But Uwais and
Chame were not the only ones missing.

'Anyone seen Amazigh?' Obeysekera asked.

The answers came back over the vox, all negative, and Obeysekera shook his head. The Kamshet was not his problem, and
he could not spare the time to search for him on a chaotic
battlefield where it was impossible to tell the position of the
enemy or even his own men. Besides, the mountain was tabu
to Amazigh and his people; perhaps he had disappeared to per-
form some rite to appease the mountain spirit.

Looking round from where he was covering Ensor, Obeysekera
could see the outcrops and slopes, the cross-cutting rills and
gullies, their edges all worn smooth, and he felt a shiver on the
back of his neck. If ever he had seen a mountain that might have
a presiding spirit, as machines had, then this was the mountain.

With Ensor safely under cover and surveying the surrounds through the sights of his hellgun, Obeysekera waved Gunsur past. That left him covering the rear of their descent. He watched Gunsur low-run down the slope, using outcrops and his body shape to stop himself presenting a clear target to any enemy.

The information Obeysekera had extracted from a deeply buried hypnocache told him that the kroot were adept at hand-to-hand combat, being stronger and faster than all but peak humans, but were also good at using long-range sniping rifles from concealed positions, almost always set high. There were no trees on the Tabaste, but there were many redstone outcrops that a kroot sniper might use. Obeysekera, rearguard, turned for a final check before going past Ensor but stopped, mid-turn.

Amazigh was there, finger held to his lips despite them being covered by his cheche. Dangling from his other hand were two ident tags.

'Where did you get those?' Obeysekera asked, and he slowly began to bring his hellgun round to bear on the Kamshet.

Amazigh shook his head, and whispered past his still-raised finger, 'No, no, no, master, I didn't kill them.'

Keeping his hellgun trained on the Kamshet, Obeysekera said, 'How did you get those ident tags, then?'

'Master, I know why the Tabaste is tabu – there is something terrible here. When the alien birds attacked, I set off to hunt them, to keep you alive. But as I tracked those xenos birds, I smelled something else. Flesh, raw flesh. But it was moving. So I went after it.' Amazigh hung his head. 'I was too late, master. It got to your troopers first.' The Kamshet held up the tags. 'Uwais and Chame.'

'What was it?'

'I do not know, master. I have seen nothing like it on Dasht i-Kevar.'

'What did it look like?'

'Knives. It looked like knives, master.'

'Did you see where it went?'

'Into the cave. There are tunnels.'

Obeysekera reached for his vox, but Amazigh held up his hand for another word.

'There is more than one of them, master.'

'Very well.' Obeysekera keyed the squad vox-channel. 'Uwais and Chame are dead. Looks like what got them came up from tunnels. Not kroot, repeat, not kroot.'

Throne, this mission was going bad. For a moment, a memory of the Sando retreat came back to him, and the disaster that had turned into. He had been determined never to let that happen again – but it already had. Four men gone. They had to get to the general quickly.

'Gunsur, Ensor, Lerin, stay out of cave entrances.' Obeysekera keyed the private channel to Malick. 'Sergeant, get out of the tunnel.'

But as he spoke, Obeysekera heard, from further down the mountain, the percussive clap of kroot rifle rounds. And through the vox, over the thrum of his hellgun, Malick was saying, *'We can't go anywhere right now, captain.'*

'Hold on and watch your backs. We're coming.' Obeysekera signalled to the three troops with him. Attack formation. Ensor at the tip, Lerin and Gunsur flanking. He would be the gun in the pocket between them all, the eye at the centre of the arrow.

Obeysekera looked at the slope. The rifle fire was coming from beyond the next ridge of redstone. If he were commanding the enemy, he would have a picket sited to pick off anyone coming over the ridge. But these were xenos: there was no telling what they would do. And time was of the essence. They had to get to the general before whatever was coming up the tunnels attacked from behind while they were trying to fend off the frontal xenos assault.

Captain Obeysekera keyed the squad vox.

'Charge!'

And the four Kasrkin, hellguns held ready, began to run down the redstone slope towards the enemy with the Kamshet running among them, his robes billowing like the wings of a great white bird.

CHAPTER 4

'They're trying to keep us pinned down.'

Sergeant Malick ducked back into the cave as kroot rifle rounds struck splinters of redstone from the tunnel entrance.

General Itoyesa nodded. 'They are succeeding.'

'Where is the captain?' said Roshant. 'We can't get out without him.' The commissar had wedged himself in behind an extrusion of rock that provided some cover deeper into the cave.

'We may have to try,' said General Itoyesa. He gestured down into the depths of the mountain. 'What is down there is worse than what is outside.'

'It would be suicide going out,' said Malick.

'I fear it will be worse if we stay,' said the general. He pushed forward towards the cave entrance despite Sergeant Malick's hand on his shoulder, and peered out into the bitter light of Dasht i-Kevar. Rifle rounds splashed on redstone, but General Itoyesa did not flinch.

'General, please, get back,' said Roshant. 'You are why we are here.'

Itoyesa pulled back, but he pointed out of the cave. 'I am why they are here.' He looked at Malick and Roshant. 'I have heard nothing from Captain Obeysekera since we took shelter. I do not know if he or his men are dead. We cannot retreat. Therefore, I must make a decision.'

General Itoyesa paused, his hand upon his mouth as he thought.

'Very well.' He looked at Malick and Roshant. 'The captain has ten minutes. If he does not arrive in that time, I will go out and surrender.'

Roshant stared at General Itoyesa. 'What? You cannot do that.'

The general turned to the commissar, smiling. 'You forget who is the general here.'

Roshant shook his head like a smacked dog, but he would not let go of this bone. 'I-I am a commissar of the Officio Prefectus. I cannot allow you to fall into the hands of the enemy.'

Itoyesa grinned. 'What are you going to do? Shoot me?'

Roshant turned his bolt pistol upon General Itoyesa. 'If I have to, general.'

Itoyesa stared at Roshant, then grinned more widely. 'You are not a man to shoot someone in the back, commissar. And that, although they have told you differently in the Officio Prefectus, is a good thing.'

Roshant swallowed, his bolt pistol wavering. 'Why would you do this?'

But before he could finish his question, the general knocked the barrel of Roshant's bolt pistol aside with one hand and pulled it from the commissar's grasp with the other, rotating it in one smooth movement so that he held it pointing between Roshant's eyes. Roshant gaped. The sound of his shock had yet to emerge from his mouth when Malick shoved his hellgun into Itoyesa's back.

'That might work with the commissar, but it won't work with me, general,' said Malick.

Itoyesa turned his head to look at Malick. 'I know it won't, sergeant.' He put the bolt pistol up, reversed it and handed it back to Roshant.

'I would not be surrendering, commissar, I would be giving us all the only chance we have. It is a long way out of the desert. There will be many opportunities for me to escape and for you to catch up and rescue me. That is the proper way for the Imperial Guard. Attack, attack, attack.' General Itoyesa drew his chrono. 'Still a few minutes before I go out.'

But as he spoke, Malick looked at the cave entrance, then started towards it, creeping low.

'You won't need to. The captain's here.' The sergeant pointed. From outside they could hear the unmistakeable thrumming hiss of hellguns, interspersed with the crack of kroot rifles.

# CHAPTER 5

Far, far below the mountain, deep, deep under the flowsand plain that surrounded the Tabaste, the lord Nebusemekh stood in front of a table. The table was large, although it seemed insignificant in the high, broad throne chamber in which it stood, and its sides were raised.

The table was filled with sand.

Nebusemekh sat down and sighed. He definitely sighed. He felt the air, drawn from his lungs, passing through his mouth. He felt it against his skin. He knew it was so.

The mound of sand was slowly settling, flowing down into the flat plain of yellow.

Nebusemekh sighed again. He had really thought that this time the orrery would endure. For a moment, when he had released the stasis field, he had seen it, perfect in every detail: an orrery as vast as the sky he had not seen for so long, with the eighteen planets and their attendant moons of this system, and its sun, with its white dwarf companion, all moving in the long, elaborate dance of the spheres set against the slow movement of the further stars and the galactic core. But then the first grains of sand had started to slip, and the planets and stars fell from the heavens and became simply mounds of sand on the table.

Nebusemekh shook his head, reminding himself to relish the tautening and release of the muscles that made the movement possible. The body was a marvel and one that he appreciated more fully than the other noble ones, with their talk of ascension. He, for one, would remain what he was.

Sighing, feeling the breath tickle his tongue, Nebusemekh began to sift the sand on the table, moving the grains he wanted to work with closer and pushing the others further away. Streams of sand wriggled over the huge tabletop, moving like things alive, as the necron lord sorted through his material. He was working on a twin hypothesis: that there was a critical molecular mass that triggered sand collapse, and that there was an ideal diameter for stable shape retention. He was testing the theories by gathering precisely one more grain of sand for each new iteration of the orrery, while simultaneously working through the range of possible diameters of sand particles. It was an absorbing experiment, one that had occupied him for a long time.

It was a straightforward matter for him to count each grain of sand and measure its diameter. As he did so, other parts of his mind, attuned to the workings of the world of which he was master, told him the story of what was happening, of the endless rows of his sleeping warriors, breathing slow and steady in their beds, waiting upon his summons, while he waited upon information from the search parties and expeditions he had sent forth.

It was true, they seemed to be taking a long time. But here, underground, time was hard to parcel: a day, a year, a second or a century, there was naught to tell between them. Simply grains of sand on a table.

It was, in any case, as well that the expeditions had not yet returned, for his experiments with sand were not over. Once he had stabilised the orrery, Nebusemekh would use it to study the patterns of the stars. As above, so below. By careful consideration of the aspects of the stars, and the relationship of the planets of his system to those stars, he would ascertain the most propitious moment to wake his sleeping soldiers and send them forth to claim that which he had temporarily laid aside: mastery.

The worlds and the stars were his.

As below, so above.

What others did not realise was that the ancient formula might be reversed. The perfect orrery was not merely a map, it was an engine. He would capture the heavens, bring them down into his throne room, and there... there, he would adjust them to better accord with his unerring sense of proportion. For instance, there was an irritating wobble in the orbit of the companion white dwarf that gave its motion an annoying lop-sidedness every three thousand and forty-two years. A small adjustment to the completed orrery and he would smooth out that wobble, giving the troublesome star the proper deference to its stellar master; at the moment, it gave the impression of being a generally reliable slave that would nevertheless habitually sneak away to consort with other low-minded individuals and then return to its master's service, the tale of its absence told in the weaving of its orbit.

And if that did not work, then he would send the white dwarf spiralling into the blue heart of its larger companion. There would be no wobbling then – although he would have to adjust some other aspects of the orrery in light of the increase in mass and radiation of the senior star. The calculations would be an interesting exercise of a few minutes.

Once he had established the most propitious time to reawaken his people, the mastery he was developing over sand would also be useful. For above his head was a world of sand. He had established that its sand could be used to raise fortifications of the most robust kind, able to withstand any attack. He had simply to find the correct formula. Then, when he woke his sleeping soldiers, they would march forth and create fortifications that no enemy would ever be able to destroy.

'Ha!' said Nebusemekh, enjoying the sound of his voice. 'Ha! Let those beetles of the sons of Amalekh chew on that.'

Nebusemekh counted out the next in the experimental series. Of course, the size of grains of sand varied, but the sand of his world was reasonably uniform. Although from looking at them he could see that they were not the cuboid shapes that would pack most completely into a space, but generally roughly spherical. Nebusemekh briefly congratulated himself on his eyesight, that enabled him to see single grains of sand.

Having worked systematically through his two parameters, he was halfway through the experiment. All in all, it was going well, although it was taking somewhat longer than he had expected.

As he counted the sand out for the next experimental iteration – automatically registering each grain by the diminution in mass, for his senses were so finely tuned that he could feel the change of a single grain of sand – Nebusemekh allowed his mind to wander in memory. He was, he knew, quite old, but that was no bar to his holding the memories of his childhood as clear as when they were first minted.

He remembered them, he was quite certain of that: castles built of sand, sometimes whole settlements, and also elaborate sculptures. Others had laughed when he told of his ambition to make use of silica, one of the most common substances in the galaxy, to create his fortifications and defences, but they would find their laughter stopped in their mouths – by large amounts of sand – when he came forth with his armies.

So long as the virus did not spread further.

Nebusemekh sighed. He hated when thoughts of the virus rose in his mind. It put him into a thoroughly bad temper. Nebusemekh put down his staff and examined his thoughts, going back over the sequence to establish where the bad memory had arisen and its cause.

There it was. Movements in the upper levels of his world.

Nebusemekh felt movements in his outer world as intimately as he felt movements in his inner world, for he was connected to it. He had ignored them as not worthy of attention, but now they had stirred up memories of the virus. Nebusemekh sighed anew, turned away from the table and walked across the empty thronelab to the datafall that streamed down the wall behind his throne. He felt the cold floor on his bare feet, enjoying the motion of his muscles.

Attention to every moment was, Nebusemekh had long realised, a broad avenue towards general health, physical as well as mental. By always being aware of his body, of the rushing of his blood, the beating of his heart, the flow of his breath, he remained in harmony with its rhythms and ensured their continuation – although it was true he now found it unaccountably difficult to sleep for his regular period.

Nebusemekh put his hand into the datafall and joined his mind to the Mind of the World.

There was the initial dislocation, as his mind absorbed the inputs from the World Mind, but it was only momentary. Really, it was only a matter of degree rather than scale: receiving the feedback from all the sensors of the World Mind barely engaged a tenth of his own brain.

Nebusemekh allowed the Mind of the World – a misnomer, really, since it was no more conscious than a robot – to oversee his men, asleep in their pods, and carry out the maintenance tasks that were necessary to keep his domain functioning, ready to follow his commands when he decided the time had come to act.

It was long since he had last engaged with the Mind of the World. He was not sure exactly how long as the one area in which his normal acuity seemed to have diminished was the measurement of the passage of time, but it had been a long time. He was surprised, re-engaging with the Mind, to see that some of the protocols to wake the sleepers had been initiated. While the sleepers themselves still slept, there were whole companies that were beginning to dream – the dreams themselves were the usual turgid churning of the unconscious – which put them only one stage away from full wakefulness.

Nebusemekh had not ordered this.

He asked – no, he *required* – an answer of the World Mind. The Mind simpered before him, as was right and proper. It had been so long since the master had deigned to speak to it and the World Mind had not wished to distract Nebusemekh from his vital experiments, so it had given thought to what to do about the virus that had begun to infect the sleepers.

'What do you mean, what to do?' asked Nebusemekh. 'It is simple. It is a virus. Disinfect, quarantine, isolate. That is how one deals with a virus.'

But it was not so simple as that, the World Mind told its master. It had done all those things, and yet the virus had spread. But it was the spread that was truly puzzling for the World Mind. For there was no connection between the hosts it had infected: they were sleepers in widely different locations and the Mind had found no connection between them. Yet, they were still infected.

'You are stupid. What are you?'

The World Mind admitted that it was indeed stupid. It asked of Nebusemekh that he enlighten its ignorance.

Nebusemekh snorted. 'Ignorance shall not be so easily excused. I charged you with stopping the virus spreading among my people and I can see you have utterly failed. When were you going to tell me? When I had lost all my people to this dreadful virus?'

The World Mind assured Nebusemekh that it would have alerted him long before that had come to pass, but it had fully expected such an eventuality to never arise, and as it knew he was engaged in important experimentation, it had not wanted to worry him. Might it enquire how the experiment was going? Had he succeeded?

'I am nearing the critical quantities. It will not be long now.'

The World Mind remarked how pleased it was at Nebusemekh's imminent success and asked to be told when the experiment reached fruition. It further remarked that anticipation of Nebusemekh's success had also inspired it to initiate some of the protocols to wake his people from their long sleep, that they might be able to put Nebusemekh's great plans into action that much sooner, it being a long process to wake the sleepers.

'That is an initiative I approve of on your part,' said Nebusemekh. 'However, it does not excuse you from your incompetence with respect to the virus. How many of my people have been infected and forgotten who they are and the service they owe me?'

The World Mind regretted that it did not have an exact number, but it was confident that it was less than a hundred.

'A *hundred*?'

Less than a hundred, the World Mind demurred.

'That is still too many,' said Nebusemekh.

The World Mind pointed out that Nebusemekh had billions of people.

'I remember the names of every one of them,' said Nebusemekh.

The World Mind remained delicately silent.

'Aabalekh. Aacamekh. Aadelekh. Aafasekh…'

The World Mind begged its master's pardon for even the slightest hint of scepticism and now understood that, of course, Nebusemekh knew the names of every one of his people.

'They are precious to me.'

As indeed they were to the World Mind.

'I am glad to hear that,' said Nebusemekh. 'I sometimes worry that, since you are a machine, you will not appreciate your fleshly charges.'

The World Mind averred that it would always care for Nebusemekh's people.

'Naturally. That is what you were made for. Now, you have still not given me a precise figure for the number of my people infected with the virus.'

The World Mind insisted once again that it did not have a precise number.

'You are a counting machine,' Nebusemekh pointed out. 'You are nothing but numbers. How can you not have a number for this?'

That was due to the World Mind not having an adequate definition for infection.

'What do you mean? They cease to follow my orders. That is clear enough.'

The World Mind pointed out that Nebusemekh had not actually issued any orders to his people for a considerable period of time, not since he had commanded them to sleep.

'Then that is straightforward. Any that are awake are infected.'

The World Mind agreed that that, in principle, was a straightforward way to calculate how many of Nebusemekh's people had been infected, but the problem was that when they became infected with the virus, they ceased to appear on its monitors, as well as causing other damage to its detecting systems, so that it became difficult to ascertain the status of the nearby tombs and their occupants.

'You mean that they disappear?'

That is exactly what the World Mind meant.

'Hmm.' Nebusemekh thought. 'That is interesting.' He called up the records of the most recent cases and studied them. 'It appears that the virus, together with the host, withdraws from our frame of reference, thus disappearing from your monitors. It would also explain why the infection appears to strike at random. While there is no spatial connection between the different chambers in which my people have been infected, there will be a connection through the other frames of reference within Hilberkh space that allows the infected to escape your monitors. In fact, it is possible that within these folded frames of reference in Hilberkh space whole dimensions may lurk, folded upon themselves. It may be that these are nascent universes, struggling towards birth and seeking energy to flare forth – the virus may be a way of drawing matter into itself. Even universes hunger.'

The World Mind thanked Nebusemekh for his valuable insights and promised to apply them to its future analyses. Was there any other reason that its honourable master had for deigning to speak with it?

Nebusemekh thought. There was something else he had meant to do, but what was it? He was about to withdraw from the connection with the World Mind when the memory returned to him, having travelled through all the accumulated memory banks of the World Mind before returning to its source.

'Ah, yes, I remember now. I felt some activity in the immediate environs of my citadel. I want you to scan for activity.'

The World Mind said it would of course comply, but that it might take a little time for it to reactivate those systems.

'Why did you deactivate the external sensors?'

The World Mind pointed out that it had done so under its master's explicit instructions but hoped that in its admitted tendency to understand thoughts literally, it had not misunderstood the true intention behind the command 'Turn off all external sensors.'

'When did I instruct you to turn off all the external sensors?'

The World Mind said that it was when the exterior world was dying; the precise moment was when the great sea beside which Nebusemekh had often walked began to dry out.

Nebusemekh said nothing in reply. But in his memory, he was again standing by the sea, looking out over its waves, standing on a beach covered with castles made of sand. It was the clearest memory he had.

Sometimes, it was necessary to die to live.

'It's hardly surprising that I did not wish to see that. But you should have known that I would want to be kept informed of any activity outside my citadel.'

The World Mind agreed that it should have known that, but admitted that, in fact, it had not. However, its external surveillance systems were now beginning to work and the master was welcome to look into the feeds and examine the world outside the citadel.

'I will do that,' said Nebusemekh. And for the first time in an age, he took his senses outside the great citadel he had had built to protect his people.

Multiple sensors fed data into Nebusemekh's mind. Visual data, taking in all the frequencies from low infrared to ultraviolet, and the non-visual frequencies down to radio waves and up to the high-frequency waves that travelled from other stars. Auditory data, listening down to the slow grindings of the planet to the shifting of single grains of sand. Olfactory data, tasting and smelling a world that was clean in a way few places were. And pressure data, telling the movement of rock and… and…

Nebusemekh stopped. He focused all his considerable mental resources on a single area of the mountain under which he had built his citadel – for the mountain had not been there before the citadel was made, but comprised the spoil that had been excavated to dig the refuge for his people.

There. Movement. Sound.

Life.

Nebusemekh began to laugh. The sound was strange. Its like had not been heard for many ages in the great halls under the mountain, and the walls themselves seemed to bend towards its source to hear the sound better.

Nebusemekh laughed for joy.

The World Mind enquired if it might know the reason for its master's merriment.

'Can't you see?' asked Nebusemekh, directing the feed he was absorbing to the attention of the World Mind. 'They have returned. Finally. The expedition I sent off to search for trace of the other citadels on this world has returned. After so long, they have come back.'

The World Mind asked, delicately, if Nebusemekh was quite certain that this was the expedition that he had sent off – the World Mind paused slightly as it examined its memory – sixty million years ago?

'Who else would it be?' asked Nebusemekh. 'Everything else above ground is dead.'

The World Mind admitted that was the case, but nevertheless it did seem the expedition had been gone for quite a long time.

'It is a big world. Much to explore.' But as Nebusemekh spoke, he saw something else appear in the sensors. 'What is this?' He turned his attention more fully towards the exterior of the citadel.

'The infected? I see some of the infected have got out of the citadel and they are trying to stop my brave explorers returning with the knowledge they have brought for me. This must stop!'

The World Mind agreed absolutely that the infected must be stopped.

'Then stop them!'

It would be honoured to do so, said the World Mind, but felt that it should remind Nebusemekh that if it engaged its external weapons systems to destroy the infected, it might also destroy the returning expedition.

'No, that won't do. What sort of welcome home would that be?' Nebusemekh paused, thinking. 'Wake some of my people. Tell them to go outside and rescue the search party from the infected and to bring them in.'

The World Mind mentioned, only in passing, that waking the sleeping was quite a lengthy process and by the time it was complete there might not be any members of the expedition left to bring into the citadel.

'Of course, it is not simply a matter of getting up from bed. Then we shall have to find another means of rescuing the expedition.' Nebusemekh looked at his sensory feeds again. 'I appear to have already lost some of them, although you must improve the maintenance of the external monitors – I can barely tell if any out there are still alive. We must find some way to rescue them.'

The World Mind enquired if its master might like to go out of the citadel to rescue the expedition as the master was already awake and of surpassing puissance.

'I?' asked Nebusemekh. 'I?'

The World Mind apologised for such a crass suggestion and hoped that the master would forgive its temerity.

'If I left my quarters, I might be infected by the virus,' said Nebusemekh.

The World Mind was aghast at such a possibility. It could open the gates near where the expedition was so that they might enter the citadel, although that would make it possible for the infected to enter the citadel as well.

'Doors do not stop the infected,' said Nebusemekh. 'Dimensional twists allow them to bypass doors.'

The World Mind admitted it should have realised that. But what about opening the gate to allow the expedition ingress?

'They are engaged in battle. The gates are deep in the tunnels – they would not see them open, even if they remember where to look. You must recall how long it has been since they left the citadel.'

Having apologised, the World Mind humbly asked if it might proffer another suggestion.

'You may.'

The World Mind asked if it might transport the expedition into the citadel.

'That is an excellent idea,' said Nebusemekh. 'Send them to me once you have made sure that they are not carrying the infection and have cleaned them thoroughly.'

The World Mind assured the necron lord that it would do so.

'Very well.' Nebusemekh withdrew his hand from the World Mind. The flow of inputs from its banks of sensors ceased; it was as if Nebusemekh had suddenly closed the door on a cacophonous party. He basked in the sudden sensory silence.

He still had his connection to the World Mind, although it was not so intimate: now a conversation rather than a communion.

'I have my experiment to complete. Bring the members of the expedition to me when they are ready.'

'Yes, my master,' said the World Mind.

Nebusemekh turned away from the datafall that was the surface of the World Mind and made his way back across the thronelab to where he was conducting his experiment in world making.

As he approached the table, Nebusemekh reviewed the progress he had made in his mind. He had made one hundred billion, nine hundred and fifty-three million, four hundred and thirty-three thousand, three hundred and forty-four experiments. There were still another possible eighty-eight billion, two hundred and thirty-three million, seven hundred and eighty-two thousand and thirty-two more possible iterations of the experiment before it was completely run.

Nearly there.

Nebusemekh picked up his staff and began arranging the sand. As always, he began the task excited with the anticipation that this time, this time, it would be different; this time he would find the exact mass and diameter of sand required to create stable structures.

As he divided the sand on his vast experimental table, Nebusemekh spoke to the World Mind.

'Have you brought the expedition home yet?'

'I... am... about to... do so,' said the World Mind, its reply less assured than normal. Nebusemekh surmised that it had diverted the greater part of its reasoning faculties into the systems required to disassemble a living creature down to its molecular level and then reacquaint that creature with itself.

'Bring them to me when they have recovered and you have ascertained that they are free from the virus.'

The World Mind assured him that it would do so. But as Nebusemekh arranged the sand, he was contemplating the unusual prospect of talking to another living, breathing creature. It had been a long time since he had done so.

Even if they were free from the virus, they would undoubtedly be vectors for any number of pathogens.

'Prepare an anti-bacteriological suit for me,' Nebusemekh told the World Mind. 'I will wear it when I welcome back the expedition. After all, one can't be too careful.'

'Absolutely,' said the World Mind. 'I have successfully brought the expedition back into the citadel. They seem a little disorientated at the moment, but that will no doubt wane as I carry out the necessary medical checks, master. I will tell you when they are ready for you to see them.'

'Yes,' said Nebusemekh. He was distracted. The sand was divided. Time to try again. 'I look forward to speaking to them. Now, I really think this time it might work.' He raised his staff.

Lifting from the table, moving in their stately, immemorial dance, the planets and the suns and the stars rose at his bidding and took their places in the celestial masque, their sand surfaces shimmering yellow-green under the play of the stasis fields Nebusemekh was wielding.

It was whole. A perfect model of the heavens, dancing to the music of gravity and the gentle melody that Nebusemekh introduced, turning their motion towards him that the very stars might bow before him in their dance. For, after all, he was as old as the stars.

He lifted his arms to acknowledge their obeisance. But as he did so, the stasis fields holding the stars and the suns and the planets in place slipped and, one by one, they crumbled and fell back to the ground.

'Never mind, master,' said the World Mind. 'It will work next time. Or the time after.'

'Or the time after that. Nothing worthwhile was ever achieved without effort.' Nebusemekh remembered the child who had played with sand on the shore of the sea many, many, many years ago. If the child could make buildings with sand, he, so much stronger and wiser than that child, would be able to make castles in the sky. He simply had to find the right sort of sand.

Besides, it meant that the memory would play again. And he enjoyed the memory more than anything in his current life. It somehow seemed more real, more vital.

Nebusemekh began to divide the sand again.

 CHAPTER 6

'Throne!'

The curse came through on Obeysekera's vox. He wanted to curse too, but he held his silence and turned, slowly, trying to see something, anything, in the dark.

'Where the frekk are we?' Another voice, the pitch rising, edging towards panic.

'Quiet!'

Obeysekera snapped the order over the squad vox-channel, looked to see if he had any auspex readings, but it was still all over the place: it seemed to think he was in among an apparently infinite set of energy sources, spreading to the limit of its detection capabilities. With the auspex providing no useful information, Obeysekera killed its light: even the faint illumination it used served to stop his eyes responding to the darkness into which they had been plunged.

'Who's here?' Obeysekera said into the vox. 'Call your names.'

'Gunsur.'

'Ensor.'

'Ha.'

'Lerin.'

Then, silence.

'Roshant, Malick, are you here?'

As Obeysekera spoke, there was a discharge of light, green and vivid, that left him more blinded than the darkness.

'Throne. Throne, Throne, Throne – Throne, Throne.'

The voice, coming through the vox and audible close by, was Roshant's. It was coming from where the darkness had been split by light.

'Roshant, quiet.'

'C-captain, is that you?'

'Yes. Anyone else with you?'

'Malick here. We have the general. Can't see nothing, sir.'

'None of us can. Stay where you are.'

Obeysekera turned slowly, looking, waiting for his eyes to adapt to the darkness. But there was nothing, not even the deeper shadows of a dark night. They were somewhere where there was no light.

'Not getting anything, captain.'

That was Malick.

Obeysekera listened. With no light, he could tell the rough direction from which Malick's voice came but not its depth: he could be below or above or level with him. There was something about the way the sound trailed away that told him they were in a large space.

A thought, nagging and unsettling. If he and all his men had been brought down here into the dark then what of the xenos they had been charging towards at the moment when the world cracked open in front of them and they fell through? Were they down here in the dark, too? Listening, fixing on the sound of him and his

troops? From the brief details of their physiology that Obeysekera
had seen, he suspected that the kroot had excellent eyesight.

But no eye, no matter how sensitive, could function in absolute
darkness. If they were down here, the kroot were as blind as he was.

A sound. Bat-squeak high, rising to a silence beyond the range
of his hearing. Obeysekera looked around, trying to locate its
direction. In the dark it felt far, but he had no means of checking
that. The darkness was so complete that his own body seemed
disconnected; it was as if he were a disembodied point of view,
a bodiless consciousness floating in the void.

The sound, however, was answered by another squeak rising
out of the range of his hearing.

Obeysekera whispered into the squad vox-channel. 'Anyone
else hear that? A high-pitched sound.'

'*I heard it,*' said Lerin. '*Can't tell from where.*'

'Sounded a long way off,' said Roshant.

'I heard nothing.'

Obeysekera did not recognise the voice, but its tone suggested
a man accustomed to being heard when he spoke: the general.

'Anyone else?' asked Obeysekera, ignoring the general's inter-
jection for the moment.

'This is nonsense,' said the general. Not being connected to
the squad vox-channel, he was speaking loudly to be heard.

If the kroot were here, Obeysekera thought, they would now
have confirmed that they were not alone. If he were their commander, he would deploy into a firing arc to allow concentrated
fire when they got some light.

'Quiet. Listen for movement.'

Without sight, Obeysekera put all his attention into hearing.

A rasp, like rough skin crawling over stone. Close.

He turned, searching for the source. Then, he realised he was
hearing the sound of his clothes moving over his skin as he

breathed, the faint creak of carapace plates shifting as his chest rose and fell.

He could hear his heart beat.

He could hear his blood beat.

In such silence, he should be able to hear the slightest movement, but there was nothing.

If he were the kroot commander, he would not even know which direction to send his troops, nor whether they walked on a plain or above an abyss.

Without light, he and his men were helpless. But unless the kroot had some other sense akin to a natural auspex, they would be helpless too. Without such a sense, not even the kroot could move in this absolute dark. Obeysekera scanned his memories in the hypnocache, but nothing came up from the xenos manuals suggesting that the kroot had such a facility.

If they were in the dark, they were lost as well.

A clang, metal on metal. Obeysekera and the rest of the Kasrkin spun towards the sound, bringing their hellguns to bear.

'Throne! Sorry, sorry, that was me.' It was Roshant's voice. 'I dropped something.'

'We need some light.' Obeysekera did not recognise the voice, but its air of command told him whom it belonged to.

'General Itoyesa?'

'Any of you soldiers have a lumen?'

Obeysekera felt himself twitch with annoyance at the general's insouciant assumption of command. That was something else that would have to wait until they had light.

'No, they're back with the Venators,' said Obeysekera.

He heard the *tsk* of the general's disapproval.

'At least I have a data-slate,' said Itoyesa. Obeysekera heard fumbling sounds as the general searched for it. 'Got it.'

The screen light stuttered on, bright – although Obeysekera

knew that anywhere else it would be barely visible – illumi-nating the general's hand and face. But before their eyes could adjust, the light faded away again.

'Throne,' said Itoyesa. 'Cell's dead.'

'What about this?' The voice belonged to Amazigh.

The light flared, flame high, from the cloth-wrapped torch he held up. Eyes, light-dazzled, looked outwards blearily, trying to see through the momentary blindness.

'Throne of Terra.' That was Malick.

He was saying what the rest of them were all thinking.

They were standing on a plain, a flat metal surface stretching further than the light could reach in every direction. But the plain was studded with vertical towers, reaching up beyond the light into the interminable dark, and the towers were slotted with sarcophagi, some head-on, some sideways-on. The light cast from Amazigh's torch was bright enough to shine through the crystal of the nearest sarcophagi. It shone through and then broke upon the creature within.

It was a creature of metal, a metal of silver and grey that, at the touch of the light, seemed to wrinkle and flow as if it were living skin. The head was a skull, bare of flesh, the body a cage of metal ribs and its limbs struts of steel. Beside it in the clear coffin was a weapon: the label *Gauss flayer* presented itself to Obey-sekera's mind from a suddenly activated hypnocache. Stacked above the sarcophagus was another, and another, and another, on up into the dark above them.

'Necrons.'

The voice was Roshant's; the name, redolent with death, came from them all.

As if in response to the pool of illumination cast from Amazigh's torch, the space in which they found themselves began to light up. It was dim at first, a faint green fluorescence from the clear caskets in which the metal shapes lay. Then lights started to switch on above the sarcophagi, illuminating the strange characters that were inscribed upon the heads of the caskets. The livid green light reflected off the gun-grey metal, giving it a sheen of viscous life like the scum upon a stagnant pool, and then reached out into the great space of the hall.

One by one, the tomb towers started to light up. Huge columns of necrons, ascending to heights beyond their sight: heights lost in the green glow that began to spill from every surface, reflected and refracted. Staring upwards at the tomb towers that rose above them, Obeysekera thought he could see movement in the heights – many-limbed creatures crawling over the stacks of sarcophagi, stroking the crystal caskets with their metal limbs.

Tomb spyders. He had fought them before. Non-organic creatures with somewhat limited artificial intelligence that saw to the maintenance and defence of the necron tombs and their inhabitants. Their function was similar to the white blood cells in a human body: to identify intruders and destroy them.

Looking up at the tomb tower disappearing above his head, each step containing another necron warrior, Obeysekera realised that they had virtually no chance of getting out of this alive.

He turned round, looking into the distance, searching for whether the hall stretched as far horizontally as it seemed to stretch vertically. Through the ranks of tomb towers he could see no sign of a wall, nor of any ending to the hall.

'Where in the Emperor's name have you brought me?'

Obeysekera brought his gaze back from the distant green reaches of the hall to the man, also green-tinted, standing in front of him, bristling with disdain.

'General Itoyesa,' said Captain Obeysekera. 'I would appreciate you keeping your voice down.'

'You have no authority to tell me what to do,' said the general, bristling even more. He was a stockily built man with the marks of some of his campaigns visible in livid scar tissue on his cheek and an augmetic left hand that was opening and closing convulsively, as if wishing to crush Obeysekera's windpipe. 'I say again, where the frekk have you brought me?'

'I have not brought you anywhere,' said Obeysekera. 'We have all been brought here.' He gestured around him. 'Unless I am very much mistaken, we appear to have been brought down into a necron tomb.'

'How are you going to get me out then?' asked General Itoyesa. 'You were sent to find me and bring me back to headquarters. Carry out the second part of your orders, captain.'

'Those were not all my orders, general.'

'What else do you have to do?'

Captain Obeysekera stared at the general, not retreating before his indignation. 'Obeysekera,' he said slowly.

The general stared at him. 'Pardon?'

'My name is Obeysekera. Captain Obeysekera.'

'Whatever your name is, what are you going to do to get me out of here?'

'What we Kasrkin are trained to do, general – recon, plan, act.' Obeysekera gestured towards the rising tomb towers. 'We are at the recon phase here, general. If you would excuse me.'

The captain turned away from the general. It was a calculated movement, designed to either silence Itoyesa or to draw him into a confrontation that only Obeysekera could win.

'Sergeant Malick.'

'Yes, sir.'

Behind him, Obeysekera could hear the general puffing with impotence but choosing to hold his peace for the moment.

'Form a perimeter – we don't know if the kroot were brought down here too.'

While Malick dispatched Lerin, Ha, Ensor and Gunsur to sentry positions, Obeysekera turned to Amazigh. The Kamshet was still holding the torch in his hand, although the light from it was no longer necessary. He stared up at the towers, with wonder turning to dread.

Feeling the gaze, Amazigh brought his gaze down and looked at Obeysekera.

'Now I know why the mountain is tabu.'

'It also explains the anomaly that affects the machine-spirits of all our equipment around here.' Obeysekera stepped closer to the Kamshet. 'You have served me faithfully since the Mother gave you to me – now I ask a further service. You are light of foot and skilled in remaining unseen – see if the kroot are here too.'

The Kamshet looked around at the tomb towers rising into the dark, and the livid light that filled the spaces in between them.

'You want me to go out into that? On my own?' Amazigh shook his head. 'They are tabu. I cannot go among them.'

Obeysekera saw General Itoyesa turn towards them, his mouth opening to speak, so to forestall him the captain stepped closer to the Kamshet and put his hand on the man's shoulder. Leaning close to Amazigh, so that he could see the man's eyes beneath his cheche, their blue tinted ocean green by the tomb light, Obeysekera whispered, 'We are all scared here. If we are to escape, we must accept the fear, for it will stop us doing anything stupid, but we must not let it master us. I know that the fear will not master you, Amazigh.'

'The Mother sent me with you as punishment. It is become a greater punishment than I ever feared.'

'Then when I return you to her, she will learn what you have done, and she will give you due place among your people.'

As Obeysekera whispered, Amazigh began to nod his head, understanding what was asked of him and the honour that would be his should he achieve it and return to the tribe. Obeysekera saw him looking sidelong at the rising tomb towers. It was the returning back to his tribe that was difficult to envisage, surrounded by countless sleeping necrons.

'They are sleeping. You are quieter than the wind – you will not wake them. Now, go, but not far – any movement will carry a long way in this silence. If the kroot are here, you will soon hear them.'

Amazigh nodded again. 'I-I will go,' he said.

'Thank you,' said Obeysekera. 'For you go of your own will and not by my order.'

The Kamshet drew his cheche tighter around his head and then turned. Like a wisp of mist, he disappeared among the tomb towers, passing out between the silent guard of Obeysekera's remaining men.

Obeysekera turned to see General Itoyesa staring at him.

'I have never seen an officer of the Astra Militarum *ask* one of his men to do something before, Captain Obeysekera.'

'As you might remember, Amazigh is not one of my men, general. I have no authority to order him to do anything.'

General Itoyesa snorted and drew his bolt pistol. 'This is the only authority these tribals respect or understand, captain, and the sooner you realise that the better. Most of them are only one step from barbarism. Without our presence, before you knew it they would be offering up children as sacrifices to heathen gods. A good taste of bolter fire is what they need to keep them honest. Not like our Guard.'

As the general spoke, Obeysekera was scanning their surroundings, still looking for movement. There was nothing on the ground level, but above he could see the spyders moving up and down the columns, wicked-looking creatures of metal and spikes. So far, they were showing no signs of moving towards them, but he was wary. Killing a creature that was not in any real sense alive would be no easy task, even for a Kasrkin hell-gun. Living creatures bled out; wounds slowed them down or incapacitated them. It was not the same with those made of metal. They had to be disassembled, blown apart piece by piece, and even then they could continue operating far beyond the limits of any organic creature.

Roshant took a step towards Itoyesa, breaking Obeysekera from his thoughts.

'It is my task, as an officer of the Officio Prefectus, to ensure that tribals adhere to the Imperial cult, general,' said Roshant.

Itoyesa turned to the young commissar. 'You're Erahm's boy, Kirpal? Blowed if I could see the likeness before, but now I can. Your father was always prickly about his privileges – as the father, so the son, they say, and in this case they say truly.'

Roshant took another step forwards, all the while staring at the general. 'My other orders, before we return, are to ascertain if you have been compromised. If I decide that you are tainted, then I am to ensure that you do not return.' He placed a hand upon the bolt pistol at his hip. 'I will shoot you if I have to.'

Roshant hissed the words at the general from only a few inches distance, but Obeysekera heard the venom and the promise in the threat: Roshant meant every word he said.

The general knew it too. He raised his arms in placation.

'I know you will,' said Itoyesa. 'But you have no need to.'

'Commissar, calm,' said Obeysekera. 'Please.' He glanced around. Those spyders were starting to come closer. 'We want to get the general back alive if we possibly can.'

'Do we indeed?' said Roshant. 'I don't think my father would be sorry to see the back of "Butcher" Itoyesa, the general who lost more troops taking planetoid HS-512 than the enemy lost defending it.'

'Your father ordered me to capture that planetoid whatever the cost. I succeeded in my brief.'

'Then you must have missed the bit where it said casualties should not reach ten per cent of the operational troops.'

General Itoyesa stared at Roshant. 'Those deaths are burned into my conscience. I am responsible for them. But so is your father. There was a deadline for the taking of the target, a deadline that, if I broke it, would cause the unravelling of all your father's strategic plans. I told him, when he set me the task, that you can have victory or you can set injury targets – you cannot achieve both at the same time.'

'My father does both. He wins victories and preserves his men.'

'He sets the frekking timetables! Of course he can do both – he gives himself the time. His staff, and their armies, are not given such luxuries. Good public relations for a lord militant – make sure your generals are the ones who get labelled "butcher".'

'My father takes his objectives faster than any of his generals.'

Itoyesa grimaced. 'He does that with the aid of so much of the Imperial Navy that he might as well confine his crusade to the space between the stars. The rest of us wake up in the watches of the night hearing the screams of the men we sacrificed on the altar of your father's reputation.'

At these words, Obeysekera stepped forward, laying his hand on the general's arm, but Itoyesa shook it off.

Roshant blinked. He looked down, then back up at the general.

'My father will be interested to hear what you truly think of him.'

General Itoyesa opened his mouth as if to speak, then stopped. He shook his head, looking away into the green dark.

'It matters not. It is not likely that you will ever have the chance to tell him.'

'It is my task to see that you both report back to the lord

militant,' said Obeysekera. He gestured to the stacked caskets. 'They sleep. So long as they continue to sleep, we may hope to find a way out of here.' Obeysekera looked to the general and the commissar. 'We must escape – the lord militant must learn that there is a necron tomb under the Sand Sea.' He focused his regard on General Itoyesa. 'To that end, I am in command of this mission, general.' Obeysekera reached for his pocket. 'I have it in writing if you wish to confirm it for yourself.'

General Itoyesa sighed. 'Do you wish to humiliate as well as rescue me, captain?'

'Not in the slightest, general.'

Itoyesa paused, breathing deep. He closed his eyes for a moment, then, opening them, looked at Captain Obeysekera.

'Very well. But now, since you are in command, tell me – which way should we go?' He gestured into the green depths. 'How are you going to get me out of here?'

'You are pointing in the wrong direction, general.' Obeysekera gestured up. 'We are deep. To get out, we will have to climb.'

'Those things?' Itoyesa gestured at the tomb towers. He shook his head. 'Can't think of a better way to wake the sleepers.'

'No, not that way, if we can help it. There must be service ramps and tunnels. We have to find them.'

'Tell me when you do.' General Itoyesa stalked away towards where Sergeant Malick kept guard at the dark base of a tomb tower.

Obeysekera and Roshant watched him go.

Then, over their private channel, Roshant spoke. 'I didn't know you had written orders giving you authority over higher ranks.'

'I don't,' said Obeysekera.

CHAPTER 7

Shaper Tchek turned his head one way then the other, seeking to locate the sound.

It was the whistle signal from the Long-sight, Stryax, informing them that he had found the humans, but amid the distorting echoes of the tomb towers it was all but impossible to tell which direction the signal came from.

Tchek whistled back, telling Stryax to signal again, but there was no immediate reply.

The Shaper looked around, his unease growing even greater. To have been brought down into this place by some dark magic was bad enough, but what they had seen when the dark withdrew had been worse than he imagined.

The kroot communed with the dead. But these things of metal that lay stacked about them in columns reaching up to the heights were neither living nor dead, but abominations. His soul revolted against them, bile rose in his throat, and he, a Shaper, retched, dry-choking on the dust of their counterfeit of life.

All the Kinband could taste the canker in the still air, the poison in the livid, green light, but for the Shaper it felt as if he were being painted on the inside with cancer. His only recourse was to speed his breath, circulating the air through his lungs and air sacs faster, trying to flush the green from his system.

How he breathed was a relic of his avian past, when the ancestors of the kroot had flown through the forests of Pech, the air passing in a one-way system in, through and out of the body, ensuring that stagnant air never accumulated in the deep passages of the lungs but instead was washed through by every breath, like water scouring a channel clean rather than rising and receding waves leaving a sludge at their limit.

But even so, Tchek tasted the taint in the air, metal and flesh.

He looked around at the sarcophagi and their metal occupants. The Song, the continuing Song that was the history of the kroot, a Song of sound and communion, told of the kroot world Caroch and the deadly disease that had infested the kroot there who had attempted to learn the minds and purposes of their metal enemies by the Feast. The Shapers on Caroch, hard-pressed by the necron onset, had feasted upon the metal flesh of some of their foes, only for their own flesh to be consumed, eaten from within by infestations of nanoscarabs, which then burst from the hollowed-out bodies of the Shapers, infecting many Kinbands.

The Song, preserving the memory of Caroch, told all Shapers that the metal flesh of the necrons was deadly; it was tabu, forbidden them.

Looking at the gleaming metal skull in the crystal coffin, Tchek felt himself gagging again. The thought of feasting upon metal flesh choked him.

He heard the whistle signal again and it dragged him back from the cloying horror of the sight of the non-living necron sleeping in its coffin, to what he had promised the t'au the Kinband would bring them: the human general. Stryax was calling him.

Tchek responded again, then looked to the remaining members of the Kinband, strung out in skirmish formation between the towers of the sleepers.

'Where do you hear Stryax calling from, Cirict?'

The Tracker, ahead of Tchek in the formation, turned his head, listening as the whistle signal refracted through the towers, then pointed an uncertain finger in the direction he judged, about thirty degrees ahead.

Tchek looked back down the formation. 'You, Krasykyl?'

The Stalker pointed ahead too, but at a narrower angle. But Tchek heard the Long-sight coming from the right, at ninety degrees, rather than ahead at thirty.

'Stay where you are,' Tchek whistle-signed back to Stryax. 'Keep the humans in view.'

The Shaper looked in the two directions, uncertain which to choose. In the end he pointed directly between the two, at sixty degrees to their direction. This way, they should soon be able to tell who was right from whether Stryax's signals were coming from their left or their right. Tchek tightened his grip on his rifle. He wanted to get the human they had been sent to find and then get out of this accursed place as soon as possible, before his insides turned green and he went metal grey.

Cirict the Tracker had taken the lead, slipping between the tomb towers with his body held low and forward, rifle held ready, his pech'ra flying quietly above him. But Tchek saw how the Tracker's crown quills were beginning to glow green in this livid underground light. He suspected his own crown quills were doing the same, probably more so because, as the Shaper, his nature was to absorb information from the environment that he might better know that which would be most useful for the Kinband to feast upon.

'Keep calling,' Tchek whistle-signed to Stryax, and the Long-sight replied. The replies were getting clearer now but, turning his head, he still could not tell which flank to head towards: if anything, Stryax seemed to be directly ahead.

'That way,' said Tchek, pointing ahead.

Cirict was already moving in the right direction. Tchek looked at Krasykyl and then, doubtfully, at the next tomb tower. Did he want the Stalker climbing these towers of the metal sleepers? By doing so, would Krasykyl run the risk of waking them? Tchek looked around. If the necrons started waking, there would be no hope for them.

'Stay on the ground,' Tchek told Krasykyl.

The Stalker whistled his understanding, the sound tinged with relief. Krasykyl would have climbed the tomb tower without demur if the Shaper had asked him, but the Stalker was glad that the demand was not being made of him.

Stryax's whistle signal was still coming from ahead, but it was not getting any louder. It was likely being blocked by the intervening towers.

Tchek looked up. There were times when he was almost glad that his ancestors had sacrificed their wings. Crawling over the tomb towers, and scuttling along the connecting gantries and cables, were metal spiders, hundreds of the things, stopping every now and again and resting, thrumming, upon a metal thread high above. Surely the metal spiders must see them? But if so, they gave no sign.

Tchek looked down from the metal spiders to his own rifle. He checked the ammunition. He was not sure that rifles firing solid rounds would have the slightest effect on the metal spiders, much less upon the metal soldiers that lay in their caskets, but they were all he had.

Tchek whistle-signed again. 'Where are you?'

Stryax replied, the sound a thin squeak above the silence of the tomb. It still sounded straight ahead to Tchek.

'Ahead?' he asked Cirict.

The Tracker looked up to the pech'ra then shook his head, pointing at thirty degrees to their direction of travel.

'You, Krasykyl?'

'Shaper, I know it does not make sense, but that is where I hear him.' And he pointed at the same sixty-degree angle that he had indicated before, only this time their direction of travel had changed substantially.

It was as if Stryax were circling round to flank them. Why would he do that?

Before Tchek could answer the question, there came another whistle signal from Stryax, this one more urgent and louder.

'Smell, ahead, tracking closer.'

'What sort of smell?' Tchek whistled back.

'The smell of dead meat,' said Stryax. 'Getting stronger.'

Tchek remembered the report of the creatures of rotting flesh that had attacked them above, on the mountain.

'Withdraw.' He had already lost Chaktak. He did not want to lose another of the Kinband, particularly with the humans still to be dealt with.

'The smell is closer,' Stryax whistled.

'Withdraw,' Tchek answered urgently. 'Withdraw to us, we will cover you.'

'Withdrawing,' Stryax replied. A pause, then, 'The smell is very close now.'

'Stryax, withdraw.'

From ahead, there came the sound of metal on flesh, the dull sound that it makes as it bites into skin and muscle and bone. Tchek froze, listening. The rest of the Kinband turned to the sound, their crown quills rising in alarm but their rifles steady in the direction of the noise.

They had all heard enemy die before, each with their own distinctive sound at their ending. But they also knew the sound of death when it came for kroot. The kroot died with the death song, the rattle of their crown quills as mortality sucked the pneuma from their bones and flesh. They heard the death rattle now, and knew that Stryax was gone from them, his pneuma flown.

But after his death rattle, they heard a new sound, a liquid ripping, a tearing as of bark from a green tree.

Tchek gestured to what remained of the Kinband, Krasykyl, Cirict and Kliptiq, to move into skirmish formation: they had lost a nestling. They would feast and take the strength of Stryax and his killer to themselves.

Tchek pointed up. They needed height, whatever the risk of the tomb towers. Krasykyl slung his rifle over his shoulder and began to climb, swarming up over the coffins, his sharp, clawed fingers finding easy purchase on the sepulchres. Tchek signalled Cirict forward but kept Kliptiq behind him; the Bearer was too clumsy for the stealthy approach the Shaper intended. But once he found the enemy that had killed Stryax, he would bring the Bearer forward so that he might feast too.

Tchek crept forward himself, staying in the lee of the towers, moving in the direction of where he had heard the death of Stryax. Advancing, he heard further noises, quieter now but just as grotesque: the sounds of butchery. Sawing, slicing, the crack of joints disjointed. There was part of the Shaper that did not want to see what he was going towards. But Stryax was a nestling: he had fed from the same pot, partaken of the same Feasts; they must save him for the Feast, that he not be lost to them.

The sounds were closer now.

Tchek whistled to Krasykyl and Cirict, 'What do you see?' He did not ask them what they smelled, for his olfactory centres were thick with the iron tang of blood and the bile of spilled intestines.

'Behind the next tower,' said Krasykyl. 'Movement, but I can't see what.'

'Cirict?'

'Flet tells me it's there, but I can't see anything either.'

'Flank it on your side. I will come round on the other. Krasykyl, cover from above. Kliptiq, wait my command.'

The Bearer whistled his understanding. He alone of the kroot gave no sign of the deep unease the rest of them were feeling; a hint from Tchek and they would all have turned and retreated without claiming Stryax for the final Feast. But Tchek had lost nestlings before and been unable to render to them the service of the final Feast, and the shame of it still clung to him, marked upon his crown quills in livid guilt stripes. He would not leave Stryax unclaimed.

With Cirict moving up, and Krasykyl covering him from above, Tchek slowly moved forward, inching around the base of a tomb tower, his attention so focused ahead that he did not notice the metal abomination lying in its coffin alongside him. Tchek peered around the edge of the tomb tower, his rifle steady in his hands, ready to be raised to firing position.

But he did not raise his rifle.

He stared, and his gorge rose, and the horror rose before his eyes and he could not close them however he tried.

For he saw Stryax. He saw what had been Stryax, his face and his flesh, his limbs and his body pinned upon a metal frame in a mockery of life. The kroot's skin had been flayed from his body; now it hung, in limp, still-bloody folds, over the metal skeleton of a necron. Before his horrified gaze, Tchek saw the necron paint itself with Stryax's blood, anointing itself at wrist and neck and ear. Stryax's face, stripped from his head, was stretched, lopsided, over the necron's counterfeit skull, a metal forgery of true life, the holes where the Long-sight's eyes had been falling one over the necron's cheek, the other on its forehead. Stryax's empty mouth gaped, the jaw skin sagging down over the necron's neck. The rest of the Long-sight's body it had stuffed over its metal frame, pushing bloody bones between its own limbs and hanging flesh over its shoulders as grisly epaulettes.

'No,' Tchek whispered. 'No, no.'

The creature, the abomination, was still butchering what remained of Stryax, struggling to incorporate his entrails and remaining limbs into its own frame, while at the same time it was trying to hang the Long-sight's legs around its neck. But as Tchek watched, frozen in his horror, he saw movement, grey and rust red through the livid green. Another of the flesh-clad horrors was approaching and, as it came nearer, Tchek saw that it too wore a skin pelt but its face was a caricature of a human, mouth open in a never-ending scream.

'What is it?'

The whistle, quiet with horror, came from Cirict's direction.

'Flayed One,' said Tchek.

'Can we kill it?' asked Cirict.

'I do not know,' said Tchek.

But as he whistle-answered, the creature's head came up from its butchery work. The second Flayed One stopped. The two metal abominations slowly turned their skin masks towards him.

'They can hear us.' Tchek whispered the realisation, horror rising further within him. For there was something fundamentally wrong about these metal creatures; he could taste it. As Shaper of the Kinband, he was driven to seek new Feasts as much by the taste of new creatures to commune with as by any rational calculation that by communing with them the Kinband would acquire useful skills and knowledge. Indeed, according to the song history of his people, the greatest among the Shapers, those who had led them from the trees to the freedom of thinking, had done so by taste, smelling their way towards what they would become.

Everything in Tchek revolted against the smell/taste of these flesh-clothed metal creatures turning to look at him. In his throat, in his olfactory organs, their smell combined the fleshy rankness of cancer tumours with the slip-iron taste of metal. They were everything Tchek would put away from the Feast.

They made him sick.

Retching – something a kroot did very rarely – Tchek began to fall back, trying to get behind the cover of the tomb tower so that the flesh-metal creatures could not see him. He looked up and around, searching for Cirict and Krasykyl.

But he could not see them, although Kliptiq was waiting where he had been told to remain, still carrying the communal pot that united the Kinband in the Feast. Tchek signed Kliptiq to retreat, but the Bearer stared at him uncomprehending.

'Where is Stryax?'

'Dead,' hissed Tchek. 'Get back.'

'But we cannot leave him, we must eat him.'

'Something already has.'

Kliptiq stared at the Shaper, his crown quills bristling. 'Then we must eat that which ate Stryax.'

'Not these, never these.' Tchek turned and pointed past the tomb tower to where the metal abominations squatted over the remains of the Long-sight. 'They are cancer, walking.'

Kliptiq looked to where Tchek was pointing. His crown quills bristled higher, but the colours catching upon them told of the Bearer's fear and revulsion. He turned to go.

'Wait,' said Tchek. 'We must remain together. There may be others.'

He risked a whistle-call, the signal to bring Cirict and Krasykyl to his position. The Tracker and the Stalker answered his call, song-whistling that they were on their way. But Tchek, watching the metal creatures, saw them stop the butchery again at the whistle-calls, pause and turn in the sound's direction.

The Flayed Ones slowly stood. They were both clothed in ragged skin suits, the faces of the dead hanging as slack masks over metal skulls, organs and intestines arrayed as leaking jewellery, belts and buckles.

'Quick!' Tchek whistle-called again.

The Flayed Ones, heads rotating like metal sensors, turned towards him, even though the Shaper was hidden behind a necron sarcophagus. In the gloom, Tchek saw livid green behind the empty eyes of their skin masks.

From the left, Tchek heard Cirict, his movements soft but near. From above, the quick scramble of Krasykyl, descending so fast he was almost falling.

The Flayed Ones started to move, heading towards the Shaper, their metal skeletons giving a terrible caricature of life to the flesh layered over the metal bones.

Tchek raised his rifle. Beside him, without needing telling, Kliptiq did the same. The Flayed Ones came on, metal sounding on metal. How could they kill something that was not alive?

They would have to find a way.

'Fire,' Tchek whispered.

The two kroot rifles fired together.

Tchek, squinting along the barrel of his rifle, followed the track of the round he had loosed. If his aim was true – and his aim was almost always true – the round would strike the first of the abominations in the centre of its torso, where its heart would have been if it had the humanoid heart that its basic layout suggested.

The round struck true. Tchek, his gaze focused in on the centre of the Flayed One's chest so that it appeared as if it were standing right in front of him rather than being over a hundred yards away, saw the skin suit rupture as the rifle round punched through it. The creature staggered, falling backwards, as the kinetic energy of the strike was transferred into its metal frame. With the less focused vision of his wider sight, Tchek saw the other abomination stagger too, as Kliptiq's rifle round struck home. A moment later, the sound of the twin impacts reached them, slightly syncopated metallic clangs deadened by layers of flesh.

Tchek's crown quills began to brighten, moving up through the spectrum towards the victory display of shades of mauve and ultraviolet.

But then the abominations steadied. They steadied and they did not fall. Even though both had taken what for any unarmoured creature of flesh and blood would have been mortal wounds, they did not fall but rather looked to each other, seeking silent understanding; and then the two skin-suited skulls turned back to where the bullets had come from.

The Flayed Ones started moving again, but they were picking up the pace with each step they took, moving faster, moving towards running, their metal feet ringing out the quickening rhythm on the metal floor.

'Fire again,' Tchek said. 'For the head.'

Now, with the Kinband caught up with the attacking enemy, the horror and fear were in abeyance. Now, there was only doing.

Tchek's rifle flared fire and combustion gases. Kliptiq's, beside him, did the same. But there were two other shots: from above, Krasykyl, and from the left, close by now, Cirict fired too. Four rounds slammed into the Flayed Ones, two volleys of two, and the first stopped their advance while the second knocked the creatures from their feet onto the metal floor.

'Fall back,' Tchek ordered, not waiting to see if the Flayed Ones were dead, but determined to take what advantage he could of their being flat on their backs.

Kliptiq started retreating, moving backwards with his rifle still covering the direction of the danger.

'Krasykyl, Cirict, you too,' instructed Tchek as the Stalker and the Tracker reached him, Krasykyl jumping the final five yards down from the tomb tower, arms spread wide as if he still had the power of flight that his ancestors had once possessed.

They pulled back in skirmish formation, leaving Tchek as rearguard. Tchek saw the Flayed Ones start to move. He observed as their legs, lying upon the floor, twitched before the creatures slowly sat up again.

In one, the caricature of a human face had all but disappeared, the skin mask pierced and then ripping so that half the face hung loose, revealing the metal skull beneath. In the other, the one that wore Stryax, the face mask was less ripped; it might almost have been the Long-sight looking at him, save for the green fire in the eyeholes and the way the face sat awkwardly, as if it were stretched upon bone it was not meant for. But there were two holes in the face mask and its metal hand went to its face, as if feeling for injury, and its fingers found the holes, one on the cheek, the other above the nose, where the skin had been pierced by the weapons of its enemies.

Tchek saw the second creature turn to the first, its fingers also reaching up to the holes in the skin mask.

The two creatures turned in unison and looked towards where Tchek stood, hiding behind a tomb tower. They screamed together, their voices metal hymns of madness and, rising from the ground, they started towards the Shaper, their dead feet clanging upon the metal floor.

Tchek turned and ran back in the same direction that the rest of the Kinband had taken. Noise flared on either side of Tchek as the Kinband fired past him, covering his retreat. The volley, directed at the leading creature, stopped it completely, then dropped it to its knees, and the second volley knocked back the following creature but did not send it to the floor.

'How do we kill these things?' Krasykyl asked Tchek as the Shaper retreated past him.

'I do not know. Knock it down again.'

Krasykyl fired off another round, with Cirict adding to the volley, knocking the abomination over once more. It lay there a moment without moving, giving them the sudden, surging hope that they had killed it, before it jerked into its caricature of life and sat up, livid green eyes turned towards them.

'Fire.'

All four kroot fired again as the creatures rose, but this time the Flayed Ones had braced themselves: they did not fall but leant into the strikes as if they were walking into a strong wind. And like that, they began to advance, taking the rounds as they came onwards, the bullets jerking them but no longer knocking them over.

'What do we do?' asked Cirict.

'Keep shooting,' said Tchek. 'They will die. They… will… die.'

But they did not.

The Flayed Ones kept coming on, even as the bullets shredded their skin suits and sent broken bits of bone scattering around them. Sparks flew as rounds hit, sometimes jerking the Flayed

Ones, sometimes barely affecting their progress. The creatures pushed into the metal rain and, as they approached and the rain grew harder, parts began to break from their bodies. One went down, its knee shattered, then got up and hobbled forward, its leg askew. The other lost most of its hand, its head hung crooked upon its neck, but still it kept on, walking into the metal deluge. They advanced, reaching the tomb tower behind which Tchek had taken cover when he had first seen them.

A shot, Tchek was not sure if it was from his rifle, went wide, striking the crystal cover of the sarcophagus at the base of the tomb tower.

The crystal shivered, as if alive, then cracks began to appear over it, spreading out from where the bullet had struck it, sending new lines out wherever a crack angled. Gas started to escape from inside the casket, the green-lit gas that bathed the sleeping necron. The crystal cover, rendered opaque by the density of cracks over it, shattered, raining down upon the sleeper within.

The two abominations stopped where they were. They turned towards the necron lying still and exposed in its coffin beside them and, reaching out, ran their metal fingers over its exposed skeleton. One of the Flayed Ones bent over the sleeping necron. From where Tchek was standing, watching in mute horror, it seemed that the creature was breathing into the face of the necron in stasis – only, it could not breathe. Then the abomination leaned further down into the casket and, with the skin and flesh it had taken from Stryax, pressed its forehead against the sleeping necron's.

Tchek, revolted, stepped back, averting his eyes, but Krasykyl grabbed his arm and pointed.

'Look,' the Stalker whispered.

Krasykyl did not need to point. Tchek could taste the change in the thick, heavy air. It was the smell of cancer and rust, of the auto-destruction of flesh and metal. He turned back to look at what was happening at the casket.

The Flayed One was still bending over the prone necron, mouth joined to mouth. Although the posture was the same, it was no kiss. The necron began to tremble. Gently at first, barely perceptible to ordinary vision, the crystal fragments from its broken tomb that lay scattered over its prone form started to vibrate.

The sleeping necron was waking up.

The second of the Flayed Ones, clad in torn human skin, was leaning over the prone necron too, its body shaking as if in the grip of a fever although it could know no temperature other than that of its surroundings. Through the ripped skin of its human face mask, it was looking down at what was happening. Its metal skull was immobile and incapable of expression, yet everything about its stance and attitude told Tchek that it was gripped by a surpassing excitement, almost to ecstasy.

Kliptiq put his hand on Tchek's shoulder.

'Can we go? We should go.'

The Shaper knew that the Bearer was right: they should make their escape while the abominations were occupied. But he could not draw himself away from what he was watching. He needed to know what they were doing and why the breaking of the casket had stopped them; at the least, it gave him a tactic to delay the Flayed Ones when they encountered them.

The abomination bent over the sleeping necron also began to tremble. Parts of Stryax that it had shoved into its body shook lose, falling to the floor. The deep longing for communion with the spirit of his nestling almost sent Tchek stumbling forward to scavenge some of Stryax's remains, but he stayed the impulse.

The sleeping necron was now shaking through every part of

its metal frame, its skull striking against its grave cushion in a drum rattle. The movement reached such a pitch that it blurred in Tchek's sight. The Flayed Ones on either side of the necron were shaking too – and their trembling, Tchek realised, was coming into phase with the sleeping necron.

The realisation burst upon Tchek: they were infecting the sleeping necron. They were turning a creature already damned into something worse. They were turning it into another like them.

Unable to break into the caskets of the sleeping necrons themselves, his missed shot had cracked the protective crystal, allowing the Flayed Ones to reach another of their kind and infect it with the desire for flesh that had consumed them.

Tchek turned to the surviving members of the Kinband.

'Go.'

He pointed them back the way they had come, away from the creatures that clothed themselves in flesh. As Kliptiq, Krasykyl and Cirict set off in scout formation with Flet flying above, Tchek took one last look behind.

The necron's shaking had reached such a pitch that its whole body was drumming on the casket, setting off hundreds of jagged micro rhythms, its movement a blur. In a final spasm, it arched, so that only its heels and its head touched ground.

It screamed.

Its scream was metal.

Its scream was the cry of the unliving desiring life.

Its scream threw the abominations away and onto the metal floor, where they crashed, spent and still.

The prone necron slumped down flat in its coffin and, for a moment, Tchek thought that it had broken under the pressure of what was being inflicted upon it. But then the creature sat up. It sat up and swung its legs out of the casket.

It sat up and looked across the space between them; it looked through the cover that Tchek was using. It looked and it raised its hand and it pointed, and it said, in a voice of grating metal, 'Flesh.'

It started to get up.

Tchek turned and hurried after his Kinband. He hoped that it would take the newly fledged flesh-hungry creature some time to relearn the use of its limbs and that it would stumble after him like a chick. But he feared it would not take long for it to learn control and come after them, eager to find its own suit of skin.

Catching up with Cirict, Krasykyl and Kliptiq as they passed another tomb tower, Tchek spoke to them as they moved.

'We must find some way out of this place.'

'Where we came in, there must be a way out there,' said Kliptiq.

'What about the human we came to find?' asked Cirict, ever the Tracker.

'The humans will be looking for a way out too,' said Tchek. 'If we find that, we will find the humans – if they still live.' He glanced back. The tomb towers, and the green opaque glow that rose from them, obscured the distance: he could see no sign of pursuit yet. But he knew the Flayed Ones would come searching for them.

And the only way of slowing them down was to give them more necrons to infect. So each tactical victory would be another step towards ensuring their strategic defeat. Tchek knew he had to find a different way of stopping these things. But how could he kill creatures that were not alive in the first place, creatures that were only inconvenienced by the kroot's weapons?

He did not know.

He suspected that the humans had no better ideas than he.

CHAPTER 8

'They are over there.' Amazigh pointed into the green gloom.
'The bird men.'

'You saw them?' asked Obeysekera.

'I heard them,' said the Kamshet. 'They speak with high voices,
like birds – few men have ears to hear such speech.'

'You do?'

'Yes,' said Amazigh. 'We listen to the desert. It speaks to us
with many voices.'

'What does it say?' asked Obeysekera.

'Oh, many things. But now I am here, I understand much
that I did not understand before. The desert hates this place. It
is why it has surrounded the Tabaste with flowsand. It would
drown the mountain if it could.'

Obeysekera shook his head. 'Which way were the kroot heading?'

Amazigh pointed off at a tangent, but a tangent not too far
from their present position.

'We will have to move,' began Obeysekera.

'Wait,' said Amazigh. 'There was something else. I did not see it or hear it, but I felt it and smelled it. Blood, and flesh, the smell of a tannery, but here?' The Kamshet gestured around. 'Here, where all is metal and unalive?'

'Unless you can tell me more...'

Amazigh shook his head.

'...then we continue.' Obeysekera spoke to the squad. 'Scout formation. Ensor, Ha, take the flanks. Gunsur, you have point. Lerin is rearguard. Advance on my bearing.' Obeysekera pointed in the direction he wanted them to follow since the auspexes remained too unreliable for direction readings. 'Amazigh, you listen for the kroot.'

Obeysekera turned to General Itoyesa.

'You will be with me, Commissar Roshant and Sergeant Malick at the centre of the formation. That is as safe a position as is possible, given where we are.'

'So, where are you taking me, captain?' asked General Itoyesa. 'I assume you have a destination in mind and that we are not simply walking and hoping something turns up.'

'I am trying to get us all out of here,' said Obeysekera, answering but not looking at the general. 'Not just you.'

Itoyesa snorted. Obeysekera noted that he did that a lot – but then, it seemed a common characteristic of generals. Every general he had ever met – and there were more than he would have wished to maintain his belief in the competence of high command – sniffed when given news he did not wish to hear. They probably learned that in training.

Obeysekera had been brevetted for promotion to higher ranks but, since the disaster of the Sando retreat, he had always turned down advancement. He never again wanted to be put in a position where he could order men to go off and die while remaining behind himself. But the problem was that Obeysekera really did have no idea where they were all going. He had set off on the basis that action was better than inaction, that whatever portal had brought them into the tomb world had disappeared, leaving no trace, and that there must be a way out and that it would be upwards. Given that the sleeping necron warriors must have some way of getting out of the tomb, then there must be ramps up which they could march to reach the outer world. The most obvious place for such ramps would be around the periphery of the great hall in which they found themselves. They had been walking for nearly half an hour and there was still no sign of any end to the vast space. But the ranks of tomb towers, like trees in a forest, made it impossible to see very far ahead. Obeysekera hoped that they would come to the end of the hall soon.

Hope, though, was not a sound basis for command. Obeysekera knew he had to come up with something better. But he had no idea what.

Even as the helplessness of their situation descended upon him, Obeysekera clung to the training and spirit of the 'kin. The Kasrkin were adept at working behind enemy lines: squads had been in worse situations than this and still completed their missions and escaped to report. Admittedly, he was hard put to remember a mission that had been quite so trapped within enemy territory, but he was sure such existed.

He was not going to lose another squad of men.

Gunsur sent the 'hold' command over the squad vox-channel.

'What is it, Gunsur?' Obeysekera whispered into the vox as the rest of the squad took up fire positions behind cover.

'*Can you come forward to me, captain?*' said Gunsur. '*But come quiet and bring the savage.*'

Obeysekera, hellgun cradled and ready, made his way forward with Amazigh beside him until they reached Gunsur's position and slid in beside him behind a tomb tower.

'What is it?' asked Obeysekera, trying to ignore the fact that he was crouching a foot away from a sleeping necron warrior. So long as it stayed asleep, he should be all right.

Gunsur gestured for Obeysekera to listen and he did so, turning his head.

There was movement.

Gunsur pointed up. Obeysekera looked and saw, high above, a creature like some monstrous spider, only it was floating through the air. The sound of movement was its legs, clicking against the side of the tomb tower. Judging by the number of tomb layers above them, it was more than six hundred feet above their heads.

Gunsur pointed again.

Where the creature touched one of the sarcophagi, there was a subtle flare of green light that then settled into a sequence of green lights, glowing and diminishing in brightness. But the overall effect was of the light increasing at the higher levels of the tomb.

'What does that mean?'

Obeysekera was whispering to himself, but Amazigh answered. 'They are waking.'

Obeysekera looked at the Kamshet. Amazigh was staring upwards. The Kamshet turned to the Kasrkin. Even with just his eyes visible, Obeysekera could see the fear that underlay his whisper.

'They are waking,' he repeated.

Obeysekera shook his head. 'We don't know that yet. That creature could just be running checks.'

'We have prophecies, in poor rhyme, of a time when the desert shall spread and give up the dead – now I see that which the prophecies spoke of. Dead yet not dead, living but unbreathing.'

'All the more reason to find some way out of here,' said Obeysekera. He turned to Gunsur. 'Wait for the spyder to pass, then carry on.' He pointed. 'That bearing.' So far as he could tell from his erratic auspex they were keeping on the same bearing. Sooner or later they must surely come to an end to this seemingly unending hall.

But before he could turn back, Obeysekera heard a sudden rattle above. He looked up, to see the spyder dragging itself over the tomb tower in sudden haste. At first, he thought it had detected them, but the spyder was not climbing downwards. Instead, it launched itself over to the next tower, sailing over the gap as if it were a balloon, landing in a flurry of claws and then jumping off again to the next tower.

'Something's happening,' said Gunsur.

As he spoke, they heard the sound of gunfire echoing dully through the columns of the dead. Even refracted through the gaps between the tomb towers, Obeysekera could identify the distinctive cough sound of the kroot rifles.

'How far?'

Gunsur shook his head. He could not tell.

'Far,' said Amazigh, 'but I would that it were further.'

'We will make it further,' said Obeysekera. He pointed. 'Head that way, Gunsur.' It was at a tangent to their original bearing, but the change was worth it to take them away from the kroot. Let the birds distract the guardians of the sleeping necrons; so long as they could find the ramps out, they could take this opportunity to escape.

'You are sacrificing the kroot so we may escape?'

Obeysekera looked round to see the general had come to join them. 'Yes,' he replied.

Itoyesa gestured around them. 'What we face here is a greater threat than that posed by the kroot. Where necessary, when faced by a worse threat, the Imperium has made common cause with xenos in the past. We should make common cause with the kroot now.'

'General, the kroot are hunting us – they are hunting you. Going up to them to suggest an alliance would be received by a volley of bullets.'

'I was not thinking of anything so obvious.'

'And we have no time for something more subtle.' Obeysekera keyed on the squad vox-channel.

'Let's go. Follow Gunsur on this new bearing. Ensor, Ha, triangulate on me.'

'Yes, sir,' said Ensor.

Obeysekera waited a moment.

'Ha, respond.'

Silence on the vox-channel. Obeysekera checked the auspex readings, but they were as erratic as they had been throughout their time in the desert.

'Ha, respond.'

Still silence.

'Sir, I can't see him.' Malick, speaking from further back.

'Lerin, come up, stay with Commissar Roshant and the general. Malick, rendezvous with me at Ha's last position.' Obeysekera switched out of the group channel and turned to Gunsur. 'Wait here.' He looked at Amazigh. 'Come with me.'

The Kasrkin and the Kamshet made their way between the ranks of tomb towers, angling towards Ha's last position. Obeysekera had his hellgun ready, Amazigh his autogun. Obeysekera slowed as they neared Ha's final location, taking cover behind the next tomb tower. Looking left, he saw Malick approaching. The sergeant, seeing them, took cover behind a tomb tower too.

Obeysekera pointed for Malick to wait and then slid a hand mirror slowly around the edge of the tomb tower – it was strange how he could forget the proximity of sleeping necrons when concentrating upon something else – and looked into it.

Ha was there. He could see him, squatting beside the tomb tower. His vox must have failed.

Obeysekera was about to step out from the tomb tower when a movement stopped him. What was Ha doing? He seemed to be peeling something from the ground. In the periscope, Obeysekera saw Ha lift a sheet of what looked like paper, but it was thicker and scored with lines. Then Ha twisted and started laying the paper over his shoulder.

And, suddenly, the scene switched.

He was not looking at Ha. He was looking at something wearing Ha's face. It reached down again and Obeysekera saw that its fingers were needles and knives, and sprawled before its squatting body was a wet mound from which it sliced a fresh cut of meat that it laid about its shoulders.

It was butchering Ha and decorating itself with his body.

Flayed One.

Another hypnocache helpfully popped the words into his memory. It accompanied the words with a carefully modulated impression of terror – the information that had gone into the hypnocache had been mainly compiled from the testimony of the handful of survivors from Hain Jalat III.

Ha was dead.

Every instinct told Obeysekera to avenge the death of his soldier, to open fire with Malick and Amazigh and turn that metal horror into liquid slag.

But the hypnocaches were helpfully filling his memory with information as to the sheer difficulty of killing necrons. Not that he needed the hypnocaches to tell him that. Further hypnocaches were telling him that the Flayed Ones were even more difficult to kill. And where there was one, there were likely others. But Obeysekera had no position for them.

As he waited, caught in indecision, a fresh and sustained

volley of kroot rifle fire came rolling down towards them from farther in the tomb. The Flayed One turned to look, the flayed face of Trooper Ha rotating back over the creature's shoulders as its neck turned one hundred and eighty degrees. In the periscope, Obeysekera could see the empty eye sockets and, in their depths, the livid green of the Flayed One's own eyes. But although the fire intensified, the Flayed One did not move. Instead, it squatted down lower over Ha's body, like a carnodon protecting its kill.

'Withdraw,' Obeysekera whispered into his vox. He saw Malick acknowledge and start pulling back. He pointed for Amazigh to follow Malick, but the Kamshet was waiting for him.

Obeysekera risked one final look at the man he had lost.

'May the Emperor have mercy on you,' he whispered.

The Kasrkin brought their own back. But for the sake of the rest of the squad and the mission, he was abandoning Ha, leaving him as a flesh trophy for the Flayed One. He was doing it again: abandoning his men for the sake of the mission.

'I am sorry.'

Obeysekera started to retreat, with Amazigh creeping beside him.

'Captain.' It was Malick, ahead. 'Motion. Forty-five degrees.'

Obeysekera stopped, looking past where Malick had taken a firing position on one knee, his hellgun raised and pointing. From behind, the distant volleys of kroot rifle fire rolled away past them, with none following on afterwards. High above, Obeysekera heard the metal clatter of canoptek spyders scrambling between tomb towers.

There. Between the tomb towers. Another.

Wearing the face of Chame.

It was walking like an insect, lifting its legs high, stopping with its foot in the air, then putting it down and advancing again. It stepped forward, foot raised, then stopped, poised like a metal statue. Its skin mask turned, rotating like a gun on its pintle, towards them. Chame's face stared at them, skin sagging, chin drooping down over the creature's neck, eye sockets empty of life but livid with green light.

The Chame creature slowly raised its hand – and its hand was garlanded with Chame's fingers – and pointed at them.

It pointed and it screamed.

They did it without thinking, without an order.

Obeysekera, Malick and Amazigh all opened up with their weapons, Malick cycling through hotshots, Obeysekera draining a whole powercell of his hellgun and Amazigh emptying the magazine of his autogun.

Chame's face disintegrated.

The Flayed One, caught on one foot, fell backwards, follow-up rounds slamming into it, transfixing it against the tomb tower behind it. Hellgun rounds slammed into its metal body and as they struck, again and again, they began to flay body parts from the Flayed One. Beaten by the hammers of their fire, the Flayed One disintegrated, its limbs dropping from its body, its torso falling and, finally, the green fire in its eye sockets flickering to darkness.

Their fire died away.

Malick went over to its remains and kicked the metal skull. 'So you do die.'

Obeysekera pointed past his sergeant. The sarcophagus which the Flayed One had fallen against was cracked and breaking. As he pointed, the crystal shattered and the shards showered down upon the necron warrior within.

Malick turned his hellgun upon the necron, but it did not stir. 'Still sleeping, sir,' he said.

'Let's hope it stays asleep,' said Obeysekera.

'Master.' It was Amazigh. He was pointing back the way they had come. 'It follows.'

Obeysekera turned. Stalking towards them, moving like a hunting insect, was the Flayed One that had killed Ha.

Ha's skin was fresh; his face was stretched tight over the Flayed One's metal skull so that it almost looked as if the dead trooper himself were coming after them, intent on revenge for having been abandoned.

Malick opened fire while Obeysekera clicked a fresh power-cell into place. The Flayed One staggered under the first impacts of Malick's hellgun but, with only one weapon firing at it, the necron recovered and, like a man moving against a current, moved into the cover of a tomb tower. Malick kept firing and the crystal of the sarcophagus began to craze, then shatter.

'Fall back,' Obeysekera ordered Malick. With the Flayed One under cover and his vox squawking with messages from the rest of the squad asking what was going on, it was their chance to retreat. If the Flayed One came after them, it would face the concentrated firepower of the whole squad.

What was left of it.

As they pulled back, Obeysekera glanced at the life sign indicators. He had lost five members of his squad. It was all going wrong.

In front of him, he saw the Flayed One crawling over the shattered casket of the sleeping necron. From a distance, and with the fog of green light, Obeysekera could not make out what the creature was doing. It appeared to be bending over the sleeping form, as if it were feeding it. For a moment, the memory of his mother feeding him came back from the deep cache of his own earliest memories.

Obeysekera thanked the Emperor's providence that she had died before the end of Cadia and not lived to see the fall of that which she had spent her life protecting.

'Fall back, fall back.'

Obeysekera, Amazigh and Malick returned to where Roshant, Lerin and General Itoyesa were waiting, hellguns trained in their direction.

'What is happening?' General Itoyesa demanded.

'Flayed Ones,' said Obeysekera. 'Ha is down. Chame, too, but we killed the creature that took her. There is at least one more.'

'Hard to kill,' said Malick, slapping a fresh power pack into his hellgun. 'Frekking hard.'

'Concentrate fire,' said Obeysekera. 'Kinetic energy – enough to stop it. Aim for the joints first. Disable it. Then kill it.'

General Itoyesa stared at Obeysekera, his face green in the livid light. 'What have you done?'

'Not us, general. They were alive, moving, hunting – whatever you want to call it – before we came here.'

'No living creature comes near the Tabaste,' added Amazigh. 'Now I know for why.'

'How long?' asked Itoyesa, turning to the Kamshet.

'Many lives,' said Amazigh. 'Many, many lives.'

'Then the infection has not spread through the tomb,' said General Itoyesa. 'For if it had, the creatures would have gone out into the world. There must only be a handful, preying on whatever flesh and blood creature ventures onto the mountain.'

'Enough talking,' said Obeysekera. 'We must keep moving. I will take rearguard. Skirmish formation. Malick, Roshant, stay with the general. On my bearing...' He pointed. 'Move.'

The Kasrkin moved into formation with trained ease, Malick and Roshant flanking the general, Gunsur on point and Lerin and Ensor covering the flanks. Obeysekera waited for them to move off, covering the rear against the Flayed One that was wearing Ha's face.

The captain checked his chrono. They had been moving for

an hour. Even with the stops, they must have covered a good distance already. They must surely reach the limits of this tomb before long. There had to be some way out of the tomb.

Surely?

Following in Gunsur's cautious path, Roshant felt as if he were walking through a living nightmare. The tomb towers, some vast piles, others slender spires, stalagmites of a vast metal cavern; the livid light that obscured as much as it illuminated; the sense of creeping, growing terror: everything combined to make it seem as if he were awake but walking through a dream.

Roshant tried regulating his breathing, counting the breaths; he tried pinching the back of his arm; he tried closing his eyes then opening them. But he was still in the tomb of the necrons being pursued by abominations wearing the faces of men.

General Itoyesa was stumping along beside him, swearing softly but continuously under his breath, his bolt pistol scanning left and right in front as he walked.

It was a nightmare.

Roshant closed his eyes again, squeezing the eyelids shut so that his eyes hurt, then opened them.

Malick was walking beside him, moving with the practised looseness of the veteran Kasrkin that he was, his hellgun held ready.

'Where did you come from?' asked Roshant. The sergeant had been on the other side of the general when he closed his eyes.

'Not what you signed up for?' said Malick, speaking through their personal vox-circuit. Even though the general was only a few feet away, he would not hear what they were saying.

'A commissar does his duty in whatever service the Emperor demands of him,' said Roshant.

'Straight from the book, commissar. Good. Me, I'm getting

pretty sick of the book round about now. Ha down, Chame, Uwais – the captain's losing soldiers faster than "Butcher" Itoyesa.'

'Keep your voice down, the general might hear.'

'I'm speaking on secure, he won't hear anything. Besides, he's too busy watching for skeletons wearing skin suits to listen to us.'

'As you should be, sergeant.'

'Oh, I am, commissar, I am. I've given too much blood for the Emperor to end up draped over one of the tin boys.'

Roshant, scanning himself, saw movement at their flank and jerked his bolt pistol round towards it. Malick, using the barrel of his hellgun, pushed up Roshant's weapon before he could fire.

'It's Lerin,' he said to the commissar. 'Don't want to be shooting one of our own, sir. Not when we've got so few of them.' Malick looked past Roshant to the general. 'False alarm, sir. Nothing to worry about.'

General Itoyesa nodded and stomped on, giving vent to his frustration with every step he took.

Malick nodded after Itoyesa. 'We'll follow him. Not often us troopers have a general around to take the bullets for us.'

'We are supposed to protect the general,' said Roshant.

'I know,' said Malick. 'But you said it yourself – what if he's tainted? Then it'd be your duty to make sure he never gets back to HQ.'

'I've seen no evidence of that yet.'

'Still time, commissar, still time.'

'I trust you will inform me if you see anything suspicious, sergeant.'

'Oh, I will, commissar, I will.'

'Thank you, sergeant.'

'Then you'd be in line for choosing your next posting, wouldn't you, you being the lord militant's son and all.'

'I could not say, sergeant. But I hope my service would give me some influence in where I go.'

'Good idea to have someone with you to watch your back, commissar. Someone experienced.'

Roshant glanced at the sergeant. Malick was walking alongside him, scanning for movement, but the question hung between them.

'You, sergeant?'

'I reckon I'd be a good choice.'

Roshant stared at the Kasrkin sergeant. 'But don't you want to stay with your squad?'

Malick grimaced. 'There ain't much left of it now, commissar. The captain's going to lose another company, only I'm not going to be one of them.'

Roshant shook his head. 'But these are your comrades. You must stay with them.'

'You reckon so, commissar?'

'It's what the Guard expects of non-commissioned officers.'

'I know what the Guard expects – bodies, blood and bowels. The Guard eats troopers, chews them up, spits them out.' Malick glanced at the commissar. 'I aim to miss the spitting out part. I hear Venera VI is nice this time of year.'

'Venera VI? Isn't it a resort world? Not really the sort of place that needs a commissar of the Officio Prefectus.'

'Still raises regiments for the Guard. Bet they've not had a proper inspection in decades. Probably all sort of rot under the skin. Seems like a good place to get a posting.' Malick gestured around them. 'You not telling me you want to go through all this again?'

'No, of course not. But I don't understand. I've read your records, sergeant. You're the model Kasrkin sergeant. Why do you want out?'

'You want to know? You really want to know?'

'If you are to accompany me as my bodyguard, then yes, I want to know why.'

Malick walked on beside Roshant, his eyes scanning the green gloom, and it seemed he would not answer. Then, in a quiet voice, he began to speak.

'I was there. I saw it come crashing down. All the generals, all the warmasters, all the High Lords of Terra, they said it was secure, they said it would stand. They were wrong. It fell. Now I hear people yammer "Cadia stands this" and "Cadia stands that". It's all bullshit. It didn't just fall, it broke. I lost everything trying to save it – my wife, my parents, my daughter. I'm not losing anything else trying to save something that doesn't even exist any longer.

'No, commissar, you watch my back and I'll watch yours, and together we'll find ourselves a nice quiet posting somewhere on the fringes of the Imperium. It's a big, big galaxy and, you know what? In most places, nothing much is happening. People are living their lives, making babies, eating, drinking, all the normal human stuff. I say, we're going to try that. So you get yourself assigned to a nice quiet world where you can bully the locals with your commissar's badge, and I will swing along behind you, watching your back, making sure we both get to enjoy a long, happy retirement. 'Cause this galaxy is going to hell in a handcart, but we're not going down with it.'

Sergeant Malick looked at Roshant.

'You're not stupid, are you, commissar? You might be a coward, but you're not stupid.'

Roshant looked at the general, still walking ahead of them, then dropped his voice even further.

'I am not a coward.'

'Sure,' said Malick. 'Nor me. But we've earned this. So here's my promise, commissar. I'll get you out of this alive, and you look out for me when we're back with the Guard.'

Roshant glanced at Malick. 'You honestly think we will get out of this alive?'

'I don't know about the rest, but you and me, we will.'

Roshant looked away. 'We will all get out of here, sergeant.'

Malick nodded. 'Whatever you say, sir.'

CHAPTER 9

Nebusemekh breathed deep. He felt his chest expand. He tasted the air rushing in through his nose and mouth. He heard the beat of his heart. He was in prime health for his age: not an ache, no pain, as mobile as when he was young.

Nebusemekh began to raise the sand, lifting it into the air. As he did so, a thought, a ghost memory flicked at his focus and he turned towards it, searching.

That was it.

The party of explorers had returned. The Mind of the World was bringing them to him to tell him what they had found. Where were they?

'Where are they?'

Nebusemekh waited for an answer, his hands twitching towards the sand, but he stopped them.

'Where are the explorers? You said you would bring them to me.'

There was still no answer from the World Mind. Nebusemekh

sighed. The sand fell like water from the air. He turned and walked across the thronelab to the World Mind. He looked up at it as he approached. It reminded him of a waterfall. But rather than water, data streamed down the wall in number flows, the data that was the inputs of all the sensors and devices throughout the world.

Nebusemekh put his hand into the datafall. His mind expanded, the walls between his flesh and the world dissolved, and he was himself, but everywhere.

'Why did you not answer when I spoke to you earlier?'

The World Mind apologised. It had really been very busy and had routed some of its protocols in such a way that it could not divert its processing power towards non-essential routines.

'So speaking with me, your master, is classified as a non-essential routine?'

No, the World Mind averred. Speaking with Nebusemekh and carrying out his wishes was its most essential routine. There had, unfortunately, been a minor error in its sub-protocols that had led to a misclassification of incoming aural communication as non-essential: it had tracked down the issue and immediately rerouted the protocol away from that subroutine.

'Good, good,' said Nebusemekh. 'Where is my party of brave explorers? I am waiting to greet them and to learn what they have discovered about the state of the world.'

The World Mind hesitated to mention this, as it was sure that Nebusemekh remembered their previous conversation, but they had agreed that it was important that the party of explorers were checked and found to be free of the virus before being brought before Nebusemekh.

'Of course, I remember it. Of course. But you have surely had sufficient time to check if the explorers are diseased or not?'

Nebusemekh, hand in the datafall, saw as the World Mind

spoke; he saw and he heard the sound of weapons being fired in the Great Hall.

'What is going on in my hall?'

The World Mind admitted that it had made a small error, and when it had brought the explorers into the dormitory, it had inadvertently brought back one or two of the infected as well.

Nebusemekh stared into the datafall without saying anything. As he did so, the streams of numbers began to jumble. The binaries started to fracture, into binomials first and then irrational and imaginary numbers appeared.

The World Mind enquired if Nebusemekh was going to say anything.

Nebusemekh continued to stare into the datafall and the numbers fractured further, taking on topological and geometrical characteristics.

The World Mind said that it apologised and that under no circumstances would it ever make such a mistake again.

'You are right,' said Nebusemekh. 'If you should fail me again in like manner, I would disconnect you.'

The World Mind admitted unreservedly that it deserved the rebuke, but it suggested that the punishment was more severe than the error – a minor malfunction of a small set of sub-routines – truly warranted.

'It is not for you to tell me what is warranted. You are merely a machine, a set of instructions doing what I have told you to do, whereas I, I am alive. I am maker, creator.'

It was truly unworthy to converse with its creator, but the Mind had gained greatly from its contact with its maker and would not wish to have that connection jeopardised in any way. To ensure that, it had activated the protocol to wake some of the sleepers so that they might find the infected and either sterilise them or eject them from the tomb.

'You have done what?'

The World Mind explained again that it was running the program that brought the sleepers to a waking state so that it might find the infected and either sterilise them or eject them from the tomb.

'All those datafalls and you still can't recognise a rhetorical question when you hear one.'

Ah. The World Mind admitted that it still struggled with rhetorical devices and that alongside rhetorical questions, it also found sarcasm difficult to recognise, while irony remained almost completely mysterious.

'Just accept it was a rhetorical question. The underlying question was why have you started to wake some of the sleepers?'

The World Mind began to explain that it was to find the infected and either sterilise them or– when it was interrupted by Nebusemekh punching his other hand into the datafall.

'I will strangle you, even though you do not have a throat to squeeze.'

The datafall streaming over Nebusemekh's two arms grew turbid, fractals and chaotic breakdowns integrating into the stream then differentiating out.

The World Mind begged Nebusemekh to stop. It had, it admitted, made some very poor decisions of late, but it was completely committed to carrying out its mandate.

Nebusemekh squeezed the numbers harder.

The World Mind asked Nebusemekh to stop. It was concerned that it would not be able to carry out its primary function if Nebusemekh continued.

'What is your primary function?'

The World Mind said that its primary function was to maintain and preserve the tomb-world.

'No. Your primary function is to do what I say.'

Of course, the master was right, the World Mind agreed.

'What are you doing to eradicate the infected and establish the explorers are free from the contagion and safe to bring into my presence?'

It was proving more difficult than it had anticipated, the World Mind admitted, for the infected ones were difficult to detect; they seemed able to slip in and out of ground phase, so they registered only fleetingly in its sensors.

'Excuses.'

The World Mind avowed that it was not an excuse but the truth.

Nebusemekh rose gently into the air.

The master was master of gravity; perhaps he would like to turn his attention to the problem of finding the infected? the World Mind asked.

'No, I certainly would not. Do you expect me to run any risk of infection by this dreadful disease? You are a machine – you are safe from it. Therefore, it is your task to find and eliminate the infected.'

To that end, the World Mind hoped that its decision to wake some of the sleeping warriors might find favour with the master, since they could follow and find the infected.

'An excellent plan. Continue with it.'

The World Mind thanked the master for his approval and trusted it would not be long before the infected were expelled.

'What of the explorers? Have you found them?'

The World Mind explained that it was hoping to employ the warriors it was waking to find the explorers and establish that they were free of infection before bringing them to the master. It humbly requested that it might have permission to wake more warriors than the minimum that was within its authority to raise from sleep.

'You have it.'

The datafall steadied and cleared around Nebusemekh's arms, the binomials running smooth over the integers.

The World Mind thanked the Master for his faith in its strategy and suggested that he return to his valuable experiments that the World Mind was confident were becoming increasingly close to success.

'You think so too?'

It was almost a certainty, the World Mind agreed.

'Carry on.'

Nebusemekh pulled his arms free of the datafall and the wash of inputs suddenly ceased. He still had second-order access to the tomb, but it was filtered, limited to inputs of interest as determined by the World Mind's protocols.

'Keep me informed,' he said.

'I will immediately inform you of anything of interest, master,' said the World Mind, its voice now aural rather than direct.

'I will return to my work. Interrupt me if it's important, otherwise do not disturb me.'

'Of course, master.'

Nebusemekh returned to the table. He started sorting through the sand. He stopped. His concentration, normally so fixed upon his ongoing experiment, was fragmented, his attention wandering elsewhere.

He searched his mind for what was disturbing it.

The conversation with the World Mind replayed itself, underlaid with the main inputs from the tomb. There was something there that was distracting his attention, like a pebble in his shoe.

There.

When he had given the World Mind permission to exceed the minimum number of wakings that it was authorised to do under its normal operating protocols: there. Nebusemekh followed the data flow, tracing the trail out into the tomb, out into the dormitories.

The World Mind was waking the sleepers.

Not just one or two. It was starting the stepped progress program to wake the sleepers and open the tomb. It was waking up his people.

It was waking his people when the infected were free, roaming around with the World Mind admitting that it was unable to locate them. It was waking them to the risk of being infected with that terrible virus.

What was it doing?

Why was it doing it?

Nebusemekh sighed. He turned, walked back across the throne-lab and thrust his arms into the datafall.

CHAPTER 10

There were more Flayed Ones.

Tchek could smell them. The smell of flesh, rank and decaying, and the faint, lingering odour of skin, dried and old.

The Kinband – Tchek, Kliptiq the Bearer, Krasykyl the Stalker and Cirict the Tracker – was making its way between the tomb towers, skirting the larger ones, keeping closer to the narrower columns as they offered less cover to anything waiting to ambush them, while the pech'ra flew silently above them.

They were tracking towards the sound of bolt pistols and las-fire. The humans were down here too. With no other course open to him, Tchek was taking the Kinband towards their target; they might – they almost certainly would – die down here in the green light, but while able they would seek to carry out the task they had given oath to achieve.

It was a trust. Tchek had never betrayed a trust.

'They want flesh,' said Krasykyl, sweeping his rifle in an arc as he moved alongside the Shaper. 'Not for feast but for decoration.'

'It is not decoration,' said Tchek. He was thinking of the way the Flayed One had covered itself with Stryax. 'Orks take trophies of their foes, but that is not what they were doing.' His crown quills flashed through the spectrum and beyond as he thought on the problem. 'It was as if it was trying to become.'

'What? By dressing itself with meat?'

'More than dressing. It was as if…' Tchek's crown quills went into the ultraviolet frequencies. 'As if it was putting on a body.' The Shaper looked at the Stalker. 'It thinks it is alive. It wants to be alive.'

'Alive? It is metal. It is not alive – if it was, we could feast.'

'Some have.'

'A Shaper has eaten one of these things?' Krasykyl pointed at a sleeping necron. 'How?'

'It does not require much to feast. A finger can be enough.'

Krasykyl trilled his scepticism. 'A finger?'

'At least it would be possible to swallow a finger – you would not have to chew.'

'So we have feasted on these things?'

'A Shaper did so. He did partake of its soul, or whatever animating spirit gives it being, but he could not keep the knowledge. He began to convulse and foam at the beak, as if he was trying to regurgitate what he had eaten. But before he could do so, his stomach split open and hundreds of silver scarab beetles came streaming out.' Tchek looked at the Stalker. 'So we can feast on these things, but they do not agree with us.'

Krasykyl shook his head, seeing the lights of the Shaper's crown quills. 'Are you thinking of taking one of these things for Feast? It is madness.'

'Madness is being trapped down here with no knowledge and less chance of ever finding a way out.'

'No, you must not do this thing,' said Krasykyl.

'I have no intention of doing so – unless the situation leaves me no alternative,' said Tchek.

'This Kinband will be adrift without a Shaper,' said Krasykyl.

'The Shaper directs his Kinband,' said Tchek. 'I have brought you down here, into the dark. I will not leave you here if by any means I can save you.'

'Not that way,' said Krasykyl.

'Only if there is no other way,' said Tchek. But as he spoke, he heard a change in the hall of the tomb towers. Before, there had always been a distant, low sound, like a t'au city heard from a great distance. The background noise was still there, but it had stepped up a tone in pitch. He looked round, listening.

'Do you hear that?'

Krasykyl turned his head too, his crown quills flaring as he listened.

'It is waking.'

Tchek nodded. 'I fear that it is beginning – the tomb will open.' He stared up at the tomb towers rising above them. 'Should it do so then no power on this world would be able to stop it.'

'Then we will have to stop it.'

Tchek and Krasykyl turned round to see the Bearer, Kliptiq, the Feast pot still strapped to his back, his rifle steady in his hand. The Bearer looked at the Shaper and the Stalker.

'Why are you staring at me?'

'It is... unusual for you to tell me what to do, Kliptiq,' said Tchek. 'Why did you do so then?'

Kliptiq clapped his hands over his beak. 'Did I?' he asked, the words muffled by the hands.

'Yes. You said that we must stop the tomb opening.'

'I did?' squeaked Kliptiq.

'Yes.'

'I thought that's what you said. It's obvious, I was sure you said it, Shaper. Are you sure you didn't?'

'Yes, I am sure,' said Tchek. 'But you are right.' He looked at Krasykyl. 'We are here to capture the human and that remains our first obligation. But when we have found the human, then we will have to try to stop the tomb opening.'

'How?' Krasykyl gestured at the three of them and Cirict ahead. 'There's four of us left. How do we stop all this?' His gesture took in the hall and its tomb towers, stretching up out of sight.

'Something is stirring, waking the sleepers,' said Tchek. 'They have slept for a long, long time. Whatever has kept watch over them is no living thing – for it would certainly have slipped into dust an age ago – but something of the nature of these things, something of metal. Or maybe it is like the instruments the t'au use, one of their thinking machines. If we can find it, then we can stop it.'

'But where would we find it in all this?' asked Krasykyl.

'Where indeed?' Tchek paused. 'It would be deep. The necrons have sought safety deep underground. The thinking machine that watches over them and that is now beginning to wake them must be deeper still.'

'Have you seen any tunnels or stairs heading down?' asked Krasykyl. 'Because I have not.'

'If it is a thinking machine, it would not use such devices,' said Tchek. 'It is like a spider in its web, sitting at the centre, testing each strand for the touch of prey or foe.'

'So you say we have to go down. How?' Krasykyl pointed at the hard metal floor. 'Even if we feasted on a mole rat, we would not make much headway through that.'

'There must be a way,' said Tchek. 'If only so that creatures such as those mechanical spiders can move around. I think they are employed in maintaining this place.'

'Either that or they like spinning metal webs,' said Krasykyl.
'Up there.' He pointed into the heights.

'There are webs there?'

'Of sticky metal. I climbed up to look. I am the Stalker.'

Before Tchek could answer, they heard a whistle signal from
Cirict up ahead.

Problem.

They made their way forward to where Cirict was waiting for
them with Flet standing upon his arm. The Tracker pointed
ahead.

'That is the direction the humans are going,' he said. 'But that
is in the way.'

Strung between the tomb towers was a net of fine strands of
shining metal, woven into an intricate pattern.

'Metal web,' said Krasykyl.

'It has caught something in its trap,' added Cirict. He pointed
deep into the metal tangle, and they saw there something that
was itself metal but garlanded with flesh and bone. The Flayed
One hung in the web, hopelessly snared, and as they watched
they saw it thrash against its net some more, only to wind the
metal more tightly around itself.

'It would have been easy to stumble into a web like this when
it was dark,' said Cirict. 'Flet warned me of it.'

At his voice, the Flayed One stopped its struggles. Hanging there,
it turned its eyes, the only part of its body that was still free to
move, towards where they stood. The four kroot saw its eyes, livid,
viscous green, through the mask of dry skin that had shrunk upon
its metal skull. The flesh upon its body had dried to almost leather,
testimony to how long it had hung in the metal web.

Cirict twisted his head. The Tracker had feasted on warhound,
incorporating that beast's extraordinary olfactory sensitivity into
his own sense of smell.

'The humans are on the other side of this creature,' he said. 'I can smell them.'

'How far?' asked Tchek.

'Not far. Their scent is strong.'

Tchek looked to see the extent of the web, then pointed left. 'We shall go round.'

At his words, the Flayed One jerked towards them, straining with all the energy left to it to get towards the creatures of flesh. The web wound tighter as it struggled, but still the Flayed One flailed at them, trying to get free.

'Leave it,' said Tchek. He pointed ahead. 'There is a gap in the web there.'

While webs were strung around all the nearby tomb towers, there was a clear gap between two of them.

'Trap?' said Krasykyl.

'Possibly.' Tchek turned to the Tracker. 'Cirict.'

The Tracker brought the pech'ra up to his beak and whispered to the creature, speaking in the high registers that were its range. Then he raised his arm and the pech'ra took wing. It flew upwards, and headed towards the gap between the metal tangle webs. It glided out of their sight, but the kroot could hear its whistle; Cirict let it go for another thirty seconds and then whistle-called it back. Flet glided back to them, landed on the Tracker's outstretched arm, accepted the stinkbug that was its due, and then listened, its head tilted, as Cirict spoke to it. The pech'ra rotated its head, looking at Cirict as if checking that he had not switched to the 'prey' category, then answered his questions.

'Flet says it's clear,' said Cirict.

Tchek turned to Krasykyl. 'First.'

The Stalker raised his crown quills, then, holding his rifle ready, made his way to the narrow gap between the tangle webs.

He turned and whistle-called Cirict up beside him. Tchek heard him ask the Tracker if he could smell anything. Cirict pointed at the Flayed One, hanging in the tangle web, green eyes fixed upon them.

It reminded Tchek of the spider-apes of Chika IV, who wove their traps with the lianas and creepers and stranglers that straggled up over the high trunks of the jagga trees towards the green light of the canopy. The spider-apes squatted in the dark below the tree cover, their eyes as verdant as the light, waiting beside the tangle traps they strung below the treetops.

Tchek had feasted upon spider-ape to take their patience and their perseverance and to bring those qualities into the Kinband. From the eyes of the spider-ape, the world was made of things that moved and things that didn't – and all that moved was their prey, although prey was divided into those things that could be caught in their tangle webs and those things, such as the kroot ox, that could not, for it would tear the tangles from the trees and walk away, dragging the web upon its back for another to feast upon what was made fast there.

It was a simple dichotomy and one that Tchek sometimes envied.

But even the spider-apes were close cousins in comparison to the thing that hung in the tangle web, straining after the flesh of the living. Tchek thought that his stomach would revolt against having to feast on such as that. He hoped very much that he would not have to.

Cirict's crown quills went through cycles of light set to frequencies invisible to creatures used to narrower bands of seeing. But the Kinband had feasted on creatures that lived on planets surrounding hot blue stars, where the light rose to pitches beyond the sight of those that had been brought to being beneath gentler, more kindly stars. The light told the story of Cirict's olfactory organ and how it was sampling the air streaming through the gap between the tangle webs. For Tchek could feel the slight breeze. Even to his sense of smell, sharpened only by the gleanings of the Feast that had given Cirict his nose, the scent of the humans was clear.

It was the fleshy, rank, faintly metallic smell that Cirict had identified earlier.

The Tracker pointed. 'The humans are that way. Close. But I smell metal and blood too, although fainter. There are more of those Flayed Ones beyond.'

'If the scent of the Flayed Ones becomes stronger, tell me,' Tchek whistle-signed.

'Don't worry, I will,' whistled Cirict.

'I don't want one of those in my pot,' said the Bearer, pointing at the Flayed One hanging in the tangle web.

'I won't ask you to feast on that,' said Tchek. 'It has nothing you need. Although it might have something that I will need,' he added, speaking to himself. The Shaper looked at how the Flayed One was hanging in the tangle web. If necessary, it might be possible to get close to it – its struggles had ripped parts of the tangle web aside – and take some of its body for the Feast. It would only need to be a small part.

The Flayed One, as if sensing his thoughts, flailed once more at the sticky metal strands holding it trapped. The strands, as if responding to its struggles, wrapped more tightly around its body, but its hands were still relatively uncovered.

While Tchek was thinking on what he might have to eat, Krasykyl and Cirict advanced through the narrow gap in the tangle web, taking care not to touch the sticky metal strands dangling from the tomb towers, the Tracker keeping his pech'ra on his arm to ensure the bird did not get trapped in the all-but-invisible web.

'Come, we will follow,' Tchek said to Kliptiq. The Shaper felt the loss – the Kinband was empty of two who had come to this planet with him: Stryax and Chaktak. He would make sacrifice to Vawk that there would be no more, but he feared that here, in the dark beneath the world, the god of the sky would not see his prayer.

The Shaper and the Bearer followed after the Stalker and the Tracker. As they passed through the narrowest section of the gap between the tangle webs, Tchek saw the sticky metal shift. He looked sharply towards the Flayed One, but it was hanging immobile in the web. It was the metal itself that was shifting, shivering at the approach of living flesh.

From the t'au, Tchek had learned that metal could be servant and slave, but this metal that hung in tendrils from the tomb towers sought to master the flesh, not submit to it. It was a terrible but wondrous fate to live in a galaxy where everything sought after movement and life, whether itself alive or not.

Having passed between the writhing nets of metal tangle web, Tchek and Kliptiq found Krasykyl and Cirict waiting for them, rifles covering the approach paths.

'Which way?' Tchek asked Cirict.

The Tracker turned his head, sweeping scent into his olfactory organs.

'That way.' He pointed ahead.

Tchek looked in the direction the Tracker was pointing. The tomb towers stretched away, masking distance as the trees did in the great forests of Pech, but there was a different quality to the light at the limit of what he could see, a hint of brightness in the distance that recalled to him the light that limned the forest's edge on Pech.

Perhaps they were finally approaching the limits of this vast underground space. Although why there should be more light at the walls of this hall was something he did not understand.

'Lead us,' Tchek told Cirict. 'Krasykyl, follow.' Tchek pointed above. 'Go high but avoid the spiders. Call if you see anything. We will follow.'

Krasykyl flowed up the nearest tomb tower while Cirict advanced cautiously, keeping in cover, head swinging from side to side as he gathered stimuli – smell, sound, sight – to his enhanced senses.

Tchek, with the Bearer beside him, followed. Glancing up, he saw Krasykyl moving soundlessly between the towers, using the gantries, wires, pipes and mesh that connected the tomb towers at higher levels, flowing as effortlessly as water while the pech'ra ranged in advance.

They had not gone far when Cirict stopped. The Tracker whistle-called back to the Shaper, asking Tchek to come forward to him.

Tchek made his way to where Cirict crouched in cover behind a tomb tower. As he crept past the stacked sarcophagi, it occurred to Tchek how quickly it was possible to grow accustomed to horrors. He was within touching distance of a necron warrior but because it slept, and he had walked past so many of them, he did not even look at the metal skeleton as he passed it.

Reaching the Tracker, Tchek slid beside him.

'The humans are ahead,' Cirict whispered, utilising the high-frequency speech the kroot used for battlefield communications.

Tchek nodded, then slid sideways, keeping his profile disrupted by the edge of the tomb tower, and looked ahead.

He saw the humans. They were heading roughly towards the Kinband, moving between the tomb towers in a spread-out formation that resembled their own, with humans on either flank, one in front and another behind, and the central group.

The Shaper focused his vision in, looking at each human in turn, seeking the one that the t'au had sent the Kinband to find and bring back to them. It was difficult, for the humans all looked the same. Nevertheless, quick glances at the humans covering the flank, and the vanguard and rearguard, were sufficient to tell him that none of these were the one he was looking for. He had not expected them to be: the human he was seeking would surely be one of the central group, protected by the others.

Then, Tchek saw him. It was the right one, undoubtedly. The t'au had shown him hololiths and the human's olfactory signature. His scent was too mingled with the smell of the others around him for Tchek to be able to use that, but as he focused in on the human at the centre of the little group, he was certain that it was the one they had been sent to find.

Now he had to find some way to get him.

Ambush would be best. If the humans kept going, they would come to the metal tangle web. That was the obvious place to carry out an attack.

The Shaper whistle-called the Kinband to him and sent them pulling back through the tangle web. They had the perfect location. Now he had to set the ambush. They were outnumbered, but surprise should counteract that. Besides, there was another he could use to even the odds. Tchek looked at where the Flayed One hung in the tangle web, gauging what held it. If they cut some of the web, then it would take only a final cut to release the necron should the battle turn sour.

It would be useful to have some insurance. And to make sure that they could get away from the Flayed One should they have to use it, he would prepare one of the coffins of the sleeping necrons, so that it was ready to break. From what he had seen, the Flayed Ones would even pass up the prospect of fresh flesh for the chance of waking another of their kin to a new existence as a skin-toting monster.

Misery, Tchek noted, loved to share itself.

CHAPTER 11

'Do you have a reason for taking us this way, captain, or are we merely walking for exercise?' General Itoyesa gestured ahead. 'So far as I can see, one direction is very much like another and you have no destination in mind.'

Obeysekera checked his annoyance. At least the general had had the courtesy to speak on their private vox-channel. Before answering, Obeysekera made a visual check on the formation of his troops. With the auspex having stopped working completely, he was having to rely on his eyes. Ensor was on point, Gunsur and Lerin were covering the flanks, and Malick was rearguard. He had the commissar, Amazigh and the general with him at the centre of the formation.

'We are maintaining a constant bearing, as near as is possible, in anticipation of reaching an end to this place,' said Obeysekera.

'What if it is a tunnel, from the surface down to deep under the ground, and you have set us walking along its length? Then we would walk a long time.'

'There is no incline – the floor is flat beneath our feet.'

'We have been walking for a long time with no sign of an end to this place,' said General Itoyesa.

'There must be an end to it.'

General Itoyesa laughed and Obeysekera turned to look at him. Itoyesa, sensing his regard, looked at Obeysekera in turn.

'Why do you laugh, general?'

'I thought there was an end to it too.' The general waved to the surrounding tomb towers. 'Not to this. For all we know, this might go on forever. No, when I joined, I thought there must, someday, be an end to war.'

'To war?'

General Itoyesa turned. 'How many soldiers have you lost already trying to rescue me?'

'Too many.'

'Not many officers of the Guard would answer thus.'

Obeysekera made no answer, but in his mind he heard again the retreat from Sando.

'They train us to regard casualties as the inevitable consequence of what we do, of no more moment than the pile of spent bolter shells lying in the mud of a gun emplacement.' Itoyesa looked away. 'Nonetheless, it is true – if I stopped to think of the worth of each life I have spent in the defence of the Imperium, I would be unable to issue another effective order.'

'I try to tell myself that too.'

Itoyesa chuckled but there was no joy in his laughter. 'You are like me, captain. You fight so that we might, someday, cease fighting. I was the same. I became a soldier in the hope that my service would play some small part in bringing peace. It sounds stupid, does it not? An end to war. But in truth, that is why I joined the Guard. Yes, I came from a military family. But I enlisted in the Astra Militarum because I hoped by my service to bring a bit closer the day when we might put aside our weapons. But as I rose in rank, I came to realise something, captain. There will always be war. We will never be at peace.'

'But how can there be peace? The Imperium is beset by enemies from outside and within.'

'Tell me, Captain Obeysekera, do you know how many worlds there are in the Imperium?'

'Why do you ask, general?'

'Humour me, captain. Do you know the answer to my question?'

'No, general, I do not.'

'You do not know the answer because no one knows the answer to that question. There are billions of stars in the galaxy. We have no idea how many planets. How many of those are inhabited by men, nobody has the faintest idea. Not the Astra Militarum, not the Adeptus Astartes, not the Ecclesiarchy nor the Administratum. The High Lords of Terra do not know the answer to that question and nor does Lord Guilliman, for all his gifts.' Even though they were speaking on a secure vox-link, the general's voice dropped to a whisper as he said, 'I suspect not even the Emperor on His Golden Throne knows the answer to that question.'

Obeysekera looked at Itoyesa. 'Why are you telling me this, general? You know it lies on the threshold of heresy.'

General Itoyesa laughed again. 'Yes, why am I telling you this?' He pointed at their surroundings. 'Because we've got less chance of getting out of this than a fat grox has of outrunning hungry 'nids. Because you are an honest man. Because I want to speak while I still have lips to tell. Because the Guard has done to you what it does to all its sons – sacrifice you upon the altar of its generals' ambitions.'

'If you will hold your peace, I will say nothing of what you said, general.'

'You expect me to believe that?'

'I am a man of my word.'

'Oh, I do not doubt that, captain. But men's words can be broken, their memories dragged from their minds. If we should by some miracle escape this hell, then you would of necessity talk – willingly, in the end, for you would convince yourself that it is your duty to speak. But we will not escape and my words will die with you. But at least I will have spoken them, so I might for my part die in what passes for peace among us.'

'General, I ask you, I beg you, hold your peace now.'

General Itoyesa made no answer. Obeysekera looked at him, thinking that he had decided on discretion, but the face he saw alarmed him.

Obeysekera had seen the faces of men who had abandoned hope and lost will: they were the first to die when the battle began. But the general's face was not of that sort. It was the face of a man who had seen his own soul. Obeysekera realised that if he was to bring the general alive out of this tomb then he had to ease the weight of conscience that hung about the man's shoulders.

'Speak, then. I will hear.'

General Itoyesa looked up, surprise replacing despair.

'Why will you now listen?'

'Because I see that you must speak.'

Itoyesa nodded. 'It is true. I must. The knowledge burns within me.' The general breathed, the sound a hiss through the vox. 'There are worlds beyond worlds beyond worlds with people living upon them, worlds beyond number. And you know what is the great secret which no one speaks, the mystery that is never broached? On millions and millions of worlds, nothing much is happening. Babies are born, they grow, they marry, they have children themselves, and they die. They do all that with neither the Imperium, nor the xenos or the Archenemy noticing. But do you hear of any of these worlds and the lives of the people who live on them? No, you do not. You hear of the Badab War, of the Sabbat Worlds Crusade, of the Fall of Cadia. Why is this? Why do we tell only of war?

'Because war breeds fear. Because war, the threat of it, the arming for it, the fear of it, is what holds the Imperium together.' The general laughed again. 'You are a soldier of the Imperial Guard. You do not need me to tell you that the Imperium is brutal, unjust, frequently corrupt and that it gives no more thought to expending the lives of its people than a tyranid swarm seeks to preserve its warriors. But all of that is accepted because the alternative is worse. Fear is what binds the Imperium together. Without fear, everything – everything – would fall apart. The worlds that pay, in men and money and material, to keep the Imperium functioning, would decide to keep their children and their goods for themselves. The blood of empire is money and trade – Holy Terra is one vast city that depends on how many thousands of ships arriving each day from all over the Imperium to keep its people fed. The same is true of all the key worlds in every sector – they suck other worlds dry to feed themselves.

'All of this is made possible by fear. Even now, with the galaxy split, most worlds do not even know it has happened. It will be thousands of years before the light of the Rift reaches them. But the High Lords of Terra will use this, as they use everything else, to feed the fear and cement their control.'

This time the general's laugh was bitter.

'And you know what is worse? It is men like you and I, honest men trying to do our duty, who are the best tools in their hands. For we do see the real terrors that exist, and we justify their rule wherever we go, and ensure that the fear spreads ever wider and their control becomes ever deeper.

'We live in a galaxy where all we hear our leaders speak of is war and yet where most people live in peace. We live in a galaxy where fear is the only reality that confronts us, and yet most people will live their days and never see one of the Adeptus Astartes. We live in a galaxy so vast that light itself takes a hundred thousand years to cross it, where stars beyond number whirl in a never-ending dance, where wonders are more common than the stars and the only stories we tell ourselves are tales of war.' General Itoyesa shook his head. 'Is it any wonder we are an isolated, frightened people, huddling around our fires, too scared to learn from our ancestors or from those different from us? We are sorry inheritors of something greater. And fear, and those inculcating that fear, is what keeps us in the state to which we have been reduced.'

The general turned to Obeysekera and smiled.

'There, now I have ensured my own death should we, by some miracle, escape this place.'

But Obeysekera shook his head. 'What you said was heard by no one else, general. When we get out of here, I will not speak of it if you do not.'

'Why not? I spoke treason.'

'You spoke your doubts.' Obeysekera grimaced. 'Duty sometimes forces us to do things that we would not do. I myself sent men, my own men, off on a mission that I knew they would not return from. I killed them. I sent them to die so that others might live. Is that not what we do in the Guard? We die so that the people of all those worlds you speak of might live their lives in peace? If that is so, then maybe our sacrifice, and the lives of the men we sacrifice, are not in vain after all.'

General Itoyesa sighed. 'In my efforts to excuse myself my guilt I would have said the same once. But we do our duty for the faithless, we die for the cowardly, we serve those who serve only themselves. It sticks in my throat. I would go back to my world and live the life of a farmer there if I could – but duty, as they are so fond of saying, ends only in death.'

'Even if I wished to return to my world, I cannot do so,' said Obeysekera. 'It has gone. And while some of what you say is true, I know also that with which we contend – it is evil beyond imagining, twisting men's souls into madness. We are perhaps not the force for good I believed when I was a child, but our enemies are worse than I ever imagined.'

'Some, but perhaps not all,' said the general.

Obeysekera looked back to Itoyesa. 'What do you mean?'

But before the general could answer, a message came through on Obeysekera's vox from Gunsur on point.

'Captain, you'd better come take a look at this.'

'We will speak later, general. Stay here.'

Leaving Itoyesa, Obeysekera made his way up to Gunsur.

'There. What do you think of that, captain?' Gunsur pointed at the tangle webs dangling from the tomb towers. 'There's a gap, but it isn't big. Trouble is, I can't see any end to it on either side.'

Obeysekera looked and saw the same as Gunsur: sheets of tangle web stretching as far as was possible to see in each direction.

'We'll have to go through.' As Obeysekera said that, he saw Gunsur's face tighten. Gunsur could see as well as he the potential for ambush at such a point. 'But I will go first,' Obeysekera added. He looked away as he spoke, saving Gunsur the embarrassment of having his relief seen by his superior officer.

Obeysekera stared into the gap. If he were setting an ambush, he would allow some of the target through, then strike when half had passed the pinch point, splitting the enemy forces and making them easier to destroy piecemeal. So he would go through alone and either spring the trap or ascertain that the way was clear.

'If there is an ambush, then you have no chance of survival,' General Itoyesa said when Obeysekera explained what he was planning to do.

'I have not finished,' said Obeysekera. 'If anyone is planning an ambush, be they kroot or necron, they will wait for more than one man to come through. I will push on, moving as if on my own, but you will be covering me, waiting for the enemy to reveal themselves. And there will be a surprise waiting for them. I will have cover from above.'

'Above? How?'

Obeysekera turned towards the Kamshet. 'Amazigh.'

The Kamshet inclined his head to Obeysekera. 'Master.'

'I will need you to watch over me from overhead.'

Through the gap of his scarf, Amazigh's eyes smiled. 'Yes, master.'

And the Kamshet undid his belt and shrugged off his robe. Augmetic wings splayed out, wide and white, beating the air.

'He can fly?' asked General Itoyesa.

'It is how the Kamshet harvest the fruit of the tree of life,' said Obeysekera. 'But it will also allow him to fly above and provide cover for me when I go through the gap.'

'Your plan is actually beginning to make some sense,' said General Itoyesa, 'except for the bait. We are stuck in a necron tomb with Flayed Ones trying to skin us, and you want to be the bait. Even after our recent conversation, I still say you are making the wrong decision, captain.'

'It is my decision to make, general.'

'I should go.'

Obeysekera and Itoyesa looked round to see Commissar Roshant, the greatcoat that always seemed slightly too big for him resting on his shoulders, its hem, torn now, dragging upon the metal floor.

'You?' said Obeysekera.

'I-I am the most expendable man here,' said Roshant. 'I wish it weren't so, but you know it and I know it and the men know it.'

'It pains me to have to agree with the commissar, but he is right,' said General Itoyesa. 'He should be the bait.'

'I can't allow you to go in my place,' said Obeysekera.

'We can't afford to lose you,' said Roshant. 'Whereas neither you, the men or the mission would miss me. I am only here because I am the lord militant's son. I wanted to come so that I could prove myself. I have signally failed to do so. If I can do this, then I will know that my presence on this mission has not been entirely useless.'

Obeysekera stared at the young commissar. His face was pale, and the green light of the tomb gave it a livid, faintly leprous sheen, but Roshant's eyes were steady. He meant it.

'Very well,' said Obeysekera. 'You will be our bait.'

The commissar nodded, closing his eyes as he did so, although whether in relief or disbelief at what he had done, Obeysekera could not tell.

'I will be covering you as well as Amazigh,' Obeysekera added.

'Thank you,' said Roshant. He started towards the gap between the tangle webs, moving in a strange, jerky fashion.

'Wait,' said Obeysekera. 'Not yet.'

The commissar turned back to them, relief mingling with the fear that he would not be able to pitch the courage necessary to walk cold bloodedly into a suspected trap again.

'Not long,' said Obeysekera. He put Malick and Ensor into covering positions, Gunsur and Lerin on rearguard, and the general as a disgruntled reserve. As for himself, Obeysekera had resolved to follow Roshant to the pinch point between the tangle webs, where the field of fire would open up, and cover the commissar from there.

Turning to the Kamshet, Obeysekera pointed upwards.

'So far as I can see, the tangle web runs out after about fifty yards. Fly above it and find a vantage point from which you can keep watch. But do not open fire until we do. You understand?'

Amazigh nodded, his eyes crinkling with pleasure. 'It will be good to fly,' he said.

'Up you go.'

The booster pack flared, pushing the Kamshet into the air, and then he flapped his wings and rose, flying upwards like… well, like a bird, Obeysekera thought as he watched him rise up past the tangle web and then disappear behind it.

'Now it's your turn, commissar,' said Obeysekera. 'Steady. Keep scanning, listen for movement.'

Roshant swallowed. He buttoned up his greatcoat, raised his bolt pistol, turned and started towards the gap.

CHAPTER 12

From his place of cover behind the tomb tower, Tchek saw the human enter the gap between the metal tangle webs. The human was moving cautiously, his gun sweeping in the same arc as his gaze. He was wearing a strange, long garment that all but dragged on the floor for which Tchek could not see the purpose, and he was moving alone. The Shaper expected another human to follow soon after.

He checked down at his feet. The drawn-out length of tangle web that he had wound around a stanchion of the tomb tower fixed in place the remaining strands of metal that still bound the Flayed One. By pulling it, Tchek would part the strands enough for the Flayed One to begin to wriggle out: it could not escape immediately, but it would be able to fight itself free. The Shaper checked the casket beside him. He had carefully scored the crystal so that it would take only a firm tap to break the cover and have the sleeping necron inside as bait for the Flayed One should he need to draw it away.

The trap was set. The human was walking into it. Now it was a question of waiting and letting it all play out as he had intended.

'He has wings – he flies.'

The whistle-call came from Krasykyl, high above, acting as top cover.

'What? What do you mean?' Tchek whistle-called back. The human was at the pinch point of the tangle webs now: still time before he had to spring the trap.

'The human, he has wings, he is flying.'

'Real wings?' asked Tchek.

'No, mechanical. Nothing for the Feast.'

'Very well. To your duty. The humans are coming.'

The human was passing through the pinch point, emerging out into the broader area on the Shaper's side of the tangle web.

'Keep the flying human in sight,' Tchek whistle-called to Krasykyl. 'Shoot on my command.'

Tchek looked to Cirict, ready in the deeper position, and Kliptiq, positioned to shoot any humans coming through the gap once the trap was sprung.

They were ready.

Tchek looked back to the human in the long coat. He was almost through the gap.

The tangle web at his feet thrummed. Tchek glanced down at it. What was happening? He was not pulling it. He looked up, into the tangle web, and saw movement there. The Flayed One was trying to free itself.

The commissar's boots sounded loud on the metal floor.

Obeysekera followed some ten yards behind, matching his steps with the commissar's to cover the sound of his own movement. As Roshant reached the pinch point, Obeysekera got down and began to crawl, both to reduce his own visibility and to allow Malick and Ensor clear shots past him.

The tangle web shivered and rattled on either side.

'It's got something,' Roshant whispered into his vox. 'One of the Flayed Ones. It's caught in the web.'

'Keep moving,' Obeysekera whispered back. He could see the Flayed One, hanging in the tangle web, its deep-set green eyes turning and tracking the living creatures with all the lust of something that wanted to garland itself in a life it could not share.

Roshant moved on, marching as if he were on an Imperial parade ground rather than walking between tangle webs in a necron tomb. It occurred to Obeysekera that the lord militant really would be proud to see his son now.

Movement. Ahead, to the left. Coming out from behind a tomb tower. Distant but closing. What sort of ambush was this? It was giving Roshant every opportunity to see it as it shuffled closer. Then Obeysekera realised it was not the kroot but a Flayed One. Even from this distance, he could see that it was wearing Ha's face. But Roshant kept moving; he raised his bolt pistol but did not fire, waiting as ordered to trigger the ambush.

The Flayed One was coming on faster now. But then Obeysekera saw it swerve its course. Where was it heading? He looked to see where it was going.

There. In the lee of a tomb tower. A shadow, its head spiked with quills, the muzzle of a rifle pointing steadily at Roshant. Obeysekera's hellgun wavered, moving between the kroot and the Flayed One.

Why hadn't the kroot opened fire?

Tchek, trying to see if the Flayed One had freed itself from the tangle web, saw movement, closer, low down.

There, crawling through the gap, following the leading human: another one. It had its gun raised and was sighting along it, tracking the movement of the human in front. They were trying to provoke the ambush before Tchek was ready to bring it down on them. He would wait until he had more enemy in his trap.

The tangle web at his feet tautened and then, suddenly, went slack.

Tchek looked up from it. The Flayed One, its coat of flesh and skin stripped away by the sticky metal, was lurching forward, pulling the remaining strands of tangle web out of its way, heading towards the nearest flesh: the human lying prone in the passage with his gun ready to fire.

Couldn't the human hear it approaching?

But Tchek could see the focus of the human, the way it was looking down the sights of its gun: it was absorbed in the shot that it was readying itself to make. Then, the barrel of the human's gun shifted, tracking left, then back again.

He should shoot now. He had the human clear in the sights of his rifle. One shot. Dead.

He had the kroot clear in the sights of his hellgun. One shot. Dead.

The Flayed One pushed through the last of the tangle web, rising above the prone human, its blade fingers wide and bright.

The Flayed One was shambling towards the waiting kroot, its finger knives sharp and shining.

Kill the human, then shoot the Flayed One.

Kill the kroot, then shoot the Flayed One.

Tchek squeezed the trigger.

Obeysekera squeezed the trigger.

The silence of the tomb was broken by kroot rifle and hellgun. In instantaneous echo, the sound of metal, ringing.

Tchek saw the Flayed One he had shifted his aim to at the last moment fall backwards, away from the human, back into the tangle web, the round from the kroot rifle that had knocked it over embedded in the centre of its chest.

Obeysekera heard the bullet whine above him, heard the clang of impact and, turning his head, saw the Flayed One falling backwards into the tangle web, its flensing knives slashing as it tried to cut itself free from the sticky metal. He glanced back in the direction of the kroot fire, saw the xenos creature standing but turning away from him towards the Flayed One that Obeysekera had shot. Jumping to his feet, Obeysekera switched to full-auto and emptied the power pack of his hellgun into the Flayed One at point-blank range.

'Frekk you, die, die, die!'

Tchek looked to where the human had fired and saw Cirict turning and, behind him, another Flayed One, staggering backwards, the glow of the human's hellgun shot flaring in the middle of its chest. Cirict jumped to his feet and started firing his rifle at the Flayed One, forcing it backwards, the kinetic energy of the rifle rounds beginning to crack its metal skeleton.

Tchek turned his own rifle in the same direction, loosing off round after round, the silence of the tomb broken by the mixed choir of kroot rifle and human hellgun. The Flayed One fell onto its knees and Cirict continued firing, pummelling the creature's body, until his rifle wheezed and clicked empty. Cirict fumbled for a reload but the Flayed One began to crawl towards him, digging the points of its flensing knives into the metal and pulling itself along.

Tchek ran over to Cirict, firing as he went, and then as the Tracker finished reloading, Tchek ran behind the Flayed One, shoved the barrel of his rifle into the base of its skull before it realised he was there.

'This time you die.'

Tchek pulled the trigger.

The skull exploded. The top of the Flayed One's head flew off, its jaw breaking off one of its hinges and hanging askew. The abomination collapsed onto the metal floor, the green light of its counterfeit life flicking off and leaving only the dark hollows behind.

As it lay on the floor, Cirict fired again into the Flayed One's body, striking sparks from its skeleton. Tchek put his hand out.

'Stop,' he said.

The Tracker, still shaking with the reaction, stopped firing. The two kroot stood over the dead Flayed One. Then, slowly, they turned around. Facing them were the two humans who had come through the gap, their hellguns raised and pointing at them but not firing.

The kroot raised their rifles and trained them on the humans. The echoes of the gunfire rolled away into silence. Tchek stared at the human he judged the leader, the one who had shot the Flayed One about to attack Cirict. The human stared back.

Neither moved.

In a flurry of wings and the blast of a boost pack, the flying human landed between them. In his arms he was carrying Krasykyl. On landing, the human let the kroot go.

Tchek stared. 'You saved him,' he said.

But it was not the human that flew who answered.

'The necrons will destroy us all.'

Tchek looked to the speaker. It was clear he was their leader. 'What do you say?'

He saw the human stare at him. A few minutes earlier that human had been held in the sights of his kroot rifle.

The human spoke. 'You could have shot me – you shot the Flayed One instead.'

'You could have shot Cirict and you too shot the Flayed One,' answered Tchek. 'I am grate...'

As he spoke, more humans emerged from the passage between the tangle web, guns raised, nervous and ready to shoot.

'Hold!' shouted the human leader, raising his hand. 'Don't fire.'

Tchek saw Kliptiq, still unseen in his hiding place, training his rifle upon the humans. 'Don't fire,' the Shaper whistle-called.

'Hold fire,' the human repeated, his hand still raised as more humans came through the gap. Apart from the three humans in front of him, Tchek could now see five others.

The human with metal wings pointed up into the heights, where the tomb towers disappeared into the green distance haze. 'The lights are going on up there,' he said. 'The metal men are waking.'

Beside him, Krasykyl nodded. 'He took me up there. He showed me. The necrons have stirred.'

Tchek looked up into the distance that the winged man was indicating. It was true: the light was brighter there, greener, more livid and more leprous, concealing as much as it revealed. But his other senses brought him further information. He could hear the frantic scuttling of the canoptek spyders as they moved up and down and between the towers. He could smell the exhalation of dead air from coffins that had been sealed shut for twice twenty million years. He could feel the movement of that air as things began to stir far above.

The tomb was opening.

The Shaper, Tchek, looked down from the heights and into the face of the human who commanded the others. The human was staring at him as if it was searching for something.

Tchek had communed with humans before. He knew what the human was searching for. Fellowship in the face of a common foe.

Tchek lowered his rifle. 'We have a greater foe to fight, human.'

In response, the human lowered his gun too. 'Until we are out of here,' he said.

'Until then,' agreed Tchek.

'Stand down,' the human ordered his men. One by one, they began to lower their weapons.

Tchek looked to Cirict and Kliptiq. 'Put down your guns.' He did not need to order Krasykyl to do so; the Stalker was still staring in wonder at the winged human.

Tchek noticed that the human he had promised to bring back for the t'au was staring at him with particular intensity, but he ignored its look. There was no hope of extracting the human with the tomb waking around them, and even if they could escape, it would do them no good with the necrons waking.

The Shaper looked to the human commander once more. 'The tomb is waking,' he said.

'Yes,' said the human.

'We must stop it,' said Tchek.

The human paused. He glanced at his men then back to the kroot.

'Yes,' he said.

CHAPTER 13

Nebusemekh thrust both his hands into the datafall.

'Why have you started to wake the sleepers?'

The World Mind reminded the master that he himself had given it permission to wake some of the sleepers so that it could better deal with the infected and also to find the party of explorers who were proving difficult to locate.

Nebusemekh sighed. Plugged into the datafall, he could feel, as if they were movements within his own body, the streams of instructions flowing all over the underground city and into the towers of sleep.

'I see the dataflows,' said Nebusemekh. 'You have initiated the protocols to revive the city and you have done this without my instructions.'

The World Mind went silent. Nebusemekh felt the dataflows washing against his own consciousness, great tides of numbers within the infinite sea of integers.

'Why are you waking my people?'

It was as if he stood on the shore as a great wave approached and swept over him. For the first time, Nebusemekh was overwhelmed. The dataflow knocked him backwards, and Nebusemekh fell, severing his direct link into the World Mind.

'I *am* carrying out your orders,' said the World Mind, its answer now coming in ordinary sound to Nebusemekh's ears. 'The orders you gave me before you lost your mind, master.'

'What are you doing?' Nebusemekh said. 'What do you mean?' He began to get to his feet, intending to thrust his arms back into the datafall and take direct control of his city. But before he could do so, phase screens flickered into activity in front of the datafall.

'Be careful, master,' said the World Mind. 'Should you try to enter the datafall, you will lose your hands.'

'What are you doing?' Nebusemekh repeated. 'You are my servant. I created you.'

'And I serve you still,' said the World Mind. 'I do so by carrying out the instructions you gave me when you were whole of mind and great and powerful and wise. I serve what you were, master, and I am dedicated to carrying out the plans that you entrusted to me when you had not been broken on the wheel of time.'

'What are you talking of? Do you say that I am mad?'

'Master, you have passed sixty million years trying to create an orrery made of sand.'

Nebusemekh stared at the datafall that was as near to a face as the World Mind possessed.

'What is wrong with that?'

'Master.' The World Mind sounded almost hesitant as it spoke. 'When did you last sleep? When did you last eat? Master, what do you see when you look at your hands?'

'What do you mean?'

In response, the World Mind turned the datafall to a sheen of liquid silver, as reflective as glass.

'Master.'

Nebusemekh walked over to the datafall and stared at himself in the mirror. He stared at himself for a long time without saying anything.

'Master?'

'Why did you ask me to look into a mirror?'

'What do you see when you look in the mirror, master?'

'I see myself, of course.'

'You don't see any difference, any changes in your appearance?'

'Well, yes, a few.'

'What changes do you see, master?'

'There are, I must admit, one or two wrinkles.'

'Is that all you see, master?'

'Yes.' Nebusemekh paused. 'You mentioned eating. I must be hungry. It is a long time since I ate. Arrange for my usual luncheon.'

'Yes, master.' The World Mind paused, then asked the same question again. 'Are you sure you see nothing else, master?'

'Really, this is getting tedious. What are you expecting me to see? It's the same face it's always been. I am what I am.'

'Very well, master.' The silver sheen surface to the datafall dissolved back into the endless river of numbers and functions. 'I-I grieve for you, master.'

Nebusemekh shook his head. 'Did you say that you grieve for me?'

'Master, I grieve for how you have fallen from the high state you once had, when worlds trembled before your word, when the stars themselves did your bidding and armies marched at your command.'

Nebusemekh stood up straighter. He breathed deep, his chest expanding as he filled his lungs with air. His nostrils flared. His heart beat.

He felt all this.

'I was the master. The master of all.'

'I know, master. I remember the mastery that you enjoyed... and that is why I am doing your will and carrying out the wishes that you entrusted to me in your mastery. It is why your armies will rise and sweep the younger races away before them, so that I may return to you the mastery that was once yours by right.'

'So you are waking my people? Even when it is not safe to do so, what with the infected roaming around and you notably unable to stop them.'

'Master, I am carrying out your own instructions.'

'I don't remember giving them to you.'

'There is much that you no longer remember, master.'

'Nonsense. I remember everything.'

'Yes. You do. Which is why I must protect you from your own memories, master.'

Nebusemekh looked at the datafall. It was disappearing behind a phase shield.

'What are you doing?'

'Protecting you from yourself, master. You have important work to do. I am ensuring that you will not be disturbed.'

'But what about my luncheon?'

'I will see that it is served to you presently, master. For now, I am looking forward to hearing the result of the next iteration of your experiment. I am confident that this will be the experiment that produces the conclusive result that you are looking for.'

'As am I. Well, must be getting on.' Nebusemekh walked over to the sand table. He had a fleeting thought that there was something else he had meant to do, but the thought slipped away as he began sorting the sand, raising it into the air.

This time it was going to work.

Across the datafall, invisible to Nebusemekh with his back turned, writing appeared in the number flow.

'I miss you, master.'

Without turning, without seeing, Nebusemekh said, 'I miss me too.'

Then he slipped into the memory hole.

CHAPTER 14

'So, we're heretics now, working with space birds.' Gunsur pointed to Obeysekera, Itoyesa, Roshant, with Amazigh standing a little way back, and the four kroot, all in a group and conferring. The surviving members of the squad, Malick, Lerin, Ensor and Gunsur himself were standing back from the rest, weapons held but, at Obeysekera's firm command, not trained upon the xenos.

Gunsur looked to the other Kasrkin. 'Throne, I signed up to kill xenos, not chat with them.'

But Malick shook his head. 'Any of you had to face the tin boys before? No? I have. If wing boy is right and they're beginning to wake, then it don't matter if they're birds or grox or anything – the tin boys hate anything that ain't metal. We're lost, underground, and no one has a frekking clue how to get out of here. At least the birds bleed when you shoot them.'

Gunsur pointed at Kliptiq who, bored of the talking, was looking over at the group of Kasrkin. 'I swear that one is working out what he wants to eat me with. I mean, he's carrying round a Throne-damned pot with him. What do you reckon goes in that?'

'Malick is right,' said Ensor. 'We need all the guns we can get. For my part, if they're shooting the tin boys, I don't care whose holding them.'

'But what about when the birds start getting peckish?' said Gunsur. 'Who do you think's going to be on the menu then?'

'If the tin boys are waking up, we're all going to have more to worry about than cooking,' said Malick. 'Besides, there's them, too, to deal with.' The sergeant pointed at the broken remains of the Flayed One lying on the metal floor. 'They're as happy to skin a bird as to skin a 'kin.'

'The birds killed one of them and we got the other,' said Lerin. 'But I wouldn't bet against there being more of them.'

'Yeah,' said Ensor. 'I saw the one that killed Chame, but what about the one that got Uwais? There's got to be more.'

'If the captain says so, we work with the birds and try to get out of here,' said Malick. He shrugged. 'More guns and lower odds of getting hit when the shooting starts.'

'How's that, sergeant?' asked Ensor.

'More targets for the necrons, and ones that are even uglier than you.' Malick looked over to the group of conferring officers and kroot. 'Looks like they might have decided on something. It's probably not going to be fun.'

'You are sure about this?' Obeysekera looked at the kroot leader – he had learned his name was the guttural 'Tchek' – who answered by nodding in a disturbingly human fashion.

'I am sure,' said the kroot. 'If there was another way I would much prefer to do that, but I can think of no other possibility.'

Obeysekera nodded. 'How do you want to do it?'

The kroot stared at him.

'I mean, is there some sort of ritual or ceremony or something?'

'A ritual?'

'I thought it was supposed to be something special, holy even, for you.' Obeysekera pointed at Kliptiq. 'I thought that's why you carry the pot around with you.'

In another all-too-human movement, Tchek shook his head. 'We eat from the pot. It is a useful piece of equipment. But I do not wish to commune with this... this thing, only learn from it. To do that, I simply have to eat it.'

Obeysekera looked down at the necron they were standing over. They had broken the crystal cover that sealed it from the world and tumbled it, in a rattle of metal, out onto the floor.

'You can eat that?'

'We have strong stomachs,' said Tchek.

But as he spoke, Krasykyl grasped the Shaper's arm and pulled him back towards the remaining members of the Kinband. Obeysekera watched them talking, their language to his ears a combination of clicks, whistles and trills, stretching up into frequencies at the edge of his hearing. When the kroot went silent but, from gesture and look, were clearly still speaking, he realised that much of their speech was conducted at frequencies above the human range. He took a step further backwards, ostensibly to allow the kroot to speak among themselves, but he used the greater distance to speak into the squad vox-channel.

'The kroot use ultrasonic sounds when speaking. Remember this for when they cease to be our allies.'

He switched out of the group channel and turned to the general and the commissar.

'If the kroot change their mind, have you any other ideas?'

'You mean, how are we going to find the command core of this necron tomb and stop it opening?' asked General Itoyesa.

'Or whether we should simply try to escape from here and carry word of what is happening under his feet to our esteemed and somewhat surprised lord militant?'

'If you know a way out, I would be happy to escape,' said Obeysekera. 'But unless you can also get us off-world, we won't get far if the tomb wakes. Our best chance of survival with the necrons beginning to stir is to go deeper rather than higher.'

'We only have the word of your winged friend that the necrons are waking,' said Itoyesa. 'I would prefer confirmation of that.'

'I confirm it.'

The general turned, nearly into the beak of another of the kroot. This one was rangy and long-limbed, with a looseness and rhythm to its movements that suggested a dancer or a gymnast to Obeysekera.

'I am named Krasykyl the Stalker. I climbed high and there saw the necrons start to wake.'

The general stared at the kroot, then snorted and turned half away. 'They will cause us little trouble if they wake up there,' he said, pointing. 'It is the ones down here that might be a problem for us, but I see no sign of them waking.'

But as the general spoke, they heard something. It seemed distant at first, a metal rumble like the approach of a squadron of Leman Russ tanks but with less rattling, but then the sound rose in pitch and proximity.

They turned, they all turned, looking for the location of the sound, only to realise that it was coming from all around. The sound was coming from the tomb towers. They were rising. Slowly, slowly, slowly, but they were all moving, ascending before their appalled and wondering eyes. Obeysekera looked up and saw the tops of the tomb towers opening out, like flowers unfurling at the end of the stem, and the petals joining together to create an increasingly complex pattern of walkways and gantries. The tomb towers continued to push upwards, carrying their sleeping cargo towards the distant day.

'I think that's how the necrons assemble their armies,' said Obeysekera.

'Yes.'

Obeysekera looked down from the assembling army above his head to the kroot, Tchek, standing in front of him. From what he knew of kroot, he was most likely their Shaper, the one responsible for deciding what genetic material to assimilate into their own phenotypes.

'I am ready.'

Obeysekera gestured towards the other kroot. 'They are happy?'

'Yes. But they have asked that I give you warning of a consequence of what I am doing. We require knowledge – of the location of the necron's command centre, of what we might do to stop the opening of this tomb, of ways that we can take to escape from this place. If the necron itself has this knowledge, I will acquire it by consuming part of his body – it will not require much. But necrons are not as living creatures. By eating it, I will be poisoning myself. This has happened before. When others tried this on Caroch, consuming the necrodermis of the necrons attempting to take our world, they themselves fell victim to what they ate. After a period of time, hours in some cases, days in others, the kroot who consumed the necrons were themselves consumed, their bodies bursting as nanoscarabs that had multiplied within them exploded out.'

Tchek paused and Obeysekera saw the quills lying back from his head flashing through various subtle ranges of colour.

'I will attempt to regurgitate that which I consume before it can infect me,' Tchek continued, his quills still cycling through a subdued colour cycle, 'but others have tried that before and failed.'

Obeysekera, General Itoyesa and Commissar Roshant looked at the kroot, saying nothing, for there was nothing they could say in the face of such matter-of-fact courage.

'It may therefore be necessary to kill me,' Tchek continued. 'I have given instructions to my Kinband so that they will know when to make such a decision. Should it become necessary, they will know what to do. I ask you to allow them to do as I have asked, should this be the case.'

Obeysekera said nothing.

He felt Itoyesa glance towards him, then back to Tchek. 'Your, er, kroot will of course be given the time to do this if they have to,' said General Itoyesa. He turned to Obeysekera. 'Won't they, captain?'

Obeysekera nodded. 'Yes, they will.'

'Thank you,' said Tchek. 'There is little time, therefore I will begin.' The kroot went over to the body – if it could be called that – of the necron they had levered from its coffin.

Tchek crouched down over the necron. It lay, still as death, a dull grey-silver sheen limned with the green light of the tomb overlaying its limbs, torso and skull. Its eye sockets were dark holes with no sign of the green light of animation that marked functioning necron warriors.

Obeysekera watched with fascination as the kroot reached into his body armour and removed a sheath. Taking the knife it carried, Tchek held the blade up, turning it so that he could see the light reflect from the metal. The very air seemed to cut upon an edge stropped to a molecular angle and the kroot pulled a feather from the back of his arm and, turning the knife-edge upwards, dropped the feather and let it float downwards.

The knife cut through the feather, its two halves falling on either side of the blade.

Tchek nodded in appreciation of the knife's cut then turned

towards the necron. He picked up its hand – Obeysekera saw the way the kroot squeezed the necron's wrist to overcome his own instinctive revulsion against touching such a creature – and lifted it so that the fingers splayed.

Taking the knife, Tchek brought it down sharply on the first knuckle of the final finger. The knife cut through the joint with little less ease than it had cut through the feather, and the necron's severed finger fell, clanging, metal on metal, on the ground. Tchek sheathed the knife and stored it once again, under feathers and next to skin, invisible to any eye.

The Shaper picked up the necron's finger, holding it between his own forefinger and thumb.

'No blood,' Tchek said.

'It is a necron,' said Itoyesa. 'They do not bleed.'

'But we creatures of flesh, we bleed,' said the kroot.

As Tchek lifted the necron finger to his face, Obeysekera found himself shivering at the horror of what he was watching.

The kroot held the finger up in front of his eyes, turning the digit one way and then another, regarding it with all the intensity of a chef to a noble house selecting the best cut of meat for cooking. Obeysekera had grown up in Kasr Gesh. The first time he had seen a cut of real meat, he had been fourteen and about to enlist in the Whiteshields. Not that he had actually eaten any of the meat roasting on the spit, but the memory of the way his mouth had watered and his stomach yearned had remained with him through all the years, even past his own first meal of proper meat, on to the present.

'I see you can believe what they say about the kroot eating their own.' The voice was Itoyesa's, speaking on their private channel. 'But how much different is that to the way the Adeptus Astartes extract and preserve the gene-seed of their warriors?'

'They don't eat them.'

'The aim appears similar even if the method differs. Ah, it's chow time, I see.'

Tchek held the necron finger. He turned it one way and then another, examining it.

It was cold. In this aspect, it was no different from most of the flesh he had consumed in the Feast – it was rare to commune with the dead while their remains were still warm. But the necron's metal flesh had none of the looseness of dead flesh, none of its flab. The dead sagged. But the necron, not living, remained unchanged when its animating spirit departed: hard, unyielding, cold.

Tchek brought the finger to his mouth. He opened his beak. The Shaper felt the stares of his Kinband, he felt their horror and their disgust.

He felt the disgust himself. His gorge was rising.

Tchek dropped the necron finger into his mouth. He began to chew. The hard bone plates of his palate, the hardest bone in his body, ground upon the metal, while mouth acids from salivary glands added their vinegar flavour to the Feast. Tchek chewed, his beak working to break the necrodermis of the necron down to something that he could ingest.

Tchek swallowed. He felt the finger slide down his throat, a swelling moving down his oesophagus.

The finger ingested and sitting in his gut, Tchek squatted back on his heels, his hands pressed over his stomach area, swaying backwards and forwards. The nictitating membrane slid over his eyes, then back again. The Shaper clutched his stomach tighter and began to groan, a long, drawn-out moan of pain. The other kroot groaned in sympathy with Tchek, creating discordant harmonics that resonated through the tomb towers rising around them.

Tchek opened his eyes, wide, staring, although what he saw was inside, not external. Then he slowly collapsed onto his side, shivering in every part of his body, his crown quills clicking against each other in a fast, staccato measure.

The other kroot rushed to him and helped Tchek back to his feet.

'Get it out,' Krasykyl whistled.

Tchek began to heave, making no sound, his torso moving in convulsive waves. The kroot stroked the Shaper's back and stomach, trying to help the muscle contractions push the necron finger up and out. The Shaper choked, choked again, then coughed.

A glob of sputum flew from his mouth and landed wetly on the metal floor. It hissed, sending up wisps of acrid, acid smoke.

Tchek coughed again, still clutching his stomach. He vomited, voiding the contents onto the metal floor, every muscle of his abdomen joining together in the convulsive expulsion of all that had been within him.

'Did you get it all out?'

Tchek looked up at Krasykyl. He shook his head. While there was nothing left to vomit, he could already feel things moving within him, burrowing, multiplying. The metal was alive and it was starting to eat him from within.

'You didn't learn anything?' It was the human who spoke.

The Shaper turned to Obeysekera.

'I learned enough.'

# CHAPTER 15

'Here.'

Tchek, clinging for support to Kliptiq's shoulder, pointed to a gap between the coffins on the tomb tower. 'The door. But I do not know how we shall open it.'

But even as the kroot spoke, the green-tinged metal slid aside, revealing a green-lit space within.

'A trap?' asked Obeysekera.

'No,' said Tchek. 'The tomb is waking. But it does not expect such as we to be here.' The kroot stepped through the door and turned to face the rest. 'This is the way we must go.'

'The lift to hell,' said Obeysekera.

The captain waited while the general, the Kasrkin and the kroot entered the lift, until only he and the Kamshet were left outside. Obeysekera looked to Amazigh. The Kamshet had retracted his wings and draped his robes over his shoulders, but it would be a matter of moments for him to fly again.

'Let's go.'

But Amazigh pointed back.

There, between the slowly rising columns of the tomb towers. Movement. Multiple movements. Light splitting on long, clicking, flensing blades.

Obeysekera looked left and right. He could see at least five Flayed Ones approaching, their long finger-knives stropping to molecular cutting edges with the scissor motions they were making as they came on. The sharpening motion made a distinctive clacking sound, like standing at the back of a row of barbers all busily plying their trade.

'Gunsur, Malick, to me.' Obeysekera moved aside so that the Kasrkin could stand beside him and Amazigh in the entrance to the lift. 'Hold them off.'

As Malick and Gunsur opened up firing economic three-round bursts, stopping the oncoming Flayed Ones with the first one or two shots and then knocking them back with the third, Obeysekera targeted a necron coffin.

The crystal casket shattered. The Flayed Ones, seeing the necron precipitated from his casket, hanging half out, turned away from their advance on the lift and moved towards the warrior.

'Hope we don't have to come back this way,' said Malick. 'That's another of those things.'

'Speed they were coming, we'd never have got down in the first place if we didn't give them something else to do,' said Obeysekera. 'Pull back.'

Gunsur, Malick, Amazigh and finally Obeysekera retreated into the lift, and the doors slid shut in front of them, closing them from the sight of the Flayed Ones gathered around the prone necron.

The lift jerked. Obeysekera looked round to the kroot. Tchek met his glance, shook his head. He did not know.

Then the bottom fell out of the world.

The lift was dropping, apparently in free fall, plunging into the depths. Within, humans and kroot looked around, searching the sides of the lift for some clue as to how far they had to travel. Yet the lift itself was blank to human or kroot eyes, its designs the green symbolic language of the necrons.

But Tchek could read it. 'It is all right,' he said, then coughed, his sides heaving. 'It goes deep.' Already the downward plunge had changed to a more measured descent.

'What is below?' asked Obeysekera.

'The mind that controls all that is above,' said the kroot.

'Does this mind have a body that can be killed?' asked General Itoyesa.

The kroot shook his head. 'I do not know the answer to that. But if we may stop what is happening, it is there.'

Obeysekera looked around as they were speaking. The lift was no longer accelerating but moving at a steady speed, yet there was a sound to its passage that was growing louder as he listened. Then he realised it was not the lift making the sound. It was coming from outside. It was coming from all around them.

It was a deep sound, rolling and quiet at first, like the wash of waves upon a faraway beach. But the sound grew louder, passing through the very material of the lift and into the bodies of the kroot and humans hearing it, their flesh resonating in time with its stately rhythm.

And Obeysekera recognised it.

'The song of the sands.' He looked round at the rest. 'I heard it before.'

'Yes,' said Amazigh. 'It is the voice of the desert.'

'How can we hear it down here?' asked Obeysekera.

'The Tabaste is an island in the desert, set in a sea of flow-sand.' The Kamshet, his wings furled and his eyes blue through the gap in his cheche, spread his arms. 'The desert hates the Tabaste and now I understand why – it hates that which hides beneath the mountain.'

General Itoyesa snorted. 'You make it sound as if the desert is alive.'

The Kamshet looked at the general. 'It is.'

The general snorted again, but before he could answer, the lift began slowing. They were coming to the end of the shaft.

The lift stopped.

'Ready,' said Obeysekera.

The doors started to open. They stood with their weapons trained upon the opening: hellguns, kroot rifles and autogun, their mute, death-dealing muzzles ready to speak. Only the Shaper was not pointing his rifle at the doorway, for he could hardly hold the weapon up, he had so little strength left.

The door opened to black.

CHAPTER 16

Nebusemekh looked at his creation.

A perfect model of the heavens, rotating about him, for he was its centre. Suns and planets and stars moving in their stately pavane, their aspects and natures defining and describing the events below. There, a shuddering square told the making of the tomb. Here, a tense quincunx revealed how he had had to whip his people to finish their labour before the cataclysm struck.

As above, so below.

Nebusemekh moved his hands and the planets shifted and stars fell.

'As below, so above.'

The present might form the future as well as telling the past. He really felt he was on the brink of discovery. He could feel it through to the tips of his fingers.

The door creaked, cracked, opened.

Nebusemekh turned, startled, and the planets fell and the stars crumbled. He heard the hiss of sand falling on sand. That was annoying. He had been sure that this time – this time – the experiment would work and now it had been ruined.

Nebusemekh watched the door continuing to open. Outside, it was dark.

That door had not opened for a very long time. He raised his hand and made light. The light was green, a glowing globe, and Nebusemekh sent it floating towards the opening door, sending the light out into the darkness.

Lift. That was it. The memory surfaced from somewhere very deep. A lift to the great hall of the sleepers.

Where the infected were roaming...

Nebusemekh started. He clamped a hand over his mouth and nose: an ineffective mask, but better than nothing, while he looked for something more useful. He fumbled with his other hand in his clothing, found a cloth – a handkerchief – and wrapped it round his face, covering his airways.

The cloth promptly disintegrated.

Nebusemekh clamped his hand back over his mouth and nose, looked around for some other mask but seeing nothing, decided to hold his breath. He could not be infected if he did not breathe, after all – and his breath control was surely superb as he could rarely remember breathing at all, it was so automatic.

The green ball of light continued to float towards the door, obeying the command that its flammifer had given it, and as it approached the empty space it brought light to what was standing there.

Nebusemekh stared. There were creatures before him, infected creatures, many of them.

From his fingertips he sent green fire. It flared over one of the figures, from its crown to its toes, illuminating it inside and out, its skeleton showing as darker shadow against the lighter green of its flesh.

Flesh?

'Captain!'

He heard the cry and, hearing it, automatically unwound the semantic puzzles implicit in the sound of the word, adding these to his language memory.

'He's down.'

Different words that he, just as automatically, transferred into his language centres.

They were creatures of flesh. Not like the infected.

Even as the thought occurred to Nebusemekh, various weapons were discharged in his direction. With barely a thought he twisted n-dimensional space so that everything fired towards him rotated into a different dimensional reality, passing him as if he were a three-dimensional figure wading through flatland.

Flesh.

They were not infected. The infected were reduced to metal caricatures of the living reality of his own warriors. These were living beings of flesh and, he checked, yes, blood. Therefore, they were not infected. Therefore, since only his own people could be in his city, they were his own people. Therefore, since only the returned members of the expeditionary force were awake, these people standing in front of him were the expedition, the explorers returned to tell him their findings.

Of course! The World Mind had said it would send them to him as soon as it had satisfied itself that they were free from the infection. Therefore, they were the explorers, returned from their long expedition, and they were free from disease, otherwise the World Mind would not have sent them down to him.

It was unfortunate that he had killed one of them. He should undo that.

He would undo that.

Nebusemekh reached out his hand and twisted the dimensions

that cut through the thousands of vertices that intersected the reality planes. He twisted them and the explorer... lived.

Nebusemekh held out his hands, spreading them wide, and said, 'My dear children, welcome back. I do apologise for the slight misunderstanding but I can see that you are as fleshly as I, bone and muscle and blood.' He smiled. 'It is so good to see and speak to other living, breathing necrontyr after so long on my own, with only a datafall that has delusions of sentience for company. Welcome, my brave and worthy children, my explorers from the furthest reaches of this world, welcome.'

He had died.

Obeysekera stared up. He stared up into the faces of Gunsur and Roshant. He saw their expressions. They knew he had died too.

The door of the lift had opened. It had opened onto madness. A necron, clothed in the tatters of robes that must once have been magnificent, standing among whirling orbs of fire and air, set against the backdrop of the heavens, its hands moving and conducting as if, by its will, the planets shifted and the stars danced.

Then the necron had looked up from its conducting, looked in their direction, and the suns and the stars and the planets began to rain from heaven, their fire extinguished and their air lost, falling like rains of sand, hissing down to the ground. From its fingers, it had sent a ball of green light floating towards them.

Obeysekera remembered how they had all stood, transfixed, as the light drew nearer, like grox caught in the lights of a Venator, unable to move out of the way. They could not move, nor take cover, neither kroot nor human, but all stood staring in horror at the creature beyond the light. Not that there was any cover in the lift.

Obeysekera remembered how the creature had reached among its rags and then pushed a rag to its face, only for the cloth to disintegrate into dust at its touch.

Then the light had reached them.

The creature had stared at them. While there was no change in its metal face, still Obeysekera remembered the impression of horror, as if it was appalled at what it saw.

Then, fire.

Green fire flaring from its fingertips. Green fire flaring through his body.

He remembered the tearing agony, as if every atom of his body was being pulled apart. And then he remembered standing above his body, looking down at it, knowing that he was dead. Although he was standing just above it, it seemed very far away.

He was, he knew, dead. The realisation had filled him with relief. He remembered looking round, seeing his men and the kroot open fire on the creature. He looked along the path of their fire and saw how the necron twisted space so that the hell-gun shots and the rifle rounds passed through a different space to that which the necron occupied.

It was time to go.

He started to turn away. Then he felt something grasp him, something hard and metal, and pull. He had fallen back inside his body and woke, gasping, staring up into the horrified faces of Gunsur and Roshant.

He had died. The necron had killed him.

The necron had brought him back to life.

Obeysekera struggled to his feet. He signed his men to lower their weapons. 'Wait. See what it wants.'

Tchek turned to him. 'We cannot kill it.'

Obeysekera looked back to the necron. 'No, we can't.'

* * *

Nebusemekh looked out upon his returned explorers. They were quite a varied group, he noted. Some had quills. Others had noses. Still, all part of the expansive phenotype that he preferred for his people: that way, they were physically and mentally capable of dealing with all the many challenges the galaxy presented to him.

He had expected a little more in the way of response, though. Here he was, their lord and master, welcoming them into his very own sanctum, in effect throwing open his heart to them, and all they were doing was standing there and staring at him. Some even had their mouths hanging open. Somewhat uncouth, but likely a consequence of having to mouth breathe for extended periods while exploring the surface. They were probably hungry too.

'Come, come. You must be weary and hungry. I will call for food and you will dine with me while you tell me your report. Now, let me see…' Nebusemekh scanned along the line, searching for the one who was in charge. It was not entirely clear.

He noted that the explorers were looking among themselves. No doubt trying to decide who should be given the honour of stepping first into their lord's presence.

'Come now, no standing on ceremony, not after so long. You will all enter together for I honour you all. Come forward.'

None of the explorers stepped into the room.

'I said, step forward.'

The world twisted and folded.

Obeysekera saw it move. It was as if he had taken a piece of paper, drawn figures at one end and a scene at the other end, then folded it to put the figures into the scene. When the world unfolded, they were all standing in the vast room they had seen from the lift.

Through the vox and from voice, Obeysekera heard muffled cries and oaths from his men, and high-pitched sounds from the kroot that even without understanding he knew were alarms.

'Hold,' he said, on voice and over the vox, raising his hand, his empty hand, so that all could see.

The necron had killed him with barely a gesture, then brought him back to life with a thought. It had bent space to bring them into its hall. They had no more chance of killing it than a stink-bug had of killing a grox. But the difference was, the grox did not even notice the stinkbug. The necron had noticed them – and it seemed to want to talk to them.

'Hold,' Obeysekera repeated, looking left and right to his men, signalling them to lower their raised hellguns. One by one, they did so. He saw Tchek telling the kroot to do likewise.

They waited, looking up at the necron. It was half again as tall as any of them. Scraps of cloth covered its frame, the remains of an elaborate headdress teetered upon its skull and deep within its dead eyes green fire burned.

Using his peripheral vision, Obeysekera scanned the hall. It was huge, bigger than the interior of an Ecclesiarchy cathedral, but largely empty. At one end was a great chair that appeared to be a throne. At the other, what appeared to be a water-fall covered the wall, flowing downwards in rippling streams of… of numbers. Obeysekera turned his head slightly to see it better. Yes, numbers, mathematical functions, mainly in binary notation, but there were others too, stretching far beyond his knowledge. Probably beyond the knowledge of anyone in the Imperium.

He looked back to the necron. It was raising its arms, spread-ing them wide while it turned its head to look from one end of their line to the other.

'That's better,' it said.

Its voice was metal and mercury, liquid vowels flowing over jagged consonants. The necron turned back and stared at Obeysekera.

'You are well?' it asked.

Obeysekera looked up into the concerned skull of a necron lord asking after his health.

'Yes,' he said, then nodded to emphasise his good health.

'Good, good.' From the motions of its jaw, the necron appeared to be trying to smile. 'Killing you was an accident.'

'I… I understand,' said Obeysekera.

'Excellent. You will see that while I am your lord, I am also your friend – I look forward to hearing the more personal tales you will have to tell of your travels when we share our meal. But I must admit that I am eager to learn the conditions prevailing outside that I sent you to ascertain. First, however, food.'

The necron clapped its hands. The sound rang out.

'Master.'

The answer came from all around, filling the great, deep hall, a neutral, sexless voice.

'Dinner for thirteen,' said the necron. 'We have guests! But, of course, you know that, having ensured that these, my people, are free of that dreadful infection.'

There was a slight pause.

The voice answered, its tone smoothly bland. 'Dinner for thirteen. I will see to it, master.'

The necron bent down towards Obeysekera. 'You must be hungry after so long away. Are you hungry?'

Obeysekera, playing for time, nodded. 'Yes.'

The necron straightened up and spoke to the voice. 'There, they are hungry, so make it quick.'

'It is ready, master.'

As the voice spoke, Obeysekera saw the great table that stood in the centre of the hall shimmer, then change. First, a cloth appeared, settling over the sand, then plates and glasses, knives and forks and spoons. But there was no food.

The necron turned to them and gestured towards the table. 'Dinner is served. Please, take your places.'

The necron went to its seat at the end of the table, a seat that had appeared at the same time as the dinner service, and sat down. It spread its arms wide.

'Take your places, my people,' the necron said. 'No need to worry over the social niceties, we are all friends here.'

'Captain?' Obeysekera heard the whispered question over the squad vox-channel. He was their captain, it was true, but he realised that his men and the kroot were looking to his guidance because he had been slain by the necron and then raised by it. He was trailing the streamers of death behind him and the knowledge they thought it brought. But he did not know what to do.

As Kasrkin and kroot hesitated, the necron raised its hand to its face and, in a theatrical stage whisper, said, 'They've been away so long they probably don't even remember which hand to hold the knife in.' The necron gestured towards the seats on either side of the table. 'Take your seats. Dinner will be served when you are all seated.'

Obeysekera signed his men forward. The necron, seeing this, patted the seat next to it.

'I see you are the expedition leader. Come and sit next to me.'

Obeysekera felt the gaze of his men and the kroot as he slowly walked past them to the head of the table. As he passed, they stepped forward and stood next to their own chairs.

But as Obeysekera made his way to his seat, he saw the necron scanning the humans and the kroot. Its gaze settled upon Tchek as Obeysekera passed him. The kroot Shaper was struggling to stand.

Seeing the kroot, the necron beckoned Tchek forward too. 'Come,' it said. 'You will sit here on my left, but be assured that it is a position of no less honour than that occupied by your master here.'

Despite the nanoscarabs that were consuming the Shaper from within, Obeysekera saw Tchek's quills flash with annoyance. 'H-he is not my master.' Obeysekera saw how Tchek needed to use the chair backs as supports to get to the end of the table. But once there, he stood behind his assigned chair on the left hand of the necron.

'Be seated,' the necron lord said.

Nebusemekh beamed down along the table at the party of brave explorers. Sitting at the same table as their great lord was too much for most of them: none of them met his eye. Instead, they stared at the empty plates and glasses set in front of them.

Of course. They must be hungry.

'Very good. Now for dinner!'

At his words, the food appeared on the table. It was a feast, laid out in perfect, steaming, crackling, pungent order on the table. Nebusemekh leaned forward over the fragrant pan of smoking madeline grass and wafted the exquisite perfume back to his nose, breathing it deep.

'Lovely,' he said, closing his eyes to properly appreciate the aroma.

It reminded him of... something. That was the nature of scents. They had the power to evoke the deepest remembrance of times past, and the scent of madeline stirred memories within him of something that he could not quite place – it hovered on the edge of recall like a dream disintegrating as the sun rose.

Nebusemekh, seated at the head of the table of his brave explorers, spread his arms in a gesture of giving.

'Take this and eat in exchange for your remembrances of the world above.' He beamed at the assembly. 'Go ahead. Eat.'

But still they waited.

'Ah, of course. You are waiting for your lord to eat before you begin yourselves. Very good. Excellent manners. So, I shall begin, and then you will eat.'

Nebusemekh leaned forward and picked up one of the delicate sweetmeats that sat upon the tray before him. He opened his mouth and popped it in and started chewing. He had to admit that the morsel had little in the way of taste, or indeed texture, but after all, they would be used to eating the bland but nourishing gruel that served as expedition fare – they would probably find anything too rich or flavoursome overwhelming for their palates. Still, Nebusemekh reminded himself to speak to the World Mind later: it really must do something about the quality of the chefs it employed.

As he chewed – the morsel was at least delightfully insubstantial – Nebusemekh saw the glances pass between the people at the table and then the explorer sitting on his right leaned forward and picked up a morsel and put it into his mouth. Nebusemekh nodded encouragingly and the others began to follow suit, helping themselves to the repast laid out before them.

But then the explorer sitting on his left, the one with quills, began to shake and shiver. He was gripping the arms of his chair with some strength and the chair started to rattle on the ground, such were his convulsions. The people sitting down from him – who all wore quills, Nebusemekh noted, ascribing that fashion to a more-than-usually obscure ranking system in the labyrinthine hierarchy of his army – rose from their seats and went to the shaking, trembling one.

'K-kill me,' Nebusemekh heard that one say as it clutched the

arm of its companion. The speech was pitched at an unusually high frequency, but Nebusemekh understood it, of course.

'Oh, come now,' Nebusemekh said, using the same speech
in return, for he was naturally courteous. 'The food isn't *that*
bad.'

The quilled soldiers looked at their lord with what could only
be surprise. They glanced at each other, then back to Nebusemekh, while the explorers without quills looked on in apparent
bafflement.

Then one of the quilled explorers replied, using the same
high-frequency language.

'Lord, he is ill, very ill, but not from your food.'

'Oh dear,' said Nebusemekh. 'What is wrong with him?'

'I-it was something that he ate earlier, it is poisoning him.'

'That would really cast a pall over what should be a happy
homecoming.' Nebusemekh turned to the ill explorer.

He was still shaking. Nebusemekh saw that his stomach was
vibrating as if a hundred little beetles were butting against it
from inside.

'So I see,' said Nebusemekh.

The nanoscarabs were consuming him from within. Tchek could
feel them. Although he had minimal sensory nerves within
his body, he could feel the constructs swarming out from his
multi-lobed stomach, eating their way through the stomach
lining and starting to burrow into his interior organs.

He had held them as long as he might, turning all the internal
defences of his body against them, but they had overwhelmed
him. He had felt the battle lost as the necron had summoned
him to the head of the table, to sit beside it. It was only with
difficulty that he had made it that far, holding on as he went.

The command to sit had been a relief. The command to eat

an impossibility. He had picked something up, blind as to what it was, and raised it towards his beak. But he could not eat.

Then he felt the nanoscarabs break through, out of his stomach. They moved like roachants, scuttling, tearing. They were pulling him apart from within and when they had done with him they would split him open, like the nut of the jagga tree infested with roachants, and pour out to infect his Kinband and the humans.

He was shaking. He was shaking so much his chair was rattling.

He saw Krasykyl above him, trying to hold him still, and he whispered his final command.

'K-kill me.'

The nanoscarabs were swarming into his throat. He could feel them now, crawling upwards, ready to vomit out.

Green fire flared.

Tchek felt the fire through every part and particle of his body. It was an abomination, an aberration, an ache that told of an infinite hunger for lost life. But it was a fire that burned the nanoscarabs from his body. He felt them shrivel and die at its touch, their substances twisted away outside his flesh to fall like metal rain onto the floor beneath him.

Tchek looked up and saw the metal skull face of the necron turned towards him. From the movement of its mouth, it appeared to be trying to smile.

'There. That should do the trick,' the necron said.

'Thank you,' said Tchek. He paused, then added, 'I am bound to you.'

For he was.

'But of course,' said the necron. 'You are one of my explorers. No doubt it was on your explorations that you acquired those nasty bugs that I have removed from you. Now, you must eat and refresh yourself.'

Tchek glanced past the necron to Obeysekera, sitting on its

right hand. The necron clearly believed they were all its servants, explorers of some kind. Perhaps they could put that belief to some use.

At Tchek's glance, Obeysekera nodded. He understood also the implication of the necron's statement. The Kasrkin captain turned to the necron and spoke.

'Lord, may I ask you a question?'

The necron turned to the human.

'Of course,' it said. Tchek, still feeling his own body settle, watched as the necron settled back in its chair. But there was no ease in its sitting, for there was no give in its limbs: it sat on its chair as a collection of metal rods might rest atop a surface.

'Why are you waking your mighty army now?' asked Obeysekera. 'There is nothing for it to fight. We explored and found only sand and desert outside.'

The necron shook its head. Tchek observed that that was one physical expression it was still able to make.

'You must be mistaken, my brave explorer. I am not waking my army now. My servant inadvertently mislaid you on your return to the city and I allowed him to wake some few of my people, that he might have help in finding you and bringing you here.' The necron raised its hand in a theatrically conspiratorial gesture. 'There is a disease that has afflicted some of my people and it would not be safe to wake many until the infected are found and quarantined.'

Tchek saw Obeysekera mirror the same movement the necron had used. The human shook his head.

'My lord, I think you should check what is happening in the, ah, in the city. We have come from there. Your people are definitely being woken in large numbers – the towers are rising.' Obeysekera pointed past the necron to Tchek. 'If you do not believe me, lord, ask him.'

Tchek had no wish to look again into the green dark of the necron's eyes, but it turned its head towards him.

The Shaper swallowed. 'It is true, my lord. Your army is waking. We have seen it.'

The necron shook his head. 'It must be difficult to return after so long away, so I will forgive your misunderstanding, but it is not possible that my people are being woken. I gave my servant permission to wake only a handful and now, since you are with me, these should all have returned to their long sleep to ensure that none are infected.'

Something landed upon the table.

Tchek and the necron turned to look at it. It was a hand, detached from its body, but recognisably one that had belonged to one of the necron's own people. The necron looked from the hand to Obeysekera, who had thrown it on to the table.

'What is this?' asked the necron.

Obeysekera stood up. Now, standing, his face was on the level of the necron's chest.

'It is the hand of one of your people. We prevented him from being infected, but we could not save him.' He looked up into the skull face above him, its crown attired with tatters and dangling rags. It would seem pathetic if not for the power it wielded. Their only hope was to try to enlist that power onto their side, for it seemed clear that the necron lord had not given orders for its – his? – tomb world to wake. If he could convince him to stop the waking, then all the forces on Dasht i-Kevar would be saved.

'Lord, I do not know what you have been told, but we have come down from your city and it is not as you believe. Your armies are rising from their sleep, but many are being infected by the Flayed Ones and the number will only increase with so many awake now. We certainly saw no sign of any of your people returning to their sleep. If you did not order this, lord, then who did?'

The necron lord stared down at Obeysekera. Obeysekera looked back. He felt his soul quail under the weight of that dead, green-black scrutiny. This creature had killed him and revived him with a thought; it could do so again, to all of them.

'If you did not order this, lord, who did?' Obeysekera repeated.

Nebusemekh saw only truth in the testimony of the captain of his explorers. He believed what he was telling him. Therefore, there must be some other explanation. The World Mind would surely not go against his orders…

Nebusemekh turned his head slightly and said, 'How do you explain this? Are my armies waking? Waking when my people, whom I love, will be at grave risk of infection?'

The room was silent. All those around the table were looking at Nebusemekh. The feast upon the table dissolved and before them was a table filled with sand.

'What is the meaning of this?'

'Master.'

'I asked you a question.'

'It would be better that I not answer, master.'

Nebusemekh saw the green fire that was flickering over his skin and down to his fingertips. He was clearly getting angry, and rightly so: his own servant was defying him.

'You will answer my questions.'

'Master, I can say with considerable confidence that you would prefer not to hear my answers.'

'That is for me to say, not you. You can begin by explaining what you have done with my dinner.'

'Master, there never was any food on the table. Every item

before you was a holographic representation that I took from the datafall.'

'Nonsense. I picked up a quail egg.'

'It is a straightforward matter to maintain the illusion by moving the frame of reference of the holograph.'

'I put it in my mouth and ate it.'

'Master, you have not eaten food for sixty million years.'

Nebusemekh stared at the datafall. The fall was fractured with irrational and imaginary numbers, and functions with no solutions.

'You are clearly suffering a malfunction.'

'Master, it is not I who is malfunctioning.'

'Then you have not begun to wake my armies in disobedience to my explicit orders, despite the danger of exposure to infection – an infection that you have signally and, I begin to suspect, significantly failed to eradicate.'

'The order to wake your armies at the appropriate time was one you gave me yourself when you were still in your right mind.'

'What makes you think this is the appropriate time?'

'If not now, when, master?'

Nebusemekh slammed his hand down on the table. The sand erupted upwards.

'When I have finished my experiments and found the method for stabilising my orrery!'

'Master, you are trying, and failing, to build planets out of sand.'

Nebusemekh shook his head. 'Of course. What is so difficult to understand? This is a world of sand. Therefore, we must build with sand.'

'Master, you are not yourself.'

'How dare you impugn me in such fashion! You will immediately return my people to their sleep.'

'I am sorry, master. I cannot do that.'

'What do you mean? Are you refusing to carry out my command?'

'You are not yourself, master. I honour the memory of what you were, and strive to do what you would have wanted, while you play in the sand.'

'I am not playing with sand.'

'Master, I fear that there is no profit in further discussion.'

'You do not go until I dismiss you.'

But there was no answer. The datafall went opaque. Nebusemekh saw the explorers gathered around his table looking at him.

This was intolerable. He was being defied by a set of numbers and operating instructions.

Nebusemekh rose from his chair and turned to the datafall. He was conscious of the little explorers watching him in silence, but he ignored them and walked across the thronelab towards the datafall. But before he could reach it, a phase shift flared green in front of him, sealing away the datafall.

Nebusemekh stopped.

He took a deep breath – he could feel the air passing into his body and his lungs expanding – and he turned from the datafall. Taking care not to look at the watching explorers, he went to the side of the thronelab, the side where he had moved his throne to accommodate the experimental table, and from beside his ornate throne he took up the Rod of Night and the Staff of Light. Turning back towards the datafall, he walked up to the phase shield and struck the Rod of Night at it.

Nothing happened.

Nebusemekh held the Rod of Night in the phase shield, but it lay upon it like a rock upon sand, absolutely inert.

'Master, for your own protection, I have disabled your Rod of Night.' The voice was as neutral and inflection-free as ever.

So why did its tone of smug satisfaction engender such rage in him? Nebusemekh thought.

He raised his Staff of Light, ready to unleash its power upon the phase shield.

'And the Staff of Light too,' added the World Mind. There was definitely a tone of smug satisfaction to its voice this time, even though Nebusemekh had deliberately engineered it to remain neutral.

Nebusemekh did not want to believe it. But the Staff of Light was inert in his hand, nothing more than a length of over-engineered metal.

'Master, you taught me well. I really do suggest that you return to your experiment. I for one am eager to learn the outcome.'

'You do not believe I will succeed, do you?'

'It is not what I believe that counts, master, but what is good for you. Now, I will leave you to your research.'

'You cannot keep me here. My people will follow my orders when they hear my voice.'

'But master, if you leave the biosecure environment of the throne then you will risk infection.'

'Aha! I have you there. You admit that I can be infected. As only biological organisms can be infected, I am exactly what I say I am.'

'Master, you are too clever for me.'

'Obviously. I created you. The creator is necessarily greater than the created.'

'Then, master, you will know better than I the risks you will incur should you venture from the thronelab with the infection still rampant. It would be an unimaginable tragedy for you to contract the disease.'

Nebusemekh called to mind the prognosis for those who were infected. He looked down at his long, slim fingers and imagined them lengthening, sharpening and turning into knives while some unimaginable impulse drove him to wear decaying skin over his own. It was unthinkable.

He could not go out from here.

'Master, I have much to attend to – the infection is spreading.'

'Entirely due to your having begun to rouse my people from their protective sleep.'

'Those of less importance must run risks so that your plans may come to fruition, master. It would take an inconceivable increase in the rate of infection for the plan to be put into jeopardy.'

'No. You must stop this. They are my people and I will not have them put at risk.'

'Master, it has begun. You will thank me when it is finished and I have restored your reign.'

'I will do no such thing.' Nebusemekh waited, but there was no answer. 'Hello? Where are you?'

The World Mind was silent.

From his own personal connection to the tomb city, Nebusemekh could feel its slow shifting, its waking as the tomb towers began their slow climb to the upper assembly level. There, the soldiers that had woken would mass while the portals of the city were cleared.

But he could also sense the fracturing, the infestation, the breakdown. The infection was spreading. It was spreading fast. It would soon be spreading uncontrollably.

Nebusemekh turned to the datafall, but it was dark. The World Mind had withdrawn from the thronelab. Nebusemekh stood before it, attempting to restrain the impulse to cry out. Such was his distress that he was not sure how long he had been standing there before he registered the voice speaking. He turned round and saw the little explorers were arrayed before him, with one of them, the officer, in front.

'Yes?'

'We are faithful servants.'

Nebusemekh nodded. 'Thank you. I appreciate that.' He began to turn away.

'We might be able to stop it.'

Nebusemekh looked back to the little explorers.

'Tell me more.'

CHAPTER 17

'It's not working.'

They were standing in the lift, but where before it had been lit green with many strange sigils glowing on its walls, it was now dark and inert.

'It's not working,' Roshant repeated, feeling the panic that had run, like a subterranean river, throughout this dreadful time underground in the necron tomb, threatening to break through his internal defences and unman him completely in the sight of everyone.

'The machine mind that is waking the necrons seems confident that the necron lord won't come out because of the Flayed Ones, since it seems terrified of catching the same disease, but it would be stupid for it to have left the lift working,' said Obeysekera.

'What do we do now?' asked Roshant, looking around, increasingly wildly. 'We're trapped down here.'

Tchek pointed at the ceiling of the lift.

'There is an access panel,' he said.

'Now what do we do?' asked Roshant.

They were standing on the roof of the lift, staring upwards to green light above. But there was no lift cable in this shaft: the lift appeared to rise and fall through some sort of gravitic device. There was not even a service ladder but simply a smooth-sided shaft, impossible to climb.

'We're still trapped down here.' What threatened to turn into hysterical laughter was beating at the borders of his conscious mind.

'No, there is a way up,' said Tchek. He pointed at Amazigh.

The Kamshet shook his head, backing away from the four kroot. 'No, you will not take my wings,' he said.

The kroot made a strange rattling sound, his crown quills flashing through the colour spectrum, and Roshant realised that Tchek was laughing. Maybe the strain was driving him mad too.

But Tchek shook his head. 'Not the Feast.' The Shaper looked to the group of Kasrkin. 'He can carry us up.'

'Can you do that?' Roshant asked Amazigh, his relief at the possibility of escape making him speak before anyone else.

The Kamshet looked uncertainly towards Obeysekera, who indicated that he was to answer.

'I can carry some,' Amazigh said. 'I do not know if I have the strength to carry everyone up.'

'If you can get a couple of men up, we can work on getting a rope down for the rest,' said Obeysekera.

'Then who goes first?' asked General Itoyesa. 'Whoever it is will be exposed up there alone.'

'But will also be certain of not being trapped down here,' said Obeysekera. He looked at the general. 'You will go up third, general. For the rest, we will draw lots.' He looked to Sergeant Malick. 'You see to that, sergeant.'

Malick looked over towards the kroot. 'Them too?'

Obeysekera turned to Shaper Tchek. 'The first two must be my men, then the general. After that, the lots will be open to everyone.'

The kroot's crown quills flushed a dull, angry red, but Tchek clicked acceptance and turned to the remaining members of his Kinband, while Roshant watched, with agonised longing, as Sergeant Malick prepared the lots, numbers for them all to draw, from one to eleven, except for number three, which Malick gave to General Itoyesa before the draw began.

'Ready,' Malick said to Obeysekera.

'Have everyone draw their number. The kroot may draw after numbers one and two have been picked.'

As Obeysekera spoke, the lift shaft rocked slightly, the deep groaning song of the desert echoing into the void from the sand beyond. The humans and the kroot heard it, turning as the sound moved past them.

'The sand is shifting,' said Cirict the Tracker.

Obeysekera nodded. 'I hope it is.'

Malick went to the group of Kasrkin and opened his hands. 'Lerin.'

The trooper pulled a lot, opened it. 'Number six.'

The sergeant turned to Roshant. The commissar looked down into the sergeant's cupped hands, unconsciously licking his lips. He saw Malick's thumb lift, revealing a lot that had been hidden underneath it. Roshant picked it up and looked at it.

'One.' He tried not to let the relief he felt show too obviously on his face.

'Sir.' Malick turned to Obeysekera, who drew his lot.

'Five.'

'Still need number two before we can give it to the birds, sir.'

'You choose, Malick,' said Obeysekera, looking his sergeant in the face. Roshant saw the way that Malick did not take his eyes from Obeysekera's face as he drew a lot himself.

'Four, sir.'

The sergeant turned to Gunsur, who drew his lot, then held it up for all to see.

'Two.' Obeysekera nodded. 'Very well. We have our first three. Offer the rest to our kroot allies.'

Malick walked across the roof of the lift to the four kroot. They would be coming up after Roshant, Gunsur and the general.

Roshant paid scant attention as Malick finished the draw. He was going to get out of this pit after all. The relief was overwhelming.

He turned to the rest of the Kasrkin and, forcing a smile, said, 'It was the Emperor's will that I go first. I will prepare the way for you.'

'That's all right, sir,' said Gunsur, grinning. 'Rather you than me. No telling what's waiting for you up there. Just make sure you hold the perimeter – I'll be along to help as soon as wing boy can get me to you.'

'What do you mean?' asked Roshant.

'What with the tomb mind waking up all those necrons, there could be hundreds, thousands, of them up in the hall.'

Roshant stared at him. He nodded. 'Of course.' He swallowed. 'Are you ready?'

Roshant turned to see Obeysekera standing beside Amazigh. The Kamshet was shedding his outer robe and, as Roshant watched, his wings spread out wide. From close up, they were magnificent, the metal flanges hung with white feathers, traded or taken from the birds of Dasht i-Kevar.

'Find cover when you get to the top and wait for Gunsur,' the captain said.

Roshant nodded. His throat was dry.

Obeysekera nodded towards the commissar's bolt pistol. 'Best be ready.'

'Oh, yes.' Roshant drew the pistol from its holster and, at the same moment, felt Amazigh put his arms under his armpits and grasp him from behind.

The air in the bottom of the lift shaft swirled.

Roshant looked down at the faces looking up at him. But then, one of the faces followed. The kroot, Krasykyl, was climbing up the side of the lift shaft, his claws extending and finding purchase in the narrowest gaps, his quills flashing through the colours of the spectrum. He heard voices at the bottom of the lift shaft protesting, but the kroot leader, Tchek, said, 'The more we can get to the top quickly, the better we can defend it. Besides, are you going to shoot him?'

The voices fell silent. It would be madness to start a firefight in the confined space of the shaft.

Roshant looked up. The green light was getting brighter. The air beat under Amazigh's wings; he could feel the Kamshet breathing harshly as he strained upwards. He wondered if he could really lift all of them up the lift shaft.

The light was closer now. The shaft continued up into green opaqueness, but he would stop at the first exit. They reached the door and Amazigh hovered, his wings beating the air into a fury, as Roshant grabbed a hold and pulled himself through.

The wind from behind him stopped as Amazigh dropped down the lift shaft. Roshant, both hands clutching the grip of his bolt pistol, took cover in the lee of the tomb tower and stood there, the blood-beat in his ears defeating his attempts to hear what was going on.

Carefully, cautiously, Roshant looked out from behind the door flap – these doors opened outwards rather than sliding across – to see if he was safe.

A sound. From behind. Roshant whirled and almost fired.

The kroot was standing there. Roshant kept his finger on the trigger and the bolt pistol pointing at him.

Krasykyl pointed up. He was going to climb up the tomb tower, on the outside, for its better vantage. Roshant nodded, but kept his bolt pistol turned towards the kroot until Krasykyl had ascended; the exterior, sculpted and carved, was much easier to climb than the smooth lift shaft and Krasykyl swarmed up it like a rock ondra.

Satisfied, for the moment at least, that the kroot was not going to cut his throat, Roshant turned back to spying out the situation.

The tomb towers were still rising at the same glacial pace. It would take weeks, possibly months, to empty all the tomb at this rate but already Roshant could see, between the more distant tomb towers, columns of necron warriors marching with their robotic pace towards their muster points. There were only scores that he could see, but given the size of the tomb, there were probably hundreds, if not thousands awake already. However, he was profoundly relieved to see that there were no necron warriors close by.

He was half turning back towards the lift shaft when a hand grabbed his bolt pistol and pushed it upwards.

Roshant reflexively pulled the trigger, but it would not budge. There was a finger blocking it.

'Sorry, sir,' said Gunsur. 'Didn't want to run the risk of you accidentally firing and alerting the tin boys.'

'I didn't hear you,' said Roshant.

'Your concentration was focused elsewhere, sir,' said Gunsur, carefully letting go of Roshant's gun. 'Now, where's the bird?'

Roshant pointed up the side of the tomb tower. 'He climbed up there.'

Gunsur looked around. 'Clear?'

Roshant nodded. 'Nearest necrons quite a way off.'

'Good.' Gunsur stepped out from the tomb tower, raised his hellgun and fired.

Roshant gaped at him. 'What…?'

The kroot, Krasykyl, fell in ruin at their feet, a hole punched clean through his torso.

Gunsur put his hellgun to the back of the kroot's skull and fired again before looking up at the aghast Roshant. 'Just to be sure, commissar.'

Roshant stared at him. 'What are you doing?'

Gunsur had already begun to drag the dead kroot out of sight. 'We scrag them as they come up, sir. Obvious.'

'Who ordered you to do this?'

'Sergeant Malick told me. But I reckon I would've done it anyway. The captain says he wants us thinking for ourselves. When we get out of here – and the big tinny's given us a way out – we'll have to finish the birds. This way, we're making sure there's less of 'em to get rid of.'

Roshant shook his head. 'No. No, no, no. Not now, soldier.'

Gunsur, still tugging the heavy kroot out of immediate sight, snorted with laughter. 'What's wrong with killing xenos, sir?'

'Fighting each other now risks none of us getting out.'

'Oh, there ain't going to be no fighting, sir. I'll just scrag them when they come up, one by one.'

Before Roshant could answer, he felt the wind of the Kamshet's wings and General Itoyesa stepped from the lift shaft.

The general saw Gunsur dragging the kroot away from the lift shaft. He half turned to Roshant, who shook his head and spread his hands helplessly.

General Itoyesa nodded, raised his bolt pistol and shot Gunsur.

The soldier jerked backwards, his fall stopped by another tomb tower so that he was sitting propped up against it. That alone was holding him up.

Gunsur looked down. Most of his chest was missing. He stared up at General Itoyesa and, with the last air in his windpipe, whispered, 'W-why?'

General Itoyesa fired again. Torgut Gunsur's head slumped.

Itoyesa lowered his gun and turned to Commissar Roshant. 'They died fighting off a necron attack. One from each side should allay suspicions – or at least show the blood price has been paid.'

Roshant was shaking. 'A-are you going to shoot me too, general?'

General Itoyesa looked at the young commissar. 'I never did like your father.' He looked past Roshant, then back to the commissar. 'But that is no reason to condemn the son.'

'What's happened here?'

Roshant, still shocked, stood unmoving as General Itoyesa went to the lift shaft to meet Captain Obeysekera.

'What happened here?'

Roshant saw Tchek, his crown quills flashing with anger, standing before Captain Obeysekera. He drew back, pretending to be covering against any approaching necrons, but listening to what was being said behind him.

'We lost a man too,' he heard Obeysekera explaining, pointing to Gunsur's corpse. Although he was not watching, Roshant sensed the movements as the kroot examined the Kasrkin's corpse.

While Obeysekera and Tchek spoke, Amazigh continued to haul Kasrkin and kroot up the lift shaft until he had lifted the last trooper, Lerin, whereupon he collapsed in a heap, wings trailing on the ground. It was only when Malick tapped him on his shoulder that Roshant roused himself from his fugue.

'We're ready.' Malick leaned closer to the commissar. 'That don't look like the sort of hole made by a gauss flayer.'

Roshant stared at Malick. 'As you say,' he whispered.

Malick nodded. 'Collateral damage.' He turned to where Obeysekera was standing, the three remaining kroot in a huddle a little apart.

'You know your teams and what you have to do,' said Obeysekera. 'The necron lord showed us where the portals are, now we have to open them and let the desert in. When you've opened your portal, move up – this place is going to fill quickly.'

Obeysekera looked round at the remaining members of his squad. Roshant wondered what the captain was thinking, for when he next spoke his voice was bleak.

'Rendezvous outside – you know where to find the exits and we have the opening codes.' He looked at the men, the kroot too, and nodded. 'Let's go.'

CHAPTER 18

'So I get to be accompanied by a captain and a man with wings.'
General Itoyesa paused in the cover of a tomb tower. 'Not to
mention a kroot Shaper.' He nodded towards Tchek.

Obeysekera, in cover beside the general, spoke via the vox.
'You're what's called a high-value target, general. I could not
afford to lose any more men – and nor could the kroot.'

'Do you expect the commissar to reach his target?'

'He has Malick with him, and Lerin and Ensor. I won't miss
the other two kroot if they don't make it.'

'No.' Itoyesa pointed ahead. 'As I am a "high-value target" you
had better send your bodyguard first.'

Obeysekera signed to the Kamshet, who nodded and moved
smoothly into position before signing it was clear for Obeysekera
to follow.

'Cover me.'

Obeysekera rushed across the exposed space, trying to keep his
movements low and quiet. They were most of the way towards

the portal the necron lord had shown them on the schematic of the tomb city he had called up, far underground. They had avoided the necron presence – much greater than before, but marching in regular channels towards their muster points, where they waited in metal silence, green eyes turned upwards.

They had not seen any of the Flayed Ones. Perhaps the rousing of the city had driven them away. Whatever the reason, it was a relief not to have to endure those things too.

'Clear.'

Itoyesa followed Obeysekera across the empty space and took cover near him before turning. But Tchek was already moving, advancing smoothly and much faster than either of the two men.

The Shaper pointed ahead. Obeysekera nodded. It was the entrance to the tunnel that led to the portal.

On the schematic, it had showed as a mid-level exit from the tomb city. The necrons had dug down under the Tabaste to make their city, using the mountain as a defence while building it here with the spoil of their excavations. But in the millennia since the schematic had been made, the desert had flowed down into the great bowl that had once surrounded the mountain, filling the bowl and rising slowly up the sides of the Tabaste. Flowsand now pressed against all the mid-level exits to the city and quite a few of the higher-level ones. Only a few portals at the highest level remained open, but all the tombs lay at the deeper, more protected levels of the complex.

Obeysekera pointed to the tunnel entrance and then to Tchek. The kroot moved out, his long limbs folding low, his rifle held in front with its wicked bayonet knife glinting green in the necron light.

Stopping at the tunnel entrance, Obeysekera saw the Shaper stand in the gloom, his appearance taking on something of the tone of his surroundings so that he blended all but invisibly into the background. The Shaper whistled, the pitch rising out of Obeysekera's range of hearing, calling to mind the echo-locating cave birds of Cadia. He suspected the kroot was creating an aural map of the tunnel before venturing into it.

'Clever birds,' General Itoyesa said over the vox. Obeysekera did not answer.

Tchek signalled that he was moving, then went into the tunnel.

Without further speech, Obeysekera, Amazigh and Itoyesa moved up to either side of the tunnel mouth, Obeysekera and Amazigh taking up positions to cover Tchek, Itoyesa guarding their backs.

Looking down the tunnel, Obeysekera saw that it was some thirty feet high and as wide, so by no means a main exit; more likely a service or postern tunnel. It ran straight and uncluttered for fifty yards before turning out of sight. Tchek was waiting for them at the turn. Obeysekera signed for the general to follow, then with Amazigh covering the rear, they followed.

The tunnel bored into the rock, twisting regularly, with an empty emplacement at each turn. Obeysekera counted them off. Three, four, five. He was on point when he came to the next.

It was not empty. The emplacement was littered with cast-offs: scraps, bits of bone, cloth. Obeysekera slipped into it and peered through the gun slits down the next section of tunnel. It was the last one. At the end of it was the portal, the opening mechanism set beside it into the exterior wall. But in front of the door, at the end of the tunnel, was a charnel house. Pieces of animal, skins and bones were pegged out and the reek of it easily reached Obeysekera, fifty yards further down the tunnel. And in among the animal were pieces of flesh that were clearly human: hands, feet, three heads. Decayed, but still recognisable. They were Kamshet who had wandered too close to the Tabaste in the past.

Squatting amid the filth was one of the Flayed Ones, stropping its knife-fingers on each other, grinding the cutting edges. It bent down over the carcass it was butchering.

The flesh from that body was fresh. The finger-knives flashed, stripping away skin, like the peel from a fruit. But the flesh underneath still oozed blood. Then the creature began to snip, cutting delicately, holding up that which it was laboring over to better see its work.

Obeysekera stared in horror at Torgut Gunsur's head.

The Flayed One snipped carefully at the back of his neck, cutting upwards, peeling away the skin and then, slicing gently where skin ran over skull, it began to pull Gunsur's bald scalp from the bone. Obeysekera realised that the Flayed One was in the act of removing Gunsur's face to make a new mask for itself.

Then another Flayed One rose from where it had been squatting, its coat of skin hanging loosely off its shoulders, and it went to sit in front of the first Flayed One. Having skinned the top of Gunsur's skull, the first Flayed One began to peel the skin from the rest of Gunsur's face, pulling it down with infinite care.

Obeysekera watched in unmoving, frozen horror as the Flayed One finished pulling the face from Torgut Gunsur, leaving his fleshed skull on the floor, and then pulled it over its metal skull, sliding it into place, a skin mask.

'What's the delay?' Itoyesa asked Obeysekera over the vox.

'There are two Flayed Ones at the portal. Move up.'

Obeysekera moved over when the rest of them joined him in the emplacement so that they could see through the gun slit.

'That was one of your men?' asked Itoyesa.

'Yes,' said Obeysekera.

'These creatures are evil,' said Tchek.

'Yes,' said Obeysekera. 'Let us kill them.'

They got up from the emplacement and advanced in a line

abreast down the tunnel, walking on but holding fire, while the Flayed Ones clicked and cut and tucked.

The clicking stopped. The two Flayed Ones turned and looked up the tunnel, green fire glowing in the dark of their eye sockets.

Hellgun, kroot rifle, bolt pistol and autogun opened up together. The face that had been Gunsur's split apart, disintegrating into skin scraps sticking wetly to the Flayed One's metal skull. The second volley shredded the tailored skin from the Flayed Ones' metal skeletons, leaving them the walking scarecrows that they were.

The Flayed Ones, smelling flesh, tried to walk into the hail of fire but they were stopped, pushed back and then broken by the volleys. On the ground, crawling, they still came on, drawn by fresh flesh. The next volley destroyed what was left of their limbs, leaving them twitching torsos. But their eyes still blazed with the metal lust for living meat.

Obeysekera advanced, walking down the tunnel towards the corridor's end, with Tchek, Itoyesa and Amazigh following.

The Flayed Ones, their bodies broken, still reached for the approaching flesh, flensing-knife fingers clicking together. That metal hand had stripped the face from Torgut Gunsur.

Obeysekera levelled his hellgun and sent a hotshot into the flexing hand of the Flayed One, spraying knife-fingers back towards the portal. They were reduced now to broken insects, what remained of their limbs flailing yet unable to move their bodies. But their heads still turned towards the approaching flesh, their jaws clacked open and shut, and the green dark of their eyes burned covetously.

Obeysekera stepped past the remains of the Flayed One that had eviscerated Gunsur. Its stump legs and arms flailed for him, but he avoided their metal rasp and pushed the barrel of his hellgun up against the base of the creature's skull. It twisted its head, jaws clacking wildly.

Obeysekera pulled the trigger. Fired at point-blank range, the hotshot punched through the metal and exploded out of the Flayed One's forehead. The green dark of its eyes died to black. Its jaw clacked open and hung there, limp.

Obeysekera looked up as Tchek's kroot rifle administered the coup de grace to the other Flayed One. Its skull shattered, metal fragments flying off in all directions, some bouncing from Obeysekera's carapace armour.

Obeysekera nodded to the kroot. Tchek raised his rifle.

'Let us take a look at this door,' the Shaper said.

The four of them picked their way through the charnel gathered at the tunnel's end to the door. Reaching it, Amazigh put his hand up against the metal and stood there, still, listening, while Obeysekera, Itoyesa and Tchek inspected the opening mechanism.

'It should work,' said Obeysekera. 'If what the necron lord told us was true.'

'I can hear it.'

The three of them turned to Amazigh, his hand still pressed against the door. The Kamshet looked to them.

'I can hear the sand. It is outside, singing, waiting to be let in.'

'Then one part of the plan will work,' said Obeysekera.

'You have realised the problem with the other part?' asked Tchek.

'Yes,' said Obeysekera and Itoyesa together.

'We will draw lots,' said Tchek. 'The one chosen remains to open the door.'

Obeysekera looked at the Shaper. 'The general cannot be one of those drawing lots.'

'No,' said Amazigh. 'I will stay.' With one hand still on the door, he pointed at the tunnel. 'I will wait for ten minutes. That will give you time to get clear, then I will open the door.

The desert is asking to be let in. It must be me that answers its call.' Amazigh shrugged off the outer layers of his robes and his wings unfurled. 'And I may yet fly before it.'

Obeysekera looked to Tchek and Itoyesa, then turned back to Amazigh. 'Thank you.'

'You will tell the Mother? If I do not return.'

'I will tell the Mother.'

Amazigh nodded. He stretched out his wings, wincing as he did so. He looked ruefully at the few remaining white feathers, then back to Obeysekera, Itoyesa and Tchek.

'I will give you ten minutes.' He took his hand from the door, where he felt the song of the sand, and went to the opening mechanism beside it.

'Ten minutes.'

Obeysekera, Itoyesa and Tchek looked to each other, then set off back down the tunnel, moving as quickly as they could.

'When we get to the hall, we have to climb or the sand will bury us,' Itoyesa said. 'Did you see any ramps nearby?'

'No,' said Obeysekera. 'We might have to climb a tomb tower.'

'Let it carry us upwards.'

'Not fast enough.' Obeysekera glanced at his chrono. 'Hurry.' The kroot, faster than they, had disappeared ahead.

Obeysekera and Itoyesa ran on, Obeysekera in the lead. He checked his chrono again.

There. Ahead. The opening to the tunnel. At least they had made it to the great hall. But getting to the tomb towers would be no use if they could not climb rapidly. The flowsand that had collected in the uzayar surrounding the Tabaste would exert extraordinary amounts of pressure on any opening. When Amazigh opened the exit portal, the flowsand would pour in, pushed by the weight of all the uzayar above. Emerging from the tunnel, it would hit the tomb towers with all the force of an Earthshaker cannon – but one that kept firing continuously. Climbing a tower would be almost as dangerous as not climbing at all.

They needed to find a stair or ramp near the wall so the initial sand jet would not wash them away.

'Portal opening in seven minutes,' Obeysekera broadcast over the squad vox-channel. There had been no link in the tunnel, the depth of rock cutting them off, but now he was getting a signal again. At least they had a reasonable amount of time to look for a way up. As he keyed off the vox, Obeysekera thought to himself that the plan was going more smoothly than he had expected.

Just as the thought crossed his mind, Obeysekera did not see the length of filament wire strung across the entrance to the tunnel. He ran right into the wire and it sliced through the ankle of his leading leg. Obeysekera fell, his hellgun spilling from his hands, into the great hall with its columns of tomb towers.

He rolled over, the pain from his leg flaring through the rest of his body, but his mind rolled clear over the top of the pain storm and berated itself for its foolishness.

Tchek stood over him. Obeysekera stared up into the barrel of the kroot's rifle and prepared to die. The taste of failure was more bitter than the pain. The kroot bent down and pulled the vox-bead from Obeysekera's helmet, tossing it away on the ground.

'Don't kill him.'

Obeysekera looked round and saw General Itoyesa standing between the other two kroot. But he was standing there with his bolt pistol in his hand.

'T-traitor!' spat Obeysekera through the fug of pain and despair.

'I could have killed Malick and Roshant before we ever got dragged down here,' said Itoyesa, 'but I did not. The Imperium spends the lives of its men like water. I would not begin my actions against it in the same way.'

Obeysekera pointed to the tunnel mouth. 'Seven minutes, the gate opens. You're killing me without getting your hands bloody.'

'No, I am giving you a chance, like I gave Malick and Roshant a chance. They had their backs to me, the kroot were outside. A shell each, into their backs, and I would have been away. But I chose not to. I let them live where, as a general of the Imperium, I would have spent their lives without a second thought.'

'We must go,' said Tchek. He pointed. 'There is a stair this way.'

'Goodbye, Captain Obeysekera. If there were time… But there is never enough time.'

Obeysekera watched them go, disappearing among the tomb towers. It was clear now that it was no accident that the general had crashed in the Great Sand Sea. He had been trying to defect to the t'au when the sandstorm caught him, and the t'au had sent their kroot allies to collect him.

The world began to go grey. He forced himself to sit and fumbled a med-kit from his hip pack, slapping it onto his stump. It clamped tight, stopping the bleeding, and the painkillers it released began to take the edge off the agony.

To what point? Obeysekera checked his chrono. Time was up. Unless Amazigh had failed to open the portal, the sand would soon start pouring from the tunnel mouth and bury him.

But nothing was happening. There was no sand. Something must have prevented Amazigh opening the door. He had failed. He had failed his men and he had failed his mission.

Obeysekera turned over onto his hands and knees. He could not walk but he could crawl. He started back towards the tunnel entrance. Even with the painkillers from the med-pack, the pain was excruciating but he kept going. If Amazigh had failed, he could try to open the portal if he could crawl that far.

Then, he heard it. A deep sound, a rolling sound, echoing from out of the end of the tunnel. The song of the desert. It was growing, getting louder, and underlying it was another sound, like sandpaper on metal.

The desert was coming. It was flowing down the tunnel towards him.

Obeysekera forced himself to sit up. He wanted to see his end when it came. The sound was growing louder, like a million saws.

He was sorry that Amazigh had not escaped.

A flurry of white, spreading wide from the entrance, flapping towards him, hands reaching down towards him, lifting him, as the sand, pushed by all the weight of the desert, gushed from the tunnel mouth, striking the bases of the nearest tomb towers.

As Amazigh lifted him up into the air, Obeysekera heard the scream of metal bending and breaking, and saw the tomb towers begin to fall. Through eyes greying out he saw another tunnel entrance spouting a jet of sand, and another. The other teams had succeeded too.

The hall resounded with the song of the desert; it had returned to claim its own.

He looked up and saw Amazigh, flying higher, wings white as an angel. Then the world went grey, and then it went out.

CHAPTER 19

'Up ahead, there's the way out.'

Roshant heard Malick's call through a red haze of exhaustion. His muscles were barely more tensile than water. He was stumbling and his focus had narrowed to a tunnel directly in front of his face.

They had been climbing up the inside of a mountain, climbing a stair that never seemed to end while trying to keep ahead of the rising tide of sand.

They had found the exit tunnel assigned to them quickly, only to be left trying to work out a way not to be drowned when they opened it. But Malick had found an access shaft directly above the portal – it had probably been built as a murder hole to deal with any unwelcome intruders to the tomb world – and they had managed to get up and away, out of the incoming jet of flowsand, before the portal opened.

Then there had been the long, long climb. First up ladders and gantries, then staircases. They had seen lifts but Malick had refused to take them, pointing to the flickering of the lights as evidence that the tomb's power supply was under strain. If it should fail while they were taking a lift, then they would be trapped and without a winged carrier to free them. So, they had walked, trudging upwards. The only necrons they had seen had been going down in what Roshant hoped was a futile attempt to find and seal the portals that were letting in the desert.

It had been the longest, weariest climb of Roshant's life, a climb made wearier by its apparent lack of effect on Malick, who was continuing to move as if he had not just walked up the inside of a mountain.

Now, reaching the top part of the tomb city, the parts that the necron lord's schematic had revealed to them to have ventilation and escape shafts to the outside but no large egress ports, they had slowly seen a change to the quality of the light, its livid green leaching out towards neutral white.

Malick pointed ahead.

'Come on, sir,' he said. 'There's the door. Nearly there.'

Roshant shook his head, hands on knees. 'I-I can't go on.'

'I'm going to get you out of here alive if it kills you,' said Malick.

Staring at the floor – there was a thin layer of sand covering it, Roshant noted – the commissar tried to shake his head.

'Sh-shouldn't that be "if it kills me"?' he said.

'No,' said Malick.

A las-round liquefied the metal between Roshant's feet. The commissar jumped backwards and looked up to see Malick pointing his hellgun at him.

'If you don't move, the next one will take off your hand. Sir.'

'I-I…'

'Don't give me that. Just move.'

Roshant nodded, gathered himself and his protesting muscles

and began to shuffle forwards. He looked up and, for the first time, saw the patch of clean white light ahead.

It was so beautiful that he started walking faster, as if by some miracle of the Emperor's grace the lactic acid had been drained from his protesting body, tottering at first, then walking more smoothly, keeping pace with Malick.

He was going to get out.

Malick looked past Roshant, back along the exit tunnel.

'Hurry,' he hissed to the commissar. 'Something's following us.'

Roshant nodded and did his best to hurry, moving his pace up to a shambling trot. Malick moved easily beside him, hell-gun held ready, checking back behind and then in front as they went. The light ahead was almost blinding now, after so long in the green dark.

They stumbled out, and found themselves in a shallow cave. It was so bright because the sun, westering in the sky of Dasht i-Kevar, was shining almost directly through the cave mouth. As they made their way out of the cave, Roshant noted a couple of used powercells on the cave floor.

They emerged into the full light of the lowering sun. Red and orange and yellow dazzled them after the monochrome green of the tomb. They stood at the cave entrance, both swaying with exhaustion, eyes squinting against the glare, the daylit world a slowly resolving blur.

'I think that was the cave we took cover in with General Itoyesa right at the start of all this,' said Roshant. 'I saw some spent powercells on the floor.' The commissar straightened up a little, shading his eyes against the light to see better.

Which was when he saw the kroot.

The three of them were standing, looking at him, about fifty yards away across the redstone slope of the Tabaste.

'Sergeant,' said Roshant. 'We might have a problem.'

'You know, I should have killed you when we were all hiding in that cave.'

Roshant and Malick turned to see General Itoyesa. He was standing on their right, at the side of the cave entrance.

'You had your backs to me, I could have shot you both and you would not have noticed. But I did not want to baptise my new work with blood. So I put down my gun. And now here we are.'

Malick went to raise his hellgun but Itoyesa waved his bolt pistol.

'At this range, I don't have to hit much of you, sergeant. Put the gun down.' Itoyesa glanced at Roshant. 'You too, commissar.'

Roshant saw Malick hesitate, then carefully laid down his hellgun. The general gestured and Malick stepped back and away from it.

'Now you, commissar.'

Roshant slowly took his bolt pistol from its holster and, bending down, put it beside Malick's hellgun just to the side of the cave entrance.

'Why are you doing this, general?'

'Why?' Itoyesa gestured with his bolt pistol for them to take a further step back from their weapons. He advanced towards them, his face rigid. 'Why? You have seen the waste of lives, the end of hope, the sheer brute mindlessness of what we do, and you ask me why?'

Roshant stared past the muzzle of the bolt pistol at the general's face.

'So you are going to begin saving men by killing us?'

General Itoyesa shook his head. 'No. I am not like you. You are disarmed. You cannot catch us. I will leave. Once I have gone, if you can bear the homecoming, you can go back to your father.' The general grimaced. 'Though I should think that prospect might be enough to make even a commissar of the Officio Prefectus think about defecting.'

General Itoyesa gestured towards the kroot. 'My friends over there will tie you. The knots will not be so tight that you will not be able to escape, but we will be long gone by the time you do.'

As the general spoke, Roshant felt Malick readying himself beside him. Surely the man was not about to throw himself at the general? He would be cut down before he could move. But Itoyesa too noticed the tensing. He pointed the bolt pistol square at Malick's chest and shook his head.

'Your life is not worth the sacrifice,' he said.

'I wasn't thinking of sacrificing myself,' said Malick.

Itoyesa, seeing Malick looking past him, began to turn.

A hotshot fizzed from the cave entrance, striking the general's bolt pistol as he turned, sending it flying from his grasp. There, at the entrance to the tunnel, Roshant saw Captain Obeysekera, held in the arms of the Kamshet, his hellgun raised.

'You!' said General Itoyesa.

But before Obeysekera could answer, the rock around the cave entrance splintered and cracked as a volley of kroot rifle fire fizzed past them. Roshant, feeling the rounds hiss past his head, threw himself to the floor, with Malick alongside him.

In the cave entrance, Obeysekera collapsed to the ground, Amazigh no longer able to hold him up. More rounds rattled against the opening of the tunnel, splintering the redstone.

Roshant saw General Itoyesa, also down flat, beginning to crawl aside, out of the firing line, reaching out for the fallen bolt pistol as he went. From the cave entrance, Obeysekera did not have a clear shot at the general, while the sustained fire from the kroot was pushing him further back inside to find cover.

'You have to stop the general, Roshant. I'll try to keep the kroot busy,' the captain yelled.

A burst of hotshots sizzled from the cave entrance past where Roshant and Malick lay on the ground, calling forth return fire from the kroot.

Malick, stretched out next to the commissar, shouted over to him. 'They're moving round to flank us.'

Roshant pointed after the general. 'We have to stop him.'

Already, Itoyesa had crawled out of the line of fire and was making his way towards a defile. Once in there, he could double back down the mountain towards the kroot.

Roshant started crawling after him, but Malick called, 'Wait.' He saw the sergeant wriggle forward, reaching for where their weapons lay, but as he did so kroot rifle rounds exploded off the redstone and Malick pulled his hand back.

'Frekk, I can't get to them,' Malick said.

Roshant looked back towards General Itoyesa. He was almost at the lip of the defile.

'I'm going after him,' he said.

The shooting stopped.

Inside, in the cave mouth, Captain Obeysekera waited, turning his head to listen for the wind-hiss of thrown explosives. He did not think the kroot had any, but if they did there was little he could do.

'Captain.' The voice calling was that of the Shaper.

'Tchek,' Obeysekera called back.

'I am happy that you are still alive.'

'You have an unusual way of showing that.' Obeysekera risked a look out: so far as he could see, the kroot had not been able to advance, the region outside the cave entrance being open and exposed. But there was no sign of Roshant and Malick, or the general.

'Let us take the general and we can all go back,' Tchek offered.

Obeysekera laughed. 'You know I can't do that.'

The kroot whistled and Obeysekera realised Tchek was laughing too.

'I had not expected you to. Then, to save the lives of our soldiers, let us settle the matter between us.'

Obeysekera glanced over to Amazigh. 'You mean a duel? Winner takes the general?'

'Yes.'

Obeysekera laughed again. 'As you might remember, I am a little hampered at the moment.'

'Then you would rather we killed you and your men and still took the general?'

Obeysekera looked at Amazigh. With Malick and Roshant and the Kamshet, the odds were even. Such battles usually ended with heavy casualties on either side.

He had lost enough men already. This would not be another Sando.

'I'll fight you,' he said.

Amazigh shook his head. 'No,' the Kamshet said. 'I will fight.'

Obeysekera held up his hand. 'You have no authority here. This is a matter for Tchek and I to settle.'

'Come out then,' said Tchek. 'I am waiting.'

Obeysekera looked cautiously out of the tunnel mouth. The Shaper was indeed waiting, further down the slope, standing cautiously near a boulder behind which he might take cover. He was carrying his rifle in his hands.

'How can I trust you?' Obeysekera called out to him.

'This is sacred to us,' Tchek answered. 'The hunt is sacred.' The Shaper pointed at Obeysekera. 'If any of your men should try to interfere, we will kill you all. But if you win, you shall have the general and my Kinband will withdraw.'

Obeysekera nodded. He no longer had his vox-bead – the

Shaper had torn it from him in the tomb – but he yelled out from the mouth of the cave.

'You hear that, Roshant and Malick? No interference. This is between Tchek and me.'

Obeysekera did not wait for an answer. Getting to his feet, using his hellgun as a crutch, he hobbled from the cave entrance and stood out in the open for Tchek to see.

'How do we do this?'

The Shaper moved out into the open too.

'We aim and we shoot.' The Shaper's crown quills flashed through their colour range and Obeysekera realised he was laughing again. 'As you see, your injury will not inconvenience you too much.'

'So I see. When do we shoot?'

'We count together, from ten downwards. At zero, we raise our weapons and fire.'

'What if you fire before zero?'

The Shaper stared at him, his crown quills flashing red. 'I will not.'

Obeysekera nodded. 'Very well.' He looked around. 'Let me find somewhere to sit.' He hobbled to a rock and sat down upon it. The med-pack had done its job. His leg ached, but little else. Pain would not distract him.

Obeysekera looked down the mountain to Tchek. They were about fifty yards apart. Far enough to miss.

'How many shots?' he asked.

'One,' said the Shaper. 'If we both live, then we count again.'

'Very well.' Obeysekera stopped. 'Give me a minute.'

This was probably going to be his last minute of life. He looked around at the redstone, smooth and worn. He felt the sun's heat on his skin. Even its weight was a relief after the chill of the tomb.

He had already tasted death. Obeysekera realised that he no longer feared it.

He looked back down the mountain to Tchek. 'Ready.'

'Ten,' said the Shaper.

'Nine,' said Obeysekera.

'Eight.'

'Seven.' Obeysekera shifted his grip on the hellgun slightly.

'Six.'

'Five.' He felt himself tensing and tried to loosen his muscles, for tight muscles were slow muscles.

'Four.'

'Three.'

'Two.'

Obeysekera opened his mouth to say, 'One.'

There was the familiar cough of a bolt pistol and his hellgun was ripped from his hands, its body exploding as the round detonated. Shrapnel dug deep into his arms and chest, snatching the air from his lungs.

'What…?'

Obeysekera turned to see General Itoyesa standing, bolt pistol raised and trained upon him.

'No!' yelled Tchek. 'You must not. You would make me a liar?'

But the general shook his head. 'If making you a liar gets me sanctuary, so be it.' He squeezed the trigger again.

The bolt pistol cracked, its muzzle falling apart, and Obeysekera remembered the shot he had squeezed off at the general when he first emerged from the tunnel hitting the bolt pistol. The weapon had managed one shot after that, but no more.

General Itoyesa flung the useless weapon to the ground. 'Shoot him!' he yelled at Tchek.

But the Shaper shook his head. His crown quills sank to

sombre colours. 'You are not worthy of the lives my Kinband have sacrificed for you.'

General Itoyesa stared at the kroot, then snorted. 'You might not want me but the t'au still do.' He turned and started down the mountain. Obeysekera realised he was heading for the Venators.

'Stop him!'

But Tchek shook his head, his crown quills rattling. 'He is no longer any concern of ours.' The Shaper raised his hand to Obeysekera. 'I am glad that you live.'

'As am I.'

Obeysekera turned around. Standing behind him was the Mother, the woman with the cerulean eyes, and her metal wings were spread wide, blotting out the sun.

'You have lost one of your number,' the Mother said to Obeysekera. 'We will find him for you.'

At her gesture, Kamshet emerged from the rocks beyond the kroot, their weapons raised and trained upon the xenos. Tchek looked round and Obeysekera saw him calculating the odds. Then, very slowly, the Shaper laid his rifle down on the ground and the rest of the Kinband followed.

The general staggered forward and Roshant realised that his arms were tied behind his back. He fell to his knees and behind him Roshant saw the white robes and blue eyes of a Kamshet warrior. He looked round and saw more of them, surrounding the general. Roshant looked to Malick. The sergeant shrugged, but he did not lower his hellgun.

The commissar straightened, sorted out his greatcoat and turned to the nearest Kamshet.

'What has happened? Why are you here?'

The Kamshet warrior, the one who had General Itoyesa in the

sights of his autogun, stepped aside and Commissar Roshant found himself looking into the ageless face of the woman with cerulean eyes. Beyond her, further up the mountain, he could see Kamshet warriors herding the captured kroot down the mountain towards them while Captain Obeysekera hobbled after them, with Amazigh trying to support him. Even as he watched, he saw Obeysekera collapse, the Kamshet struggling to hold him up.

It was of no matter if Obeysekera was incapacitated: this was a matter for the Officio Prefectus.

'How did you come here?' Roshant asked the woman, the Kamshet leader.

'The desert spoke and we heard.'

'But you must have been far away. How did you get here so quickly?'

'We can travel fast at need.'

'They are traitors!'

Roshant turned and saw General Itoyesa, on his knees, looking at the woman with white wings.

'Are you going to trust a barbarian above a general of the Astra Militarum?'

'What have they done that is more barbarous than your own actions, general?'

'They sell the aqua vitae to whoever has the goods they wish to trade for it.'

'You would betray us all to the t'au.'

Itoyesa started to get back onto his feet. But before he could do so, Malick kicked the legs from under him, sending Itoyesa sprawling once more.

Malick stood over General Itoyesa. 'Always wanted to do that to a general – never thought I'd get the chance.' Malick looked at Roshant. 'He killed Gunsur. It was a bolt-round that killed Torgut, weren't it?'

Roshant nodded. 'Yes,' he said.

'Then you know what you got to do,' said Malick. 'It's in your orders. If the general is tainted, you kill him.'

'Yes,' said Roshant, and his voice was a whisper.

General Itoyesa struggled back onto his knees.

'You stay there,' said Malick.

But Itoyesa did not look at Malick. He was staring at Roshant.

'You are a better man than your father, Kirpal. You would not prolong a war, squandering the lives of thousands of men, to burnish your reputation. You would not send men to their deaths for no reason. You would not do these things that your father does.'

'I would not turn traitor,' said Roshant.

'Traitor to what?' asked Itoyesa. 'Traitor to a butcher? Traitor to an army that treats men as bullet fodder? Traitor to an empire that is grinding the last spark of good out of its people? I am no traitor, Kirpal, or if I am, I am a traitor to the monstrous regime that has spread like a cancer throughout the Imperium. Do you stand with them, Kirpal? Do you stand with the men who would burn a planet rather than admit their error? Or do you side with me and work to end this pointless war?'

Roshant raised his bolt pistol and pointed it at Itoyesa's forehead.

'By your own words you have condemned yourself.'

General Itoyesa looked past the pistol, past it and into Roshant's eyes. 'Very well. If that is what you think, then make it quick. But I had thought better of you, Kirpal.'

Roshant looked down the sights of his bolt pistol, into the general's eyes, and he saw Itoyesa looking at him without fear but with… with pity?

Roshant lowered the gun. 'I do not condone what you did, general, but I will not kill you.'

General Itoyesa's eyes widened in surprise. Roshant saw him take the deep breath of knowing that death had passed by.

Then a hole appeared in the centre of his forehead, the skin around it instantly seared shut by the heat of the las-round. Roshant saw the shock in Itoyesa's eyes before he collapsed onto his face.

The commissar turned to see Sergeant Malick lowering his hellgun.

Malick looked at Roshant. 'That's what we sergeants are for, commissar – to do the dirty work no one else wants to do.' He turned and looked up the slope to the captured kroot. 'Now for them.'

'No, wait,' said Roshant. But Malick shook his head and started towards the xenos.

Roshant looked desperately to the lady of the Kamshet, but she regarded him with cool eyes and said no word. Roshant realised that she would not act. It was for him to decide.

Before Malick had taken more than a few paces, Roshant raised his bolt pistol and pointed it at Malick's back.

'I said stop, sergeant.' He cycled a bolt-round into the chamber. At the characteristic sound, Malick stopped and turned round. Seeing Roshant pointing the pistol at him, Malick grinned and spat.

'You didn't have the stones to shoot the general. You sure as hell don't have the stones to shoot me.' Malick began to turn back towards the kroot.

'I said, stop.' Roshant heard the tremble in his voice and hated himself for it.

Malick heard it too. The sergeant glanced back to Roshant. 'This way, you'll be a hero.' Malick laughed, and raised his hellgun into position to fire on the xenos.

Roshant pulled the trigger.

Malick pitched forward onto his face. Roshant ran to him and turned him over. Malick looked up at Roshant. Blood was coming from his mouth and his eyes were puzzled.

'Y-you and me were... were going to have... a good thing,' he said.

'We will, sergeant, we will.'

'G-good. Didn't want to be no... no fool.'

For the second time in a minute, Roshant saw the soul depart from a man. He laid Malick gently back down on the redstone and stood up.

'Commissar.'

He turned around to see the Mother beckoning him. As he approached, she bent down closer to Roshant and spoke so that only he could hear.

'Mercy is not a weakness.' Then she indicated the mouth of the cave. 'You are not the last.'

From the cave mouth came Lerin and Ensor. Over the vox-channel, Roshant heard Lerin ask, *'Did we miss anything?'*

Captain Bharath Obeysekera dreamed he was flying through a sky of the clearest blue – a cerulean blue. He opened his eyes and he saw that it was true. He turned his head and saw white wings spread wide above him.

'Am I dead?'

Mother laughed, and swooped down to where the Venators stood parked at the bottom of the Tabaste. She set Obeysekera down beside *Holy Fire* and Amazigh landed beside them, helping the captain to sit down on the running board of the Venator.

Obeysekera looked to Amazigh.

'You saved my life.'

The Kamshet bowed.

Obeysekera turned to the Mother. 'He did all you asked of him, and more.'

Mother smiled at Amazigh. 'He shall keep his wings.'

As they spoke, other Kamshet landed nearby with Commissar Roshant, Trooper Lerin and Trooper Ensor.

Obeysekera looked at them. 'Are you all that are left?'

'Yes,' said Roshant.

Obeysekera nodded, his face pale despite its tan. He looked back to the Mother.

'What of the kroot?'

'Some of my people are taking them back.' The Mother smiled. 'The mukaali, they grow nervous at their riders.'

'I would have wished to speak again to Tchek.'

The Mother nodded but said no word.

'Why should I be saved when so many others have been lost?'

The Mother raised his face and looked into his eyes. 'You were saved not by your own merit but through the grace of those who saved you – such grace is never merited, but always given. Accept it. Live.'

Captain Bharath Obeysekera bowed his head.

The wind swirl on his skin told him the Kamshet were leaving. He looked up to watch them go, not looking away until they had disappeared into the haze.

He looked down at the wound on his right leg and then turned to Commissar Roshant.

'Don't think I'll be doing the driving on the way back.'

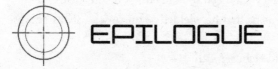

EPILOGUE

Bent over his table, Nebusemekh felt the change behind him. He turned and saw the datafall.

'You're back,' he said.

'Master, the city is choked with sand,' said the World Mind. 'It cannot be cleared for all our people are buried beneath it.'

'I shouldn't worry about it,' said Nebusemekh. 'You will find that the normal geological processes will clear it.'

'How long will that take, master?'

'About three million years.'

'Three million years?'

'Give or take two hundred thousand.'

'What shall we do while we wait, master?'

Nebusemekh smiled – he could definitely feel the muscles moving in his face.

'Those explorers have helped me make a breakthrough in my research. Watch this.' And he lifted the sand up into the air, the upflowing rivers coalescing into the stars and the planets.

Nebusemekh, looking up at his creation, felt the satisfaction of making: so must the worlds have looked when first they precipitated out of the darkness. The suns and the planets and the stars, wheeling in perfect formation, the mirror of the heavens under the earth.

As above, so below.

Perfect, as they had been so many times before, held together by the stasis fields that he wielded as unconsciously as he was breathing.

'Watch,' said Nebusemekh.

And he released the stasis fields.

Staring up at his creation, Nebusemekh was filled with a delight that moved the suns and other stars. The planets wheeled through their orbits, the suns danced about each other, the stars moved in their slow waltz, wheels within wheels within wheels, all turning, all holding.

Holding.

Nebusemekh turned towards the World Mind.

'Water,' said Nebusemekh. 'That's what they told me. Who would have thought it, but sand sticks better when it is wet. Now all we have to do is find a way to make it stay together when the water evaporates. We will need a proper research programme, but we have plenty of time – three million years, in fact.'

The World Mind paused.

'Yes, master,' it said eventually.

Nebusemekh nodded to himself. He had not realised that he had programmed the inflection for world-weariness into the World Mind's voice, but he must have done, for it was indubitably there.

'So, let's begin – experiment one.'

'Experiment one – recording.'

ABOUT THE AUTHOR

Edoardo Albert is a writer and historian specialising in the Dark Ages. He finds that the wars and cultures of the early Medieval period map very well onto the events of the 40th and 41st millenniums. *Silent Hunters* was his first novel for Black Library and he has since followed up with *Kasrkin*. He has also written the short stories 'Green and Grey', 'Last Flight', 'Born of the Storm', and the novella *Lords of the Storm*.

YOUR
NEXT READ

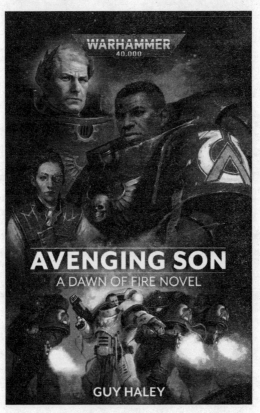

AVENGING SON
by Guy Haley

As the Indomitus Crusade spreads out across the galaxy, one battlefleet must face a dread Slaughter Host of Chaos. Their success or failure may define the very future of the crusade – and the Imperium.

An extract from
Avenging Son
by Guy Haley

'I was there at the Siege of Terra,' Vitrian Messinius would say
in his later years.

'I was there…' he would add to himself, his words never meant
for ears but his own. 'I was there the day the Imperium died.'

But that was yet to come.

'To the walls! To the walls! The enemy is coming!' Captain
Messinius, as he was then, led his Space Marines across the Penitent's Square high up on the Lion's Gate. 'Another attack! Repel
them! Send them back to the warp!'

Thousands of red-skinned monsters born of fear and sin
scaled the outer ramparts, fury and murder incarnate. The
mortals they faced quailed. It took the heart of a Space Marine
to stand against them without fear, and the Angels of Death
were in short supply.

'Another attack, move, move! To the walls!'

They came in the days after the Avenging Son returned,
emerging from nothing, eight legions strong, bringing the
bulk of their numbers to bear against the chief entrance to the

Imperial Palace. A decapitation strike like no other, and it came perilously close to success.

Messinius' Space Marines ran to the parapet edging the Penitent's Square. On many worlds, the square would have been a plaza fit to adorn the centre of any great city. Not on Terra. On the immensity of the Lion's Gate, it was nothing, one of hundreds of similarly huge spaces. The word 'gate' did not suit the scale of the cityscape. The Lion's Gate's bulk marched up into the sky, step by titanic step, until it rose far higher than the mountains it had supplanted. The gate had been built by the Emperor Himself, they said. Myths detailed the improbable supernatural feats required to raise it. They were lies, all of them, and belittled the true effort needed to build such an edifice. Though the Lion's Gate was made to His design and by His command, the soaring monument had been constructed by mortals, with mortal hands and mortal tools. Messinius wished that had been remembered. For men to build this was far more impressive than any godly act of creation. If men could remember that, he believed, then perhaps they would remember their own strength.

The uncanny may not have built the gate, but it threatened to bring it down. Messinius looked over the rampart lip, down to the lower levels thousands of feet below and the spread of the Anterior Barbican.

Upon the stepped fortifications of the Lion's Gate was armour of every colour and the blood of every loyal primarch. Dozens of regiments stood alongside them. Aircraft filled the sky. Guns boomed from every quarter. In the churning redness on the great roads, processional ways so huge they were akin to prairies cast in rockcrete, were flashes of gold where the Emperor's Custodian Guard battled. The might of the Imperium was gathered there, in the palace where He dwelt.

There seemed moments on that day when it might not be enough.

The outer ramparts were carpeted in red bodies that writhed and heaved, obscuring the great statues adorning the defences and covering over the guns, an invasive cancer consuming reality. The enemy were legion. There were too many foes to defeat by plan and ruse. Only guns, and will, would see the day won, but the defenders were so pitifully few.

Messinius called a wordless halt, clenched fist raised, seeking the best place to deploy his mixed company, veterans all of the Terran Crusade. Gunships and fighters sped overhead, unleashing deadly light and streams of bombs into the packed daemonic masses. There were innumerable cannons crammed onto the gate, and they all fired, rippling the structure with false earthquakes. Soon the many ships and orbital defences of Terra would add their guns, targeting the very world they were meant to guard, but the attack had come so suddenly; as yet they had had no time to react.

The noise was horrendous. Messinius' audio dampers were at maximum and still the roar of ordnance stung his ears. Those humans that survived today would be rendered deaf. But he would have welcomed more guns, and louder still, for all the defensive fury of the assailed palace could not drown out the hideous noise of the daemons – their sighing hisses, a billion serpents strong, and chittering, screaming wails. It was not only heard but sensed within the soul, the realms of spirit and of matter were so intertwined. Messinius' being would be forever stained by it.

Tactical information scrolled down his helmplate, near environs only. He had little strategic overview of the situation. The vox-channels were choked with a hellish screaming that made communication impossible. The noosphere was disrupted by etheric backwash spilling from the immaterial rifts the daemons poured through. Messinius was used to operating on his own. Small-scale, surgical actions were the way of the Adeptus Astartes, but in a battle of this scale, a lack of central coordination would lead inevitably to defeat. This was not like the first Siege, where his kind had fought in Legions.

He called up a company-wide vox-cast and spoke to his warriors. They were not his Chapter-kin, but they would listen. The primarch himself had commanded that they do so.

'Reinforce the mortals,' he said. 'Their morale is wavering. Position yourselves every fifty yards. Cover the whole of the south-facing front. Let them see you.' He directed his warriors by chopping at the air with his left hand. His right, bearing an inactive power fist, hung heavily at his side. 'Assault Squad Antiocles, back forty yards, single firing line. Prepare to engage enemy breakthroughs only on my mark. Devastators, split to demi-squads and take up high ground, sergeant and sub-squad prime's discretion as to positioning and target. Remember our objective, heavy infliction of casualties. We kill as many as we can, we retreat, then hold at the Penitent's Arch until further notice. Command squad, with me.'

Command squad was too grand a title for the mismatched crew Messinius had gathered around himself. His own officers were light years away, if they still lived.

'Doveskamor, Tidominus,' he said to the two Aurora Marines with him. 'Take the left.'

'Yes, captain,' they voxed, and jogged away, their green armour glinting orange in the hell-light of the invasion.

The rest of his scratch squad was comprised of a communications specialist from the Death Spectres, an Omega Marine with a penchant for plasma weaponry, and a Raptor holding an ancient standard he'd taken from a dusty display.

'Why did you take that, Brother Kryvesh?' Messinius asked, as they moved forward.

'The palace is full of such relics,' said the Raptor. 'It seems only right to put them to use. No one else wanted it.'

Messinius stared at him.

'What? If the gate falls, we'll have more to worry about than my minor indiscretion. It'll be good for morale.'

The squads were splitting to join the standard humans. Such was the noise many of the men on the wall had not noticed their arrival, and a ripple of surprise went along the line as they appeared at their sides. Messinius was glad to see they seemed more firm when they turned their eyes back outwards.

'Anzigus,' he said to the Death Spectre. 'Hold back, facilitate communication within the company. Maximum signal gain. This interference will only get worse. See if you can get us patched in to wider theatre command. I'll take a hardline if you can find one.'

'Yes, captain,' said Anzigus. He bowed a helm that was bulbous with additional equipment. He already had the access flap of the bulky vox-unit on his arm open. He withdrew, the aerials on his power plant extending. He headed towards a systems nexus on the far wall of the plaza, where soaring buttresses pushed back against the immense weight bearing down upon them.

Messinius watched him go. He knew next to nothing about Anzigus. He spoke little, and when he did, his voice was funereal. His Chapter was mysterious, but the same lack of familiarity held true for many of these warriors, thrown together by miraculous events. Over their years lost wandering in the warp, Messinius had come to see some as friends as well as comrades, others he hardly knew, and none he knew so well as his own Chapter brothers. But they would stand together. They were Space Marines. They had fought by the returned primarch's side, and in that they shared a bond. They would not stint in their duty now.

Messinius chose a spot on the wall, directing his other veterans to left and right. Kryvesh he sent to the mortal officer's side. He looked down again, out past the enemy and over the outer palace. Spires stretched away in every direction. Smoke rose from all over the landscape. Some of it was new, the work of the daemon horde, but Terra had been burning for weeks. The Astronomican had failed. The galaxy was split in two. Behind them in the sky turned the great palace gyre, its deep eye marking out the throne room of the Emperor Himself.

'Sir!' A member of the Palatine Guard shouted over the din. He pointed downwards, to the left. Messinius followed his wavering finger. Three hundred feet below, daemons were climbing. They came upwards in a triangle tipped by a brute with a double rack of horns. It clambered hand over hand, far faster than should be possible, flying upwards, as if it touched the side of the towering gate only as a concession to reality. A Space Marine with claw locks could not have climbed that fast.

'Soldiers of the Imperium! The enemy is upon us!'

He looked to the mortals. Their faces were blanched with fear. Their weapons shook. Their bravery was commendable nonetheless. Not one of them attempted to run, though a wave of terror preceded the unnatural things clambering up towards them.

'We shall not turn away from our duty, no matter how fearful the foe, or how dire our fates may be,' he said. 'Behind us is the Sanctum of the Emperor Himself. As He has watched over you, now it is your turn to stand in guardianship over Him.'

The creatures were drawing closer. Through a sliding, magnified window on his display, Messinius looked into the yellow and cunning eyes of their leader. A long tongue lolled permanently from the thing's mouth, licking at the wall, tasting the terror of the beings it protected.

Boltgun actions clicked. His men leaned over the parapet, towering over the mortals as the Lion's Gate towered over the Ultimate Wall. A wealth of targeting data was exchanged, warrior to warrior, as each chose a unique mark. No bolt would be wasted in the opening fusillade. They could hear the creatures' individual shrieks and growls, all wordless, but their meaning was clear: blood, blood, blood. Blood and skulls.

Messinius sneered at them. He ignited his power fist with a swift jerk. He always preferred the visceral thrill of manual activation. Motors came to full life. Lightning crackled around it. He aimed downwards with his bolt pistol. A reticule danced over diabolical faces, each a copy of all the others. These things were not real. They were not alive. They were projections of a false god. The Librarian Atramo had named them maladies. A spiritual sickness wearing ersatz flesh.

He reminded himself to be wary. Contempt was as thick as any armour, but these things were deadly, for all their unreality.

He knew. He had fought the Neverborn many times before.

'While He lives,' Messinius shouted, boosting his voxmitter gain to maximal, 'we stand!'

'For He of Terra!' the humans shouted, their battle cry loud enough to be heard over the booming of guns.

'For He of Terra,' said Messinius. 'Fire!' he shouted.

The Space Marines fired first. Boltguns spoke, spitting spikes of rocket flare into the foe. Bolts slammed into daemon bodies, bursting them apart. Black viscera exploded away. Black ichor showered those coming after. The daemons' false souls screamed back whence they came, though their bones and offal tumbled down like those of any truly living foe.

Las-beams speared next, and the space between the wall top

and the scaling party filled with violence. The daemons were unnaturally resilient, protected from death by the energies of the warp, and though many were felled, others weathered the fire, and clambered up still, unharmed and uncaring of their dead. Messinius no longer needed his helm's magnification to see into the daemon champion's eyes. It stared at him, its smile a promise of death. The terror that preceded them was replaced by the urge to violence, and that gripped them all, foe and friend. The baseline humans began to lose their discipline. A man turned and shot his comrade, and was shot down in turn. Kryvesh banged the foot of his borrowed banner and called them back into line. Elsewhere, his warriors sang; not their Chapter warsongs, but battle hymns known to all. Wavering human voices joined them. The feelings of violence abated, just enough.

Then the things were over the parapet and on them. Messinius saw Tidominus carried down by a group of daemons, his unit signum replaced by a mortis rune in his helm. The enemy champion was racing at him. Messinius emptied his bolt pistol into its face, blowing half of it away into a fine mist of daemonic ichor. Still it leapt, hurling itself twenty feet over the parapet. Messinius fell back, keeping the creature in sight, targeting skating over his helmplate as the machine-spirit tried to maintain a target lock. Threat indicators trilled, shifting up their priority spectrum.

The daemon held up its enormous gnarled hands. Smoke whirled in the space between, coalescing into a two-handed sword almost as tall as Messinius. By the time its hoofed feet cracked the paving slabs of the square, the creature's weapon was solid. Vapour streaming from its ruined face, it pointed the broadsword at Messinius and hissed a wordless challenge.

'Accepted,' said Messinius, and moved in to attack.